Last Man on Campus

Last Man
on
Campus

John Abraham-Watne

To: Ann

[signature]

NORTH STAR PRESS OF ST. CLOUD, INC.
St. Cloud, Minnesota

To my wife, Mary. Without you, I never would have published my first novel. You have been there for me every step of the way, and I am so grateful you decided to share your life with me. I love you.

ISBN: 978-0-87839-798-3

This is a work of fiction. Names, characters, places, and incidents are the products of the author's imagination or are used fictitiously. Any resemblance to actual events or persons, living or dead, is entirely coincidental.

Printed in the United States of America.

First edition: September 2015

Published by
North Star Press of St. Cloud, Inc.
P.O. Box 451
St. Cloud, Minnesota 56302

www.northstarpress.com

First Semester

Chapter
ONE

I WANT TO TELL YOU A STORY ABOUT COLLEGE. It begins after my senior year of high school in St. James, Minnesota. If you want a good idea of how small a town St. James is, think of the smallest town in the Midwest you have ever driven through, staring out the window and watching its bland borders pass by in five minutes. St. James was even smaller. In southern Minnesota farm country, half my graduating class lived out of town and the rest were considered "city folk." My senior class was forty-five students, the great majority of which would never see a life outside the town after we walked off that stage in their cap and gowns. I was lucky, having secured invitations to several of the finest institutions in the state. This included the University of Minnesota on the banks of the mighty Mississippi, and Saint Cloud State. I visited both schools before my graduation, and after much thought I settled on "the U" as a good enough place to procure a collegiate stomping grounds. That was before my parents intervened.

I had a rocky relationship with my parents. It seemed that for everything I wanted in life, they wanted the exact opposite. I wanted to race around the dumpy corners of our small town in my own flashy red sedan. They opted for a large, horrendous Oldsmobile the color of spilled brown paint on a barn door. They said its steel structure would keep me alive, and besides, high school students didn't need flashy cars. I wanted a job at the greasy spoon located twenty miles outside St. James in order to secure employment away from this podunk town. They decided it was for the best if I worked at the crappy discount retail store on the outskirts of the city, a Midwest retail calamity called "Pay-Go." My parents were the kind of people who were used to getting their way.

3

My father, Timothy, ran a profitable life insurance business out of a spacious white-painted building on Main Street. Tall and thin like me, he was beginning to lose hair on the peak of his head. He cleared enough money helping our town's families deal with the paperwork of their deceased to take us on a week-long vacation every other year. My mother, Elaine, a petite woman who preferred her hair pulled back in a bun most days, worked part time in the pharmacy located across from the county courthouse. This was a giant brick-and-mortar edifice dating back to the previous century and held a grand set of rusty bells in its belfry. My father told me he came from a long family line in St. James that traced its roots to the days when it was little more than a dirt road that ran through a bunch of wooden shacks and a collection of glass-fronted buildings containing men who would count up the profits of each year's grain harvest. He was accorded a certain respect around town that I never saw given to anyone else in quite the same manner. When I was six or seven, I once witnessed my father, in his usual double-breasted suit, pick up the fallen glove of a young woman as we walked on the craggy sidewalk next to the slummy pizza joint on Main Street. He called out to the young lady as his deft fingers pulled at one corner of the silk. You would've thought the pope himself had done this lady the favor of her life, so much did she say, "Thank you, Mr. Sinclair," and "I'm so glad you picked up that glove, Mr. Sinclair. It was a family heirloom." This type of behavior was not exclusive to passing maidens; the mayor oftentimes gave the same deference when we walked up to City Hall some mornings.

I'll never forget the afternoon in May when I told my parents of my decision to attend school at the University of Minnesota. I can't erase the look of horror that shot through my mother's sharp green eyes as she processed the news. My father didn't say anything at first, preferring to lean back in the old leather chair in the corner of our sparse living room, toying with the pipe he kept in a stand nearby. The loafers he wore in the evenings jutted out from the chair like small gray cats. My mother, wearing her customary blouse from the pharmacy, was the first to speak.

"Michael, you can't be serious," she said, eying my father. "The university on the river? I don't see how you'd get any studying done."

"I hear they party until all hours, and not just on the weekends," my father grunted his disapproval. My parents had a general dislike for the way kids at my school would spend their weekends popping caps off warm beers and cruising the paved main street in repetitive loops.

"It's much too big, and stretched out over the whole river," my mother said. "Your first year of college should be spent in books and in the class-room, not wandering all over the place."

"Indeed," my father said, clearing his throat with guttural efficiency. "You don't want to get lost all the time. You ought to pick someplace small. Like Malworth. It was good enough for me now, wasn't it?"

I couldn't believe what I was hearing. Malworth University was the smallest institution of higher education in the state of Minnesota. It was located in Cold River, a town three hours northwest of Minneapolis. The city's claim to statewide fame was to have stationed within an otherwise unremarkable museum the largest potato chip on record, found by some unsuspecting toddler in the 1980s. The entire town had been razed in a climactic flood during the Depression, losing much of its population in the tumultuous rebuilding period. Its population was a mere twice that of St. James. A Minnesota guidebook's description of "sleepy" was an understatement; on the day trip my parents forced me to take there in the spring I witnessed several people in tattered clothing lying on the park benches that lined the divided road leading to the school, their heads listing along with the slight wind that seemed to blow at all hours. It was a city that kids in my grade spoke about in hushed tones, considering it at once the lamest and creepiest choice for post-high school life. In short, it was the back-up choice for the back-up choice for those twenty students in my grade lucky enough to be moving onto higher education. My father never concealed the fact that he had attended this pathetic excuse for a university back in the seventies and how much it had taught him about the world. Besides this fact my parents were also footing the considerable bill for my first year of college expenses, and so had the choice in their hands. In the end, it was just one more decision they got to make for me.

"The decision is final, Michael." My father's booming voice echoed off the paneled living room ceiling, ending this discussion after a few frivolous minutes like all the others. But this time it sounded different. It was as if his voice had dropped an entire octave. I had never heard him speak like this. "You'll attend Malworth just as I did, and get the same education. After the first year you'll understand. Just like I did."

I remember sulking up in my room that night, staring at the Metallica posters adorning my walls and feeling angry at the universe for giving me such disastrous parents. After an hour of this, I gave into boredom and looked through my wooden dresser for the materials from my college trips. I gave the U of M documents a ceremonious dump into the trash and opened the tattered Malworth brochure with a deep sigh. On the front cover stood a tall brick building, its many floors lined with minute metal-framed windows. Several elm and oak trees punctuated either side of the frame. A dull gray sidewalk led up to the building and several students were frozen in time walking toward the rough wooden door in the center. I hadn't spent more than a few seconds on the scene before my eyes jolted up toward the building that towered over everything: a tall brick campanile, the looming clock's hands stuck in the ten o'clock position. I recalled seeing this structure on my visit but not how it overshadowed the campus in such a domineering manner, mocking all else around it. Looking at it in my room that night, I felt a sense of foreboding and could not for the life of me figure it out. I threw the brochure into the top drawer and resigned myself to the dreary measures of this campus. I couldn't remember more than a handful of locales I'd visited on that cold day in March. I leaned back in bed, staring once again at the posters and wishing as hard as I could for a better set of parents, or at least some that would let me decide my own fate.

I SPENT THE SUMMER before my trip to college doing tons of nothing, taking multiple trips per week to the tiny lake outside our dreary town to swim its warm waters, cruising the streets in my russet-tinged Oldsmobile and making lame attempts to pick up girls from my grade who had opted not to take the higher education path. That last summer contained some of the happiest and most relaxed days of my youth, despite the lingering form of Malworth lurking just ahead of me. By the middle of August I had almost forgotten my future until my parents decided to bring it up one evening.

"So, you have everything you need for your trip to Cold River?" my father asked in his new brooding, low-register voice, a half-filled brandy in his hand. Up until that moment my main thought was how I was going to talk Rachel McPherson, the pepper-haired bad ass who worked in her father's car shop, into the backseat of my Olds before the end of the month. My father's comment reminded me that I had not packed a thing.

"Of course I have," I lied, using a fork to push around the cold mushroom stroganoff my mother had slaved on all afternoon.

Thus commenced a day's worth of inventory. Over my eighteen years on the planet I had collected a huge amount of childish stuff, the majority of which I gave to my mother to donate at our next garage sale. After rummaging through several plastic totes of old possessions, I got down to the necessities. This included a selection of nerdy clothing I figured would be just ironic enough to get me noticed around the small campus. Besides the basics such as toiletry items, I also conspired to bring the ancient stereo my parents had bought for my sixteenth birthday in the off-chance my roommate in the dorms had no venue for playing music at unhealthy volumes. The giant box my mother allocated for this trip began to fill with odds and ends from my room: a model airplane I'd built when I was eight, a small box of LEGO bricks I convinced myself I'd need if I was bored, a collection books I thought might make me look erudite, a pair of dusty work-out shoes that needed a good cleaning. I also gathered an assortment of pens and notebooks from my desk. My parents were renting a moving truck to bring along the dark black futon I had cooped up on the side of my bedroom as well as the tiny mattress and bed frame we'd found through various inquiries in the local paper.

As I packed, my mind kept turning over the events of my trip to Cold River in March. I'd done the usual tour thing: walking part of the campus and paying a visit to the registrar's office. There a kind old woman who looked somewhat like my grandmother took down my name and information. I remembered a lot of dull red brick buildings, their cascading roof tiles arcing above me as I walked around the worn sidewalks lacing the campus. When I approached the student union a pair of jovial looking teens not much older than I ran past at breakneck speed. Several bulky uniformed guards followed in hot pursuit, their sturdy shoes pounding the sidewalk as they raced. This memory brought back one other: the tenor of the campanile bellowing out its noon-day ring across campus and the stunned silence that came afterward. No one in my immediate vicinity made a sound until the bell tower reached its zenith of rings. No one even seemed to move. I looked down and realized the cardboard moving box was full.

THE WEEK BEFORE THE TRIP to Cold River, I tied up all the loose ends I'd left floating in the wind during my last summer of freedom. On Wednesday I said goodbye to the best friend I'd had up to that point. Ben Mosey was a lean, bespectacled kid with cropped blonde hair who grew up a few houses down from me. His wardrobe consisted of striped polo shirts and black jeans, both of which attended him this evening. We stood in the middle of the small patch of asphalt and sidewalk where we'd meandered during our high school summers. We dubbed this outpost the "little square," but it had many names before we came on the scene. Mosey was matriculating to St. Cloud State, about two hours from Cold River. We bullshitted about the last few months of our high school lives while we watched our fellow classmates circle the area in their various beat up vehicles.

"Going to leave on Monday. The parents are already freaking out about me being gone for a whole year," he said. The drawl from a family of plains drifters was concealed under his voice. "Mom knows I'm comin' back for Thanksgiving, for Christ's sake."

"At least you got to choose your school," I said, leaning against the rusted hull of the Oldsmobile. I stared at the translucent windshield as a large grasshopper crawled its way up the glass.

"That sucks, man," he said. "They ever come clean as to why?"

"I figure they wanted me as far away from them as I could get. Cold River's at least four hours as the . . . how's that go? As the dove flies, or some shit? Plus my old man went there and thinks I need to do everything the same way he did. I wish the college wasn't the tiniest in the fuckin' state. Nobody else from our class is going there."

Mosey laughed, which turned into a hoarse cough in the still air. The kid had smoked cigarettes since he was a freshman in high school, just like his father, who drove trucks for a living. His large glasses caught the shine from the single lamp post at the far end of the square. "You'll have to visit St. Cloud, man. I'm sure there'll be some killer parties that first week."

"Yeah, that you won't know about," I cracked back. "To be honest, that's what scares me. Not knowin' anyone. I mean, at least you have a few dudes from our class joining you over there. I got nobody."

"I thought Claire Brooks was going to Malworth," Mosey said. "She's easy on the eyes."

"Yeah, but something came up," I replied miserably. "Said she couldn't get the college experience that way. But I think her parents didn't want her going there for some reason."

"Oh, damn," he said. "Well, you'll still have a good time up there. You'll make friends."

"Yeah, sure," I said in my glum tone. "It's so easy."

"And, hey, you ever get bored, you just call me. Like I said, I'm only two hours away."

"I may take you up on that offer," I said, swatting away the grasshopper. "Like immediately."

When the night was over, I pulled the Oldsmobile out of the parking lot to make one last circle of town, then headed to my parent's domicile. I was still pissed they had vetoed one of the biggest decisions of my life. A more mature voice in my head, one I thought was waiting for my college years, said they were doing what was best for me. My eighteen-year-old self called bullshit on that as I walked up the small stony path to our house.

Chapter
TWO

M Y FATHER LOADED THE FINAL thin desk lamp in my possession into the moving truck. "Make sure you don't drive too far ahead of us now," he said as he wiped a few glistening strands of sweat from behind his glasses and stared at me. It was the last Friday in August, a scorcher that had set heat records by eight o'clock that morning.

"Don't worry, Dad," I chirped. "It's not like I haven't been there. The route is so memorable I'm sure I'll recall every haystack and empty shack."

"Don't be a smart mouth," my father said, ramming down the metal door of the truck with a solid clang. I heard something inside latch into place, but my father still checked it to make sure it wouldn't move.

"Everything put away in there?" my mother asked, leaning out the passenger door.

"Yes, Elaine," my father replied. "Now let's get a move on before we all die of heat exhaustion."

The trip up to Cold River was about as eventful as my joke allowed. The state of Minnesota is criss-crossed with a number of boring, standard county highways that bisect a few other cities but otherwise drive straight on through long bouts of nothing permeated by the occasional rural community. I was familiar with some of these barren patches of asphalt thanks to the several trips I took in the spring to the larger universities, but this destination was a singular nightmare. I counted a grand total of two places to stop for a restroom on the four-hour journey, one of which my father allowed us to use. I moved through a good number of compact discs in the brown Oldsmobile's player during the trip. I also saw a record number of giant white windmills occupying a sparse patch of farmland about an hour outside the town. Their turbines stood motionless in the blazing summer heat.

We arrived at the town around noon. I remember the time because we drove past the main entrance sign, which contained a gigantic and hideous clock with stilted Roman numerals that directed its metal hands toward the top of the dark pewter finish. The name of the town proclaimed itself in bold letters on either side of the large face. As we blew by the sign a thought surfaced that I didn't have time to process: the numerals on the clock looked an awful like those on the campanile from the brochure.

We drove down the main street, an asphalt route with two lanes on either side of a neatly cut bed of sharp-edged grass. The tall brick buildings looked the same. A service station with some rusty old gas pumps took up a corner space near an intersection. An immense white corrugated shed stood off from the street about one football field's length. I could just make out the words "town museum" painted in dirty black paint behind the overgrown weeds. Malworth University was located west of town. The main gate stood at the end of a lengthy gravel road, wide ditches filled with lilting cattails and milkweeds on either side. A huge metal gate loomed over the road to announce the name of the school in bold, arching letters. A plaque inset into the brick portion of the gate contained a founding year that belonged to the nineteenth century. I tilted the Oldsmobile through the entrance, the moving truck pacing behind me.

The campus itself was intersected with small paved roads and tiny signs announcing speed limits not much faster than walking. Here I first saw the crowds. They were everywhere: tons of students who looked about my age, the fact that they were lost etched into their eyes even as they walked with confident steps across the sidewalks. Each kid was followed by an appropriate parental unit, and sometimes by more than one. They too had the harried and stressful look I was sure to see on my parents' faces the moment we parked. One kid with ripped jeans, a slack T-shirt with some band from the seventies on it and a dumb grin on his long-haired face almost walked right in front of my car. I gave him a brisk honk and continued on my way.

My parents tailed behind me. I saw the first of many stone-fronted lecture halls, its slanted and dingy tile roof sneering down on me as I stared in the bright sun. My eyes dipped behind it to spy one of the dormitories. I could just make out the tarnished silver metal words protruding in bold lettering from the brick framework: SCHUSTER HALL.

I parked the Oldsmobile in what I assumed was guest parking as it had no distinguishing signs. My father wrangled the moving truck in a few spots down from me. He released an epic sigh of pent up frustration as he exited the vehicle.

"Some commotion here today, huh?" he said without a trace of humor. "They all want to get into the good classes. You should too, if you know what's good for you."

"Boy it's hot out," my mother said from beside the truck. Her puffy hair stuck off at weird angles from the humidity, and she struggled to pull it back into place.

We continued on foot toward the registrar's office. This building possessed the same impending, worn look of old institutionalization but had many modern windows. Once inside I remembered learning on my previous trip that the entire building had been remodeled and contained nary a trace of what it must have looked like many years previous to my arrival. I didn't see the old woman who reminded me of a skinny version of Gram and had taken down my information on my last visit. We approached a distressed-looking woman holding down the smallest of the registration lines packed with newbie students and parents. She wore a dark-pink shade of lipstick that did not match the green frames of her eyeglasses. Her dark chocolate hair seemed to be stretched back further onto her skull than should have been possible.

"Welcome," she said with the same glassy-eyed look she had given every student up to this point. "Are you here for orientation, scheduling, or to register?"

I had managed to fill out my registration documents and had sent them to the school around the middle of August, one of the few actual accomplishments of my life during those brief summer days. I told her I was here for orientation and scheduling. She handed me some paperwork about my living situation along with a small set of worn dorm keys, which I looked over before tucking into my back pocket. The rubber key holder felt odd against my leg.

"All right," the woman said. "Marcy will take it from here. Next!"

Another woman stood up from behind her glass enshrined desk and walked across to our side of the building. There she opened a plain gray metal door, beside which read the tag line "Computer Lab." The title belied the actual contents of the room, which were five bland boxy computers, each with a student huddled before it typing at a brisk pace. I got a turn on one of the machines after about twenty minutes of waiting and next to no communication with my parents. Given that I was a freshman and had little idea what my course of study ought to be, I looked around at some extra circulars before settling on a basic cycling course for my physical education requirement and Western Civilization for the Humanities. I had one extra hour to fill so put in Creative Writing. I had a few stories I'd written outside my classes at St. James High and thought they could be of some use. I rounded out the schedule with biology and statistics, too subjects of which I had almost no knowledge. I printed out a copy for myself and my parents. My father's eyes gave a brief overview of my first semester courses before he nodded his casual acceptance.

"Ah, Humanities with Professor Deakin," he said and slapped my back. "You'll enjoy his lectures, when they're not boring you to death."

Marcy instructed that our next step would be orientation. This was held in the grand Gymnasium building across from the registrar. The entire campus had an odd aesthetic quality to it that I noticed as I glanced through the map provided to me by the registrar's office. The old lecture halls were laid out in neat, perpendicular fashion. No building seemed out of place save for the campanile in the center and a tiny shack in the upper right-hand corner. It had no label on the map, a vague oversight given that every bathroom facility, laboratory, and dormitory had been itemized.

We headed to the auditorium, a cavernous edifice that overshadowed the other monstrosities on this campus with its sheer height. Other bright-eyed freshmen began to surround us, their parents walking a few feet behind and staring at the looming distraction before us. The nearest kid, who didn't look much older than sixteen, and had long shaggy hair, gave a smarmy glance at his parents as he passed. I pulled the bronze handle on the giant oak door, and we walked inside. The smell of ancient musk and the carcasses of bugs splatted over decades hit my nostrils. The ceiling looked as black as the night sky. I swore I could even see stars shining in the upper recesses. When I looked back, they were gone. We took our seats on rickety wooden chairs. The dull pine of a basketball court lay beneath our feet. My chair let out an agonizing crack of wood as I sat down, but seemed to hold.

"So what do you think?" my father asked, looking up at the darkness with the strange downward tilt in his voice. "It's such an old campus. A lot of history here, ya know. Brings back a lot of memories."

I gave an uncaring shrug for my answer. At that moment the history of the stupid school where I'd be forced to spend the next few years was the last thing on my mind. The first thing was the distinctive lack of female presence. I wasn't so weird as to keep a running tally, but on our pedestrian jaunt from registration to scheduling to here I remembered only a handful of women. The rest were guys my age. I didn't remember seeing anyone who even looked above the age of sophomore.

"This building in particular is amazing," my father said in the low voice. He wasn't looking at me. "Back when this place used to be more doctrinal they used to hold services right in this room."

I had stopped paying attention by this point. My eyes were stuck across the room at one of the few girls. She had short locks of brunette hair and salient, bright eyes that stood out from across the universe of darkness and students. She wore a light-gray blouse and a short black skirt. Her skin had a milky complexion that indicated a life not enjoyed outside every day in the summer. Her eyes darted around until they held mine a brief moment, then looked away before she sank down into the mass of youthful faces.

"... they even had to outlaw that practice in 1899," my father said, still droning on without notice. "Some say they still perform it once a generation though. For old time's sake."

"Oh, yeah," I said, doing my best impression of his voice. "Sounds neat, Dad."

I was aware of his stern, glasses-ensconced glare heading my way. "I was talking about the rituals they used to perform here, son. Nothing to joke about. The order has of course cleaned up since those days."

I had enough time to register what he was saying when a booming voice enveloped my ears and echoed off the false night sky above. A tall man with a rumpled gray beard stood at the podium at the front of the auditorium. Dark-blue and purple robes swirled around his feet as he lunged for the microphone. He cleared his throat into the amplifier and the hall fell silent.

"Welcome to all new students and their parents!" His dusty voice pierced any remaining noise within the large room. "Welcome to Malworth University. I trust most of you have completed your registrations and scheduled your first round of classes. If not, kindly make your way there and return for the afternoon version of my great speech." A handful of confused looking students stood up with their parents and ambled out back toward daylight. The mysterious speaker watched them leave in silence before speaking again. "Now that we've cleared that up, I want to say a few words about the monument to personal betterment and education you each have made the glorious decision to attend."

I glanced at my parents as he spoke. My father was watching with rapt attention. The old man wore a tri-corner hat that matched his robes. Purple scarves adorned either side of his shoulders, and his beard edged the top of his chest when his mouth opened.

"Malworth University," he said. "The place where so many bright shining lights of this state attended. Did you all know that the great F. Scott Fitzgerald himself had a fellowship here for a while? Mary Tyler Moore spent a year here as an undergraduate. And I even heard Dylan played a secret show in town once. I'm sure each of you will add your own special light to this place in time. I am here today to talk about this school, its history, and why you made such a great choice. You see, the great Edmund Whitcare founded this place back in the nineteenth century as a place of spiritual enlightenment and edification. Why, even the very building we sit in today used to be a place for holy rituals. People would come from miles away to participate in the cleansing rites of the day. That notion worked for a half-century until people started getting . . . tired of it."

His face was starting to become familiar. The way his eyes twinkled when he moved his fingers to make a point unnerved me. "The Whitcare family started losing control of their property rights. This was a battle that would continue for the next few years." His eyes trailed up and above our heads in a wistful manner. "But where was I? Oh, yes, how this place came to become a school for all of you to attend. Around the middle of the twentieth century those who owned this ground decided the best way to attract new people was to educate them. So up went many of the newer buildings you see around you, and some of the top minds in the state were hired to teach."

I had no idea what he meant by "newer" buildings. Every hideous gaping structure I saw around this campus looked at least a millenia old. "Classes started coming and going, and before you know it Malworth was talked about in the same breath as Pillsbury's land-grant school down on the river. Word spread to other parts of the state and soon every parent wanted to send their child to this school. And to this day we carry on and we prosper. We now welcome you to our hallowed halls. I personally welcome you all as Dean Henry Moriarty." Suddenly the memory clicked. I had seen this guy's smiling, beard-clad visage glaring up at me from the back page of the brochure I had. Everyone around me started to clap, as if compelled. My parents were too, so I decided to join.

Moriarty waved his large hand, and his dark robes swayed behind him. "So go on and make us proud, students. And remember, a few of you may even make the list this year. Keep up those grades, and it could be you!" As he spoke I swear that, out of the several hundred young people crammed into that gloomy auditorium, he looked right at me. I trudged behind my parents as we headed back outside.

"Wasn't that great? Do you feel ready to learn now?" my father asked, poking my ribs. I looked at him with a sore bemusement and he fell silent, rubbing his glasses.

"I guess," I said with a slow tongue. "I still don't want to be here. I hope you both know that. But since you're paying, I don't have a choice. I'm going to find my dorm and stuff now." I shuffled my feet a bit faster so my father had to speed up as well. We walked back across campus to the dormitory where I'd been selected to live: SCHUSTER HALL.

Chapter

THREE

S WE APPROACHED THE ANCIENT dormitory, a pock-marked slab notifying its age stood out: this crumbling structure had existed on the face of the earth since the Year of Our Lord 1895. We walked under the layered shadow of the building, which looked like the cowl of Batman if his head had been crushed into a horrific diagonal pattern. Lines of tattered mortar crossed in square patterns between the ancient brick. Steel windows, some stocked with small air-conditioning units, appeared every few feet down the lengthy side of the structure. The decay of old age had long since left its mark on this edifice. The school could do nothing to make it look better. Flecks of purple paint peeled off the brittle and rusty railings, and attempts to rebuild the front steps out of cement hadn't really worked. Years of power-washing had left the outside with a scalded look, as if a century of Minnesota weather hadn't taken enough of a toll. The building was simply out of its time and should have been destroyed eons ago, but still here it was, expecting me to reside within its bowels for a full year of my life. I noticed a massive crack in the concrete spiraling upward toward the front door. Not a good sign.

"Isn't this great, hon," my mother chirped. "Such history to be found all over this campus."

"Oh, yeah," I sniped back. "I saw some of the Grecian tools they used to construct most of it on our way over here."

I used the plain copper key I'd received at the registrar's office. The metal door creaked on its hinges as we walked inside, and slammed behind us with an echoing, ethereal thud as we entered the stairwell. I could hear loud music from somewhere above where we stood. Maroon linoleum-covered stairs before us led up and down. We began our slow march upward, as I would be living on the top floor. My parents started wheezing when we reached the fifth floor. There was a newer looking pneumatic-metal door painted purple and gold at the top of the stairs. The music I noticed at the bottom of the stairs had amplified by each floor and now reached its loudest intensity here, exploding into a cacophony of drum and bass as we entered. I looked into the world I'd be occupying for the next year of my life.

Ahead a long, drab carpeted hallway stretched for fifty yards. Another pneumatic purple door sat at the far end. Tarnished wooden frames lined either side, and most rooms had the ajar look of constant traffic. Students were bringing up loads from the hallway and carrying the trappings of college life into their rooms: laundry bags, desk chairs, posters, televisions, cardboard boxes full of Ramen noodles, computers, mattresses. We were needled out of the way from behind as three kids muscled a black padded futon down the hall. I stumbled sideways into the nearest room, where I came upon a lanky fellow with short highlighted hair and a sunny disposition.

"You gotta watch yourself out there. I almost got creamed by one of those giant-ass bean bag chairs earlier," the guy said with a smile as I dodged the small office chair positioned near his built-in wooden desk.

"Sorry about that," I said. "This place is crazy today."

"I know it," he said. He wore track pants and a bleached white shirt with a phrase from a Mexican beer company on the front. The bright blond highlights streaked through his hair collected at the top, blending with the dark hair at the front. It took another minute of awkward standing before I realized that this was my dorm room.

"Oh, right," the tall kid said. "I was wondering when you'd show up. I take it these are your folks?" He had a higher register voice than I had and it cracked once in a while when his mouth formed vowels.

"Oh, yeah," I said, turning around. "This is my mom, Elaine, and my dad, Tim. And, I'm sorry, I didn't catch your name."

"It's Nick Derickson," he said, shaking our hands. "I'm from Alexandria, so not too far from this place. Isn't this building something else? I thought it was going to collapse when I shut the front door!"

"No kidding," I agreed, and could feel the consternation emanating from behind me. "But that means it has a lot of history, right? Did your parents already take off?"

"Yeah, about ten minutes ago. Sorry they missed ya. I'm trying to get settled in here now."

I surveyed the room. Nick had a good assortment of dorm room essentials laid out. A green-and-red plaid couch rested on the far wall underneath the square window that stood halfway open to let some breeze into the stifling room. A meager wooden coffee table, marked with years of knife carving and beverage stains, stood before it. Nick had commandeered the desk built into the wall on the side of the room. That meant I would get the tiny wooden desk in the back corner next to the couch. An interesting contraption towered at the front of the room where I stood. It looked like a home shop project gone awry but was a serviceable entertainment stand with plenty of platforms. Some of the white-painted edges looked like they could cause a horrendous splinter so I kept my distance. A squat black dormitory fridge fit in the space underneath the stand. A few magnets boasting about college life were posted on its door.

"You build this thing?" I asked, gazing at the apparatus.

"My dad and I, yeah," Nick said, typing away at his computer. "It may not look secure, but it'll hold just about anything."

"It looks good, man." I could feel my silent parents' eyes staring at the back of my neck and decided it would be a good time to start moving my own possessions into the room. We headed back down the linoleum stairs, avoiding another shipment of couches and chairs going the opposite way.

We unloaded most of my crap out of the truck in a couple of hours. Thanks to Nick's proficiency I only needed half of what we brought, including the metal-framed futon from my room back in St. James. I wrangled up my desk chair, some lamps, reams of clothing, compact discs, the ancient stereo, my books, and the sundry items I had packed over the summer. In the end the single large item we had to bring up to the room was the creaky wooden loft my father and I had splintered together one weekend in July, a father-and-son project done out of necessity rather than enjoyment of each other's company. It had involved him cutting the wood and me standing there watching for the most part.

"Remember, if we have our calculations right, this thing should hold both of you," my father said in the stairwell as we brought up the first long two-by-four to the room.

"If it doesn't, I guess I'll find out when I fall through and land on my desk," I joshed. My father's squinting face indicated he didn't get the joke.

"Nice roommate you got there," he said instead. "Too bad we couldn't meet his folks."

"Yeah, maybe you could swap stories about forcing your kids to attend the worst school in Minnesota," I said, less humor in my voice than malice.

"That's enough," he said, struggling to twist the wooden beam through a corner. "You don't know how good you're going to have it here."

Nick began assembling the pieces in our room. After all the pieces were complete we stood the thing up, the silver bolts poking out at awkward angles. The accompanying wooden ladder remained in place by way of a small metal hook. I climbed up first to test it out, bouncing on the cheap dingy mattress to my mother's brief horror. A slight snapping noise caused my heart to leap up into my throat, but after that it held together. Nick came up to try his mattress and when nothing else happened we called it good. Afterward I stored my clothes in the meager closet sunk into the wall and covered by a frail cloth. I thought my parents' departure was imminent.

"Well, I think I'm pretty well settled in here, guys," I said in the tame vernacular I used when trying to get them to do something.

My mother glanced at her watch. "Wouldn't you like us to buy you some dinner? We still have time . . ."

"No, that's all right," I said. "You've helped enough bringing all this stuff up here. Nick and I should be okay." I pitched a sideways glance at my new roommate. He gave me a sign of understanding.

"The boy's trying to tell us something, Elaine," my father observed. "He'll be all right. He received the history lesson today. He'll figure out the rest soon enough."

"Yeah, I have all year to find out the glorious story behind Malworth University," I said, making a slow walk toward the door. "Thanks for everything. I'll call you in a few days."

"All right, son," my father said, turning to face me in the doorway. A group of kids sauntered past behind him, their hoodie-clad faces obscured. "Now remember, always go to class. Even the early ones—I would not recommend disappointing Professor Deakin on your first day. You never know what you might miss. Don't skip meals, either. We gave you a punch card for a reason. Do your homework, all of it."

"Yeah, yeah, Dad . . ." I said, desperate to be rid of him.

"And remember," he said in his new weird low tone, ". . . you are a legacy at this institution. You're representing the Sinclair family and as such must set a good example for the rest of these . . . students. Do not fail me on this account, do you understand?"

I saw in his eyes a combination of emotions I never wanted to see again: anguish mixed with pure rage. My father and I had not been on the best of terms for most of my life, but I had never seen him look like this. "Yes, I understand," I said. "All right?"

"Ah . . . what am I saying? You'll be fine here," he said, back to his complacent self. "You'll take care of him, right, Nick?"

"Uh, yes, sir," Nick said in an absent tone. He was deep into some program on his computer.

"Be safe, Michael," my mother said. The beginnings of tears were forming in her eyes, which she would soon be dabbing away lest they interfere with the gaudy makeup she had applied this morning. "Try to meet new people. I know that's always been hard for you . . ."

"Okay, Mom, I get it," I said, herding them out the door.

"Goodbye, son," my father said as he opened the pneumatic door. "And remember: we love you, no matter what happens this year." Then they were tromping down the linoleum stairs, my Mom's pointed shoes echoing off the walls.

I waited until I couldn't hear them anymore, then returned to the room. Nick was playing a first-person shooter game. "Parents," I said, heaving my hands up and letting them drop with a deadening smack on my khaki shorts. "Am I right?"

At first he didn't seem to register that I had spoken. Then, "Oh, yeah, mine were like that too. Always have a million things to say before their little bird heads out of the nest. There's soda in the fridge if you want. I'm just finishing up this level."

I took him up on his offer and grabbed a sugary beverage. The freezing air billowing from the fridge felt great. I sat on the couch, which had a pleasant springy quality. Sipping the soda, I leaned back and considered my newfound freedom. Free at last from the two adults who had caused me such misery over the last year. But why this school? I sat there for another few minutes before Nick came to join me. We watched television for an hour before meeting our first denizen of the fifth floor. A small head with pointed cheekbones and a cropped patch of black hair poked around the side of the open door.

"Hey, guys, what's up? Gettin' all settled in?" The head was attached to a thin, muscular body clad in a "Malworth U" T-shirt and lengthy jean shorts. His charcoal eyes seemed to reach back into dull pits of nothing in the center of his head.

"Uh, yeah, we're all good here," I mumbled over the roar of the television. Nick didn't seem to notice he was standing there.

"Great, great," he said. This guy looked older than either of us and had a slight air of authority as he stood rigid in the doorway. "I'm Justin, the RA for this floor. In case you didn't know, that stands for . . ."

"Resident Advisor," Nick said in the same absent tone he'd used with my parents. His eyes didn't move from the screen.

"That's right. That means I'm a resident here, ready to assist you in any way possible. Whether that's helping to find out where your classes or the dining hall are located or dealing with some of the dreaded roommate issues," he paused for effect, his dull black eyes hoping Nick would look his way. He didn't, so Justin continued. "I'm here to help. Think of me as just another guy living here in the hall, going to school like you all, but also somebody you can always speak to regarding any problems you might have. You two dig?" His smile looked plastered on as he held his thumb up in an affirmative gesture.

Neither of us said anything. The way this guy talked it was almost like he wanted to be hated.

"We dig, dude," I said, trying not to roll my eyes. Justin didn't seem to notice, the fake plastic grin still spread across his face. I felt like a robot was standing there watching me.

"Cool, cool," he said, shifting to the other side of the doorway. He pulled out a sheet of paper from the back pocket of his jean shorts. "So, you must be . . . Derickson. And you are," he stopped, his black eyes frozen. ". . . Mr. Sinclair. It's an honor to meet you, sir." He reached out his hand. I gave him a wan shake, but couldn't look into his eyes. "Your father was a supreme legacy at this institution," he said. His voice dropped into a more reverent zone as he spoke. "I wasn't sure if you'd be living on my floor. It's a true honor. Great to meet you too, Mr. Derickson. How was the move in?"

Nick shrugged. "It was all right. We got most of it put away."

"Oh, great," Justin said, his voice tuned up again to an unnatural level of happiness. "We here at Malworth University are glad you chose us for your education. This place has been around a long time. Longer than almost any school in the state. There's a proud tradition of learning and betterment going on here, guys. I hope you're ready for the ride. I'm going to take off and meet some of the other dudes on this floor. But remember, if you need anything, have any problems, or just want to rap it out, my room's at the far end of the hallway. See ya!" Then he darted back out the door.

"What a nerd," Nick said in his monotone. "I don't think I'll be going to him for any problems, thank you. You're not planning on causing any 'roommate issues,' are you?" he asked with a glint in his eye.

"Not that I know of," I said, chuckling. "I don't think there's all that much he'd be able to do anyway."

Nick laughed, a high-pitched shriek miles away from his speaking voice. "No shit. That guy looks wussier than my sister. And she has a mean kick to the genitals to make up for her shortcomings, if you know what I mean."

We settled in to watch some more television, then headed over to the dining hall for a quick bite before turning in for the evening. I wouldn't meet any of the real raconteurs of Schuster Hall until the next day.

BETWEEN THE HOURS of one and five in the morning you find out a lot about yourself. In this case I found that I did not like sleeping in a different bed from my own back in St. James. I found out my new roommate talked in his sleep, and the bathroom for our floor was located as far away from our room as possible. By eight o'clock I was wide awake and ready to jump out of bed, leaving Nick to his pillows. Seeing as how I knew nobody on campus I decided to walk the grounds. I made a complete circle, taking in all four sides of the school grounds and locating a few of my classrooms. After paying way too much for a submarine sandwich at the student union, I made my way back to Schuster Hall. I was crashing pretty hard at this point and so opted for a nap back in our room. I woke up in my unknown, uncomfortable bed to the sun creeping down outside our window. It created a violet pink shade that shone across the upper half of our room. Nick was sitting on the couch reading a gaming magazine.

"I don't know if I'll be able to sleep here very well," I said as I jumped down from the creaky loft. "That doesn't appear to be a problem for you."

Nick uttered his high-pitched laugh. "Yeah, I know. Comes from the family. My dad once slept through a fire in his own house. He said the firefighters couldn't believe it."

"Whoa," I said, amazed. "Well, I'm going to take a stab at exploration. Want to join me?"

"Nah," he replied, waving his hand. "I'm good."

I saw a few open doors on my trip down the hall. Most rooms contained little more than the possessions of their owners: televisions, crappy looking easy chairs, stacks of tattered clothing, a few wooden or metal lofts. None had occupants. I continued until I was forced into a double take by a room halfway down. As I stuck my head back inside I heard the collective laughter of the voices within the room. Inside sat two guys wearing sweatpants and ratty T-shirts. One was situated on a love seat as old as Nick's couch. A large black chest stood in the center of the room as a makeshift table. Several signatures written in silver-gray permanent marker populated each side. The thing reminded me of a larger, dustier version of a high school yearbook. A painted wooden loft arched above the brown love seat. Both eyes were glued to the corner of the room where a kid about my size in a worn blue high school football shirt sat on the wooden desk chair and poked at the keyboard of his computer. His long face stood rapt at attention and his green eyes flowed back and forth. I stuck my head in a bit further to see what was on the screen—a musclebound dude penetrating a thin blonde chick. The guys were watching porn.

"What's up, guys?" I said as a weird mixture of shame and embarrassment caused me to glance away from the screen.

The guy on the love seat stood up to address me. A cheap-ass air conditioner was perilously situated in the window behind him, a luxury given the heat outside. This guy was taller than the kid in the corner and wore a frayed yellow baseball shirt. A patch of cropped, blazing red hair contrasted above his striking blue eyes. "Not much, man. What's your name?"

"Mike," I said. "Uh, Mike Sinclair. I live down the hall in #501."

"You mean with that other weird kid?" the kid at the computer asked. "What's his name anyway? We've just been calling him 'Highlights.'"

"Oh, yeah, that's Nick," I said. "He doesn't talk much. Which I'm fine with," I said. My legs moved back and forth in a nervous dance. I was never good at meeting new people. I'd managed to keep the same clique of friends through four years of high school, none of whom had even considered coming to this university.

"So are you gonna come in?" the red-haired kid said, watching my non-committal legs. "I've got beer getting cold in the mini-fridge. We were gonna wait 'til later to initiate, though."

I paused for another half-second to consider my option of abandoning this room and going back to watch Nick play on his computer or whatever the hell he might be doing. I walked in and grabbed the stock red plastic and metal chair that came along with each of these rooms. We watched in a creepy silence through the current video the kid at the computer had queued up before we started talking about ourselves.

"The name's Adam Baines, and this is my room," the red-haired kid said. "Well, our room. The pervert at the computer is Seth Gordon," he said with a wink. "We're both from Virginia, way up in north country."

Adam was going to school to become a teacher. Seth didn't seem to have a clue what he was doing at this school, but he had thoughts of becoming an engineer.

"Every time I go over one of the bridges up there I think, 'what if I could make somethin' like that?' So I decided, if my older brother can do it, I sure as shit could," was Seth's explanation.

I kept my story short and sweet as I wasn't sure if I could trust them with my boring high school stories. I didn't talk much about St. James and demurred on the issue of my parents. "I don't know what the hell I'm going to major in here, but all's I know is my parents are paying for it, and 'I'd better make the most of it,'" I said, wagging my finger as my father was known to do after his second brandy.

The imagery must have struck a chord with Seth because he said, "Oh, Christ, that's just how my father was, too. 'Make sure you're studying every night and stayin' away from that frickin' booooze,'" he said, elongating the vowels, "otherwise you'll end up like my good-for-nothing brother-in-law Melvin. You know how he used to hit that frickin' bottle. Don't forget you're here to make us proud!'" What I assumed to be a spot-on impression brought Adam to a chortling boil. Seth turned around and switched off the porn, opting instead for some music. "Let's get this fuckin' party started!" he clamored.

"Hell, yeah," Adam said, pulling himself up from the couch to grab some beers out of the mini fridge in the corner of the tiny room. "Grab a brewsky, Sinclair."

I had done my share of high school drinking back in St. James so I accepted a cold can from Adam's outstretched hand. Seth turned up some R&B song by R. Kelly that seemed a little inappropriate for the situation, and we raised our cans to the tiled ceiling. "To college, boys," Adam said, smiling. "The best four-to-six years of our lives."

We took deep drinks and sat on the assorted furniture. The beer tasted stale, but I didn't care. This was the most fun I'd had since my parents and I made the arduous journey to this ghost town. A few things hit me along with the alcohol. The first was that there were no parents to cramp our style. Of course, that meant there also was no one to look out for you if you made any wrong decisions. But for the first time in my life I was living out from under the thumb of disapproval where I'd spent my entire life in St. James. I took another long drink of beer as I savored the emotions.

"So, where is this St. James?" Seth asked as he sat back down.

"Southern Minnesota," I said. "Real farm country down there. The town's small as shit. Maybe a thousand people. Two gas stations and one restaurant. Plus a movie theater that showed movies three weeks after they released. What about Virginia?"

"No more than eight thousand must live there now," Adam said at my left. He held a blue pack of playing cards with a fair amount of beer stains. He laid out some cards on the rough top layer of the chest/table, pushing around some coasters and potato chip crumbles to make room. "Virginia 4 Life" was written in large silver letters where his hand rested. "My folks moved to town when I was a little kid."

"It gets smaller by the year," Seth said. "But that's what small towns fuckin' do. They die. I know we were both glad to get the hell out for a while. My folks'll stay there 'til they drop, of course."

"Mine too. I mean, down in St. James. They're pretty well known around there. Ain't nobody who hasn't heard of the Sinclair family down there." Seth's rural dialect was rubbing off on me. I felt the need to populate my diction with plenty of "ain'ts" and dropped "g"s.

"Ah, yeah, that must be rough," he said, tipping back another pull of his beer. "Thankfully my family isn't known for anything up in Virginia."

"Except for being a bunch of drunken ingrates, you mean?" Adam said, the twinkle returning to his blue eyes.

"Fuck off and deal me in," Seth yelled. "We're playing 'Asshole,' right?" I wasn't familiar with what I would later realize was the most popular college card game in the universe.

"Hell, yeah," Adam said, flicking cards around the chest. "Everybody in!"

Beers were drank, kings were crowned, music was shuffled, and I started to get drunk. As the least familiar person with the game I found myself drinking on almost every turn. By the time I cracked open my third beer Seth had turned the music down to a whisper.

"All right, shut up everybody," he admonished. "It's ten o'clock, almost time for rounds. I heard the RA on this floor is a real douche so we're going to have to keep it quiet for the next ten minutes."

My alcohol-addled mind struggled to consider what he said, so I decided to ask.

"Ah shit man, you don't know?" Seth said. "That's when 'quiet hours' are supposed to begin," he said, using his fingers to create air quotes. "The fuckin' RA's go up and down each hallway making sure doors are shut and we aren't getting too loud and crazy. They also keep a look out for this shit," he said, shaking a near-empty beer can.

"One sight of this, and you're written up. Whatever the fuck that means," Adam said.

"Right," I said. "I think I met the one for our floor today. Jacob, or Justin or something?"

Seth burst out laughing. "Oh, shit, you talked to him? We lucked out because we were both out when he was making his introductions. He makes his daytime patrol on the first weekend to meet all the new kids. My brother dealt with that Justin kid 'round here last year. He's pretty dorky, really into rules and shit. I guess you have to be if you want to do that crappy job. Had a mean streak too. Real class-A arsehole. Anyways, he and another of his kind will be coming around in like two minutes so we have to be quiet. After that we can turn the music back up, but we have to do it all over again at midnight. Once they finish those rounds we can do whatever the fuck we want 'til daylight." He chuckled at a pitch that wasn't quite like my roommate's but still scraped the ceiling of the room just a bit before landing on the edge of my ear drum.

We waited the requisite time and stayed still. We listened, but didn't hear anything outside the door. Around 10:15 the party continued, but I found myself getting tired. "I think I'll go check in on Nick," I said with a yawn. "Thanks for the beer, the game, and the, er . . . porn."

"No problem," Adam said, slapping me on the back as I stood. "Nice to meet ya, Sinclair. Come around again sometime. This type of stupid shit we'll be doing all semester."

"Sounds good," I said, bidding goodbye as I headed out the door. I didn't hear anything from within my locked dorm room. I opened it in the quietest manner possible before slipping into the pitch dark. I could hear shallow breathing coming from the loft. I turned on the small lamp on my computer desk, sat on the ugly plaid couch, and considered the events of the day. Within ten minutes I passed out. I woke up again at 3:00 a.m. and pulled myself up to my mattress. I sat wide awake for an hour before drifting to sleep.

I WOKE UP ON SUNDAY morning to the sound of people conversing and walking down the hallway, their mumbles softened by our wooden door and its purple painted outline. I rubbed my eyes and checked to make sure I hadn't imagined the time of eight o'clock blaring loud red digital numerals next to my brain. I hoisted my legs up and onto the loft ladder. The entire contraption made another suspicious crunching sound as I marched down, but seemed to hold. Nick was nowhere to be found. After putting on an acceptable outfit of workout shorts and a garish gray sports T-shirt much too big for me I flopped down on the plaid couch for some vegetative television watching and cereal eating. After about an hour in this state I heard a loud, explicit fulmination from the room across the hall.

"Fuck!" came the cry again, louder and shriller this time. It sounded like a geek in agony.

I took an apprehensive step into the hallway to gauge the scene. A thin, tall kid my age with black, square-framed glasses was bent behind his television and holding a grasp of tangled electronic cords in one hand. A patch of hair shaped into a neat bowl cut circled his head and leaned forward with the rest of him. He seemed oblivious to my presence. I padded over in my slippers, hoping he'd pop up and notice me, to no avail. He wore an ensemble similar to mine: gray shorts and a white t-shirt.

"Everything okay in here?" I said in as normal a tone as I could muster. The kid leaped a few inches backward at the sound of my voice.

"Jesus!" he exclaimed before standing upright faster than I expected. "Sorry, man. Didn't see you there. I'm having a bitch of a time getting this fucker hooked up."

"I can hear that," I said. "You raised quite a racket."

"Oh, sorry," he said with a sheepish grin. The square glasses shuffled down his nose a centimeter. "Electronics do that to me. I'll try to keep it down." He pushed the black frames up and returned to his work.

"Do you want some help?" I offered.

"Eh, yeah maybe in a second," came the reedy voice from behind the television. "Wanna plug in the red cord I'm dangling?"

I did, and we turned on the device. It seemed to function. "Congratulations," I said. "You can now watch movies."

"Yeah, and I'm damn glad about it too," he said, extending his hand now that it was free of cords. "I'm Eric, by the way. Eric Fulton. You move in this weekend, too?"

"Yeah," I replied. "Parents brought me in on Friday."

"Oh, shit, really? That's cool. You must live with Highlights, then?"

I laughed. "Boy that nickname has really gotten around. Yep, that's him. Nick is his name. Doesn't talk much. That's okay by me, though. I got to know some of the other guys on the floor last night. You met any of them yet?"

"Not yet," Eric said. "I was moving shit all yesterday, and turned in early. You're kinda the first person I've met so far."

"Really? I'm Michael Sinclair," I said. "I'm from St. James, down in the south part of the state. Where you from?"

"Eden Prairie, near the Twin Cities. You can sit down if you'd like." He motioned around his room, which I hadn't taken in since I'd set foot in it. A long padded futon resided at the far end of the room under the hinged window. This room also had a wooden loft and a couple of desks situated underneath. The futon was the major piece of furniture. Posters of Bob Marley, Tori Amos, and the Flaming Lips adorned the walls.

"These yours?" I asked, pointing.

"God no," Eric said. "Those belong to my stoner roommate. I'm sure you'll see him before long."

I let out a slight chortle. "So you're not the Tori Amos fan?"

"Fuck no," he said, plopping down on the futon. The pad was so thick it didn't make a dent. "I'm into more hard rock. I saw Stone Sour at that rock festival in Wisconsin last year."

"Oh, really?" I said, glad to meet somebody with my taste in music. "That must've been a great show."

"Yeah, it was. Corey Taylor was really animated, jumping around on stage and getting the crowd into it and shit. It was pretty sweet."

"Awesome. That's my kind of rocking. So, what are you going to this stupid school for?"

He moved his eyes away from mine. "Uh . . . I'm not sure yet. I think I want to teach, but I also kinda hate kids."

I let out a loud guffaw. "Well that may be an impediment to your future."

"I know," he simpered. "I keep hoping between now and when I graduate I'll be able to stand at least one kid. If not, I'm fucked. Plus, my parents made a big show of me going here. Not sure why—besides my dad nobody else from my family ever went here. Pretty weird, if you ask me."

"Weird, but familiar," I agreed. "Hey, you have any plans for today? I seem to have lost my roommate again and no one else is around."

"Not really. Putting that electronic shit together was kinda the last straw for me. I just wanted to watch a movie, anyway."

"Oh? What movie?"

He looked down at the bland brown carpeting with which all of our rooms had been appointed. "*Star Wars*. I know, I know, it's dorky, but I don't care. I love those old movies."

My eyes lit up. "Oh, hell, yeah, man! I love those movies too. I used to watch them on VHS when I was a kid. We'd tape them when broadcast on TV because my parents were always too cheap to buy the actual movies."

"Hilarious," Eric said. "Well, then it's settled: Let the Force be with us."

We'd reached the Death Star trench run when Eric's roommate, Jake, arrived, girlfriend in tow. He looked pretty much as Eric had described him: short, stout with smaller-framed glasses and shaggy blond hair he kept brushing to one side. He looked like he hadn't shaved in about a week. His girlfriend was a petite little thing with short brunette hair and dark-brown eyes that pierced everything they viewed. I tried not to stare at her.

"What's up, guys?" Jake asked, taking off his glasses to rub his reddened eyes. "We just got back from a walk around campus. This place is freakin' huge! Who's your friend, Eric?"

"This is Mike," Eric said. "He lives across the hall, so I'm sure we'll be seeing plenty of him."

"Oh, cool," Jake said. "What are you guys doing?"

"Nothing," Eric said before I could say anything.

"Yeah, right," Jake said. "What are you watching?"

"Uh . . . *Star Wars*," Eric said.

Jake started laughing. His eyes formed tiny slits behind his glasses. "No shit? I thought that was like a kid's movie or something."

"Yeah, well it's for all ages," Eric said, agitated. "We're almost finished."

"Oh, well, good," Jake said. His miniscule girlfriend hung behind him holding his arms. She had a large goofy smile plastered on her face. "Cuz I was kinda wondering if we could have the room for a while . . ."

A shade of anger flew over Eric's face, but then he composed himself. "Yeah, that's fine. Can we finish this in your room?"

"Sure," I said, getting up from the futon. "Nice to meet you two."

"You too, man. Hey, don't suppose you know where I can score some—"

"That's enough, dude," Eric said, the anger returning. "We're out of here. I'll give you three loud knocks when I'm ready to come back. Okay?"

"Okay, sounds good!" he said. He was already starting to make out with the girl.

"Thanks, Eric!" she said between kisses.

Eric slammed the door as we walked over. Nick still wasn't in our room.

"Just like that, huh?" I said as I plopped down on the green-and-red-plaid couch.

"Yeah, fucking great, isn't it?" Eric sighed. "I hope he transfers at the semester so I get my own room."

"That'd be awesome. Or maybe you could get a woman and do the same thing to him."

Eric scoffed. "Dude, I'm not exactly 'girlfriend' material. I'm a computer nerd who likes sci-fi films and, even worse, books. Girls don't go for that."

"Ah, come on, man," I said. "Don't sell yourself short. You seem like a funny guy. Girls do go for that kinda stuff. And we're at college! Aren't we supposed to be into books?"

"Whatever," he said. "Can we just finish watching this? I want to drown out the sounds that'll be coming from that room in a few minutes."

"Sure," I said. "But we have to figure something out so you're not expelled every night. That's not right."

"Whatever," he said again. We leaned back to finish watching Luke Skywalker save the universe. Nick finally returned just as the credits rolled. He left our door open a few inches. I could see that Eric's room was still shut.

"Where have you been?" I asked.

"Nowhere," he said in his flat voice. "Out, and around. I was checking out the library and kinda got sidetracked. Who's this?"

"Eric Fulton," I said, inviting them to shake hands.

"I live across the hall," Eric said. As he said this, his room opened, and the two disheveled characters walked out.

34

"We're all done, Eric," Jake said. His voice had a sarcastic edge to it that I didn't appreciate. We heard the purple hallway door flex open. Their footsteps echoed down the linoleum stairs.

"Was it good for you?" Eric said. Nick and I both burst out laughing. "All right, fellas, I'm heading back. Got a few chapters of Robert Heinlen to get through before bed.

"Okay, man, have a good evening," I called after him. "Good luck with first day of class tomorrow."

"I'll try. Fucking eight o'clock class is going to be a bitch. See ya!"

"So, what are you going to—" was all I could get out as my eyes traveled back to Nick. He was hunched over his computer desk, headphones on, a first-person shooter game flowing on the screen. "Oh. I guess you've got your night planned. Have fun."

I hit the dining hall for a quick snack and came back for some Sunday night television. Around ten o'clock I got ready for bed. As I brushed my teeth in the quiet, pale-white fluorescent bathroom at the end of the hall, I reflected on the fact that I had just met more new people in two days than I ever had back in St. James. When I returned Nick was already in bed, listing on his side and emanating quiet breaths. I climbed up into the loft and settled into bed. I still felt a terrible amount of loneliness. For the first time in my life I was living away from my parents and among people my own age. I should have felt elated, but the differences were all too much at this point. I told myself it must be the school, it must be because my father wanted me to attend this ancient university, but that didn't seem quite right. I wasn't ready to be on my own. Despite the tumultuous relationship I'd had with my parents over the years, I missed them. I struggled with these thoughts until a few minutes past midnight, when I drifted off to sleep.

Chapter

FOUR

HE NEXT MORNING I WOKE up to the alarm blaring near my head. I rubbed my eyes for a moment as the glowing image came into focus. The number seven stood out and pounded on my forehead, the hour sinking in with each clamoring note. I groped for the off button, my foot brushing against Nick's as I turned. He shifted close to the white painted concrete wall. I crawled down the loft ladder, opening and shutting my eyes until I could see where I was headed down the hallway. A few minutes later I ran into Seth shaving his little goatee in the bright bathroom.

"Hey, Mike," he said, raising his head and flicking shaving cream against the mirror. "Big party this Friday in our room. We're gonna try and get everyone on the floor in there. Should be fun."

I nodded as I brushed my teeth, not sure if I would make it. I liked Seth and Adam, and Eric seemed like he had the potential to be an actual friend. But the jury was still out on the rest of the guys on the floor. Most of them didn't seem to exist.

"We might even ask some of the girls on the other side to come over," Seth continued. "Adam met some of 'em last night. There are a few hotties over there, man. You should come."

"I'll see you there," I said, my apprehension lifting as I spit toothpaste into the bowl. I needed a shave too, but there was no time before my first class.

"Sweet, man!" he said, rinsing cold water over his shaver. "Good luck at class today. Eight o'clock classes are a bitch. One piece of advice my brother gave me from his time here was not to take 'em. I start out at ten each day. Much easier."

"Good to know," I said as I exited the bathroom. My mind was on the potential girls that might come to the party. I walked back to my room, threw on my old raggedy tennis shoes, grabbed the tattered book bag that had survived the journey from high school and headed down the linoleum stairs. My eight o'clock Western Civilization class was located on the west side of the campus, not far from the old gymnasium where we listened to Dean Moriarty give his history lesson. Shull Hall was half that building's size and stood in a rigid rectangule full of right angles. The front was a sheer brick wall interspersed by towering concrete columns that looked straight out of Greece. Tall black lampposts populated the worn sidewalk leading up to the building. A few young saplings lined the grassy area in front of the windows, which had odd circular patterns in their top frames.

I entered the building with a group of other students, and we filtered up the marble stairs. I noticed more than a few concerned kids my age, recognizing the scared look in their eyes as they mulled over their schedule paperwork. My only screw-up was arriving one floor above the one I needed; if not for that I could have avoided the embarrassment of walking into class after the professor started addressing the room. It was a small lecture hall, with two sets of concrete stairs leading up toward the tall windows with their circles on either side at the back of the room. The stairways were surrounded by rows of metal chairs with desktops that slid up from their sides. I scrambled up the first set of steps, feeling the eyes of fifty people, and sat down in the last row near a guy with long hair and a ratty button-up shirt. I picked up the syllabus from the chair. The professor cleared his throat from behind the lectern as I sat down. He looked about the same age as Dean Moriarty but had short white hair and thin glasses, an academic-looking sweater vest, and sharp dress slacks. He raised both arms straight out from his head, a two-handed bizarro version of the Nazi salute.

"Now that we have everyone, let's begin. My name is Professor Deakin. I'll be instructing you in the many ways Western civilization has changed the world. I trust you all purchased your textbook ahead of time. If not, you know where to locate the book store on the north end of campus.

Now then, I've been teaching here at Malworth for many years. In fact, I've been here so long they've tried to get rid of me." Mild murmurs of laughter. "However, the management has seen fit to give me one last chance to achieve tenure at this fine institution, and I dare say I intend to grab hold with both fists. You, class, are my ticket to that tenure. Therefore you must absorb every bit of information I give you with a rabid desire for educating yourselves. I intend to assist you in any way I can, but even I cannot help you if you do not show up promptly. This class begins right at eight o'clock every Monday, Wednesday, and Friday. Not 8:05, or 8:10, but eight o'clock on the nose. If you're unable to make it to class, you'll find the doors locked at one minute past the hour," he said.

The murmuring stopped. He began to pace behind the lectern as he spoke, gesturing with his arms. "And let me tell you: if you do not think you can make it to this class, if you simply are not a morning person or have an issue with Mondays, might I suggest dropping this class right now. I won't be offended in the slightest. But if you miss my class, I will be. That's all I will say on the matter." He returned to the front of the class and opened his book. "Now then. We will start with the Sumarians."

Right as the clock hit 8:50, Professor Deakin ended his lecture and released us into the wild. My eyes had begun to glaze over in the last fifteen minutes as I could not navigate a tic the man possessed. During his lecture, he would step in reverse until his back was up against the large, multipanneled chalkboard on the wall behind him. As he was making his current point, he would wave his arms around in a circle. Then he would walk forward to the lectern while doing this and take up his position there until the next trip backward. After a half-hour of this, my mind became so used to the repetitive motion I found myself zoned out until the end of class. I let most of the other students clear out before I walked down the steps. I was almost out the door when the professor called my name.

"Mr. Sinclair?" came the wizened voice from behind me. I turned around, wondering if this was going to be another lecture on puncutality.

"Yes . . . ?" I said.

Deakin let out a breath of relieved air. "Oh, thank goodness. I had so hoped it would be you."

"You had?" I said. I was still a few feet from the exit and watched the door drift closed.

"I believe your father attended this institution?" Deakin said.

"Yes, he did," I said, uncertainty rising in my voice.

"And now he is sending you to continue the blood line?"

"Um, yeah. More like forced me to attend. But something like that."

"Very good, very good. I look forward to instructing you about not only Western civilization but about other, more pressing matters," Deakin said. I couldn't tell from across the room, but it looked like he winked at me.

"I will look forward to that, too," I said, leaving the room before he could say anything else. I had no idea what this man wanted, but he was beginning to creep me out. I ran into a familiar face with black-framed glasses as I walked out into the giant hallway outside the classroom.

"Yo, Sinclair," Eric Fulton said. "What the hell? I was waving at you as soon as I saw you drag your ass in there."

"Oh, sorry," I said, surprised to see him. "I was a little worried about showing up late on the first day. I guess I'm lucky Mr. Punctual decided not to make an example out of me."

"No kidding," Eric said. "Man, is that guy weird or what? I'd hate to be the guy who pulls on that door at 8:01!"

"I know," I said. "I'd change times, but I have my schedule set up pretty well. Speaking of that, what class do you have next?"

"My natural science course. It's way the fuck over in the biology building, on the southeast side. It's a hellacious walk, but I've got an hour. How about you?"

I pulled out my crumpled schedule. "Uh . . . looks like I have Creative Writing at ten, and then Phys Ed this afternoon over at the gymnasium."

"Good luck with that," Eric said. "I got out of taking Phys Ed due to a technicality."

"What do you mean?"

"Well, I'm technically not good at sports," Eric said. "But that's not the reason. I have asthma. They gave me a waiver. I still have to take the stupid Health & Wellness lecture, though. I'd better get walking. I have to get there early or I'll never find the fucking classroom."

"Sounds good," I said, following him down the hallway. We parted ways outside the square brick corners of Shull Hall.

"Probably see ya tonight," Eric said, turning south.

"Yeah, probably," I said before remembering Seth's announcement that morning. "Oh, I almost forgot. Party at Seth and Adam's room this Friday. He said there might even be girls from the floor."

I detected the slightest hesitation in Eric's gait before he turned back around. "Oh, yeah? I haven't really met those guys yet. I suppose I'll have to drop by before Friday. What girls do they know?"

"I'm still not sure they know any," I said. "So I guess we'll see."

"Yeah, I guess," he said. "All right, I'll see ya later."

I watched him amble away until he melted into the crowd of students carrying backpacks. I turned and headed to the English building.

CREATIVE WRITING WAS MUCH more interesting than my first class. It took place in a small carpeted room in the bowels of the English building, yet another massive old brick structure on the west side of the campus. The bottom half looked even older than the others but was topped by outward radiating floors that gave it the look of an air traffic control tower. A strange art installation made of several solid pieces of concrete stuck out at odd angles and took up most of the sidewalk leading to the building. After another misfire on finding the correct classroom I walked through a simple wood panel door in the basement. My class was made up of about twenty students my age, situated in a half-circle of small desks. Thin windows ringed the upper concrete walls. The professor, Martin Ellickson, was a slight bald man with an easy demeanor who looked about fifteen years older than we were and wore thick, wire-rim glasses. He said he had been published in several literary journals in the state and was now looking to impart some hard-earned wisdom upon us young saps who thought we could make it in the writing game.

Phys Ed came down on the "less fun" side of the spectrum. After a quick lunch at the dining hall near Schuster (I ate alone since no one was at the dorms) and a change into some workout clothes, I trudged in the hot sun to the northwest portion of the secluded campus. The giant brick-and-mortar gymnasium I'd sat in on Friday remained on its moldering foundation, looking near collapse as always. The square windows looked as if they hadn't been washed in decades. The front door with the brass handle stood open at an slight angle. I slipped through and came upon the dull-brown gym floor we'd sat upon for the dean's speech. Thirty stationary bicycles that might have been new in 1970 stood in the center. A handful of nervous kids my age wearing gym clothes were milling about at the edge of the gym.

"You here for the bicycling class?" I asked in a tentative voice.

A kid wearing a torn-up white shirt with pit stains reaching outside the usual area said, "I guess so. Haven't seen the instructor yet."

"My brother told me this was the easiest Phys Ed course offered," the guy standing next to him said. He had a pair of plastic goggles with a blue elastic band strapped to his face.

"I heard that, too," I said, gazing out over the bikes. "But I'm not sure what to—"

I was cut off by a loud shout that echoed from the other end of the gym. "Gentlemen! Over here!"

The handful of us looked over. A hulking brute of a man was speed-walking across the ancient floor, blowing a whistle and shaking his fists. Arms that looked like tree trunks were somewhat contained within the bland gray sweatshirt he'd managed to pull on today. "Everybody get on a bike, now!"

We looked at each other and then acquiesced, each of us climbing up and sitting our butts down on the stiff, unpadded seats. My naive brain had been expecting a class of nice leisure bicycle trips throughout the campus. This was more like a work camp.

"Welcome to Cycling 101, or as I like to call it, ride 'til you drop," the hulk said. He resembled a shorter, angrier version of my PE coach back in St. James, but with more hair. His sweatshirt bore the Malworth University logo and tight black warm-up pants with white buttons clad his giant legs. "Start peddling, boys! And don't stop 'til I say so."

We complied, enduring the man's exhortations every few minutes. Fifteen minutes later I was ready to drop off the bike. The pedals were set to provide some resistance, and I couldn't figure out how to loosen it. My arms held the rest of my body upright as we all looked up to the coach. "Now, check your heart rate. Feel with two fingers on the big vein running up your neck here," he said, showing us. "Feel that pounding? That's what we're going for here. All right, that's enough for the first day. Next week we'll start with a longer ride. Now hit the showers!"

My companions and I slid off the bike seats, all of us in pure agony. The last thing I wanted was to find out what kind of horrific locker room facility this building had, so I made my way toward the massive oak front door. The showers in Schuster Hall were cold, barren stalls of microscopic tiles, but at least I knew them. I bid my classmates goodbye, no longer wondering why there were so few, and thanked whatever power ran the universe that I didn't have to return for a full week.

I had just two classes on Tuesdays and Thursdays, but they were twice the length of the other classes. My science prerequisite, called "Life: The Natural World," began at 10:00 a.m. Tuesday morning at the science building. It was about as exciting as it sounded. The science building, while still ancient in outward appearance, did have a number of working laboratories and chemistry labs outfitted with decent microscopes and Bunsen burners. Our class took place in a long room with twenty work tables holding the accompanying metal implements such as gas valves and sinks. Lining the entire outside wall were glass-enclosed repositories where beakers and other storage containers rested. I spied a full-size human skeleton standing at attention in the back of the room. I sat down at one of the laminated work tables with three other guys and one girl, all of them confused about what to expect. We had just enough time to introduce ourselves when the professor arrived. She appeared around forty years old. A stack of straw-like hair adorned her head, and she wore a starchy suit that appeared to be recovered from the disco era.

"Attention, everyone," she announced at the front of the lab. "Welcome to 'The Natural World.' I'll be your instructor, Professor Langdon. I'm here to teach you all about the world around you and your place within it. I trust you've all purchased the required textbook. Oh, and make sure you're in attendance every day of this class. It's only two days a week, but we will be performing experiments on almost all of them. Bring your thinking caps too, because I won't always be able to explain what we're doing—you'll have to figure that out from the readings."

I was beginning to think this was another introductory class more trouble than it was worth. The other young people at my table seemed to share my worry. The universe must have been shining on me again this day as we were let out of class with almost a half-hour to spare.

My afternoon class wasn't as bad, but the subject was. Another required topic all incoming freshman had to cover at this institution was mathematics. I had chosen statistics, despite having no idea what it might cover. I found out at 2:00 p.m. in a huge, well-lit carpeted room with tall ceilings on the first floor of the English building, one floor above where my Creative Writing class would gather again the next day. Tables and chairs lined either side of the classroom. I chose a desk at the back, and no one opted to sit next to me. The instructor came in five minutes after the class was to begin and apologized. His face looked young, but streaks of light-gray ran through his short ebony hair. Thin glasses with circular rims adorned his nose, and a thick dark beard rimmed his outer mouth. This gave him an avuncular quality that lessened my fear over the nature of the class.

"Sorry for being late," he said in a pleasant, airy voice that echoed off the upper limits of the white-painted ceiling. "Welcome to Statistics. I'm your instructor, Professor Dalton. I'm here to teach you about the many ways probability and causality affect our lives. But we won't get to any of that today. We're going to take a simple test to approximate your aptitude."

A slight groan rippled through the class, dying away before it reached my ears in the back. Professor Dalton distributed a single page to each table. It contained the sort of math problems I thought I'd left behind in high school. I left most of the answers blank and turned in the paper thinking this would be one more math class I'd fail.

"Thanks for doing this," Dalton said at the front of the room after we'd finished. "This'll give me an idea where everyone's strengths lie. I'm not just here to teach you about how many times you have to spin a die to get the number six, although we will learn that. My job is more about teaching you how to think about these concepts. Just keep that in mind, and you'll do fine. My office hours are posted on the syllabus—my office is located in this building, on the fourth floor. Feel free to stop by anytime though, if you're really stuck on something. I'm happy to help."

As put off as I was over being tested on the first day, I couldn't help but get the vibe that this man had a genuine passion for teaching. I gave Dalton a little grin as I walked out of the carpeted room, and it was returned.

SETH AND ADAM HAD BEEN TALKING up their shindig around the hall all week. Each time I ran into one or both they never failed to mention the "hotties" that would be in attendance and the copious amounts of alcohol promised to flow. By Thursday the hype machine had gone into overdrive, with Seth making a call to some unknown person as I sat next to him in his dorm room, promising to get us all "shit faced until Sunday."

I had the entire afternoon available for a nap on the plaid couch while Nick sat playing a game on his computer. When I woke up again, it was close to dinner time. Nick and I tagged along with Seth and Adam to the dining hall, the huge modern structure situated in the center of the other halls. Long, window-full skywalks held up by giant concrete pillars connected it to our floor in the old dormitory. A small store full of college staples like Ramen noodles and Mountain Dew occupied a space inside the first-floor entrance. In the actual cafeteria, a growing male could satisfy any of a hundred various appetites. Students of all ages zig-zagged among the various tables of food. Since my parents had seen fit to purchase a full year's worth of meals here, I took advantage. On this night I ate a healthy combination of pizza and french fries as my compatriots spoke of the night's upcoming adventure.

Half an hour later we stomped back through the skyway to the fifth floor of Schuster. I stopped at my room to put on a pair of slacks and one of my more stylish button-up navy-blue shirts. Five minutes later, I could hear music pounding against Seth and Adam's door as I knocked. The speaker system attached to Seth's computer wasn't huge, but he knew how to place it to create the most noise.

"Yo, Mike!" Seth announced. "Come on in! Beer's in the fridge, courtesy of my brother's friends. Also got some liquor stashed around here for shots. Have a seat. We were about to play some cards."

Before I knew what was happening a beer had bounced off my gaping hands. I reached down to grab it and pulled the tab, only to have foam spray the entire room.

"Foam party!" Adam yelled. He shook up his own beer before spraying it all over the room.

"Jesus Christ, man!" Seth yelled over the pounding bass. "Knock it off, shithead!"

I had never seen such a reckless use of alcohol but kept my mouth shut. The three of us proceeded to fleece each other in poker, going through an entire case of beer due to various "rules" we'd instated. The rule calling for a drink of beer after every swear word got to me after a while, and I felt compelled to speak up about a certain missing element.

"Yo Settthhh," I said, hearing my words slur but not caring. "Where are the 'hotties' you were braggin' about? Looks like a bunch of sausage so far."

Seth cackled over the deafening music. "Don't worry, Sinclair. Adam, why don't you head that way and see if the lovely ladies are ready?"

"Sure thing," Adam said, shoving his shock of red hair underneath a brilliant white baseball cap. He poked his head out the door, "to see if any nosy RA's are out there," as he put it, then exited. I felt a tingling sensation as he left. I'd had a few short-term girlfriends in my day at St. James so I wasn't inexperienced in the area of female interaction. But these were "college girls." That felt intimidating. I slammed the rest of my beer in preparation. Adam returned about five minutes later, two girls behind him. The first was a tall, blonde bombshell with hair that flowed behind her as she walked. She wore a smoking pink jumpsuit that had some oversized letter-jacket type letters ironed onto the front. She had sparkling blue eyes that faded once she saw the collection of goons occupying this room. The other girl I recognized from across the gymnasium at the dean's orientation speech. As soon as I saw the truncated brunette hair, I knew it was her. She had on a pretty pink blouse. and white cotton pants hugged her skinny legs. I caught myself staring into her brazen green eyes and had to look away in embarrassment.

"Gentlemen, please meet Amanda and Sarah," Adam said, beaming with drunken pride.

We all gave awkward handshakes. I made some kind of unintelligible noise as I shook Sarah's hand. Those ample green eyes poured over me, flooding out any other rational thoughts. I never had classmates this beautiful back in St. James.

"Hi, I'm Sarah Jackson," she said, grinning.

"Michael Sinclair," I said. "You can call me, uh . . . Mike, though."

"Mike," she said. "Nice to meet you. So you guys are the hooligans causing the trouble on this side?"

"Hooligans?" Seth shouted. He struck me as someone who could hold huge amount of alcohol, but I could tell he was loaded. "Who the fuck says that?"

"Oh . . . no one," Sarah said, worried. I decided to fill in the silence.

"It's probably that douchey RA down the hall," I ventured, trying to sound cool.

"Who? Justin?" Amanda asked as she grabbed Adam's tequila bottle right from his hand. He was too enamored by her beauty to do anything about it. "You gotta watch out for that guy. He pretends to be all nice and shit, but he wants to be a comedown machine for this whole floor. He warned us about playing music after ten last night. We weren't even being loud!"

"That's idiotic," Adam said. "We're fuckin' college-aged adults here. We should be allowed some leeway in our youthful adventures."

"That's what I say," Sarah said, grabbing the red plastic chair near me. I smiled inside.

"We'll just tone it down around ten, like we always do," Adam said. "You ladies likes card games?"

A few rounds later, I had achieved drunken perfection. I'd even gotten Sarah to laugh once or twice. I had never managed to get any of the girls in my grade back in St. James to think I was funny.

"So where are you from?" I half-yelled over the music. I spied Seth leaning over the wooden chair at his desk to turn up the volume on his little computer speakers.

"I'm from St. Louis Park. Know where that is?" she replied, green eyes twinkling.

"Uh, yeah," I said. "Whatdya think I am, some kind of country bumpkin because I'm from St. James?"

She blushed, making her appearance more delightful. "Of course not! Then again, I've never heard of St. James, so . . ."

I mocked being aghast. "What?! Oh, you'll have to come sometime. We only have one restaurant now, but I have it on good authority we're getting another one in a few years."

"Big town!" she said, grabbing my arm in the playful seduction of youth. I had never hit it off so well with a female before, and never in one night. In high school it was all about the pursuit: getting the girl to take a ride around the main street in town was considered the holy grail, because it meant you might shift to the back seat. Now the girl lived down the hall and had her own room. The more I watched Sarah's beautiful eyes blink as she said certain words, the more I drunkenly hoped I would get to see that room. I was knocked from my train of thought by a loud pound at the door. My eyes shifted around the room in search of a clock, but I didn't see one anywhere. Beer cans covered every flat surface, and Adam held the bottle of tequila open in his hand, mid-pour. Silence fell over the tiny dorm room as Seth turned down the computer volume. I gazed at the window, wondering how easy it would be to open it and crawl out, not thinking about the five-story drop that would happen next.

"Open up!" came the bleak voice on the other side. The hairs on the back of my neck stood straight. I could see Amanda's eyes grow wide from across the room.

"Fine! Jesus." Seth opened the wooden door an inch. "What's up?"

"The level of noise in this room, that's what!" came the voice, shaky yet sinister. I recognized it from my first day of living in the dorms. "Quiet hours have been established for . . ." there was a beat as he must have been glancing at his watch, ". . . five minutes now. I could hear your stereo all the way down the hall, isn't that right, Drake?"

There was a period of silent acquiescence from whomever else was out there. I could hear my heart beat through the tension.

"Right," Justin continued. "Plus I can smell the alcohol from here. Need I remind you that alcohol is not allowed anywhere in the grand dormitory halls of Malworth University?"

"Uh, no, you don't," Seth said, his voice dripping with condescension. "Thanks, though. We'll turn it down." He moved to shut the door. A wide palm blocke that. The sound echoed in the small dorm room.

"You'd better do more than that. Don't think I forgot how your imbecile brother was when he lived here. If I hear one peep out of this room or smell anything else when we come back at midnight, it's your ass. Do you understand me, Gordon?" Justin's voice took on a disconcerting low tone as he said Seth's last name. It was as if someone had replaced the nerdy, authority-loving douche bag with something much more devious. It creeped me out but made Sarah grab my hand, which was worth it.

"Yeah, yeah, I got it. We'll be quiet," Seth said, his voice smaller now.

"You'd better." It sounded like Justin's voice was crawling all around the door, trying to get inside. Seth closed the door and looked at us.

"What the fuck?" he said after a few seconds of silence.

"I don't know," Adam said. "That guy's a lot more mean than he lets on. But at least he didn't look inside. Now, who's up for a shot?"

"Dude, put that away," Seth said. "No more hard stuff. Plus we have to clean all this up before midnight. You know he's going to be listening."

"Man, relax!" Adam said. "You heard 'im. Quiet by midnight."

"Yeah but it's stupid 'quiet hours' now," Seth retorted. "He's just going to be looking for any reason to bust us."

Adam's face showed frustration, but he relented. "All right. But I'm still drinkin' a few more beers." He stowed the tequila in the closet.

"Fine by me," Seth said, sitting down at the computer desk.

Amanda and Sarah looked at each other using the telepathic communication known only to females. "Uh, we'd better go," Amanda said. My stomach dropped as Sarah let go of my hand.

"Sorry," she said. Her cheeks still had a touch of brilliant rouge about them.

"Don't be," I said, smiling.

"Well, it was kinda fun while it lasted," Amanda said, pushing some gorgeous blonde strands behind her ear. Seth and Adam both sat in rapt attention. "We'll have to do it again sometime. Preferably when douche-nuts isn't doing rounds."

"Sounds good, ladies," Seth said. "Thanks for coming."

As soon as they left, we all cracked another beer. The night got hazy for me as we started playing cards again and discussing which of the ladies was hotter. I remember Seth making some kind of joke at my expense—something about me using the hand I'd held Sarah's with for something despicable later. Around eleven I decided to head back to my room, making sure I had plenty of time before Justin came back. I said good night to Seth and Adam and walked down the silent hallway. I didn't hear any type of commotion coming from the other rooms. Nick was already asleep when I arrived. I switched on the television and sat on the plaid couch until I fell asleep. I dreamed about Sarah's eyes glowing like emeralds in the darkness.

Chapter
FIVE

Y SECOND WEEK OF CLASSES went a little better than the first. I made it on time each day to Western Civ and didn't get locked out of the room like Eric, who on Friday was forced to sit out in the hallway for the entire lecture and had to rely on my keen note-taking skills. Professor Dalton had graded our first-day statistics quizzes. I turned out to be in the lower third of scores. I survived another cycling class by learning how to adjust the tension speed on the metal stationary bikes and lowering it whenever "Coach" (whose name had not been asked for or given) walked away from my general area. Life: The Natural World proved to be about as stimulating as before. By the Thursday of my second week I'd already determined an afternoon of video games with Nick was more worthy of my time.

The boys of Schuster Hall continued their partying ways, always inviting Eric and me along for their debauchery but not always getting a response. I wasn't sure what to make of these kids or the fact that we still seemed to be the major contingent of human beings anywhere to be found in this dormitory. I managed to avoid Justin most days, but whenever I was trapped walking down the hallway I made sure to avert my gaze.

Sarah's gorgeous eyes were another story. I couldn't get them out of my head. I hadn't seen her since the party, so I decided to pay her a visit Thursday night under the auspices of a "study session." I took a gamble we must have at least one similar class. I also hoped she'd see through my facade. I made my way down the hall, speeding up as I walked past Justin's room. I pushed open the purple metal door and walked through to the lobby separating the two gendered sides, a slight tingling sensation crawling up my back. I had no idea which room was hers. Several doors were open in this hallway, as opposed to the total silence that came with mine. Dim light poured from a few of the rooms into the carpeted hallway. I approached the first one on my right. A pretty Indian girl with wide brown eyes and long dark hair sat on a padded pink futon reading a book. When she saw me, her eyes took on the nervous pitch of someone being stalked in a public park.

"Can I help you?" she said in a boisterous voice.

"I'm, uh . . ." I stammered, the awkwardness of the situation overcoming me. "Do you know which room is . . . Sarah's?"

She stood abruptly. "Why do you think I must know? Did she say I was her friend?" She began to walk toward me. A single drop of sweat hit the back of my neck. My sense of self-satisfaction in coming had evaporated.

"Uh, no, I guess not," I mumbled.

"Yeah, you guess not," she said. "But I'll tell you what, since I'm feeling charitable, I'll give her a message for you. She's at night class right now. What's your name?"

"Uh, Michael. Mike. Sinclair. Mike Sinclair," I garbled. "We met at the party on our side last weekend."

She started to write on a small piece of notebook paper, then stopped. "Oh. That was you guys? Thanks a lot, dumbass. Your RA is on the war path against all of us now."

"Sorry." I shrugged. "We weren't doing anything, just drinking. That guy needs to lighten up."

She started writing again. "Yeah, no shit. He's a tool. Okay, what's the message?"

I racked my brain, trying to remember why I'd taken this stupid journey of embarassment. "I wanted to see if she would be up for a study session."

"Okay, for what class?" She eyed me with an inquisitive gaze, her brown eyes dilated.

I knew my goose was cooked. Somehow I was hoping to start discussing class and then sweet talk my way into her room. "I'm not sure," I said, alarmed by my honesty. "Look, I just wanted to see her again. I don't know if we even have any of the same classes."

Her eyes relented. "All right, I'll give her the gist. It'll be less lame, though. Good night!" She shut the wooden door. The outside cork board came inches away from my face. A single blue pushpin almost made it into my nose. I turned to walk back down to the guys' side, mortified to my soul.

ANOTHER WEEK WENT BY before I got my answer. I was relaxing with Nick in our room after another boring Thursday installment of class when Sarah showed up at our door. The sight of her beautiful green eyes made me sit up in my plastic desk chair like a soldier.

"Hey, Mike," she said, inching closer to the door. She wore a giant sweatshirt with the words "St. Louis Park" on the front in red lettering, and blue sweatpants.

"Hey, Sarah," I said. "Did you, uh—"

"Get your message? Yeah, I did. That's why I'm here. After some prodding, Sidarthi gave it up. What in God's name did you say to her?"

"Uh, nothing," I said, slumping in my chair a bit. "Was that your roommate? She was weird, anyways."

"Right," she said, flashing a sharp smile. "*She's* the weird one. So how'd the rest of that party turn out?"

"It didn't really turn out into anything," I said. "After the incident with our lovely RA, things kinda wound down."

"Oh, I see," she said. "Well anyways, I do need help studying for my biology class."

"Oh, really?" It was all I could think to say.

"Yeah, dude. You have Life: The Natural World, right?"

"Oh, yeah," I said, relieved. "Do you have the honorable and grumpy Mrs. Langdon?"

"The very same. Is it just me, or does she seems unpleasant whether she's teaching or not?"

I laughed. "Oh, yeah. I don't get why most of the professors here seem to hate their jobs."

"I know," she sighed. "This whole campus is freakin' depressing. But since it was the cheapest place, my parents were attracted." She pulled on a single strand of long, dark hair. I was immobilized by the sight.

"Sorry to hear that," I managed to blurt. I realized Nick had been listening to this entire conversation. "Oh, this is Nick, my roommate."

"Nice to meet you," Nick said without looking up from his computer.

"So, when do you want to do this?" she asked. "I want to check out that library. Have you seen it? Creepiest building on campus. And that's another thing—is there a single building here that doesn't date back to the effin' eighteen-hundreds? It's like they kept everything how it was and modernized when forced to, but even that was done back in the sixties."

"Maybe that's how they keep the cost so low?" I ventured, hoping she'd find it humorous.

"Maybe," was all she said. "So you up for a library trip next week? Just make sure it's not the night I have class, Sherlock." She grinned, and a spark flashed through her amazing eyes.

"Yeah," I said, entranced. "How does Monday work? I could use a distraction after wrecking my body on the stationary bikes in the afternoon."

"Monday works," she said. "Come over to my room when you're ready."

"Oh, thanks," I said. "I'll see you there."

"Sounds good," she said. "Well, I gotta get going. See you then!"

I turned to Nick once she was gone. "Yeah, I'm trying to get on that," I said in my best manly voice. It sounded stupid the minute it escaped.

"Yeah, good luck. You sounded pretty smooth so far," he said between mouse clicks, his back still turned to me.

"Thanks for the vote of confidence," I said. My heart beat normally again as I leaned back in the plastic desk chair. I couldn't wait for Monday.

I STOPPED BY SARAH'S ROOM at seven o'clock Monday evening. My legs ached from an afternoon of sheer physical exhaustion in my cycling class.

We walked the craggy sidewalks that crossed campus, making our way to the library, an ancient, crumbling edifice situated near the center of campus. As we got closer, I realized Sarah was right to warn me about this place: it looked downright ghoulish. Tall spires rose toward the inky sky and giant wooden doors braced with rusted iron clasps stood as an entrance.

"This is unlike any library I've ever seen," I said as we muscled the giant oak door open a few feet. My calf muscles screamed fire at the movement.

"I know, right? I'm telling you, some kind of medieval-type shit went on in here," Sarah said. She shouldered a rumpled brown backpack with multiple patches sporting rock bands from the seventies stitched to the outside. A large button with a peace sign stuck out from the other side.

Inside, the pock-marked stone walls had actual metal stands for torches. Electric lighting seemed to have been installed in the 1950s and were strung down the middle of the ceiling. The carpet under our feet looked about a century old, its tarnished gold edges frayed on all sides. The distant echo of huge doors shutting surrounded us. The musty, dank smell of a thousand old books made me cough. Another smell lingered underneath the books which I couldn't place, but was pungent as an open grave. It reminded me of the smell in the gymnasium, and I shuddered.

The front lobby area looked a bit more modern and contained several beat-up metal work desks with actual computers. The stacks loomed above us through a long gap in the ceiling. A huge collection of antique wooden shelving stood on the second floor. We approached the front desk where an elderly gentleman sat on a wooden swivel chair. His eyes never left us as we approached. His receding silver hair floated over his skull like a wisp of willow. The eyeglasses that kept slipping down his nose sported black frames. The tiny, probing eyes behind them meant business.

"Can I help you?" came his raspy voice. He leaned forward, his mauve suspenders pulling taut as his pointy elbows angled upon the desk.

"Uh, yeah, we're looking for some books on biology," I said.

"Mm hmm," the man said, consulting what appeared to be the first instance of a card catalog system in existence. "Looks like . . . Level Three,

Section J. Do you need assistance getting there, my young masters?" The gleaming eyes held a trace of congeniality.

"Yeah, we do," Sarah spoke up, since I didn't.

"Take the first stairwell you see over there," he pointed with one lengthy digit. "When you reach the third level, go all the way to the western edge. There you'll find Section J. Please note: do not attempt to reach the fourth floor, as it is . . . under construction. And please let me know if you have any questions."

We looked at each other for a beat before we high-tailed it to the stairwell. Torch stands stood out from the brick wall on either side of the dark gaping maw of stairs.

"Here goes nothing," Sarah said as we entered. The chill I'd felt walking in came back with a vengeance as we started upward. The circular stairwell seemed to stretch on for an eternity, but soon enough we were at the third floor. An extraordinary chain of creaky wooden shelves stretched before us. The musty smell wasn't as bad up here, but I could still detect it as we walked in silence until we saw the "J" section. We perused a few of the major works on the natural world and selected an ancient wooden desk for our study area. A few students sat at the far end of the hall at another table. Other than them, we were alone. I put down the book I had found, a leather-bound tome with a giant picture of a maple leaf on the front.

"Is it just me, or does this place creep you out?" I asked.

"Hell, yeah," Sarah said, smiling. "It's almost like this whole campus was dropped here from a hundred years ago and we're just lucky to be in attendance."

"I know," I said. "Like it's from some time out of place."

"Or from some time that never should have beeen," she said, her eyes looking over the towering shelves. "I did some research on this place over the summer. Did you know this used to be a center for religious rituals back in the 1800s? It wasn't turned into a college until many years later."

"Not really," I said, even though I had learned just that during orientation weekend. "That's pretty crazy."

"Yeah, I know. The stuff the dean talked about . . . he didn't even touch the really weird shit that went on here. Stuff like human sacrifice, embalming bodies, secret rituals, human experimentation. And this one thing I read said there was a secret tunnel system under the whole place, so the overseers could control everything."

Something fuzzy appeared in my mind as she said it, and I couldn't shake it even as Sarah continued to speak. It looked like a square with lines drawn on it . . . a map. I was drawn to the upper right edge of it where a crude circle was coming into focus.

"Anyways, none of that stuff goes on anymore, I'm sure," she continued. "They couldn't have college kids here if it did." She opened up the book we had found. A puff of dust flew upward, making her sneeze. "Jesus, when's the last time this thing was opened—Reconstruction?"

We looked over the text for a while, trying to locate anything that could help us through Langdon's intractable class. Sarah spoke up again. "Are you going to Homecoming this year? I hear it's going to be off the chain, or whatever that expression is."

At that moment in time, any kind of school celebration was the farthest thing from my mind. But since Sarah was asking, I said, "Oh, yeah. I'll be going."

"Oh, really?" Sarah said, sounding surprised. "I didn't think you knew about it. So will I be seeing you up on the hill?"

"You probably will," I said in a clumsy voice. I could tell she was skeptical, so I folded a bit. "So . . . what all goes on up there?"

She smiled, her azure eyes catching the light pouring in from the dusty upper windows in this masoleum. "I guess you'll have to find out, won't you? I'll give you a hint. It has to do with women, and the loss of a certain part of clothing."

Hearing that focused my attention. "Really?" I said, a bit too interested. "Ok, I'll be there."

"But be careful," Sarah said. "I guess the cops crawl all over Cold River lookin' to bust people that night. Of course this is just what I've heard."

"Well, I'm sure I'll be in the mood for some type of celebratory fervor. That's like halfway through the semester, right?"

"Yep, at the end of October," Sarah said. "There's a parade downtown at noon. I hope to see you there. Now let's get back to studying. I want to get out of here at a reasonable hour."

"Me too," I said, looking over at the other table that had students at it. Now nobody sat there. I heard footsteps echo in the stairwell, and the ghost voices of other students emitted from the floor below us. After an hour of reading about different types of plant soils we'd had enough. We stepped back down the stone stairwell and made our way out through a slight space in between the giant oak doors. I escorted Sarah back to Schuster Hall until we reached my room on the fifth floor.

"Thanks for going, Mike," Sarah said, turning around. "I'll let you get back to Nick and the boys. Take care, and be careful."

"Oh, okay," I said, surprised. "I will. See ya."

And with that she was off bounding down the carpeted hallway. The small brown backpack sashayed as she walked, the peace button flopping back and forth. I watched her push through the far door before I turned my key in the lock. I was falling for this girl. Little did I know that was the best protection I could have.

Chapter

THE GENERAL ROUTINE THAT ENSLAVED most college campuses settled in around the middle of October. I made it a point to attend class almost every day. The exception was cycling, which I skipped once due to my not wanting to put in an effort. I paid for it the next week as Coach "made an example" out of me in front of my peers. I went to Life: The Natural World for no other reason than not wanting to look like an idiot in front of Sarah. The other classes were embedded into my life after a few weeks of steady attendance. The boys in Schuster Hall continued their unapologetic rampage against dormitory norms, hosting loud parties on random nights, but always keeping things quiet around ten o'clock. The few times I saw Justin in the hallway he looked like he was in a hurry for class and didn't want to speak with me.

I was getting to know Eric pretty well. He was the motivating factor ensuring I made it to Professor Deakin's class on time each Monday morning. If I hadn't vacated my bed ten minutes after my alarm I was sure to hear a blaring knock on my door. We talked about the nerdy stuff we were into on our way to class: the finer points of *Star Wars* vs. *Star Trek*, which heavy metal band ought to reunite (I always chose an Ozzy-led Black Sabbath, he a DLR-helmed Van Halen), and what it was like to occupy the illustrious halls of Schuster. Eric still hadn't gotten to know his stoner roommate very well because he was always kicking him out of the room. His temperament toward Jake was growing dark.

"Seriously, I live there too, right?" he clamored one wet and dreary morning as we walked with umbrellas purchased at the student union. "Why can't I exert veto power on his shit?"

"Because you're not the one getting laid, amigo," I said. "But I understand why you'd be upset."

"The other night, I came back from night class, and there was all this smoke billowing out the window," Eric said, exasperated. "Do you know how much trouble we'd get into if Justin saw that?"

"I know, I know," I said, flicking a rain drop out of my eye as I avoided a puddle in the craggy sidewalk. "You might want to lay down the law with him. He could get both of you kicked out."

"No shit," Eric said. "Hey, are you going to the big Homecoming shindig?"

"I was about to ask you the same thing," I said, laughing. "What is it about this 'hill' that gets everyone so excited?"

Now it was Eric's turn to snicker. "You'll see."

"All right," I said. "I'd better. Do you want to head there together? I haven't driven the Oldsmobile since I got here. I want to make sure the damn thing still runs."

"Sure, I'll go with you," he replied. "But you'd better not fucking ditch me for any hotties we may or may not encounter."

"Like I'd ever do that," I said, a wide grin on my face.

"Oh, right," Eric said. "I forgot who I'm talking to."

We walked the last few steps into Shull Hall in a whirlwind of fists and flying raindrops.

I POUNDED ON ERIC'S DOOR on the last Friday night in October as a little payback for his early morning awakenings. The sound echoed down the empty hallway. Seth and Adam had vacated for parts unknown. I was a little offended they hadn't invited me out, but figured I'd see them on this mysterious hill everyone kept talking about. I hoped Sarah would be there. I couldn't get her mention of "women" and "certain parts of clothing" out of my mind. Every time I put her in the equation I had to push the thought away. Sarah was more to me than her body, as beautiful as it was. She was a girl who didn't mind hanging out with me; back in St. James that was considered a win by my standards.

"Jesus, knock it off! I'm coming," Eric announced as he swung open the door. Behind his thick-framed glasses and thin hair I could see a pillar of smoke wafting up into the air. He wore a respectable teal button-up shirt and some old brown slacks the color of gravy. I noticed a little bulge in the stomach area of the shirt, a sure sign he was taking on the freshman fifteen.

"What the fuck is going on in there? Woodstock?" I said, my nose filling up with fumes.

Eric let out a gasping cough as he slammed the door. "They're . . . fu-fucking trying to get rid of me, the dicks. I mean: my roommate the dick and his girlfriend, the dick. I'd normally say 'bitch' but she's more of a man than I am sometimes. You ready to head out?"

"I am," I said. I had chosen a black T-shirt with white pinstripes and my most solid pair of blue jeans. "Thanks for coming with me. Do you know where Seth and Adam went?"

"With any luck, we'll find 'em down at the bars. They don't exactly shy away from alcohol."

"We'd better be careful if we go there," I said. "Sarah said the cops swarm town during this thing. Considering I don't even have a fake I.D—"

"Relax, you'll be fine," Eric said, pushing open the pneumatic purple door by our rooms. "If you want to drink, just swipe a wrist band. Everybody does it."

"Hm," I said, thinking it over. Perhaps if Sarah saw me as a cool drink-buying fellow, I'd have a better shot. "I'll see what I can do."

We jumped down the linoleum stairs two at a time and blasted open the front door of Schuster Hall. Multiple lines of students walked their way toward the main exit of the campus on the east side. We headed down the cement stairs to the parking lot where the Olds was stored. Even in the pale dusk I could still make out its horrific paint job. I unlocked it and we jumped in the front seats.

"So this is your beast from high school, huh?" Eric observed. "Bet you got a lot of play with these torn up seats," he said, fingering a gaping hole in the fabric.

"Shut up," I said. "More than you probably got in high school."

"Fuck you. I'll have you know, got my fair share of . . . oh, who am I kidding? You know me better by now," Eric said, looking downcast. The dim light outside somehow darkened his face. "I didn't get jack shit in high school. I was hoping that'd change in college, but then my parents forced me to come up to the University of Castlevania here. I've seen maybe a grand total of ten women since I arrived. That ain't right, man."

"Don't worry, dude. If there was ever a chance to score with a fine lady, it's tonight. Let's get this show on the road."

I turned the key and the old dragon fired up, belching a cloud of exhaust into the atmosphere behind us. I hit the gas, and the car sputtered, but kept running. I said a silent prayer of thanks and put it in reverse. I pulled out of the parking lot and turneddown the small paved street that ran past Schuster and the other dorm halls. I had to avoid a few stumbling revelers as we made our way to the main gate. Malworth had no sports teams, so I wasn't sure how they were treating the Homecoming event. I knew it meant previous alumni would be coming back to their Alma Matter, but in high school this thing always meant a football game and a dance afterward. I took the Olds on a slow crawl through the creepy metal gates my parents and I had entered my first day here. I meandered down the gravel road leading to Cold River. Darkness descended on my left side as the burnt-orange sliver of sun moved below the horizon at a slow clip. Several empty beer cans dotted the wide ditches on either side of the road, some caught between long reeds and blowing in the wind. A very old station wagon with wooden paneling trammeled down the road behind me. Its horn made a weird, high-pitched nasal sound as I spied it riding my ass in the rearview mirror. Realizing I wasn't going to speed up, its driver pulled around and floored by us, keeping his fist square on the horn. It was full of drunken college kids dispensing a few variations of the finger and some exhortations to drive faster than my grandfather. The driver chugged down a beer as he drove. Then they were gone, flying up the road toward the town and blowing gravel back at us. The tiny rocks dinged my warped windshield.

"Assholes," Eric said. "If what you said about the cops was true, they sure as shit better get pulled over."

"No kidding," I said, embarrassed. "They ought to be the first in line." I pushed down on the gas a bit harder and the wheels spun on the loose gravel as the encroaching night swept around us. I had made it to the end of the school's driveway when the last remnants of golden sun submerged behind the horizon. I flipped on the headlights and drove toward town. According to a drunken Seth, the "hill" was a street in the center of Cold River stocked with bars. Being as it was such a pain in the ass getting out of campus and making it there, it wasn't a major destination for most of the year. But on Homecoming night the place got packed tighter than a sardine container. Given my aversion to being in close proximity with people, at first I thought that sounded like an unnatural time. But the more I heard the stories, the more I was intrigued. Scores of college kids crowded the sidewalks. I followed them awhile before I saw the main event. I slowed to a crawl behind a four-door Ford.

A long, sloping hill lay before my car like the others in Cold River, ravaged with pot holes with only faint yellow lines down the center. On either side sat a group of establishments with names like Tony's and the Ice Castle. But the huge crowd gathered down the middle caught our attention. A few people had beers in plastic cups, some wore Mardi Gras type outfits; others wore even less clothing on this cold October evening. A parade of cops strode up and down either side, manning white wooden barricades and looking ferocious in riot gear. One celebrant tried taking his plastic cup of beer past the barricade and was manhandled to the ground. As I stared down the street, pondering where in hell I was going to park, I noticed one final thing. A girl not much older than I had managed to pull herself up onto the shoulders of a few strapping bucks in the crowd. Upon seeing this, the surrounding people started chanting something. It sounded like "throw your pits," but I knew what they were saying. The girl waved her arms, asking for beads from her devoted audience. After a few were thrown her way she proceeded to do the deed. From our vantage point it was hard to see, but I got a good enough look to know what I was missing. The car behind me gave a loud honk to let me know the light had changed. I pulled onto a residential road adjoining the hill. One of the cops glared at me as I drove past him.

"Holy shit, tell me you saw that," Eric said. "We have to get down there."

I lucked into a parking spot in front of a tall vacant brownstone. We got out and pounded up the sidewalk to the hill. We arrived between the rundown club named Tony's and a shithole called Sharkey's. The crowd was gathering momentum, and the noise drowned everything else out. A cheer rose out of the group as another girl showed off her goods. I strained to see above the heads of my fellow classmates, but saw nothing. I groaned.

"Let's find a bar," I said. "I wanna be drunk enough to enjoy this."

"Ah, man, but the show's just starting!" Eric protested. "I want to see some tits, Mike."

"Dude, the show'll go on all night," I said. "Don't you want to drink your first college beer in a bar?"

He looked at me, then back at the crowd. "Oh, all right," he said. "Let's do it. But you're doing the swiping."

My hometown had more than its share of dive bars, but none of them looked like Tony's, which was a combination club and pizza joint. A vague outline of stainless-steel kitchen equipment shown through the broad front window. Loud dance music emanated from behind the front door. We approached the bouncer's broad shoulders and bald head.

"I.D.," he spat, not looking at us.

I pulled out my driver's license, as did Eric. The brute stared for what felt like an eternity.

"Okay, you get a stamp," he said. He took a small black pad from the counter beside him and pressed a blotched image on my hand. "But I'm warnin' you. I see one drink in your hands, and you're out of here. Capiche, homeslices?"

"Uh . . . right," I groaned as we slunk by him.

We walked down the dark hallway. The kitchen equipment I saw outlined earlier sat behind huge panes of glass. I could see some pizza makers slapping dough and throwing pies into the giant oven. I pushed open the swinging door to the main bar and was bowled over by the noise. The place wasn't as full as I thought it'd be but was tough to navigate. The smell of sweat mixed with a strong scent of alcohol. A circular bar took up the middle of the room, and I could see a dance floor beyond it. There were pool tables on the other side, and steps leading to a lower area. Techno music pulsed through my brain, and I could feel a headache beginning. A young, tattooed bartender with greasy hair and a nose ring eyed us as we sat down.

"Hey, hey," he said, waving his arms as he approached. "No underage up here at the bar. Make room for the paying customers. Or go see the show outside. I mean, come on guys. Have you two ever seen a real breast?"

"Hey, fuck you, buddy," Eric said as we got up to leave. "We'll take our business elsewhere."

"What business? I wasn't going to serve you," the bartender said, one eye turning upward with the nose ring.

"I know, dumbass," Eric retorted. I snorted some derisive laughter.

We wandered around the bar amid pumping bass and strobe lights, watching sexy girls we'd never have the courage to ask to dance. We relegated ourselves to a high-top on the outskirts of the pool tables where we sat watching an old guy with a ZZ-Top beard take on a young kid with a cropped beard. As I watched them circle the table, I felt a tap on my shoulder. I looked over to see an even older guy than the pool player. His beard looked like the shaved remains of a fox, and a fluffed up mustache covered half his mouth. His blue eyes had a mysterious glean in the darkened club.

"Say, fella, couldn't help but see y'all get turned down at the bar," he yelled over the music. "I felt bad for youse guys, so I bought ya beers."

He handed each of us cold beer glasses filled to the brim with pale amber.

"Now don't go a-showin' the barkeep or nothin'," his said. His voice had a ragged edge to it, like he was hungover but out for another night. "Just set 'em on the table. If anyone asks, they's mine."

"Uh, thanks?" I said, looking at Eric and not sure what to make of our fortune.

"Not a problem. I been comin' here for years. Try to help the young 'uns out now and again. They want to get drunk and stupid like the rest of their friends." His blue eyes twinkled against the flashing lights, and I could see dirt lining the corners of his mouth.

"We appreciate it," Eric yelled over the music. "What's your name, old timer?" For someone with a short fuse, Eric was quite good at talking with strangers.

"Alfred," the old guy said. "Alfred James. Been here a long time, much longer than you two rapscallions. Before this place was even a school. Ol' Mister Ed Whitacre said he'd take care o' my problems. Instead gave me a brand new set. Lots of tragedy at this here school, my boys. Lots . . ." he seemed to be staring off into space. I looked down at his clothes. A soiled cloth suit adorned his chest and covered a torn purple vest with marble spheres for buttons. Thin torn slacks ran down his legs and two pointed leather shoes jutted out beneath them. The name he mentioned sounded familiar to me, but I couldn't remember where I'd heard it.

"But enough 'bout me, masters," he croaked over the pulsing beats. "What the hell are you two doing in these parts?"

Eric grunted. "Both our parents wanted us to go here."

The old-timer stroked his starchy beard. "Mm hm, heard that before. Gots to keep the ol' family legacy intact, 'n' all that malarky. Them's the worst."

"What do you mean?" I asked, the icy cold beer glass stopped inches from my mouth.

He looked at me with those bracing blue eyes. "Huh? Oh, nothing. Just thinkin' out loud for a spell there, junior. Well, I need to be off, gents. Gotta go haunt some other folks who think it's their destiny to be here. I stick around these here parts, so look for me if you ever come back into this saloon. I ain't goin' nowhere." He slammed both palms on the high-top and wandered in the direction of the stairs leading to the lower area. His gait seemed to favor one of his legs, as if he had an old injury. I glanced at Eric, who was as bemused as I was. When I turned back I saw something weird, and I'm pretty sure it wasn't a trick of the lights pulsating through the room. A young, blonde girl in a skimpy black dress walked up the stairs just as the old man was ambling down. As they met her shoulder and arm seemed to pass right through his instead of repelling it. A large group of guys walked in front of the stairwell right after and blocked everything from view, so I wasn't sure. But for a brief second it looked like he was translucent, which meant . . .

"What a fucking decrepit weirdo," Eric yelled, returning my attention.

"Yeah I know," I said, looking back at the empty stairwell. "What do you think he meant about our parents wanting us to be here?"

"No clue. Guy looked like he came back from the Civil War for a drink. Speaking of that, what say you and I go bottoms up before Tatooey McGinnis over there takes these glasses away?"

I looked at the pale liquid in front of me, deciding whether it was safe. The rational side of me won out so we both finished the beers. I slammed my glass down on the table and let loose a refreshing "Aahh!" The crappy beer we used to get college kids to buy for us at the gas station in St. James had nothing on this stuff.

"Well, that's the last beer we're gonna get in here," Eric said, standing. "Wanna go check the scene outside?"

"Yeah, what the hell," I said.

We returned down the long hallway and emerged outside. The number of people in the street had doubled. A huge shout began at the bottom of the hill and radiated up toward us, moving through the crowd like an stampede. I looked up and saw what to that point in my young life was the greatest thing ever: three women hoisted on the shoulders of guys tall enough to be professional basketball players, throwing their shirts off and letting them fly into the wind. I stopped, my mouth gaping at the scene. The brutal and morally reprehensible objectification of this ritual would not hit me until much later. I kept staring until Eric pushed me along down the street.

"Gotta keep moving, dude. Cops are heading this way," he said from behind me. I turned to see a sheer line of officers moving through the crowds toward the women. It appeared brief flashing was acceptable, but removing clothing and being topless was not. One of the riot cops pulled a baton from his side and held it above his head. Some drunken idiot in the crowd had the brilliant idea to grab the baton as it was raised, pulling the officer backward onto the asphalt street. I knew shit was going to get real at this point, so we turned and ran toward the last bar on the street: The Ice Castle. Steam propelled from its roof and condensation poured down its glass windows in thin lines.

"Holy fuck, dude," Eric said, looking back up the hill. I turned as we approached the front door of the bar. Madness had descended upon the group of super tall guys. The ladies began dropping from their shoulders to the street. I saw multiple kids getting beaten with batons as the remaining people cleared out in a stampede. The chain reaction pushed people toward us. I grabbed the cold handle of the door, my fingers sticking to the metal for a moment.

"Jesus," Eric said as he slammed the door once we were inside. "I thought the cops were cool with this shit on Homecoming?"

"That's what I heard too," I said. "I guess not." I walked up to the bouncer and showed my driver's license. We stepped through into a world of frozen wonder. A good-sized bar composed of sheer ice lined the room. Bartenders wearing pull-over down jackets patrolled behind it. The table tops were made of ice as well, ethereal discs floating above metal stands. College girls dressed in skimpy attire shivered as they downed shots. The music was a mix of upbeat dance music and hard-edged rock, spun by a DJ in the back corner. The temperature was the most perfect thirty-two degrees I had ever felt outside of real winter in Minnesota. We sat at a table far away from the bar, shaken from what we had witnessed.

"If that idiot hadn't grabbed that cop's baton . . ." I said over the pounding music.

"Yeah, what a dipshit move," Eric said. His glasses had already begun to fog. "I hope we don't find out tomorrow it was somebody from Schuster trying to get a better view. But what a view it was, dude! I got enough put away in the ol' spank vault to last me the rest of the school year."

"Gross," I said. "But the view was nice. You know, before the whole police riot and shit." I gazed toward the bar. A server wearing a blue coat paired with a short gray skirt darted past our table. I caught her eye and mumbled a drink request. When she saw neither of us had a wristband, she rolled her eyeshadow-covered eyes and continued her rounds.

"I don't know why you try, dude," Eric said. "We are not going to buy any drinks tonight. Might as well face up to it: the best place to get hammered is the dorms. Least 'til we're twenty-one. Which in my case won't be for another two fucking years!" He yelled the last bit, causing several people to glance in our direction.

"Shut up," I whispered. "We'll get some drinks. Just gotta find an older person to buy for us."

"What, you mean like that skeleton at Tony's?" Eric snorted. "Yeah, he was real lively conversation. I did get kinda buzzed from drinking that beer, though. Okay, who in this place looks like they'd be happy to illegally purchase alcohol . . . ?"

I noticed someone approaching our table from the bar. He appeared about a quarter the age of old Alfred, and his clothes were from a nearer era.

"What's this I hear about you gentlemen needing drinks?" he said in a smooth drawl as he reached our frozen table. He had short, slicked-back black hair and wore a strung monocle over his right eye, which he took off and cleaned before inserting in his front pocket. He wore a pressed striped suit and the gold chain of a pocket watch dangled around his waist. A translucent layer of dirt seemed to cover the jacket. His wing-tip shoes clicked as he stood at attention over our table. I reached over and grabbed his shoulder, half-expecting my hand to pass through it. When I found purchase in a very real arm I realized I had to cover for the odd move.

"Uh . . . yes, we do, old chum," I said, pretending to grab his shoulder like we were pals.

He stared at my hand, grave intentions in his chestnut eyes. When I removed it, his face regained its sunny disposition. "You're in luck, lads. I happen to have a special table in the back, if you'd like to join me?"

The man seemed about as trustworthy as our previous benefactor, but didn't appear to be a ghost. I glanced at Eric. His eyes bounced back a sudden look of worry, then relaxed. "Sure," he said. "We can always use some drinks if you're offering."

"Indeed I am," the stranger said. "Right this way, gentlemen." He waved a white-gloved hand toward a glass door I hadn't noticed upon our entrance. This whole thing seemed weird, but I didn't want to face the madness outside. We left the table and followed him through the door. On the other side was a short hallway filled with a row of wooden booths. Ancient barrels of liquor lined the walls above us, and I could hear the din of the bar beyond the walls. We sat down at the nearest booth, the stranger on one side of the frozen tabletop and we on the other. He waved his arm upward. A server in a black coat, top hat, and tails appeared at the table. Steam lifted from the icy table top, wafting around his thin face.

"Ah, Stanley. An order of your best whiskey for my two old sports here," the stranger said.

"Excellent choice, Mr. Winograd," Stanley said. He turned and headed to the back of the room, his rigid shoes sharp on the wooden floorboards, then disappeared behind a hinged door.

"Uh . . . thanks," I said, not quite sure what was happening. Winograd had a few hairs out of place on his otherwise plastered dome. They stuck out at odd angles in the frozen air.

"Don't mention it," he said. "I like to buy fledglings their first real drink. You two ever drink whiskey?"

"Love the stuff," Eric said in an honest tone. He caught my look. "What? My dad'd give me a nip once in a while. In the winter months. That was it."

"So you are familiar," Winograd said, smiling. "But you've never sampled such delicacies as this masterful establishment once provided. Such tantalizing flavors, splashing down one's tongue. Almost makes one feel alive."

My eyes narrowed upon hearing this turn of phrase. The server returned to our table with three small glasses filled with murky liquid.

"Thank you, Stanley," our benefactor said, raising his glass. "Drink up, gentlemen. The night is young, the women are showing their gorgeous physiques, and you strapping stallions need some bloody encouragement!"

Eric and I exchanged glances before raising our glasses. The whiskey went down harsh. I recoiled as it hit my tongue, but somehow managed to swallow it. Eric threw his head back, gulped, and sat the glass back on the icy table. Then he belched, a clear sound in the narrow room.

"Excellent," Winograd said. "Now then, gentlemen. What brings you to my humble Alma Mater? What drove you to attend these hallowed halls?"

I was unnerved by the question. "Well, my parents sort of made me attend here. I wanted to go to the University of Minnesota."

"Hm . . . I see," Winograd said, taking out his monocle. "I'm glad you took this path, young sir. For you see, I was lucky enough to attend this illustrious school some decades ago. Graduated with the highest honors and went on to become the top of my field of medicine out east. I trust you two hope to reach such glorious heights once you have matriculated?"

"Matricu-what?" Eric said. "Uh, I don't have anything major planned like that. My folks said this was the place to go to become a teacher."

"Indeed." Winograd leaned forward. The ice shrunk from his pointed elbows as they rested. "There's no better place to become a pedagogue than such a place of higher learning! Might I tell you about my experience here, in order to further expand your knowledge of this fine institution?"

"Uh, sure," I said, feeling he was going to do so anyway.

"Splendid! You see, I arrived here a few years after the university was founded, in the 1950s. 'Twas the glory days of my youth, lads. I don't mind telling you I was rather a looming presence on campus. My father was one of the original bricklayers of Schuster Hall. He told me he'd be damned if his son ever attended another school. Attained an degree in the practice of pharmacological medicine, went on to Johns Hopkins, and the rest was history. Surely you've heard of the great Dr. Winograd in the papers of record where you live?"

"Can't say that I have," I said, staring at the frigid table. A solitary crack in the ice had begun between his elbows and was extending to our side.

"I see," Winograd said. "Well, I saved many a man's life in Boston, and performed life-saving medicinal works. This was before the bastards stripped my licensure. But you two are young and probably don't read newspapers."

"Nope," Eric said with a short breath.

"I see," he said again. "Well, now that you know my name perhaps you'll be on the lookout. I hear there are some wonderful microfiche machines in the library. Now then, I don't want to keep you gentlemen any longer. Let's get one more . . ." he waved his white gloved hand, ". . . and I shall bid you adieu. What be your plans for the evening?"

"We were going to hit the bars and maybe watch some women take their shirts off," I said, hoping such a statement wouldn't upset this character's sensibilities. He seemed not to notice.

"Wonderful, wonderful. The saloon crawl was always my favorite. And the way those whores used to show themselves off in the windows . . . glorious! But you have to watch out for the policemen, good sirs. They were never uncomfortable using their truncheons to enforce justice."

"Uh . . . yeah. That's not quite what—" Eric started to say, but our drinks had arrived. Stanley placed them on the bifurcated crack inching its way through the table, one drink on each pointed line on its way toward us.

"To Homecoming and new family arrivals," Winograd said. "Drink up!"

I quaffed down another glass of the disgusting whiskey. Eric did the same without hesitation. My head felt very light.

"Bully!" the doctor exclaimed as we set the glasses down. The cracks were now all the way through to the other side. It looked as if the good doctor had drawn a scrawny letter Y into the glacial table. "And remember, gents, Homecoming is when all the lost alumni come back for one last haunt. If you see any of them, please give them my regards."

My brain felt like it was going to burst through the top of my skull. I could feel the motor skills in my arms and hands deteriorating. Eric waivered back and forth in his chair. "I'll be sure to do that," I said, hearing my speech slur as it came out of my mouth.

I moved to stand up, and fell back onto the hard wooden booth. After another attempt and some admonishing laughter from Eric, I made it to my feet. We walked down the tiny hallway toward the glass door and came back to the main area of the bar. We stumbled through the crowd and past the bouncer toward the front door, which was dripping with condensation and alcohol. Before we pushed through it, I glimpsed back at the glass door we'd just used. Now there was nothing there.

I heard the first person shout before I opened the freezing cold door of the Ice Castle. I looked up toward the mass of humanity rampaging all over the hill. A large beer bottle went flying over my head and shattered on the sidewalk behind us. I could hear the riot police bellowing orders to the kids running around at the top.

"Jesus Christ!" Eric exclaimed behind me. "The fuck is going on here?"

"Riot, dudes!" a kid on the sidewalk next to us yelled. He had a brick in one hand. "Everyone's goin' ape shit since the cops took down those three in the middle of the street. I heard one of 'em died." He whipped the brick across the street, shattering a small window at Sharkey's.

"We gotta get out of here," Eric said, pulling on my shoulder.

"I know, I know!" I said, a frantic tone edging into my voice. Once in St. James at my friend Ben Mosey's seventh birthday party, a kid mistook a bee hive for a piñata and swung with all his might. I was the only kid who didn't run screaming that day. I had a bunch of stings to show for my stoicism, but the incident impressed upon me the importance of remaining calm in the face of danger.

"This way," I said, pointing toward the bottom of the hill.

"That's not where you parked!" Eric said, following behind me. He had to shout to be heard over all the yelling.

"I know, but it's going to be easier going around this clusterfuck than through it!" I yelled back at Eric. What I saw behind him terrified me enough to start a brisk jog. Chaos was erupting between the mass of students and the riot police. Kids were getting their faces smashed in by batons, and those higher up the street were flinging beer bottles at the cops.

"All right, whatever! Just don't go too fast . . ." Eric cried.

We stumbled down the sidewalk until we reached the intersection at the bottom of the hill. Gas stations stood on either side, their attendants doing their best to scare away looters. I turned and headed in the general direction of the Oldsmobile. We circled around the hill until I saw the tarnished brown outline of the Olds under the dim electric pole of the vacant house. I'd never been so happy to see that piece-of-shit car in all my life.

"We made it," I said, slowing my gait as we approached.

"Thank God," Eric said, breathing hard. His teal shirt, halfway unbuttoned, was flapping in the night air. A high-pitched scream wafted over from a block away, dashed against the sounds of beer bottles shattering.

I unlocked the car and we jumped inside. I sat for a few seconds before the world began to spin. "Oh, fuck . . ." I said. "I think I'm drunk from that whiskey."

"I don't feel a thing," Eric said. "Want me to drive?"

I pondered for a minute. If Eric drove and got pulled over in my car, he'd be the one who went to jail for the night. But if I got arrested, he would have no way to get back to campus. Using the drunken logic that always looks bad the next morning, I chose to drive.

"All right, man," Eric said. "Your funeral. Or I should say jail cell. But don't say I didn't try."

"I won't, okay?" I said, frustrated. I just wanted to get the hell out of there. I turned the ignition and after a bit the Olds roared to life. I pulled onto the street and nothing showed up in my rear view mirror. I pressed down on the gas, and we were on our way. I looked back in the rear view. This time two pin points of light showed back at me. They looked like small cat's eyes in the darkness. I continued on our slow drive, passing more drunken revelers on the sidewalk. I gazed in the rear view again; this time the lights were the size of dimes. My stomach dropped a few floors until it resided on the same plain as my lower intestine. I told myself to remember the bee stings. I headed toward the street where we had first approached the hill. The large wooden barricades were overturned; one was broken in half, two of its legs standing upright and defiant. I watched another crowd of ruffians run up the street, except these kids looked different. They all wore flower-power-type baggy clothing: bell bottoms, shaggy vests, the whole thing. Their clothes were worn out, like there was a dirtiness that could never get removed from them. When they moved in front my car, the headlight beams passed right through them.

"Jesus, did you see that . . . ?" I gaped.

"See what?" Eric replied. He had been staring down the hill watching the police clear out the rabble.

"Nothing," I said, pulling the wheel and heading onto the main street. I checked the rear view. This time I saw flashing red-and-blue lights. My stomach shrunk to the size of a pea.

"Oh, fuck!" I yelled.

"Dude, I fucking told you I should have drove!" Eric screamed at me.

"Then you'd be the one going to jail?" I yelled right back. "Trust me dude, this will work out for the best. I don't think I've even that drunk anymore," I lied.

I slowed the Olds to a crawl. The cop followed, mere feet from my bumper. I found an empty spot near the town museum. The white corrugated metal reflected my headlight glare, blinding me for a moment. I felt the Olds hit the sidewalk curb so I put it in park and turned off the ignition. I was drunk enough to think of stupid ways to escape this situation. I considered getting out and running but would have felt bad about leaving Eric there. I didn't consider how the cop would have tackled me after twenty seconds. I watched him get out of his cruiser in one smooth motion. He appeared to be seven feet tall and his uniform was darker than the night surrounding us. A wide-brimmed hat sat atop his massive head. He flicked on his flashlight and pointed it right at me. A long car blew past on the street, the people jeering out the windows. I had enough time to recognize it as the same stupid wood-paneled station wagon we'd seen before when the cop arrived at my open window.

"Excuse me son, but do you know why I pulled you over?" came the voice outside my window. It sounded like a mouth full of gravel and broken light bulbs. I couldn't bring myself to look up at him.

"Uh . . . not really, sir," I garbled out. I stared straight ahead at the museum, the white steel shiny in my headlights. My heart pounded.

"Well, then, let me tell you," the gravel voice said from above. I'd been pulled over once in St. James for speeding. Our hometown cop was a friend of my father's so he let me off with a warning. "You were swerving all over the place back there. Driving slow, too. Those are tell-tale signs of . . ." his voice drifted off a moment. I saw his waist turn in the direction of the station wagon that had passed. Another scream, a high-pitched feminine warble, pierced the air in the direction of the hill. Then the flashlight came shining right back in my eyes.

". . . drunk driving," he finished, as if he had never stopped talking. I sat staring straight ahead. I could feel Eric's eyes moving up and down this situation.

"I see," was all I could eke out.

"How many have we had tonight on the ol' hill, boys?" the gravel voice continued. I peered at Eric.

"Uh . . . would you believe we were bought drinks by some older folks down there?" he blurted.

The cop's head shifted down and poked through the car window. It was a giant, ape-like visage. His nostrils flared at me as the flashlight shook in his hand. I could just make out his name badge in the dark: Officer Brady.

"Excuse me?" he said, louder than he needed in this confined space. I glared at Eric.

"We just had a few each, sir," I said. I couldn't look into his eyes. They had a dark glint about them.

"What's this about some older folks buying you drinks down there? You boys don't look the legal age. Let's see a some ID."

I pulled the St. James driver's license from my wallet and handed it over. The cop scanned it for a full minute. "Uh, my friend was talking about . . . the bartender. He never asked for ID or anything."

The cop's beady, mysterious eyes crawled all over my face. He looked perplexed and much angrier after studying my license.

"Why the hell not? He oughta know it was dangerous. I'll ask again, and I want the truth this time. How many you boys had this evening?"

"Um . . . two shots," I said, minimizing the whiskey. "And . . . a beer."

"Uh huh, that's what I thought," the cop said, straightening. He kept the flashlight right on us. "You boys wanna step out of the vehicle, please?"

I unleashed a glower at Eric that could have melted ice. I unbuckled my seat belt and creaked open the Oldsmobile's door. As I stepped out onto the pavement another car full of partiers drove by at a snail's pace, its drunken inhabitants gawking out the windows.

"All right, Mr. Sinclair. I know you're drunk, but I gotta run through these tests with you anyway," the cop said. The wide brim of his hat stood a full two feet above my head. My left hand begin to convulse, so I put it in my pocket. "Stand on one foot, please. Now recite the alphabet back-ward. Start anytime."

I failed around letter Q and returned my foot to the ground. I was still drunk enough not to retain much worry about what was happening, but it was starting to creep in all around. The thought that I wouldn't be able to drive anywhere for the rest of my freshman year hadn't dawned. Eric stood on the other side of the Olds, his hands clasped nervously on its roof.

"Now blow into this for me," the cop said, offering up a breathalyzer. I placed my lips around it and gave a pathetic blow.

"Come on, come on, you gotta blow in the godamn thing," he cajoled. "Pretend like it was your wise-ass friend here's dick from last night."

I coughed, then gave a big blow into the device. It made a tiny beeping noise. The cop pulled it away and looked at the results. "Oh, boy. You're way over here, Mr. Sinclair. Way over. I don't know what you two had down there, but it was more than two shots. You're lucky you didn't kill anyone out here tonight. Let's go."

One powerful arm grabbed my shoulder and spun me around. A freezing cold pair of handcuffs slapped down on my wrists. The next thing I knew I was pulled away from the Oldsmobile. My feet struggled to catch up with my body.

"Let's go, Mr. Sinclair. We're heading downtown," the cop said, shoving me into the back seat.

"Wait, I can explain!" I cried in a desperate voice as he slammed the door. It closed inches from my open mouth. I could see the cop talking to Eric. Eric make a long, looping gesture with this arms and his face was scrunched up in concern.

The cop walked toward the front of the police cruiser and got inside. As he closed the door, he turned his wide face toward me. "Let's go for a little ride, Mr. Sinclair," his poisonous voice spewed. It was almost as if he knew who I was. The dark glint in his eyes radiated, and I felt pure fear for the first time that evening. He turned back and slammed on the accelerator. My back was shoved against the seat. My handcuffs dug into the upholstery behind me. I watched the city's bland buildings pass by and sobered up a bit more. By the time we entered the front gates of the police station, I realized I was fucked.

Chapter
SEVEN

WE'RE HERE, SUNSHINE," came a voice of crushed shale as it pierced my drunken stupor. I opened my eyes and was blinded by the scorching light surrounding the vehicle. We were inside the garage where the police stored their cruisers. Officer Brady pulled the back door open wide, then grabbed my shoulder and gave a massive pull with his beefy arms. I had no choice but to let him maneuver me out the car door. My shoes scraped over solid cement. Brady gave me a shove in the back so I'd start walking. I heard laughter from other hidden police officers as I stumbled forth. The gleam of the flurouescents wore off as I stood before a big metal door. The cop tapped on the keypad beside it. There was a loud buzzing sound and the door unlocked. I was placed in the second holding cell. This was little more than an enclosed concrete box with a stainless steel bed, a tiny flat mattress, and a toilet in the corner.

"There," Brady said, giving me one last push for good measure. "Don't fall asleep. We have a few more questions for you." He slid the door shut behind him. The sound echoed in the small chamber.

I stood there a minute pondering my fate before I slumped down onto the flimsy mattress. There was a thick cotton blanket on top of it. I realized how cold I was and pulled it over me. Defiant thoughts ran through my head. How dare this policeman pick me up and not Eric? Or for that matter, all the other much more drunk people out tonight? How dare he not understand we didn't buy those drinks? The questions kept swirling, riding a wave of anger and confusion as I lay within this blanket that had the lingering smell of sweat embedded in it. I heard the faint echoes of other doors slamming around me as I closed my eyes. The sound of my door slamming open woke me, and I sat up to make it look like I hadn't fallen asleep.

"Wakey, wakey," Officer Brady said, standing in the doorway. In this light I could see his beady, blank eyes a little better. "We have a little interrogation before you get your beauty rest. Now come with me."

We wandered down open, bright hallways before we came to a wooden door. The cop turned a key to open it. A bland metallic table and chair sat in the middle of the room. He sat me down in the chair and assumed a position standing by the table with his back to me. My defiant mind now raced with notions of how to escape this room, the police station, this school, the country. Brady swung around, his gigantic stature towering over me.

"So, who were these characters?" he said, blank eyes peering at me.

"What characters?" I asked.

"These supposed alcohol buyers you and your dumb-ass friend were blathering about tonight. What'd they look like?"

My mind strained. "Uh . . . well the first guy was real old. He looked like he'd just stepped out of the wild west or somethin'. Had a long beard and a bushy mustache. He walked with a limp, too. Said his name was . . ." my mind faltered. I felt dehydration settling into its farthest corners. "Uh . . . Alfred. Alfred James."

Brady had been writing down everything I said on a pad of paper. When I spoke the name, he stopped. "What did you say?" he spat.

"I said his name was Alfred James," I stammered.

Brady's eyes widened, looked on fire. "That's impossible. Alfred James was . . ." he stopped. "Wait, you said he bought you some beers at the bar?"

"Uh, yeah. We were at Tony's. I tried telling you that before, but you wouldn't . . ."

"Shut up," he growled. "Very interesting. Tell me, how'd old Alf look these days? Like shit?"

I was confused by this line of questioning. "Yeah, I guess he did. His suit was all dirty, he looked like he hadn't bathed in quite some time." I neglected to mention he also may have been a ghost.

"Did he now?" Brady said. The fire seemed to dull in his eyes. "Well, that'd be about right. Do you have any idea who you brushed into at that shithole of a bar?"

"N-not really," I said. "Sh-should I?"

The fire in his eyes cooled to a slow burn. "Naw, no reason you would. He's an old-timer that shows up on Homecoming nights, just like the rest of 'em. Shoulda gone the way o' the dodo many years ago, but certain powers that be like 'im around. He entertains the youthful dumbasses like yourself, Mr. Sinclair. And your friend there, Mr. Fulton."

A chill ran down my spine at the mention of Eric. I hadn't told Brady his first or last name. "How did you . . . ?" I began.

"You said another guy bought you some drinks at the Ice Castle," the cop barked, not acknowledging my question. "You remember this guy too?"

"Uh . . . yeah. He was younger than the first guy. Doctor . . . Winograd, yeah that was his name. He had this monocle on his right eye. Said he'd gone to school here in the '50s and became a doctor."

Officer Brady once again stopped writing as he heard the name. "Winograd. Are you sure that was the name?"

"Pretty sure," I said. "He had some kind of private table in the back of the bar. He bought us a few shots of whiskey. That was it, I swear!"

The beady eyes traveled all over the room. My ears picked up a slight buzzing. I couldn't figure out what it was until I understood it to be the very low register of his voice, humming. The small eyes returned to me. The fire had gone out, but they still smoldered as they troweled over my face. He rested the palms of his hands on the metal table and leaned toward me.

"You need to be careful of that one," he said in a low voice. "You know it's dangerous to accept drinks from strangers, right, Mr. Sinclair?" he scowled. "Especially strangers like these. You have no idea who you're messing with here. Winograd isn't to be trusted. Neither is Alfred. They are remnants of a different time, you see. Can't escape, can't come back. Only on Homecoming do they get one night to indulge their flavors. And of course start riots that keep my men runnin' all over this goddamn town. Y'know, back in . . . uh, back where I used to work, I had a nice easy life. All's I had to do was watch over things. Now, I gotta not only worry about punk kids like you but all the rest of what goes on in this town. You think I enjoy this?"

My breath caught in my throat.

"Listen, Mr. Sinclair," he said as he stood to his full height. "I'm telling you right now: if me or any of my brethren ever see you on that hill again, you're done. Done with this school, done with the rest of your idiot friends, done with everything. Do you understand me?!"

The unmistakable terror I'd felt when we first encountered this guy on the main street returned with a vengeance. My hands shook in the restraints. A single bead of sweat fell out of my hair and rolled down my nose. "Yes, sir," was all I could get out. He pulled me up out of the chair and back toward the wooden door.

"And if you ever see either of those two again, you're to stay clear. I hope that's understood as well. Now, let's see if you can't sleep off this drunkenness," he said, shoving me forward. I shuffled back down the hallway, the cop pressing a large palm in my back every few feet. We reached another door at the far end. This one had a large reinforced window implanted at eye level. Brady typed some numbers into the keypad and it unlocked. The smell bowled me back into his powerful forearms.

"Don't let the stink get to ya," he growled. "They're all drunk, just like you. Don't mess with them." He pushed me forward and slammed the door. I took a gander at the population of this room. It was another enclosed concrete room like my first holding cell, but larger. Huddled on one of the metal benches in the corner were two women who looked around forty years of age. Their necks were scarred and I could see places on their arms where they had picked skin. They both looked at me, then back into the corner of the room. On the floor lay what looked like drunken hobos—men with scraggly beards and clothes that looked like they hadn't been washed in years. The alcohol smell came most clear from them. I looked over to the side of the room. A guy about my age sat on another protruding metal bench with a tiny woolen blanket covering the end. His eyes watched me as I attempted to lay down under the cloth a few feet from him. He reached out a bloodied arm, snatched the blanket off me and pulled it around himself. I lay down on the cold metal, shivering. I had one last thought as I scanned the meth-heads in the corner, the alcoholic bums on the floor and the young kid beside me, my eyes heavy with sleep: *How did I get into this mess?* I closed my eyes and slipped into a deep slumber.

I WOKE WITH A START THE NEXT MORNING, my head pounding from a monstrous hangover. As I rubbed awake my eyes, I saw there wasn't a soul in the room with me. I had been abandoned overnight. A half-hour later there was an overbearing knock on the door. Officer Brady's gravel voice traveled from behind it.

"You awake yet, Mr. Sullivan?" he growled.

I rose to a sitting position. "Yes, sir . . ." The door opened and he marched inside.

"Time to get up, drunkass," he said, bellowing laughter. "You've got to appear in front of a judge. Let's go." He pulled me from the metal bench and shoved me through the door. In the cold light of day the situation hit me like a ton of bricks: not only was I about to lose my license (my car was secondary at this point—I hoped Eric was looking after it), but these type of infractions always carried a hefty fine. The one kid in St. James who'd gotten a DWI before our graduation never made it to college in the fall. My father told me then if he ever heard of me doing the same I was not to come back home. I wasn't sure what his policy would be if he found out I'd gotten one while attending his alma mater. Brady's solid boots clicked on the linoleum behind me. He grabbed my shoulder before we approached a double door with a metal push bar.

"The judge is wrapping up the previous case," he barked. "You just sit yer ass here until you see that green light flash," he said, pointing at a light bulb poking out near the ceiling by the door. "Then you walk in there. And no smart-ass remarks about what we discussed last night, either, " he grumbled as he stomped back down the hallway.

I looked up at the darkened light bulb. Brady's final comment hadn't rung any bells yet. A scene involving two people in an interrogation room populated the cloudy back region of my mind, but I could not yet see the people involved. The light bulb flashed green before I could think of it any more. I rose and pushed through the door. I came upon a small, compact courtroom. Musty wooden chairs lined the back of it and two flat oak tables took up the space in front of the judge's bench. The carpeting was a disgusting olive color. I caught the lingering scent of old books as I moved forward. The judge, a bald old man with tiny spectacles and an even smaller mustache, waved me forward. The court bailiff, another beefy police officer, stood before his desk, eyeing me with contempt.

"Come ahead, young man. We haven't got all day," the bald judge said, irritated. "Do you think you were the only one arrested for the sin of libation last night?"

My mind flashed back to the population of the drunk tank. "No, sir," I said in a respectful tone.

"Step forward, young man," the judge said from above me. He consulted the papers before him. "Now, then. Office Brady's report says he saw you swerving in your vehicle on Main Street last night. When he pulled you over, you blew way over the legal limit. Am I correct, young man?"

I struggled to recall what all had happened last night. The alcohol we'd consumed from the strangers seemed to be a vast impairment to my memory. The interrogation room was still nothing more than a faint outline in my mind. "You are right, sir," was all I said to the judge. "I exercised poor judgment last night. I accept responsibility for my actions."

The entire proceeding was over in a few minutes. The judge ruled that I'd be stripped of my license for at least six months, "if not a year, if that's what it takes to learn your lesson," as the old bastard put it. Since this was my first offense my fine was limited, but I'd have to undergo a class in the spring to reinstate my license. I stood there defenseless as the punishment rained down from the bench, crushing my brain like a cartoon anvil but accompanied by the real pain of dehydration. When the judge was finished he slammed down his gavel to wake me from my trance.

"Am I understood, Mr. Sullivan?" the judge glared at me, his narrow eyes peering over the thin gray mustache.

"Yes, sir," I mumbled, staring at the hideous stained carpet.

"Very good. Now get out of my courtroom. I don't want to see you in here again, at least until after you graduate." I thought that was his version of a joke. The bailiff led me back to the holding cell, which was still empty.

"You get one phone call," the bailiff uttered as he opened the door. "I'd suggest it be to somebody who can pick you up from here. You have a half-hour to decide."

I walked into the cell, shock contorting my face. The reality of my situation intruded on all sides, but I couldn't wrap my head around it. A tense, careless thought about what my father would think kept pushing from the outside, but I shoved it away. I didn't have time for such matters. What was important right now was getting the hell out of this place and back into the real world. College life with all its attendant parties and girls and drinking (and classes), seemed a distant memory. What I was imbedded in now was the harsh reality of the rule of law of this city. I sat down on the metal bench and went through everything from last night. I had just started to recall the interrogation room when the door opened and the bailiff announced it was time for my phone call. I decided to call Eric's dorm. He was the closest person I had to a friend at this juncture of my university career, and had been with me last night. And he was the only person who could attest to whatever it was we saw at those bars. I thanked the stars above me when the receiver picked up. A washed out voice answered on the other end.

"Hullo?" Jake's stoned-out voice came across.

"Jake?" I said, frantic. "It's Mike Sullivan. Your neighbor from across the hall in Schuster."

A beat went past. I imagined his mind, addled by drinking the night before and a wake-and-bake session this morning, was doing its best to recall me. "Oh, yeah!" he exclaimed. "Jesus, are you all right? Eric came back at like three in the morning last night. He said you guys had been pulled over or some shit?"

"Yeah, yeah. Listen, is Eric there?" I asked. "I need to speak with him. Now." I didn't mask the irritation in my voice.

"Sure thing," Jake said. "I'll go grab him." He set the receiver down. I could hear the faint, groovy sounds of Dave Matthews playing in the background. A minute later, Eric's voice spilled out of the receiver.

"Dude, what the fuck?!" he yelled. I couldn't tell if he was mad or scared.

"Tell me about it," I said. "I'm in fucking jail, dude. What are you doing?"

"I was down with Seth and Adam. I had to fill them in on what happened."

"Oh. Did you tell them about the weirdos we met on the hill?"

A pause. I clicked my teeth together. "Uh . . . no. Didn't mention that," he said. "I thought perhaps you and I should cover that ground. Speaking of that . . ."

"Just a second," I interrupted. "First, can you come get me? I have no license, no car and . . . wait, what the hell did happen to the Olds?"

Another pause. "Um . . . well, I volunteered to drive it back to the dorms. But that cop, who was a real asshole by the way, said I was too drunk to drive. Not that he gave me a breath test. He just told me to walk back to campus. Can you fucking believe that? After you left, I toyed around with the idea of driving the Olds back to the dorm anyway. Y'know, just to get it off Main Street. But the minute I started to open the door, another fucking cruiser rolls up. This one's driven by a bigger, beefier version of the meathead we dealt with. He tells me to back the fuck off, that he's taking your car to the station. I was left standing there with two thumbs up my ass. I ended up having to walk back to Schuster, just as I'd feared. What a fucking night."

"Shit, shit," I said, stress rolling off my tongue. "So they must have it here. Tell you what, I'm not even going to worry about it right now. I need to get the hell out of here. This has been the worst fucking night of my life. I just wanted to go down to the hill and have a few drinks!"

"Me too, dude. Did they throw you in the drunk tank?"

"I'll explain everything later. Will you just come get me, please?"

"Okay," Eric said. "Just hang tight. I'll have to borrow Jake's van. It should be fine—you heard what he sounds like today." Jake yelled something derogatory in the background.

"Whatever you need to do. Just get here. Please."

"All right, man. I'll be there in a half-hour. Don't get raped or anything."

"Shut the fuck up," I said, and slammed down the receiver.

"Everything go okay?" the bailiff asked, grinning.

"Yes," I said. "He'll be here in a few minutes, all right?"

"Okay by me," he said, and ushered me back into the holding cell. As I walked into the cold white room I swore to myself I would never occupy such a space again in my life. Ten minutes later the door opened again and I was out of there. I stopped by the front desk to receive my wallet, dormitory keys and a pack of gum I'd had in my pocket. Brilliant sunshine struck me as I exited the back door of the station. I had almost fogotten I had slept and this was a new day. This place appeared to be where they dumped drunkards out after they'd overstayed their welcome in the tank. Large, nondescript industrial buildings sat on the side of the asphalt street. Eric stood outside a rickety Volkswagon bus in front of them. Steam rose from several metal grates at his feet. He ventured a grim smile as I walked toward him in the garish sunlight.

"Well well, look what the cat dragged in," Eric said, a slight smile stretching across his face.

"Shut the fuck up," I said again, more than a little tense. "Just take me home. Er . . . to the dorms."

We cycled through our versions of the evening on the drive over to the campus. I looked out the dirty windows of the VW bus, trying not to choke on the dank smell of its plush seats. The town of Cold River looked abandoned after its night of bacchanalia. A high wind blew plastic cups, beer cans, and various detritus across Main Street as we drove. I didn't see a single person on the whole trip.

"Sounds like you got the royal treatment, Mr. Drunkie," Eric said, his efforts at levity falling flat as I stared out the disgusting window.

"Does Jake ever clean this fucking van?" I asked, peevish. "But to answer your question, yes, I got the royal treatment. But here's the weird thing. I'm just remembering this now for the first time. I was interrogated."

"What?" Eric started. "You mean about the drunk driving?"

"Well, it was kind of about that," I said. "But the cop, Brady, the asshole that pulled us over and was interested in where we got the booze last night? He got a lot more interested when we arrived at the station. And when I told him the names of those two weirdos we met, that really got him going. He told me to stay away from those two."

"Wait, he knew those guys?" Eric asked as he struggled to turn the VW's stubborn steering wheel onto the gravel drive that led to Malworth. The wind blew sheets of dust across the road and into the nearby fields. "Who the fuck were they? And how did they find the only two schmucks in the place with no I.D.'s or wristbands?"

"I don't know," I said, staring forward through the windshield, which was caked with dust. "But I intend to find out."

Eric turned the van into the parking lot that ran down the side of Schuster Hall, the same place we'd left the previous night. Eric opened the front door of the building and we stumbled up the linoleum stairs, our footfalls echoing around us. I was exhausted by the time we reached the fifth floor. We came upon a very quiet hallway. I pushed open the door to my dorm room. Nick was gone, as usual. Eric muttered some profanity as he entered his room and shut the door. After shaking off my clothes and getting into some torn gray sweats, I headed down the hall toward Seth and Adam's room. I was given a prince's welcome as I entered.

"Heyooo, there's the big winner!" Adam shouted from his position on the plaid couch, a huge box of saltine crackers at his side. His torn blue sweat pants looked worse than mine, and his red hair poked out from underneath a black baseball cap.

"Holy shit, did you have a rough night!" Seth said from the computer desk, looking worried. He minimized a porn video as I plopped down on the other wooden chair with a loud sigh.

"Yeah, yeah, big winner chicken dinner, don't get to drive nowhere 'til next summer," I said.

"Ah, crap, man, that sucks," Adam said. "What the hell happened, anyway?"

"Well, I'll give you the whole sorry tale," I said, "but first I want to direct that question at you two: what the hell happened? I thought we were gonna meet you at the hill last night? Instead Eric and I found ourselves bumming around and asking for drinks from . . ." I stopped myself. ". . . from bartenders that wouldn't serve us and shit," I continued.

"That sucks, dude," Seth said. His brown hair spiked up in a few places, making him look one-quarter mad scientist. "We were right across the street. That dump of a bar known as the Shark Tank or whatever. Heard from my brother that they were gonna have drink specials. They never materialized, so numb nuts here and I just did some shots. We wandered up and down that side 'til the cops came and shit got intense. But holy fuck, did you see that trio of chicks showin' their stuff on the hill?"

I racked my brain for the image. A fuzzy scene of a bunch of police officers beating college kids sprung to mind instead.

"Wait, so you saw the riot?" I asked.

"Fuck, yeah," Adam said, leaning forward, cracker dust flying out of his mouth. "Wasn't that some shit? I'd never seen such police brutality. I don't even know how many people were hurt. That was way out of line."

"No shit," I said. "That's when we ducked indoors again. We finagled a few drinks and got pretty wasted. Well, I did. Eric seemed sober as a judge the whole evening. I'm still kicking myself for not letting him drive."

"So tell us, why didn't you?" Adam asked.

I gave them the shortest version of the story, which still turned into about a half hour's worth of talking. After about twenty minutes Seth stood up, shut the door, and opened up the black mini fridge. He handed me a glass beer bottle.

"You need this more than me right now," he said, his eyes downtrodden. I was glad to have somebody to commiserate with, even if these guys had ditched me on my night of peril. I chugged half the beer and finished the story. When I got to the point where Eric gave me a ride in Jake's shitty van, I set the empty bottle down.

"And that was all she wrote," I said, clearing my throat as I leaned back into the wooden chair. My two compatriots sat in stunned silence.

"That is unreal," Adam said. "So you lost the license, huh? That fucking sucks, man. Right when you get to college, too."

"Not like he needs to go anywhere in this shithole of a town," Seth piped in. "My brother said he hardly ever left campus because there's nothing else to do. Except go to the bars. That didn't turn out real well for you, though . . ."

I grinned, the first smile I'd felt since the day before. "Yeah, I know. Best case scenario is that I'll get it back by the time they let us go in May. But after the night I had, I don't really feel like going back to that cop shop. Even the judge was noncommittal, like, 'we'll see how you shape up first,' and shit. I can't catch a break on any of this."

"So, you tell your folks yet?" Adam asked. Here was the question I had hoped to avoid.

"Not yet," I said. "I mean, I am eighteen and can take responsibility for my actions. On the other hand, they did sort of buy me that car. To be honest, I'm kinda scared. I've never fucked up on this big a scale before."

"Yeah, that's a tough one," Seth said, looking at his computer screen. "We can't really help you with this."

"I know," I said, leaning back into the wooden chair. It now felt very uncomfortable. "I know . . ."

I felt a tug of responsibility as I walked back down the hallway toward my room. Now that I had divulged the evening's incident with the people who would judge me the least, I contemplated telling my parents about it. With the exception of a brief telephone conversation during my second week of classes, they hadn't once inquired as to my well-being on this campus. This emphasized the feeling that had grown in the back of my mind ever since they decreed I was to attend Malworth University: *they were getting rid of me.* Sure, they had made a show of missing me and making sure I found my way in this big new adult world when I moved here, but their lack of interest still puzzled me. It wasn't that I wanted to call them up every weekend with an update on my binge drinking habits, but it wouldn't have hurt to have a single conversation about my college life. I sat and watched TV for a few hours to try and sober up from the beer I'd chugged. It was around dinner time that I picked up the worn, purple rotary phone each of these tiny rooms came with and started dialing. I heard my father's gruff voice after the third ring. His throat carried the guttural sound it picked up after he'd had a glass of Scotch.

"Hey, it's me, Dad. Your son you sent away to college." I didn't mean for it to sound as trite as it did.

"Oh, hello, son," he said. "How's it going up there?"

I paused a beat. "It's going . . . good."

"Are you keeping up with all of your classes?"

"Yeah, for the most part. They're all pretty basic since I haven't chosen a major yet."

"Well, you'd better get on that," he said. His voice seemed to slow down as he spoke. "We are paying for you to go there and study but also to exit in four years with a degree. Not to while away your nights carousing on the hill, or whatever it is they call it these days."

The next words choked in my mouth. "Of course not, Dad. I'm keeping up with everything. I don't have to choose a major 'til next year anyway."

"Yes, yes," he said, sounding absent-minded. Over the crackling line I heard the clink of the ice in his glass as he raised it to his mouth. "Plenty of time. Everything else going all right? Are you meeting new people?"

"Yes, Dad. My roommate's never here, but I've become pretty good friends with the guy across the hall. There are some other kids down the hall who I've gotten to know."

"That's good. I know it's always been hard for you to leave your comfort zone for other people," he said, the gruff words biting into me. That may have been revenge for my abrupt greeting.

"Yes, well, it hasn't been as hard as you and Mom thought," I said. The events of the weekend floated around the back of my head like a fog.

"Well, that's great to hear," he said, sipping another drink. "Have you been to the library yet?"

An odd question, but not unexpected. "Yeah, I went there to study with . . ." I decided not to entertain my father with any thoughts about a future daughter-in-law, ". . . with some friends. It was kind of scary, to be honest. Like it was from another century, another world."

My father bellowed laughter, a staccato sound over the crappy phone connection. "Yeah, that's the place all right," he said, chuckling. He must have been drunk. "I know I didn't tell you much about my time there, but we used to pull this stupid prank on the fourth floor . . ."

I could hear my mother's disapproving chide in the background. Something about the number of floor he mentioned stuck in my head, but I couldn't recall why.

"Oh, all right! Your mother doesn't want me telling you. Maybe you'll find out for yourself one of these days. The pranks kids used to do around that place are almost as legendary as the campus. So anything else new? Anything you're not telling me?"

This was my opportunity to come clean, to admit to my father that I'd already messed up this golden opportunity he and my mother had given me to further my education. It didn't matter I'd only lost my license for the rest of the school year. What mattered was that I had gotten In Trouble with the Law, and that would not be tolerated. Yet I was a grown man now, and could get in all the trouble I wanted. So what if they had bought me that car? It was mine now, and I could do whatever the hell I wanted with it. These were the types of audacious thoughts rolling through my head as I mulled over how truthful to be with my father. Yes, they were mere rationalizations, covering up the fact that I didn't want to take my medicine. But they felt like true statements, assertions to myself that I didn't have to tell my parents anything about this incident. These were the people who sent me to this god-forsaken campus in the first place.

"Naw, nothing much else," I said, exhaling as I said it. I had never lied to my father before. It was exhilarating.

"Okay then," he said. His voice had the slurred edge to it that came after Scotch number two. The dullness was also there, as if he was struggling to remember how to speak. "Thanks for calling, son. Have a good night."

I hung up the scuffed phone receiver. Beaded lines of sweat ran up and down its slender, worn neck. I sat down on the plaid couch and leaned my head back, sighing. I don't even remember falling asleep.

Chapter

EIGHT

THINGS WEREN'T BACK TO NORMAL on Monday, but I was forced into a sense of normality by my schedule. My professors didn't care that I had made a recent life-altering error, they just wanted me to show up to their classes on time. Monday morning found me up bright and early and walking to Professor Deakin's Western Civ class to learn more about the Ottomans. Creative Writing was a bit more relaxed than usual, and I had a killer base for a story about a naive college kid who thinks he can drive drunk and not get caught. Cycling class was still a bitch and Coach was still an asshole, but on Tuesday my butt didn't hurt quite as bad when I sat on the hard metal contours of the stationary bike seat. Life: The Natural World passed me by without anything sticking (the better to learn with Sarah, I figured), but when I got to Stats and realized I had understood nothing about probabilities I knew I was in trouble. At the end of class on Tuesday I waited by the back of the classroom until my peers had filtered out. Then I approached Professor Dalton.

"Ah, Mr. Sinclair," he said, wide palms open toward me. His wizened beard contained little flecks of gray running in a zig-zag pattern on either side of his face. Behind the small glasses sat kind, brown eyes. "What can I do for you this fine day?"

"Well, it's the whole probability thing," I said. "I don't think I ever grasped it to begin with."

He nodded in acceptance. "I get that," he said. "Math isn't everyone's strong suit. Tell me, what classes here do you like?"

I had never been asked such a question before, and it took me back. Such interest in what I wanted came so few and far between in my life. "Well, I guess I like my Creative Writing course. I mean, I don't have to understand a bunch of complex theorems and stuff to know how to write."

"Indeed," Dalton said, leaning back against the whiteboard. His navy blazer rubbed off the equation behind him. "Writing, now that's something I could never do. You see, Mike, we all have our strengths and weaknesses. They're nothing to be proud nor ashamed of. They just are. When it comes to probabilities, it's a simple formula and can be used a thousand different ways. Do you have time to join me in my office to discuss it further?"

"As it happens I do," I said. "You're my last class of the day."

"Excellent," Dalton said, those warm eyes enveloping me. "Why don't you follow me up there and we can dig in. And please, don't be fearful of asking for help. It's never a bad thing."

As we walked up the marble stairway toward his office in the English building, I realized that not a single teacher back in St. James had ever said something like this to me. Dalton led the way into his office, a cramped, staid environment with papers and books everywhere. We spent the next hour going over how to calculate the probability of a falling die. Dalton never made me feel stupid or inadequate, only that I was learning. When I left his office that day I felt a true understanding of a mathematical concept I had never gained in my high school days. Dalton was a careful instructor, making sure I never fell behind in conceptualization. He was also the nicest person I'd come across on this dreary campus. If I gave it enough thought, even I could understand math. This was a good feeling, almost enough to make me forget my other misfortunes.

I RETURNED TO SCHUSTER that evening to find bedlam. I was appalled to hear Justin's voice screaming down the corridor as I opened the purple door on the fifth floor. He was standing at Seth and Adam's room, halfway down the hall. The back of his small neck was tensed and his shoulders were cramped up in aggravation. A campus security officer, decked out in a light-blue shirt and black slacks, stood resolute behind him with a trash bag. Justin reached in to grab something out of the room.

I could tell from where I stood that it was a bottle of Tequila. He dumped the liquid and then the bottle into the plastic garbage bag. He looked down the hallway right at me as he did this, causing my stomach to take a valiant leap into my throat. I dove into my dorm room and shut the door, not willing to see what other iniquities might be found in that room. Nick shocked me with his presence.

"Hello there," he said, staring straight ahead at his computer screen, where a first-person shooter flowed at a fast frame rate.

"Uh, hello, yourself," I said. "Haven't seen you in a while."

"I heard from Eric you had a little car trouble this weekend," he said in a monotone. "Sounds rough, man. Sorry to hear about that."

I was a bit perturbed Eric had spilled the beans, but I didn't want to brave that hallway to berate him. Even at a distance I could see the rage in Justin's eyes when I arrived. I flopped down on the old plaid couch. A piece of foam puffed out the side.

"Thanks, man. It was pretty awful," I sighed. "I wouldn't advise spending any nights in the drunk tank. Especially not in this town. But I made it through. Not without my car, though, as you probably heard."

"I did," he said. I noticed he was looking at me. I tried not to stare at the highlights arched back through his greased over hair. We were having an actual conversation.

"Oh, okay," I said. "Um . . . so I may be asking to bum a ride here and again. You know, 'til I get the wheels back."

"What, you mean at the end of the school year?"

It appeared Eric had held nothing back. "Unfortunately. Do you even have a car?"

Nick laughed, the same high pitched one that glanced off the ceiling the first time we spoke in August. "I do not. Parents wanted to save some money and all that. Of course, my sister got a car. But she's more special than me. Favoritism sucks, man."

"I guess I wouldn't know, being an only child," I said, trying not to sound dismissive. "Well, it looks like I'm finding another way of transportation. Not that I want to go anywhere in this shithole of a town. Say," I said, trying to change the subject, "did you see what was going on down the hallway?"

"No," Nick said. His eyes were back on the screen. "Heard some yelling, though."

"Looks like Justin the royal pain in the ass is cracking down on all the liquor flowing out of Seth and Adam's room. I suppose he had to—there was no way to avoid that smell."

"No kidding," Nick said, turning back to me. His eyes took on a darker shade. He looked at me with a slight squint, like he was getting ready to ask something uncomfortable. "Speaking of that . . . is our room clean? I mean, we don't have any beer or anything hiding out?"

I had never seen Nick take a drink of anything, and had never pursued the matter. Being worried about my drinking habits was something else. As far as I was concerned I could keep any amount of booze I wanted, if I could find it. "Yeah, we're clean," I lied, making a mental note to check on the bottle of Jack Daniels I'd stashed at the top of my closet a few weeks back. "Don't worry about it."

"Okay good. Not that I care, dude," he said, his eyes widening again. "It's just . . . I don't want to get on that guy's bad side. At first I thought he was a typical power-mad prick who'd rather stay here than move on with his life. But the more I see of him, the less I like. And now that he's cracking down on people for no reason . . . I'd rather be safe, is all."

"Yeah, I get that," I said. I wasn't worried. What was the worst a resident advisor could do, after all?

THAT NIGHT I WAS AWAKENED by a light tapping on our wooden dormitory door. The sound of stifled voices came from behind it.

"Yo Sinclair. Wake the fuck up!" came Seth's exhortation. Nick snored away across from me, oblivious to the world. I gave myself a light pinch on the arm to make sure I wasn't dreaming. Then I pulled myself up out of bed and wobbled my legs down the shaky ladder, almost falling halfway down. I opened the door to find the two of them wearing various amounts of clothing. Seth's wrinkled purple dress shirt suggested he'd spent a carousing night at the hill, the lucky car-driving bastard. Adam looked disheveled, drunk and tired. He had on some blue sweat pants, a dirty white T-shirt and a pair of worn brown slippers. I looked down the hallway. At the end of it towered a mass of something piled up against the concrete wall.

"What the hell's going on?" I said, squinting in the luminous hallway. Even at night the school kept its dorms lit up like the Fourth of July. As my vision focused, I could see the massive lump standing at the end of the hall. It appeared to be made up of stacked furniture.

"You like it?" Seth said. His eyes held the drunken aspiration of high school years, in which every weekend was an opportunity to steal some old lady's lawn chairs for a night, urinate on somebody's car, or steal a bunch of real estate signs. "It took us an hour to get the fuckin' thing to stand straight. We bumped douchebag's door a few times, but he never woke up."

"What did you . . . ?" I said, before putting the night's events together. They were attaining revenge upon Justin by pressing all the furniture in the study room up against his door. "Holy shit," I said.

"C'mon, you gotta check out this architecture," Adam said, his red hair leading the way down the hall. "I placed a few things myself."

A large red couch made up the backbone, straightened by the upright solid metal chairs that populated the study room I had scoped on my trip to find Sarah. They had managed to pry one of the square wooden desks against the whole thing so that it leaned against the back of the couch, which stood at an angle. The entire mess looked impenetrable.

"This is what that asshole gets for confiscating our liquor," Seth said, stumbling around the hallway behind me. "This is what he gets for fucking with us!"

"Jesus Christ, you guys," I said. Being the only person of any kind of sobriety, the idiocy of this charade was hitting me fast. Messing around with your fellow dorm-mates was one thing. Messing with this guy for doing his job, albeit a stupid one, was quite another. I decided to keep my opinions to myself until I saw the aftermath.

"I'm going back to bed," I advised as I walked back down to my room. "I suggest you all do the same."

"Yes, mother," came Seth's drunken slight as I closed the door.

I was awoke again a few hours later, this time by a horrendous noise at the other end of the hallway. In St. James I had once witnessed a house being torn down by one of those giant wrecking balls. The sound I heard that Saturday morning was quite similar, but amplified by the concrete hallway surrounding it. The bellowing shout confirmed what had occurred.

"You motherfucking prick-holes!" came the roar. It was enough to wake Nick, who jolted up in bed and stared across into my eyes.

"What the hell was that?" he asked, his eyes twitching.

"I have no idea," I lied. "Should we find out?"

More shouting from the hallway. "You dipshits think that was going to hold me? I fucking eat your barricade for breakfast! You don't got shit on me!" It was coming closer to our room.

Nick had no interest in this fracas and was back asleep within five minutes. As I did not possess such freakish abilities, I was forced to lie awake in the loft for another few minutes before there was another knock on our door. I jumped out of bed and pulled it open a few centimeters. Seth's eyes were bloodshot and his hair stuck out in several different directions. The purple dress shirt had been replaced by a ratty boat-show T-shirt that looked like it had been run through with a pitchfork.

"Holy shit, dude," he said, his breath rank with alcohol. "Did you fucking hear that display? He has no idea who did it. Even with his rambunctious show-off dumping our Tequila. No fucking idea."

"What?" I asked. "How do you know that?"

"Because," he said, coughing. I could smell the booze flying through the air at me. "You heard that shit-storm he threw this morning. The first place he would've come knocking is our room. You have to know that. And he didn't. Not a fuckin' word. We're in the clear, baby."

"Good for you, man," I said, unconvinced. I admired their drunken tenacity, but wished they would have done something a little less mean to somebody a little less volatile. I resented Justin as much as anyone on the floor, but this seemed a little out of character even for these two. Seth didn't seem to give two shits about any of it, almost as if he wanted to get kicked out of here.

"Celebration time," he said. "Can I interest you in a morning shot, perhaps?" The seriousness inherent in those reddened eyes belied the absurdity of the request.

"Uh . . . I have to go to class in a half-hour," I said, looking at the small clock on Nick's desk.

"Oh, right. All the good guys go to class in the morning, I forgot," Seth said, slurring most of the words. "That's okay, dude. We'll do some drinkin' this weekend for sure to make up for Homecoming and all of that other shit. Later."

He stumbled off back toward his room, leaving me to pack my backpack and wait for Eric to come out of his room while listening to the slow burn of Nick's morning snores. This whole incident had distracted me for a while, but I couldn't get our mysterious benefactors from the weekend out of my head. Or Officer Brady's criptic remarks, for that matter. These thoughts were roiling in my head when I gave Eric a smart-ass greeting as we headed out for Deakin's class together.

"So what the fuck was all that commotion this morning?" Eric said as we stomped down the linoleum stairs.

"You don't want to know," I said. "Seth and Adam took their revenge on Justin for taking their booze. They claim he didn't know it was them, but I have a feeling he'll find out one way or another."

"Good God," Eric said as we walked outside into the cold October light. "The way those two act, you'd almost think they want to get booted from this place."

"I was kinda thinking the same thing," I said, pulling my fleece coat snug around my shoulders. "Say, you given any more thought to our weekend?"

"No, and I'll thank you not to mention it to me right now," Eric chided, not looking at me.

We walked the rest of the cold route through campus, trampling over concrete sidewalks and brown grass in silence. Whatever it was we thought we saw that night, Eric didn't want to have anything to do with it.

THE NEXT DAY FOUND EACH DOOR of our hallway plastered with fliers in various colors. On each piece of paper were a set of typed words indicating that our resident advisor had called an emergency meeting for Friday night concerning "the furniture incident," as it was described. Attendance was mandatory. When I walked past Seth and Adam's room my feet shuffled through the tattered remains of the multiple fliers they had ripped from their door. I continued walking, sure of my mission to go on another study date with Sarah before the hammer came down and we were all sequestered in our rooms. I hadn't seen her at Homecoming and hadn't gotten a chance to tell her my sob story in the hopes of gaining sympathy. As I walked past the glass-enclosed study lounge, I noticed it was bereft of furniture. I headed down the girls' hallway to room 530 and knocked. I could hear some light pop music playing as the door opened an apprehensive few inches.

"Uh, hello?" I said. The door opened wider. Sarah's gorgeous green eyes met mine and stared right through me. She had on a pink sweatshirt and black jeans. Her short brunette hair swayed around behind her.

"Oh, Mike! Hey! How's it going? I meant to stop by your room . . ." she said, her eyes moving away from mine.

"Oh, that's all right. I wanted to see if you were free for another study session at the creepy library tonight."

She thought it over for a minute, then looked back into the room, exchanging soundless female communication with her roommate. "Yeah, that should work. It's for biology, right?"

"That's the one," I said. "Good ol' Professor Grumpypants. Have you noticed she's gotten meaner as the weather's turned colder?"

"Oh, God, yeah," she said. "I have her first thing in the morning, and boy is she ever pissed. I think she resents having to teach our generation."

I laughed, a short chuckle that was louder than I meant it to be. "You might be on to something. I'll swing by with my backpack, okay?"

"Sounds good. See you in a few."

The door closed, and I pumped my fists in the air. Amanda, the super hottie who had gone with Sarah to Seth and Adam's party, exited her room at the same time and stared at me in disbelief. My cheeks turned beat red as I fled back toward the guy's side of the hallway.

We arrived at the library a half-hour later. I managed to tell most of my pathetic Homecoming story on the way, minus our mysterious benefactors. Sarah's beautiful eyes widened to green, shiny marbles as my tale reached its denouement. When I reached the part about the holding cell, she grabbed my arm in an understanding gesture. My feet felt like they were about to leave the ground.

"I'm so sorry, Mike," she said. "I feel bad for never meeting up with you that night. We hit the bars for a few hours, but weren't feeling it. Then when the riot broke out, we called it a night. No sense in getting arrested, right? Uh, I mean . . . shit. Sorry." Watching her speak, I was struck by how awkward she had become. I wasn't used to seeing the gawky shoe on the other foot. It was a bit disconcerting, but also gave me confidence.

"It's okay," I said. "There wasn't much sense about it. I'm lucky Eric escaped and was able to pick me up the next day. I don't know what I would've done without him."

"Sounds like he's a good friend," she said. "Well, at least you can finish school, and you'll get your car back eventually."

"I hope so," I said. "I haven't exactly inquired into where it's located, but I have a feeling it's in the same place the cop took me."

"Probably," Sarah said. "I can understand if you don't want to go back there quite yet. And, hey, let me know if there's anything I can do for you. Unfortunately I don't have a car either, so I can't offer you any rides . . ."

"Thanks anyway," I said. "But I think I'm going to cool it on taking any more joy rides for the time being."

"Not a bad idea," she said, laughing. It was a delicate sound in my ears.

We were standing in front of the monstrous stone building. The large wooden doors loomed before us. "Shall we?" I asked, outstretching my palm.

She gave a concerned look but then started forward. I yanked on the brass handle and proceeded into the front area. The elder who worked the information desk was nowhere to be seen. A few students meandered the far end of the room, but otherwise we seemed to be the only people here. If the edifice hadn't been so damn creepy and retained the cold, pungent odor of musty death, I would've considered this situation a tad romantic.

"Shall we head up to the third floor, Section J?" she asked, just as I'd hoped. As much as I wanted to hang out with Sarah, I did have an ulterior motive. I wanted to see what the fuck was on the fourth floor of this library.

We headed up the stairwell we'd used the last time, our steps hollow on the sunken, worn stones. The torches from the entrance lit our way up and another set illuminated the second floor landing. When we reached the third floor entrance, I kept walking.

"Hey, where are you going?" Sarah asked, the smallest hint of angst in her voice.

"I'm going up to the fourth," I said, mustering as much defiance as I could. "I don't think it's 'under construction.' I don't think they want us up there."

"Mike!" she said, her voice little more than a loud whisper. "We can't do that! What if it really is under construction? It could be dangerous."

"Well, at least we'll know," I said. I wasn't sure why I wanted to go up there. A small, pathetic part of my lizard brain thought that an entire empty floor of the library would allow consenting co-eds to do whatever they pleased. But a larger part was beginning to get sick of all the mystery and anger surrounding this campus. I had seen too much not to become immune to the weird stuff happening all around me. It was beginning to add up: the dean's bizarre speech, our spectral benefactors on the hill, a RA going to war with his charges rather than trying to mentor them. As separate incidents, I hadn't registered them on any cosmic level, but when I considered the odd nature of an entire library floor being closed, it became too much. My father's reference to the floor on the phone had been the last straw. At the very least, it would take my mind off how terrible my freshman year of college was going. Having Sarah along for the ride was just a bonus. I continued to walk up the stairs. The soft echo of my shoes carried upward. "Are you coming?" I inquired.

After another few seconds of hesitation, Sarah stared walking. "Oh, all right, if it'll help you put this big mystery to bed, then I'll join you," she said. "But I'm telling you, nothing crazy happens here anymore. They couldn't keep the school open if it did. Did you ever think about that?"

I had, but not too much. I was convinced there was more to the picture. "Of course I've thought about that," I said, trying to sound reassuring. "But it doesn't add up with all the other crazy stuff I've seen around here. C'mon, you have to admit they seem to be withholding information from us."

"Maybe," Sarah said, her voice echoing off the stone walls. "Or maybe you're just paranoid."

"Either way, we'll find out," I said as we reached the plateau of the fourth floor. The stairwell terminated at a large brick wall. A torch holder stood on the right side, the flame illuminating the arched entrance on the left.

"Isn't it a bit odd that they left the torch going?" I asked.

Yellow tape, the kind police used to mark off a crime scene, criss-crossed the stone archway. The words "under construction" stood out in bold black type. Looking past, I could see rows of dusty wooden tables, each running the length of the floor. Rickety wooden chairs sat along the sides at intervals. These seats looked way more ancient than those on the lower floors. The room contained towering stacks just like the others below, but devoid of books. Straight ahead stood sawhorses and a few dusty power tools. A few long, wooden beams sat on top of the sawhorses and were marked with measurements. Other construction equipment littered the floor: hammers, straight edges, toolboxes, hard hats. I snaked through the yellow tape, causing one of the strands to tear from the wall.

"Be careful, Mike," said Sarah from behind me. It gave me a start, and I stumbled through the tape and into the room. "Sorry," Sarah said. "It looks like a construction zone . . . doesn't it?"

"Yeah, I guess," I said. I soldiered forth, scanning either side of me for more equipment. I saw some on the right side, down at the far end between two of the tall rickety stacks. A single construction lamp cast a bright spiral of light from that direction, as if left on by accident. A few more hard hats lay under the light. "I'm going to check that out," I said, pointing at it.

The stench up here was more powerful than the rest of the library. On our first journey here I thought it was the smell of decaying paper. Now it came to me as more alchemical, with musty and dense smells underneath. It triggered something I had forgotten about back in my days in St. James. I recalled a viewing at the town's funeral parlor when I was around six years of age. The mortician had left open a storage room in the back of the giant house and my precocious self had wandered in there, not unlike my wandering in this library. The odor on this floor reminded me of embalming chemicals, mixed with something that had been dead for many years but couldn't stay dead. Kind of like Alfred James. As I approached the construction light, I noticed a few books on the shelves. A large tome sat open on the bare third shelf of the stack, illuminated on one side by the static fluorescent light. My eyes trained over the legible side and widened as I read.

"What is it?" Sarah's voice called to me from the other end. "I wish you would have told me we were going to be exploring a dark, scary corridor. Okay, I probably wouldn't have come if you'd said that. But I also might have brought my flashlight. I see more construction equipment down there. Are you sure it isn't . . . "

Sarah kept calling to me, but her voice faded from my range of senses as I read the page. *Those who have purified their spirit and their heart may join with the illustrious members of the Malworthe Society. Every generation the mystics choose one pupil of each gender to determine their worth to join this sacred society. If at the end of their schooling they are found to be worthy, they shall join us in never-ending harmony and further the goal of everlasting darkness over the land. If no suitable choice can be made the year is forfeited and the chosen must be expelled. Such is the way of our movement: always in darkness until the end.*

A sharp tingle entered the base of my spine as I read, and I was surprised to find Sarah standing right next to me.

"What's this?" she said, her voice back to the forced whisper.

"I don't know," I said, turning to look at her and regaining my composure. "But look at this."

Sarah bent down to look at the part of the book exposed by the fluorescent light, concern on her face. I watched her verdant eyes dart back and forth. "Look at what?"

I moved my eyes from staring at hers back to the page. There was nothing there. "What the . . . ?" I said, confused. "There were words right there a second ago, I swear. Stuff about some kind of secret society on campus. I know it sounds crazy, but that's what it said."

"Are you sure?" Sarah said.

"Yes! They were right there," I said, pointing. I shuffled through a few other tattered pages in the book. They were all blank. "I'm not making this up," I strained.

"I didn't say you were," Sarah said. "But whatever you just read is no longer there. Do you know what it meant?"

"No," I said. "But I intend to find out." I grabbed the cover of the book and slammed it shut. A small cloud of dust lifted and filtered through the light. I found the small switch on the yellow pole that held the lamp and turned it off, plunging us into total darkness. My father's strange admonitions about pranks on the fourth floor rattled in the back of my head. We felt our way back through the stacks and the cautionary tape. The light from the torch in the stairwell burned out just as we started down the stairs.

"Mike, I have a bad feeling about this," Sarah said. "Why are you taking that book?"

"Because I need some answers," I said. "And as a student attending this weird-ass place, so should you."

"Answers to what?" she asked. "What the hell are you talking about?"

As we reached the warm glow from the third floor, I realized I was going to have to let Sarah in on what happened Homecoming night. I turned and faced her in the stone archway. The flicker of light danced around her gorgeous and confused face.

"Sarah, there are some things I haven't told you about what I've seen here," I began. "I didn't want to tell you because I wasn't sure I believed them in the first place. But now that I've seen this book, I'm convinced there is something more going on here. A lot more. And it involves all of us in Schuster Hall. Does that make any sense to you?"

Sarah gazed at me, her sensational eyes reflecting the sparkling embers of the torch. "Not really," she said. "But I trust you. I think."

"Good enough," I said. "Now, there's one other thing I need to look into."

We made our way down the stairwell to the first floor. The wizened old gentleman with the silver hair now manned his position behind the reference desk and its giant stack of card catalogs. A few students milled around so I grabbed Sarah's hand and wandered through the stacks, looking for an empty table. We found one at the far north side, short and squat with a plank in the middle to prevent people from looking across it. I pulled out two creaky chairs that felt loose enough to collapse in my hands. I set the ancient book down on the table.

"Now before I start another pursuit," I said, "I need to fill you in on what happened Homecoming night." I proceeded to tell Sarah about the two gentlemen Eric and I met that night, including how people seemed to walk right through Alfred James. Sarah's eyes got wider as I kept talking, then shrunk as I returned the part she knew about—the drunk driving.

"So, what does that have to do with this book?" she said, an incredulous note dancing around the edge of her voice.

"I don't know," I said. "But I think everything is connected to this school. Alfred said something about being stuck in one area of the town. And Winograd said he attended school here back in the fifties. They both have something to do with this. I need to look at one more thing."

I got up from the rickety, short table and approached the reference desk. Sarah followed behind me, her steps quick and nervous. The old man's eyes followed me as I approached, the eyeglasses edging down the bridge of his nose as he moved his head. He wore a different pair of brown suspenders tonight, and they covered a tarnished yellow dress shirt.

"Welcome, my young masters," he said in his thin voice. "What brings ye to the library at this hour?"

"Uh . . . I'm looking for books on the history of Malworth University."

His beady eyes grew large behind the small glass frames. "Are ye? And for what purpose might ye be interested?"

"You never asked why we were interested in biology last time," Sarah interjected, her voice shocking me with its strength.

The old man leaned back in his swivel chair, its rusted metal parts making a horrific screech. He ran a lithe finger through his greasy, silver hair. "I suppose you're right. Not many kids in here looking for that information. All right, let's see." He pulled out a few drawers from the cabinet with the stacks of cards. "Looks like this level, Section B." He pulled a single card from the drawer and handed it over. It read: "*Malworth University: A History.*"

"This is it?" I asked.

"That appears to be everything we have on file, my young pupils."

"That can't be right," Sarah said. I could hear sudden anger rising in her voice. "You're telling me that the entire college library contains a single book on its own history?"

"Afraid so, my dear," he said, the grin on his elderly face spreading into a comic smile.

"Well, let's go check it out," I said, bemused. We walked back through the front area between the metal tables. Section B was in the farthest back corner of the room. I scanned the area of the musty shelf where the book was supposed to be but only saw histories of Macalaster College, Minnesota State, and the U. Then I noticed a thick book jammed in at the end of the shelf. I reached over and pulled it out. After blowing dust off the cover I read the title: "*A History of Malworth University. By the Eminent Professor Henry Moriarty. Foreword by Edmund Whitacre.*"

"Bingo," I said, handing it to Sarah.

"What the..." she said, flummoxed. "Don't you find it a little funny that their own history was written by the dean?"

"What do you mean?" I said.

"I mean, do you really think we're gonna get the straight dope on this place by reading something the dean wrote? It's not like he's going to include the fact that ghosts seem to return at Homecoming. I don't think this is even worth our time."

I thought about it for a moment, but decided to take the book anyway. It had to have something valuable to our inquiries.

"Okay, but you better not spend much time reading it," Sarah said. "And make sure you study biology once in a while, since we decided to pursue your wild theories tonight."

"I will, don't worry," I said with a tiny smile as we headed back to the front desk. The old man was nowhere to be seen.

"Looks like I'm going to take these with me," I said, shoving the books into my black backpack.

"What? Why?" Sarah cried.

"I know what I saw, Sarah. I have no idea how it was done, through disappearing ink or something else, but someone doesn't want me to read this. I want to find out why."

"But maybe it never said anything in the first place," Sarah said. The incredulous edge in her voice was trying to gain one last foothold. "Maybe you just looked at it wrong."

"Sarah, I know what I read. It sure as shit wasn't blank then. Somehow it changed once I began reading it."

"Oh, all right," she said, looking down at the dusty floor. "But I don't think you should steal books from the library."

"For this, I'm willing to make an exception," I said.

We high-tailed it out of the ancient library. Dark storm clouds gathered in the west as we walked back to Schuster.

"I'll hold on to these for now," I told Sarah at the front door.

"Fine by me," she said. "You'll let me know if you find anything?"

"Of course," I said. "You'll be the first to know. And Sarah . . ."

"Yeah?" she said, pausing with her hand on the metal door.

"Thanks for coming with me."

We parted ways at my dorm on the fifth floor. I felt as if I'd been confronted by a wall of locked doors, and been given two different keys.

I CHECKED THE PAGES OF THE ANCIENT BOOK Friday morning before class. They remained blank and unknowable. As evening approached along with the emergency meeting, I worried that Seth and Adam had gone too far this time. I feared the two other friends (outside of Eric) I'd made at this shithole of a college were going to leave before I could bond with them. Nick and I exited our room a few minutes before the meeting started. As we walked past Seth and Adam's room, it opened up an inch.

"Sinclair, get in here!" whispered Seth through the crack. "We're doing a few shots to warm up for the meeting."

Nick shook his highlighted head. "Naw, man, don't think so," I said. "We're going to try and be sober for once." I didn't mean to sound like a parent, but it ended up coming out that way.

"Fine," Seth said. "See you in a few." The door pushed shut.

We walked down the hallway and were joined by a few people from the floor I'd never seen. We muffled some words of mutual acceptance about having to attend this meeting, and entered the purple door at the far end. We came upon the glass-enclosed study room. It was still empty of furniture. A few guys lined the wall, looking nervous. Nick and I grabbed a spot in the far corner, under one of the two windows. Nobody said anything. The purple door opened again, and Justin's skinny frame came marching in from the hallway. The mumbling fell to silence once he pulled open the glass door. He stood in front of us, peering into each of our faces. Anger rippled through his seething, wiry body. The dead space I once saw in his blue eyes now registered flames of animosity and dread. The indifference I felt to this guy upon first meeting him fell away, replaced by terror.

"Thank you all for coming," he said in a low, underscored voice. The blue pits of his eyes took stock of our souls. I could take it for a few seconds before I had to look down at the bland carpeting of the study room. "I suppose you've noticed there's no furniture in here. Can anybody here tell me why that is?" He gazed around the room again. Now everybody seemed to be staring at the floor.

"Anybody?" the low voice trembled. "You're telling me no one in this room knows what happened here this weekend? Hard to believe, gents. Hard to believe. Hey, wait a minute. Where are . . ."

The purple hallway door slammed open, and Seth and Adam came strolling through. Justin pivoted, moving faster than I thought was possible. Seth opened the glass door and came face to face with his nemesis.

"Oh, hey, Just-in-time. What's up? You called a meeting or somethin'?" His audacity shocked me to my core.

"Yes, I called a meeting!" Justin shouted. "Where have you two been? You're late."

"Oh, sorry 'bout that, dude," Adam said. His red hair was unkempt. "We usually are on time to everything."

They both squatted down near Nick and me in the corner. Justin's murderous gaze followed them. I feared for my own guilt by association.

"All right," he said, staring right at us, "Gentlemen, I was asking why there's no furniture in here. No tables for studying, no chairs to ease your butts. Nothing. And does anyone," he said, waving his hands wide to the rest of the group, "know why that is?"

Silence from the group. The blue eyes scanned back toward the four of us. "Anyone . . . ?"

"Jesus, really?" Seth shouted. I could smell the alcohol on his breath from where I sat. "Because we fucking piled it all up against your room, you douche bag. That's why. Big mystery."

Justin's eyes were full of red-hot rage. "What did you just call me?" he screamed. "You do not speak to your resident advisor that way. You do not speak to any member of the Malworth University family that way, do you understand? Not me, not your professors, not Dean Moriarty. Not anyone!"

"I won't, as long as they don't act like one," Seth said. My terror increased with each word spoken. I figured Seth would show up to this meeting with his smart-ass attached. This seemed like something more. Something desperate.

Justin took in a long breath and released it in a slow puff. "Anyway," he began in the low voice, "I'm here to tell you that this little stunt you pulled was the last straw. It's not my fault I had to take away your alcohol, boys. It's not allowed on campus. The same would go for anyone else caught with it on this floor."

"Yeah but you didn't catch us, you fucking opened the door and demanded . . ." Seth began.

"Silence!" Justin yelled. Seth closed his mouth. "The point is you had it. I knew you had it, and it's not allowed. End of discussion. No need for retribution, no need to settle any scores."

"Dude, how can you attend college and spout such nonsense?" Adam said. I had to cover my mouth not to burst out laughing. Nick did the same. "Guys get back at each other. Especially when one of them claims to be 'in charge' and they're really not."

"I am in charge, Adam. I am definitely in charge. And do you know what? You two just made it off the list." He pulled a small notepad from the back pocket of his black jeans. After studying it for a moment, he made two dramatic cross-offs with a ballpoint pen. "I've been waiting all semester to do that. Do you know what this means?" he asked.

"We've been crossed off your 'rape list?'" Seth said, in perfect deadpan. I covered my mouth again, sputtering behind it.

Justin's eyes narrowed into slits. "No, you didn't . . . no, you know what? Better that you don't understand. Just think of it as a list you want to stay on for as long as possible. Because once you're crossed off . . ." he glanced down at the four of us, ". . . you're done. And become fair game for me."

We all exchanged glances. I could see a sprout of worry behind Seth's dull glassy eyes. He wasn't going to be this cocky once he sobered up, if he ever did. The image of Justin crossing names off the list stuck in my head, magnified by my library discovery.

"If anything, and I mean anything else happens to me or my dorm room for the rest of the year," Justin spat, "it'll be your last prank, gentlemen. You're going to be out of here. We'll never see you again. Do you get me?"

Silence from the room. "I said, do you . . ." he repeated, louder this time.

"Yes, we fucking get you," Seth said, sounding tired. "No more stupid pranks on the douche bag RA. Is that all?"

Justin's eyes glowed a murderous shade of purple for an instant before he spoke. "Yes, that's all," he said. "I'll be watching you, gentlemen."

He turned around, pulled open the study room door and the purple door, and was gone. We could hear his room at the end of the hallway slam shut. Nobody said a word for a full minute.

"Well, that was fun," Seth said. "So, anyone wanna do some shots in our room?"

"You're kidding," I said.

"Fuck no," Adam said. "This guy can kiss our assholes. College is for having fun and pulling stupid-ass pranks like that. If he can't learn to live with that, it's not our fault. C'mon Seth, let's get the hell out of here."

Nick and I returned to the hallway in silence after they left. I couldn't shake the connection between Justin's list and what I read in the ancient book. The rational part of my brain told me there was no such connection, that the antique residing at the bottom of my dorm closet under my dirty clothes really was empty of words, that a trick of the lights had changed the writing somehow and I didn't notice. The less-rational part said that was a lot of bullshit, that I knew what I'd read, and had just seen a flash of the true motive behind this school in the form of one of its model employees. I felt a pang of worry for Seth and Adam now that they were off the list. It wasn't that I grasped what was going to happen to them, but not knowing somehow made me feel even worse. The school was demonstrating its myriad secrets, the poisonous bits just under the surface of normalcy and twenty-year-olds wrangling their way to class each boring day. But this demonstration seemed meant for me. We approached our room.

"Dude, are you okay?" Nick asked in his monotone, voiceless speech as we stood in front of the door. "That was quite a spectacle."

It shook me out of the spiral of fear. "Yeah, I'm fine," I said, trying to sound nonchalant. My stomach was attempting a handstand without any hands. "I gotta say, though: you called it on that first day. Justin is indeed a crazy fuckwad, not any kind of advisor."

"Told ya," he said, opening the door and returning to his normal station at the computer desk.

THE FIFTH FLOOR OF SCHUSTER HALL seemed to calm down after Justin's outburst at the meeting. We rarely saw him outside of when he escaped his room to go to class like the rest of us. Eric and I spied him leaving one morning before Western Civ. He appeared to turn two separate locks on the door, which was one more than we had. Then he waved his hands in a wizardlike motion toward the wooden door, pressing his palms toward it before pulling them away and retreating out of the hallway. Eric turned to me and gave his best "what the fuck?" shrug. I had no response.

"He's bizarre, man," Eric said as we walked the gritty sidewalk toward Shull Hall, shivering in the cold morning wind. My breath clouded the air ahead of me and broke up into little crystals that dissipated upward.

"You're telling me? I still can't get over what the hell happened in that meeting," I said. "I thought Seth was gonna get his ass thrown out of here."

"No shit," Eric said. Tiny bits of frost caught in the corners of his black framed glasses. The small mustache he'd started was sprouting some miniscule ice crystals. "Those two are pushing their luck. But we might be rid of them after the purge, anyway."

"The what?" I said, stammering from what I thought was the cold.

"The purge. Didn't your folks tell you about it? Why do you think there are way less people on campus these days?" He waved his arms, shouldered in a dark-brown cotton jacket as he walked. "People are leaving, dropping out or being kicked out by the other prick RA's on campus. My parents said it happens at every college. But it happens a lot more at this one. You're surprised by this?"

"Not surprised, just a little taken aback, I guess. I hadn't heard of such a thing." I factored what he was saying in with the other messed up stuff I'd witnessed this semester.

"Oh, yeah," Eric continued, wiping his nose before sniffling. "It's going to be even worse after winter break. My dad said that's when all the dumbasses make their great escape. We're left with the cream of the crop, amigo. At least that's what I tell myself. The way this year's going, you might not see me after I go home!"

"Really?" I said. "I hope not."

"Naw, dude. I'm stuck here. My parents said it was this place or nowhere. 'You wanna be a teacher, you go to fucking Malworth, and you like it!'" He pantomimed the exaggerated wagging finger that I imagined belonged to his father. "Speaking of that," he said, turning to me. "What are you gonna do for break? Not like you have a means of transportation anymore. I'll be around for Thanksgiving, but even I gotta head down to see the folks at Christmas. What the hell are you gonna do?"

I hadn't considered it. I'd forgotten I had outright lied to my parents about the DWI in October. They still had no idea I had lost the Oldsmobile. "Uh . . ." I said, trying to gather my thoughts. "I . . . I'm not sure. Can I confess something to you? I never told my parents about what happened that night. They didn't seem to interested in what I was doing up here, so I didn't feel too interested in telling them. Now what am I going to do?"

"Shit, man," Eric said. "Looks to me like you've got two choices. Either tell them, or don't. But either way they're going to be wondering why their little boy isn't coming home for the holidays."

I was drowned by the thought as we reached the front door of Shull Hall.

NOVEMBER BEGAN THE USUAL PROGRESSION into the half-year winter of the grand state of Minnesota. The leaves began their slow descent from the trees lining the brick paths of the campus, floating on the air as they spun past our heads. I managed to make all my classes on time. I even showed up to Western Civ a few times without Eric, who had after repeated knocks at the door yelled at me to go on without him, like a wounded warrior. I had even come to accept my cycling class as a necessary evil on the way to getting into shape, despite Coach's invective. I recall one trip by myself as I skirted the east side of campus, fresh crackling leaves blowing all around the rough sidewalks that looked to have been placed about five decades before my arrival. I gazed upward as the leaves trembled on the wind and saw the campanile towering high above me like some kind of strange obelisk. Seeing that clock tower in the brochure was one thing; having it oversee your every movement was quite another. It stuck in my mind as I approached, leaves shattering underfoot, as some kind of careful watchman of this institution and its residents. Watching over us all, to make sure we stayed in line, and on the list.

The two books sat in my closet at Schuster, one with pages mute to me and the other divulging little in the way of truth. I'd read the introduction to *Malworth: A History*, written by Dean Moriarty and had learned the school was originally built in the 1950s, just like he said in his speech. There was no mention of anything prior to that time, let alone our two benefactors, but I was going to keep at it.

I hadn't seen Sarah much around the dormitories since our last library excursion. I wondered if she had forgotten, or chosen to forget, what had happened. Seth and Adam also made fewer trips outside the confines of their room. It was as if the easier choice was to button up and stay indoors, away from prying authority or conspiratorial leanings. I felt very alone stomping through the leaves that afternoon, the cold gray wind biting at the back of my thin brown coat.

Thanksgiving at the dining hall was a feast fit for a king, or at least a small hoard of hungry college students. I'd come to know this place, situated in the center of the main dormitory halls, as a slight refuge from the drama of our hall and the people living there. I made a cursory trip down the hallway, asking if anyone wanted to join me for an engorgement. Seth and Adam's room sounded empty. Eric left a note pinned to the cork board adorning his door stating that he'd taken a trip to the library to study. I considered a pathetic trip over to the girl's side to ask Sarah if she'd join me, but the stink of desperation from the plan was too much for even me to bear.

The delicious smells wafted my way as I mounted the linoleum steps that led to the front of the dining hall. I was met by a wondrous combination of fresh carved turkey, hot mashed potatoes and gravy, and stuffing that looked homemade. The disheveled woman with the hair net behind the glass buffet line asserted as much to me. I piled high a plate, grabbed a smaller one for cranberries, and situated myself in a corner of the large, bright room. Groups of students sat all around me chortling and yelling to each other, friends coming together in this time of thanks. I reflected on how the people I'd met here weren't even around for a simple dinner. I let that thought push out those about the books as I dove into the meal. Thirty stuffed minutes later, I hobbled back to Schuster and ensconsed myself in my room. Nick had decamped back to Alexandria for the weekend so it was just me. I wondered for a few minutes if any of my friends from St. James had returned there from college at this time. I considered what old Ben Mosey might be up to this week. I called his house, but got the machine. I didn't see the point of leaving a message. I then considered calling my parents, but I remembered I'd have to address the fact that I wouldn't be coming home for the break, so decided against it.

After another few minutes of digestion, I looked at my closet. I pulled the ancient, vacuous book from its hiding place behind my clothes basket. Still nothing on any page. I took a lemon I'd secured from the dining hall and gave it a good hard squeeze. I'd seen this done in a movie once and naively thought it contoured with reality. A few drops of transparent liquid dotted the page. For the briefest of moments I thought I saw some kind of lettering appear, but then I realized it was a manifestation of my wishful thinking. Those words had somehow been willed to disappear. Getting them back would not be easy. I returned the book and flopped down on the plaid couch for some football watching as I drifted to sleep. A few leaves brushed the window of my room before my eyes closed. I dreamt about what it would be like to attend a normal university.

Chapter
NINE

ECEMBER BROUGHT WITH IT an icy chill that people on the frozen plains of Minnesota knew as the first shot across the bow of winter. Everyone I passed on my way to class had an immediate addition of clothing—large, down-filled coats and slick black and brown boots that kicked puffs of snow in their wake in the winds between the brick buildings of campus. I had my own ensemble to show off to my fellow classmates: a disgusting yellow hooded jacket my father had forced on me during one of our college shopping trips. My boots were the same pair I'd had in high school: high strung things made of a tarnished leather.

The talk around Schuster concerned our plans for the two-week break between semesters. I had yet to tell my folks I had no means of traveling anywhere. Eric had offered to show me a good time down in Eden Prairie but I declined, with respect. I had almost put our mysterious Homecoming benefactors out of my mind. I considered how a trick of light in that darkened bar on the hill could have made me think I saw one extremity pass through another human being. It couldn't have happened.

I knew I'd have to face the music with my parents. One week before the end of the first semester, I made a monumental phone call. I wanted to make the call in relative privacy so I walked down the hallway to the main lobby area between the gendered sides, where a pay phone resided near some upholstered furniture from the seventies. As I walked by Justin's door I noticed the two locks. One appeared to work from the inside, yet I had seen him operate it from the hallway. The faint smell of burned marshmallows over a campfire after a slow rainfall enveloped me as I walked past.

I grasped the receiver with a shaking hand and inserted a few quarters. I had never lied to my father in such a brusque manner before that fall. There was an incident from my high school days that involved alcohol found buried deep in the back corner of the Oldsmobile's trunk. In that case I'd tried to bend the truth, but as usual my parents saw right through the mystique and grounded my sorry ass. This time was different. My father seemed disinterested in most of what I was even doing up here at his alma mater, the school he'd forced me to attend against my wishes. Some angry part of me felt glad his trust had been dashed so much—perhaps now he'd realize what he'd done to me. This antagonism fell away when I heard his voice crackle to life over the line.

"Hello, Michael," came the gruff voice. This phone's connection was a bit better than the old rotaries in our rooms, but it carried with it a pinch of static every once in a while.

"Hey, Dad," I said, leaning up against the concrete wall.

"How's my big man on campus these days?" he said through the static. It made him sound even more distant. "Still making it to all your classes? You're about to finals, aren't you?"

"Yeah, about a week away," I said, folding the phone cord around my knuckles until they turned white.

"Haven't failed anything yet, I presume? This school cost your mother and me a lot of capital. I'd hate to hear you were goofing off with your newfound friends up there." The dour note of his voice indicated he was once again drinking as we conversed.

"Nope, not yet. My statistics teacher has been very helpful. He's taught me stuff I never thought I could understand."

I considered delving into this topic, but knew I had to take my medicine. "Actually, Dad, the real reason I'm calling is—"

"Been to the library yet?" came the voice.

"I told you, Dad, I have."

"And what about the forth floor?"

I held the receiver for a moment. His insistence was maddening. "Yes, we, er, I even checked it out. There was nothing up there but construction equipment. Looks like they are remodeling it or something. Although the whole building could use about a hundred years' worth of upgrades."

My father chortled, a disconcerting noise that ended with a series of hoarse coughs. I'd never heard him make such a sound. "Well that's unfortunate. Wish you could've seen that floor back in my day. We had some good ol' times up there, boy. But enough about the past. You said you had something you wanted to say?"

This was my moment, and I froze. My knuckles had lost some feeling due to the cord wrapped around them, and I almost dropped the receiver. I switched hands and brought it back to my mouth. "Dad, listen . . . I won't be able to make it back to St. James for Christmas. I'm sorry."

Silence on the other end, then a clinking of ice into a glass. I hoped this was only his second drink. "I see," came the voice. "Well, that makes this a bit easier, then. I'm glad you said something. Your mother and I won't be here anyways."

I almost dropped the receiver a second time. "You what?" I said.

"We won't be here," he repeated. "You see, the insurance folks ran some kind of contest, and it seems I've won. We've been given a trip on a cruise ship around the world. We ship out from California on the last day of the semester."

"You . . . you're going on a—"

"Cruise, that's right. So it's a good thing you're going to stay up there with your friends. I hope you have a good time."

"Um . . . yeah. My friends." The misery I'd felt leading up to this conversation began a fast descent toward rage. There was a longer pause on the line than I expected.

"I'm sorry, son," he said, his voice taking on the dull tone I remembered from our last conversation. "I didn't think you'd mind. Besides, I want to make sure you understand the nature of this university before you're fully accepted into its society."

I was stunned. It sounded like he wanted me to stay here. *Accepted into its society?*

"Was there anything else you needed to tell us before we leave? Any exciting news on the girlfriend front?"

"No, no updates there," I said, slapping the concrete behind me with a flat fist. "Well, it sounds like you've got your plans made. I guess I'll see you in the spring." I hung up the phone without his reply. I didn't need it.

Tears stung the edge of my eyes as I walked back down the hallway to my room. My father and I had never seen eye to eye, but he and my mother had raised me. And now he couldn't bear to be in my presence because of some stupid fucking cruise? Why wouldn't he care that I couldn't come home? My fear of telling the truth had been buffeted by a small hope he would have offered to pick me up for the break. Now I was looking at spending two weeks in Schuster Hall alone.

I ignored Seth's cry to join him and Adam in their room for a drink and continued on toward mine. I slammed the door shut and jumped up onto the loft bed. Nick didn't ask if anything was wrong. I pushed my head into my ratty pillow and tried to hold everything within myself. I lay that way until I fell asleep.

I TOLD ERIC THE NEWS the weekend before finals.

"Ugh, that is borderline psychotic, or something," he said, angling his glasses up so he could get the full measure of my pained face. We were sitting on the giant padded futon in his room.

"Tell me about it," I said. "We went on vacation all the time when I was in school. Now that I'm away, they think it's the perfect time to decamp for a world tour?"

"That's messed up," Eric said. "Well, the offer to join me in Eden Prairie still stands. My folks might be a little surprised, but—"

"No," I said, cutting him off. "They made their choice. I'm making mine. We'll see how they like knowing they made their only child stay two weeks in an abandoned dormitory."

"Sounds like they don't really care," Eric said, trying to get a laugh. He shut up when I narrowed my eyes in his direction. "I mean, yeah, that'll show 'em," he stammered.

"It might give me some more time to catch up on a project I've started, anyways," I said, getting up to leave. "Good luck on your finals."

"You too," Eric said, his face torn with concern. "Oh, and we won't be seeing Jake around here next semester. Got kicked out last week for smoking in our dorm. I was lucky Justin didn't throw me out, too."

"Good for you, but bad for him," I said from the doorway. "So you getting a new roommate or something?"

"Nope, now I get my own room. Pretty sweet. Almost makes up for all the times he kicked me out."

"Indeed," I said as I headed down the hallway toward the girls' side.

I gave a few brusque knocks on Sarah's door. Sidarthi, the gorgeous Indian girl who'd given me such a hard time before, answered. She sighed long and loud when she saw who had graced her room with his presence once more.

"She's not here," she said, rolling her eyes so I could see them fall back in her head. "But, she did leave a message for you in case you stopped by. You know, I never thought in my wildest dreams college would teach me to become a courier for two grown-ass adults."

I almost said something, but decided against provocation. I just wanted to see Sarah. "What's the message?"

"She's at the campanile," Sidarthi said. "She goes there a lot these days. Sits there on one of the benches and just stares at it. Weird behavior, if you ask me. You two seem made for each other. Now goodbye!" The door slammed in my face.

I put on the old leather boots and hideous yellow coat and started on my trek. The soaring tower sat almost dead-center of campus, surrounded by a wide field populated by maple and evergreen trees. It was a brick-and-mortar obelisk that featured a wide clock's face on all four sides and a terrifying belfry that led up to a peak covered in adobe plates, which today were blanketed in an inch of snow. Three concrete sidewalks merged into each other at the south side of the imposing structure, their cracked and worn paths split by decades of rain. Metal benches were situated at random angles near its base. I recognized Sarah once I entered the clearing: she sat on a green metal bench staring upward at the edifice. She wore a pretty pink coat with traces of white on the sides, and a tight black wool hat that looked quite warm. Even from a distance I could see those beautiful green eyes reflect the snow and radiate toward me.

She saw me as I crunched through the snow toward her. "You got my message, I take it?"

"Yup," I said, plopping down next to her. "Your roommate is a real piece of work, you know that?"

She chuckled. "I know. And I swear she's got a new guy in there every week. Everyone wants a 'taste of India,' apparently. Shit . . . was that mean? I don't care."

I bellowed laughter in the clear daylight. "I was just wondering, given how she treats me when I attempt to see if you're around. Nice to know you feel the same way."

"Yeah," she said. Her breath made a circle of frozen drops in front of her tiny mouth. "Say, you ever look at this thing? I mean, really look at it?"

I turned and glanced upward. "Uh, no. Not really. Just another creepy building from another century, like the rest of them."

"I don't know," she said, angling her head up. "This one seems different somehow. Like it doesn't quite fit in with the others." I watched as she scanned it up and down, zooming in on any perceived imperfections.

"I've never noticed," I said. "But I'll have plenty of time. I'm going to be stuck here over the break."

Sarah's gorgeous eyes widened as they returned to mine. "What?"

"Believe it. My folks are going on a fucking world cruise. I didn't even get to tell them I couldn't come back cuz of the DUI. What the hell, right?"

"Yeah, I'd say so," she replied, looking worried. "That sucks, Mike. Well, I'd invite you to come back home with me, but my parents are going on vacation too. They're bringing me along, of course."

I leaned back against the hard, cold steel. "Of course," I said. "That's what good parents do."

"Mike, I'm really sorry. I wish I could stay here to keep you company."
The idea comforted me. "Thanks," I said. "But I'll be fine. It'll actually
give me some time to work on . . ." I lowered my voice, as if we weren't
sitting on a bench in several hundred yards of open space, ". . . the books."
"Oh, yeah?" she said. "Any luck deducing their secrets yet?"
"Not yet," I said. "But I have a few ideas."
Sarah gazed over the expanse of frozen landscape before us. The fact
no other students were around should have unnerved me, but I didn't
even register it. "That's why I wanted to meet you out here. I was going
to ask if I could take the blank book with me. You know, to study it. See
if I could get any answers."

I sat up and gave her a sidelong glance. "Oh, really? So now you think
you have something to bring to the table? Well, all right. I can grab it from
my dorm when I get back. You won't leave it at home or anything, right?"
"Duh, of course not! *I* don't steal library books, remember?"
"Right," I said, issuing a sad smile. "But you give me a call the second
you get that sucker to reveal anything. You got me, Ms. Jackson?"
"I got you," she said, grinning.
"All right," I said. "I guess I'll keep the one that actually has words in it."
We spent another few minutes in peace, staring up at the clock tower
in the dimming light.

FINALS WEEK ARRIVED, and with it some germane versions of the tests that
I was used to back at St. James High. Professor Deakin handed us all a long
"bubble sheet" where we'd fill in our answers, and a short stack of papers
crammed with questions. Ellickson's last assignment for Creative Writing
was a short story with a topic of our choice. I had decided to delve into the
world of dormitory living, with mixed results. Coach rode our asses as we
clocked in a full twenty-miles on the exercise bikes, with full resistance.
Thanks to his intense pressure I managed to complete the ride without losing the contents of my lungs. When it was over he didn't say "good job,"
but exited the gym like any other day, telling us to hit the showers as usual.

My Tuesday/Thursday classes took up the most of my concern, but it was only the Natural World that gave me the biggest hurdle. Since our discovery at the library, Sarah and I had not been back there to study, and it showed on my final. Statistics was much better, thanks to my weekly sessions with Professor Dalton in his office at the English building. He taught a similar class on Probability he said he'd try to squeak me into based on my final grade. I considered myself a success, in that I didn't fail any classes my first semester of college. I didn't excel in any either, but I chalked that up to the fact I had more on my mind, like who was choosing students to join this wonderful "society," and how my father seemed to be aware of the same basic concept. Thoughts kept collecting in the back of my mind like driftwood, splinters and spikes fitting together to create something terrifying.

I SAID SOME AWKWARD GOODBYES to Seth and Adam before they headed up to Virginia for the break.

"Sorry you can't join us, Sinclair," Adam said as he shrugged a giant blue-and-green backpack over his shoulders. "Make sure Justin Douchman doesn't try to suck your blood or anything."

"Or your dick," Seth said, emanating hysterical laughter.

"But that's pretty fucked up about your parents," Adam continued. "Almost like they don't want you around or something."

"I know," I said, trying to hide the bitterness in my voice. "Not everyone gets to have parents who welcome them home from college with open arms, I guess."

"Well, I'm all set. You ready to party your ass off with the old crew?" Adam said.

"Fuck, yeah! Let's get this show on the road," Seth replied, shutting and locking their door.

"All right Sinclair, hold down the fort 'til we get back."

"If we get back . . ."

"Yeah, whatever."

They pushed through the pneumatic purple door, and I watched it glide back closed, returing the hallway to silence.

Nick had left for Alexandria that morning, so my room was empty. I had just sat down and was staring at the closet that held *Malworth: A History* when I heard a knock on the wooden door. When I opened it, Justin's creepy visage stood there, grinning. His face appeared more gaunt than usual, and his hair like it hadn't been combed in several days. The bleak anger circling his dark-blue eyes at the floor meeting seemed to have resided.

"Hey, Mike," he said, his voice back to the fake sweetness I'd heard the day Nick and I had met him. "So I hear you're the only one left up here for the break. Pretty rough, man. I'm sure your parents had a good reason for leaving you here, though."

I was taken aback for a moment. "What do you know about my—"

"Don't you worry, Mr. Sinclair," he continued, rolling right over my question. "I've been selected to be the 'stay-behind' over the winter break. You're not the only one who gets to bum around this place for the next two weeks. There's a girl staying on the other side as well. So the powers that be have decided I am to sit right here. You know, in case either of you try anything stupid."

I stared at him for a moment, not sure what he was telling me.

"Uh, I mean . . . not that you would," he continued. "Malworth holds such high standards for its students, that I'm not expecting anything from you. And, hey, speaking of that—great work on your finals, Mike. Looks like you showed up to almost every class this year."

"Wait, what? How did you . . ."

He kept on speaking, as if he was a robot. "Many of your other dorm mates couldn't achieve such discipline, so you won't be seeing them next semester. I've already had to remove one undesirable element," he said. I watched as he brought up the small notepad he'd brandished at the floor meeting the previous month. A few other names I couldn't read were crossed off the list. "And more to come," he said, nodding his head in the direction of Seth and Adam's room.

"What the hell are you talking about?" I stuttered, still not sure if I should be trusting a word coming from this asshole.

"Oh, nothing," Justin said as he placed the notepad in his back pocket. "Just giving you notice that you're ahead in the rankings with your school work completed. Keep it up next semester and you'll be set on joining . . . er, getting out of here with a great grade point average." He stretched his mouth into and unrecognizable, unnatural smile.

"Uh, thanks for your support. I'll try to stay out of your way," I said, attempting to shut the door. Justin lifted a flat palm to stop me.

"That'll be a good idea on Friday night. But any other time, I'll be around as your resident advisor, ready to assist in any way possible. Whether that's helping you find your classrooms next semester, where the dining hall is located, or dealing with some of the dreaded roommate issues," he said, almost repeating what he'd said the day I had met him, "I'm here to help. Think of me as just another guy living here in the hall, goin' to school like you all, but somebody you can always speak to regarding any problems you might have. You dig?" His smile had receded to more like what a mental patient might flash at some orderlies.

"Uh, yeah, I dig," I said, trying to shut the door again. I found it near immovable.

"Just not Friday night, as I'll be . . ." he said, and then placed a skinny hand over his mouth. "Nothing, nothing," he said, releasing the door so I could push it shut with a slam. The noise echoed in the hallway. After I heard his footsteps moving away, I flopped down on Nick's plaid couch and tried figuring out what the hell I had just witnessed.

THE NEXT FEW DAYS PROVED more boring than anything I'd ever experienced. I had not realized how much I had come to depend on other people in this building to enliven my evenings and provide me with some discussion. I found myself reflexively standing up and walking to the door to head over to see what Eric was doing every few hours before I had to put a note on the door saying I was all alone. Television during the day was more boring than I remembered, but I did enjoy a few games of *The Price Is Right*. The dining hall remained open and retained a minimal staff so I didn't starve to death. Each trip through the glass-enclosed hallway that led over to the giant modern dining hall felt like a solitary trip through time as I exited one ancient building for one that had actual conveniences. I watched the sapling trees in the grassy yard below as I returned to Schuster each evening, their young branches twisting in the biting winter wind.

On Thursday I decided I'd had enough of my own presence and decided to walk around the dormitory to see if there was anyone else left worth conversing with. I headed down the bland carpeted hallway toward Justin's room. It was locked shut as usual. The strangeness of his last words still hung in the back of my mind like rotting meat on fish hooks. They meshed too well with my father's final statements on the telephone. I skipped past the study room, still bereft of furniture. I pushed through the lobby and over to the girl's side in hopes of running into my one other companion on this floor. I noticed a single door open at the far end of the hallway.

Soft rock music spilled outward, so I approached with caution. I peered across the doorway to see if anyone was inside and came across Amanda, the gorgeous blonde I'd met at the first dorm party at Schuster. She sat on plush pink futon, her blonde hair flowing behind her and her head swaying to the music on the stereo. Her sparkling blue eyes widened when she saw my dorky ass approach in sweat pants and an oversized gray sweatshirt. She turned the volume down on her stereo and looked right at me.

"Uh, hello?" she said, her perfect lips moving in synchronicity.

"Oh, um, hi. I just wanted to see who else had the pleasure of staying around this place over the break. I'm Micheal Sinclair. You might remember me from the party we had last fall?"

She gave me a withering glance, one I'd become familiar with among a certain caste of girls in St. James, made from a hefty dollup of pity and a slight dash of contempt.

"Oh, right. I'm Amanda, since you probably don't remember due to how drunk you all were that night. My parents died when I was young, and my legal guardian just had to go out-of-state for some ghastly reason, so I'm freakin' stuck here. With you."

"Gee, what a shame," I said, giving her my best sarcasm.

"Sorry," she said. "I've just been bored out of my mind these last few days. You can come in and chill if you want, but don't try anything you might regret. I have a boyfriend back home."

I'll admit the thought had crossed my mind upon seeing this stunning creature in her natural habitat. But I knew when a girl was out of my league. Still, it was nice to have some type of companionship that wasn't weirdo Justin. I sat on a wicker chair propped up in the corner of the room. The dirty brown cushion exumed dust.

"Don't worry," I said, trying to sound important. "I'm considered a perfect gentleman."

"Right," she said, rolling her eyes. "You and the rest of those dumb-asses. So who all is left around here? Are any of the RA's still here?"

"Yeah, only Justin from our side," I said. "The guy who almost busted us at that party, remember?"

"Oh, yeah," Amanda said, her eyes narrowing. "I haven't really talked to him since then. He came to our room back around the first part of the semester to say 'hello' or something. He seemed nice, I guess."

"Well, he's not," I said. "He's actually a total fuckwad, throwing away my friends' alcohol and acting like a total weirdo. Although I'd be pretty pissed if I had a bunch of furniture propped up against my door, too."

Amanda chuckled, a dainty laugh that sounded like dropped China plates. "No way. You did that?"

"Well, not me, but some guys on my floor. Seems they've begun a little feud with the guy, and it ain't pretty."

"I see. Our RA isn't even here most of the time. She's too busy going to the hill to find another guy of the week to get on her. I don't even know her name."

I didn't even realize there was a resident advisor on the girl's side. Sarah had never mentioned one. "Well, is she nice to you girls at least?"

"Fuck no," she said. "Treats us like shit most of the time. Like she doesn't even want to be here herself. But who can blame her? This campus fucking sucks. When was it last updated, like fifty years ago?"

I thought we'd reached a rich strain of conversation topic. "Oh, I know," I said. "And what about that library? Have you seen the place?"

"No," she said. "I don't really study. Plus some jerks got all the furniture banned from our study lounge . . ." she smiled at me, causing my insides to backflip. "So I just do most of my reading in here. My roommate transferred the hell out of here at the end of this semester, so it'll just be little old me here from now on."

I pushed away the thought of this girl becoming so bored over winter break she begged me to come to the girls' side for her entertainment. I tried to focus on Sarah, and what she might be doing instead. "Well, you should check it out. The oldest fucking building you'll ever have the displeasure of entering. But stay away from the fourth floor. It's under construction."

She gave me a weird look and said, "I already told you, I wouldn't be caught dead there."

She seemed bored by this point, so we listened to her music for a dull hour. When the pink bubble clock on her wall hit six I asked if she wanted to hit the dining hall.

"Uh, no I don't like the food there," she said, pulling a package of Ramen from the wooden shelves next to a closet stuffed with a massive amount of clothing. "Plus the store in that building sells some crazy good cheap shit. Like this. Just add water!"

If I wasn't so transfixed by her beauty I would have been struck by how feather-brained Amanda seemed to be. I didn't recall any of this from the party, but then again I didn't recall much of anything that night. She got up from her seat and headed out to grab some water from the drinking fountain in the hallway. Thinking I may have overstayed my welcome, I started to get up when I heard a familiar voice outside her door.

"Hello there." It was Justin.

"Uh, hello," I heard her say in almost the exact tone she'd used with me.

"I'm Justin, the RA for the guy side. Everything going okay over here?"

"Um . . . yeah. Everything's fine. Just getting some water for my Ramen." I could hear the annoyance gathering in her voice.

"Oh, great. But you know the dining hall is open throughout the entire winter break, right?"

"Yeah, I heard. I might check it out tomorrow."

"Tomorrow? Tomorrow is . . ." he stopped, and it sounded like something stuck in his throat. ". . . is a good day to go there," he finished. His voice had a scratchy, raw quality now.

"Good to know," Amanda said, her voice moving back to her room.

"And let me know if you need anything else over the next week. I'll be around as your resident buddy, ready to assist you in any way possible. Think of me as just another guy living here in the hall, goin' to school like—" he stopped when she reached her room. Justin gaped at my presence on her wicker chair.

"What's he doing here?" he accused.

"I don't know," she said, rolling her eyes toward me. It seemed she had found an even more bothersome guy in this dorm hall than me.

"I see," Justin said. His eyes changed in an instant, from firey red to the black pits of charcoal I'd noticed on our first meeting. "Please recall that gentlemen are not allowed in lady's rooms past curfew, Mr. Sinclair. I'd hate to come back here during rounds and find you taking up this wonderful woman's time. Isn't that right, Ms. . . . ."

"Thank you," Amanda said in her most smarmy voice yet, closing the door. "What a fucking weirdo," she gasped, turning to me.

"Yeah, that's our RA," I said. "Interesting human being, isn't he? If he's even human."

She laughed again, the China plates dropping. "You know, I'm kinda glad y'all tried trapping him in his room."

I guffawed louder than I should, a nervous tic I had around gorgeous women. "Yeah, maybe that's a little clearer now. I can't believe he caught you in the hallway like that. What is he, spying on you or something?"

"That'd be creepy," she said, placing her bowl in a small white microwave on top of her dresser. That reminded me I needed something to eat of my own.

"Well, I'm going to head over to the dining hall. I eat there most days, if you're ever interested," I said as I got up to leave.

"I told you, I don't eat there," she said, pushing back a lengthy strand of golden hair. "But I suppose I could make an exception. We're kinda like the last two people on earth for this week. Us and that space alien."

I laughed. "Yeah, well try to forget about him. And if you're ever bored, I live down in 501 on the guy's side."

"Oh, I thought you lived on the girl's side," she said, attempting some of my brand of humor. I couldn't turn away from her smoldering eyes, and forgot to laugh.

"Oh, right. Good one," I said as I exited. "I'll see you around."

"Okay," she said, shutting the door.

I gazed down both sides of the hallway for any sign of Justin before I walked out toward the dining hall.

FRIDAY DRAGGED ONWARD as I reached the limits of my abilities to entertain myself. I'd almost memorized the schedules of each of the five local TV channels Malworth had granted upon its dormitory residents. In between mindless clicks I came across weather updates that looked bad every hour. A major winter storm was heading through the Dakotas and would be gaining steam right around the weekend. The forecast was for ten inches of snow at least, with more coming after it. This was the type of storm Minnesotans dreaded every year. Since I didn't have a car and had nowhere to go, I paid little heed as the local news forecaster became more harried by the hour. By suppertime I was ready to be done with it all, and so headed back to the dining hall for an unhealthy meal of pizza, hash browns, and a small bowl of cereal. Not having any parents around meant I did a piss-poor job of feeding myself.

I wandered back through the glass-enclosed hallway from the dining room, my eyes trailing over the darkening skies above as they twisted and contorted, awaiting the dumping of snow that was to come. The clouds looked even more ominous as they towered and danced over the old buildings of campus. I made sure to stroll through the girls' hall in the scant hopes I'd run into Amanda, but her door was shut tight just like the rest of them. I had not yet ventured to the other floors to see what denizens might find themselves trapped here with me, but I wasn't that desperate yet.

I resigned myself to sitting on the ugly plaid couch in my solemn dorm room, the Malworth history book open in my lap. I flipped through a few pages until I came across one in particular that stopped me. It was a group of what looked like soliders from the Civil War posing for a photograph on a dirt road slanted downward. Something was familiar. I stared at each grizzled face, wondering what they would tell me if I could reach them. As my corneas strained to the end of the line, I felt a twinge of recognition. Standing at the back of the line, moustache bushy and beard protruding just as they had on Homecoming night, was Alfred James. I blinked once, then twice, but the image didn't change.

"Holy shit," I said to myself and my room. I looked at the caption of the photgraph. It stated that this was the final group of soldiers admitted to the "Malworthe Institution of Healing." My eyes moved to the passage below.

The Malworthe Institution of Healing was born of necessity. In the mid-nineteenth century many a plague scandalized the Midwest region of our fair nation. Out east, the country was preparing for an inevitable civil war. In the land of Minnesota plagues of sickness and death were everywhere. Travelers were passing away from cholera, dysentery, the myriad strains of the flu, and other more serious maladies. And the land itself was being protected by sacred and ancient Native American rites. Some even describe these as a curse placed upon the very land of the institution.

Only our great founder, Edmund Whitacare, saw any value in this land. He brought the first healers and priests to begin the society of healing on this very land. He constructed the great temples, and invited all who were weary to come and partake in the first trials. These were trials to destroy the evil terrorizing our fair land. Sometimes this required giving up that which the patient loved most. But those willing to give it all often saw remarkable progress. The lame were found to walk again, those plagued by maladies found vigor returned, and some even claimed they had seen the great beyond during their trials.

"What the fuck," I said, glancing at the photograph. Alfred's grim mug stared right back at me, along with nine other dirty and tarnished faces. I turned the page and continued reading.

The institution gained prominance in the war, but fell out of favor after its conclusion. Investigators from the east coast began to look into our practices and means of health, and the institution was shut down in 1867. The land would remain barren and unclean until the founding of the university close to a century later.

I shut the book, stunned by what I'd just discovered. Alfred James wasn't just any old supernatural creation. He was part of the final group of men admitted to whatever nuthouse existed on these grounds back then. The final group before it was shut down for good. This was too much to process, and I had no one to talk to about it. Amanda would think I was a raving lunatic, and Justin . . . was he in on the whole thing? I had to block out encroaching thoughts, so I turned on the television and shut off my mind as best I could. I fell asleep in front of Nick's white-painted ramshackle entertainment center, the screen a mesh of white static. I pulled myself up the creaky loft ladder, ignored the large snap it made as I slumped onto the mattress and closed my eyes before I even hit my ratty, torn pillow.

I was charged awake by a loud thunder of movement against the wooden door. It was a force big enough to shake my entire room, including my loft. My eyes shot open in the darkness, and I reoriented toward the small digital alarm clock that rested on the wooden post beside me. It read 3:00 a.m.

"What the . . . ?" I mumbled as I registered the time. "Who . . . who's there . . . ?"

I shuffled my legs around, wheeling them toward the ladder. I crept down, slipped on some black mesh shorts, and pulled on my rubber sneakers. My heart pumped hard, beating like a fist against my ribcage. I unlocked the door and pulled it open a few inches. The light from the hallway spilled in, illuminating my room and blinding me for a few seconds. I noticed a slip of paper floating in the crack between door and concrete wall. It was a piece of one of the fliers Justin had papered all over our floor. I pulled the door open further and opened my eyes as wide as I could.

The entire corridor was a mess of paper and trash. It looked as if somebody had run through the dorms with a full wastepaper basket and gone to town. Posters and notifications some guys had placed on their bulletin boards had been shredded and tossed around. Some bits of paper still floated through the air, as if they had just been loosed upon the earth. The noise of sheets brushing against concrete and settling down were all I could register above the silence that permeated the hallway. The brilliant fluroescents gave the scene a bizarre daylight quality, as if this was just one more prank perpetrated by one dorm room against another. Except no one was here.

I moved one foot into the mess, my sneaker ruffling notebook paper and a coupon for Tony's on the hill. As I moved to shut my door I noticed the malicious nature of the perpetrator: the schedule Nick had placed on our bulletin board had a giant "X" ripped through it and was hanging off the door. Whoever did this meant to agitate everyone. Seth and Adam's bulletin board had been torn from their door, the dried remains of the wood glue used the single trace of its existence.

I kept moving, one cautious foot over the other, paper scattering every which way as I walked. I spied Justin's door at the end. It was locked and bolted. I continued through the purple door at the end of the hallway, toward the empty study room and into the carpeted lobby with its art-deco furniture and wide windows. The large room appeared to be untouched by the paper massacre. I decided to see if anyone was around even as my heart continued to punch its way out of my chest. I had no idea who or what could have done this but thought there must be evidence somewhere. I pushed through the pneumatic door in the middle of the area and headed down to the main lobby of the building, my sneakers squealing on the linoleum stairs and echoing all around me. A single bead of sweat poured down the center of my forehead.

I pushed through the main lobby door. The lighting was dimmer here; the main office dark and desolate. My eyes darted around trying to catch any movement. I thought I saw something outside the window. On the far side of Schuster Hall a craggy, broken set of concrete stairs led under an awning to the main lobby area. I avoided entering the building this way as the rust-addled railings and cracked steps seemed about a minute away from total collapse. It was also a popular destination for the three or four people in the dormitory who needed quick access for a smoke break (another reason I avoided it). I approached the metal door leading outside. A small puff of smoke drifted upward outside the window in the door. I froze and waited. After a few minutes I crept forward again, this time spotting through the window a hooded figure standing at the bottom of the concrete stairs, facing away from the building. Pieces of large snowflakes fluttered above the dark fleece hoodie, some attaching to its contours, melting and dripping down toward the ground. A big gloved hand moved a cigarette in a slow arch up toward the hood. A few seconds later a puff of smoke wafted up into the air, dispersing among the white dots of snow. I stood at the door and stared at this figure as it repeated the motion three times without doing anything else. My heart was beating so hard it was actually causing my thoughts to dance as they trekked through the forest of figuring out who the hell this person was and what they were doing. I didn't recognize the stature from this view. The figure took one more slow drag on the smoke.

"What are you doing down here?" came a low voice from behind me.

I jumped and almost sliced off the tip of my tongue as my jaw clamped shut. After settling back to earth and turning around, I saw Justin sitting in one of the ugly art-deco chairs.

"I said, what are you doing down here?" he asked, his face shrouded in darkness. I turned back around to face the metal door. The figure was gone. Snowflakes drifted to the ground in the space where he stood. There were no footprints.

"N-nothing," I said, too stunned to move for a moment. I didn't notice my heartbeat anymore. It was as if this last scare had caused it to cease functioning.

"Doesn't look like nothing," came the voice, buttressed above on either side by the two purplish dots of flame that made up his eyes. "Did you see what happened upstairs?"

"Yes . . . I did," I managed to reply. "Did you do that?"

He leaned forward. The moonlight shifted on his face and illuminated his tiny eyes. He looked like a creature out of Lovecraft. "Do you think I would do such a thing to this dormitory? My *home*? I think not. Say, what were you looking at out there?"

I glanced one final time at the rugged concrete stairs, their metal banisters shedding purple paint. "Nothing," I repeated.

"Didn't look like nothing," he said, still leaning forward. After another pause, "Big snow coming this week. Hope you're ready."

My heart slowed. I somehow found the wherewithal to extract myself from this horrifying situation. I made a brusque turn back in the direction of the stairwell from which I'd entered, pulled open the pneumatic door and high-tailed it back up the linoleum stairwell. All I knew was that I had to get away from Justin. When I reached the fifth floor and its trash-strewn hallway, I felt a strange sense of déjà vu. I opened the door to my room, threw myself inside, and slammed the door shut, shoving the dead bolt in place. I crammed onto the plaid couch and sat there like a deer, wide-eyed and afraid, until I collapsed from exhaustion.

I woke in a pool of sweat and drool. My head had landed on the right arm of the plaid couch at an extreme downward angle that hurt when I moved. The night's events swelled in my mind, then disappeared, as if a dream. All I could formulate was Justin sitting in that hideous lobby chair, asking me what I was doing down there. I cranked my head against the pain and looked out the window. White strips of snow outlined the rectangular design, their bumpy edges sticking out as more snow attached from above the pane. Huge snowflakes drifted downward lazily and collected in the large oak trees outside Schuster Hall. The silence was miserable and served as a helpful reminder I was all alone here. Except for him. And her.

Amanda. Her door had been shut the night before. But might she have seen anything? I calculated the risk of running into Justin in the hallway versus finding out if she had some insight into the crazy scene. In the end I went against my better judgment and opened the room door at a snail's pace before peering down the hallway. The first thing I noticed was how clean it looked: as if the mess of assorted papers and fliers I'd seen covering the corridor had never existed. I made a beeline down the hallway toward the purple door next to Justin's room, which sat silent and locked. I pushed through to the lobby. The girls' side was just as deserted as mine. I approached Amanda's room and saw the door was ajar by a few inches. I pushed it open a few more inches and spoke a quiet greeting. There was no one in the room. Disappointed, I headed back to my room. I had nobody to talk to about what I saw last night, not that Amanda would believe me. I wondered if Seth and Adam would when they got back. I wasn't sure Eric would, given his inability to grasp what we saw Homecoming night. What I now had proof of in that book. I shuddered as I thought about Alfred's pale face staring up at me. I entered my room and locked the door.

I DIDN'T LEAVE THE ROOM much after that, using the restroom when necessary but avoiding my routine trips to the dining hall. It's not that I was afraid of Justin, but what I had seen shook me to my core. I couldn't get the hooded figure off my mind; how it just disappeared into the snow without leaving footsteps. Just like Alfred moving through that girl's shoulder. Just like Winograd disappearing behind that hidden door at the Ice Castle. Three instances of paranormal behavior, three events I couldn't corroborate with anyone else on this campus. And one crazy-ass RA who seemed intent on getting rid of students rather than assissting them. And of course, there was the list. Whatever "society" Justin was gaming to put us into, I could never be a part of it.

My decision to not leave my dorm was reinforced by the snow, which continued to fall all weekend and buried the campus in a heavy layer of white. When I peered out the dorm window Monday morning, the strips of snow had doubled in size, limiting my view to a few square inches of frame. What I saw scared me: the entire campus was a pale outline of itself. The huge old dormitory buildings were almost unrecognizable among the staggering whiteness. The few cars remaining in the parking lot were buried in several feet of snow. They looked like boulders with wheels stuck in marshmallows. The rest of the campus faded in and out through the frosty air, illusions of sanity. Even the campanile was gone in the mist.

I made a stealth run over to the dining hall on Monday afternoon. I hadn't seen Justin since my bizarre encounter and thought my luck was good. As I speed walked through the girl's side of the dorm I noticed Amanda's door was now closed tight. I knocked twice, but no one answered. The window-lined corridor leading to the dining hall was a freezing tunnel of darkness. The wet snow poured down its sides, blocking the view. I decided the best course of action would be to get in and out as quick as I could. I hit the little convenience store on the bottom floor for all the potato chips, frozen mini-pizzas, and soda I could carry.

"Sucks bein' stuck here over the break, don't it?" said the pimple-faced kid manning the register by himself. He looked a decade too young to be attending college.

"Yeah, especially when you've got . . ." I stopped myself, knowing a disclosure of what I'd seen might be dangerous. My paranoid mind said I should keep this information to myself. "Uh . . . nothing to do," I finished. I grabbed my items and marched the hell out of there.

When I got back to the room I checked the bolt twice. Then I proceeded to gorge on all of the food my parents warned me against eating. I figured it served them right for abandoning me to this icy tomb. I sucked down the last bit of sugary soda from my second can and slumped into the plaid couch, attempting to stay awake for the weather report from the one local news channel still broadcasting to the campus. I grabbed the history book from my small desk and started plunging into the next chapter. I had almost reached the Depression era, when the Moriarty family began to get involved in creating the school, when I feel asleep.

Three pounds of a fist on my door woke me up an hour later. The history book had slumped out of my hand and onto the floor, still propped open by my foot. My heart lept into my throat as I sat up straight, re-injuring my neck. I stared at the door a full minute before three more knocks chilled me to my spine. I pushed myself off the couch and approached the door and clicked the deadbolt. My hand was shaking as I turned the copper handle of the door. Something inside must have snapped because the next thing I did was pull open the door as fast as I could. There was no one there, and no sign of anyone in the hallway.

"Hello?" I cried, my voice tiny in the echoing corridor. "Who's there?" Nothing. I scanned as far down as I could. Still nothing.

I pushed the door shut and locked it once more. My hand had a slight shake to it even as I sat back down on the plaid couch. I thought a drink might help calm my nerves, so I pulled the bottle of Jack from my closet. I grabbed the cleanest plastic cup I could find from Nick's closet and poured myself a tall drink. I chugged half of it. I flipped through a few channels on the television; they were now all static. Just to confirm I was living in an actual horror film, I picked up my hardscrabble purple rotary phone from its receiver. No dial tone. I poured myself another steep drink and sat on the couch, considering my fate. One more drink after that and I was passed out. The fluorescent light above me flickered as I slipped the coils of consciousness and entered drunken dream land.

BY WEDNESDAY I HAD VERY LITTLE liquor left to drink. I decided drastic action was needed. I opened the room door and looked out into the hallway. I walked down to the other end and kept going until I reached the lobby, where I stopped to take the stairs. I went down to the first floor and came upon the place I'd seen Justin on Friday night. There was no one here; the office was dark and empty. I headed to the guys side of the first floor.

"Hello?!" I yelled down the passage. It had the same bland yellow paint that covered every hallway in this structure. My call came back to me in a weird reverberation that made me sound like a giant with a cold. I listened for a full minute to make sure I didn't miss any voices. Resigned, I headed over to the first floor on the girls' side. Again I yelled "Hello?!" After a full minute there was no response. I repeated the same sorry procedure on both sides of the second, third, and fourth floors. Again and again there was no response. I was alone. I trudged back to my room, never feeling so solitary in all my time on this earth.

I must have slept through the night on the plaid couch because I was awakened again Thursday morning by three sharp knocks on the door. My back arched as I rubbed my eyes open to see. I rubbed my neck, still in pain from the previous nights.

"Sinclair! I know you're in there," came Justin's voice. "Open up!"

I sat staring at the door, my heart picking up beats and my feet beginning to tremble. This was the moment I'd been afraid of: Justin was finally coming to eliminate me before the break was over. He'd give some bullshit story to the school and my parents, and I'd be gone without any trace.

"Mr. Sinclair. I'm not messing around here. I need to talk to you."

His formal summon was unnerving. I figured I might as well accept my fate, but on my own terms. I got up from the couch and twisted the bolt on the door. I pulled it open a few inches, and some kind of hot breath flooded in through the crack. It smelled like singed hair.

"What's the deal here?" Justin's winy voice protruded. "I just want to make sure you're all right."

"I'm fine," I said, keeping the door propped against my palm. The next second I found myself shoved backward onto the couch as the door flew open against me. It was the same move he must have used when his own door was blocked with the study room furniture. I struggled to grab onto the couch for leverage so I could sit up and face him. He wore the same "Malworth U" shirt he'd worn when Nick and I first met him. His eyes were their normal dull blue, but throbbed with anger. I grabbed onto the right arm of the couch, terrified.

"Mr. Sinclair, I'm disappointed in you," he began, taking a few steps into my room. The small muscular outlines of his pectorals flexed underneath the T-shirt. "You have such great potential, if you'd only use it."

"What are you talking about?" I yelled at him. "What were you doing last Friday night? Who was that hooded figure?"

His gaze moved right through me, as if my concerns were a fly buzzing in his ear. "So much potential." He began to amble around the front part of our room, taking in the large white entertainment center, Nick's desk with its assortment of video game controllers, the closet where I'd stored the Jack. "And yet you keep ruining it. Running to places you're not supposed to be, getting in all sorts of trouble with the law. Didn't I tell you not to disturb me on Friday? A simple request, but you couldn't handle it. I'm beginning to see why others wanted you off the list."

"What list?" I cried, terrified. "What the hell are you talking about? Where's Amanda?"

"What, that slut?" he said in a casual voice. "Don't you worry about her. She got exactly what she deserved. But you . . ." his dull blue eyes bored a whole through me. ". . . you are a much bigger concern. If you hadn't buckled down and done so well on your finals, I would've had no other choice than to eliminate you from contention."

"Contention for what?!" I screamed. The confusing nature of his responses was making me incensed. Despite his level of strength I'd just witnessed, I wanted a piece of this guy. At the moment I didn't care if it would have cost me my life. "What the fuck is this 'society' anyways?"

Justin was in the middle of flicking away a piece of white peeling paint from the entertainment center when he looked right at me. "Where'd you hear about that?" His voice had taken on the low, demeaning tone it had on Friday night.

I froze. This was confirmation this asshole didn't know quite everything. "Uh . . . nowhere. I think I heard Dean Moriarty say something about it."

Justin rubbed his chin with two thin fingers. "Hmm . . . he isn't known for making sloppy statements like that. I'll need to speak with him. It matters not, anyway. You're a prime candidate, my boy. Good grades all throughout your primary education, strong pedigree in your father. Strong pedigree. I thought all of this would add up to something, but I'm just not seeing it. You need to demonstrate true leadership to be a part of this society."

"I have no idea what you're talking about," I said. "But there is no way you're getting away with this. You, and whoever else is attached to this plot. I'll tell my parents, first of all—"

Justin chortled from deep in his gut, a scorching melody of malice. "Your parents? Ha! Why do you think your father sent you here in the first place? Foolish child. Your parents won't give a thought about you. And even if they do, we've made sure all of their desires are being met on their trip. In fact, they may even be seeking an extension. They've almost blocked you from their memory."

"That's bullshit!" I yelled. "They'll be back. And when they come back, I'm letting them in on your little scheme."

"You go right ahead," Justin said. "Like I said, why do you think your father sent you here? To get your laughs and to see a few tits down on the hill? Play some stupid pranks in the library? No, I think not."

I struggled to hold back the tears burning the edges of my eyes. I could feel my fists shaking with rage and panic. "Well, there are going to be a bunch of people returning to this campus in a couple of days. Most of the guys on this floor already know what a prick you are. My story will be the last thing they need to revolt on your sorry ass." I wasn't sure if any of that was true, but it felt good to say.

Justin met this with an even heartier chuckle that echoed in the small dorm room. He sounded possessed by a laughing demon. "Your friends? You mean those pathetic excuses for students that drank themselves stupid every night? I'm afraid you won't be seeing many of them back here. I decided to make a phone call to the parents of Mr. Gordon and Mr. Baines over the break. I informed them of their children's various misdeeds with alcohol and with me. I regret to inform you that neither of those idiots will be making the trip back for second semester. The possessions in their room will be turned over to the school or rubbished."

"What? No! You can't do that!" I hollered. "You can't!"

"Oh, but I can," Justin said, licking his lips. You think those two would have gotten the better of me?"

"What . . . what about Eric?" I babbled.

"Alas, he still remains a viable candidate. Couldn't get rid of everyone, could we? I'm sure he'll remove himself from contention eventually. The Fultons were never well bred, like your family."

"And Sarah?" I asked.

Justin sighed. "Yes, Ms. Jackson as well. If I were you, I'd stay away from her. And if you know what's good for you, you won't mention that other whore's name in her presence. Remember, she got what she deserved."

I pounded one of my curved fists against my leg. "You bastard. And what about Nick?"

"I'm afraid he has transferred out as well. Turns out his family didn't think he was getting a good enough education at this blessed institution. Not much of a loss though. It was just a matter of time before he saw he didn't fit in around here. I'm told he's having everything in this room that's his packed up and shipped to whatever second-tier establishment he considered to be a good fit. That's why I'm here, you see. To let you know that your chances have improved dramatically. As long as you follow the rules. So far it looks like you have. But if you stray from the chosen path, Mr. Sinclair, if you follow the lustings of your heart or the sorrows of your head, you too will be crossed off the list."

"What list?" I shouted again, even though I knew it sat in his pocket.

"Don't be coy, Mr. Sinclair," Justin barked. "You know exactly what list. Now I must bid you adieu. I suppose it goes without saying, but if you breathe one word of this to anyone you're off the list."

I clenched the cushions of the hideous couch that wouldn't be here much longer as I watched him leave. The door somehow pulled shut behind him. I got up to lock the dead bolt, then collapsed back onto the couch, shaking. I must have fell asleep again because when I woke up it was dark outside the window, and snow had begun to fall once more.

I WOKE UP FRIDAY SOMETIME still clutching the couch. I shook my head a few times, hoping to clear away what must have been a nightmare-induced discussion with Justin. When it didn't leave my mind I knew it was very real. I looked behind me out the window. The jagged edges surrounding the four panes were a few inches thick now, but the snow had stopped. I stared around the room, my eyes misty. Justin said Nick was sending a crew to pack up his stuff. Could it be true?

I ate the last remnants of potato chips out of the final bag and tossed it into the trash. I was famished after my week of terror, and so decided to make one final surreptitious trip over to the dining hall. I sprinted down both hallways, noting that Amanda's door was shut tight. I jogged across the glass walkway and into the dining hall. The gigantic room was devoid of students but remained lit from one end to the other. I peered around at the hundreds of metal tables and plastic chairs where so many students sat just two weeks ago as I ate my few pieces of stale pizza. I snagged a few cookies on my way back toward Schuster and sprinted back to my room. I had never felt the need for a human connection as bad as that night, alone and terrified sitting on the plaid couch. I couldn't bring myself to read the Malworth book any more; it was becoming a part of my own life.

Eric arrived on campus Saturday afternoon. I would've heard him hauling up several tote bags worth of Christmas presents, including a new DVD player and speakers, but since my door was still shut on Justin and the rest of the world, I had no idea he was even there. He knocked twice on my door, scaring me out of my skin. I pulled it open an inch and saw three-quarters of a frame of square black glasses and newly shaved head.

"Yo, Sinclair, open up! It's me!" he shouted through the narrow space.

"Eric? Is it really you?" I don't know why I said this.

"Uh, yeah. What other balding geeks with glasses do you know on this floor? Open up, dipshit."

"Just a minute. Let me come into your room. We're safer in numbers," I said, aware of the paranoia coursing through my voice.

"Uh, okay," he said. I opened the door just enough to squeeze through, made sure I locked it, and walked into his room and closed the door.

"Jesus Christ," was all I could say. "Jesus H. Mother-Loving Christ."

"What? What's wrong, Sinclair?" Eric said. "Did something happen here over the break? I had a great one, man. It was so nice to get back among actual civilization. Did you catch this sweet new speaker system . . ."

"Dude, I'm trying to tell you something here!" I shouted. Eric's eyes turned pale as they widened behind the glasses.

"Something did happen, didn't it?" he asked.

"Yes," was all I could say. "Yes, something happened." Justin's exhortations to keep the list to myself echoed in my ears. But I had to tell someone about what happened before his little visit.

"Okay, so what? Justin didn't try to rape you or anything, did he?" Eric said, cracking a small smile. It faded once he saw the look on my face.

"Nothing like that, but . . . look, something did happen while you and everyone were gone. I think you're the only other person I can tell this to, all right?"

"All right, fine, whatever. It can't be that bad . . ." Eric said, leaning back into his padded futon. "Okay, you go first, but then I get to tell you about all the loot I got for Christmas."

I proceeded to tell him what happened last Friday night, starting with the hallway full of paper and the mysterious hooded figure outside, and finishing with Justin sitting on the first floor. I left out any mention of Amanda or Justin coming into my room two days prior. Eric's eyes retained their widened gaze but shrunk as I spoke. My hands were shaking as I recounted the end of the horrendous night, the weird knocks on my door that followed, and the snowfall. I could tell he wasn't buying any of it by the time I finished speaking.

"Well, that sounds like quite a time," he said, folding his hands beneath the scraggled beard he'd grown over the break. "Have you told anyone else about this shit?"

"No," I shrugged. "You're the only person on this side of the hall who would believe me. You know, given what we saw on Homecoming."

He looked askance. "Yeah . . . about that. I'm not so sure it wasn't the alcohol messing with what we saw that night. You were pretty loaded, as the cop found out."

"Dude!" I said, throwing my hands up in the air. "You're caving on me with that stuff? I know you saw the same fucking thing as I did."

"I don't know anymore, Mike," Eric said. "I think it was one night, and one night only. I think alcohol was involved, and will tarnish any version of that story. Oh, shit, you haven't told that to anyone, have you?"

"No, of course not," I lied. "But what if I told you I could prove to you it was a ghost?"

"Uh . . . I'd say you were even more nutty than I thought," Eric said, trying not to laugh. "In fact, I'm going to say the same about this whole fiasco. It's not that I don't trust you. It seems a little far-fetched. Some hooded guy disappearing outside just as you turn away? I mean, what's up with that?"

"I'm telling you what I fucking saw!" I said. "Do you think I'd make this up?"

"No, at least not on purpose," Eric said. "But I also know you were by yourself all week before this happened. People in seclusion can get kinda batty. Ain't you ever seen *The Shining?*"

"This is not cabin fever, Eric," I said, flustered.

"Okay, okay," he said, showing me his palms and trying to get me to settle down. "Well, whatever happened, you don't have to worry about it now. Justin wouldn't try anything stupid now that kids are starting to come back to campus."

"You don't know that."

"No, but he wouldn't be able to get away with anything with so many witnesses and stuff."

"You don't know that either. There was this girl . . ." I stopped myself.

"What girl?" he said, confused.

"Nothing," I said. "Don't worry about it. Clearly you have enough on your mind right now than to have to worry about my silly ass. Did ya know Seth and Adam got kicked out of school? And Nick isn't coming back either? That means it's just you and me left."

"Wait, what?" Eric said, confused.

"Justin kicked Seth and Adam out, and Nick isn't coming back either."

"Well, they were warned about messing with alcohol. And Nick wasn't exactly Mr. Congeniality around here. I don't see it this as any big loss."

"Of course you wouldn't," I said, irritation shattering my voice. "Sorry I even brought it up."

I whirled and charged out the door. I didn't hear any protestations from Eric. After a minute of looking for my dormitory room key I managed to get back into my room. A few minutes later Eric knocked on the door, muttering some kind of apology, but I didn't answer. I'd had the most terrifying experience of my life, and the one friend I thought I could rely on didn't even trust me enough to believe it had happened.

SARAH ARRIVED ON CAMPUS the next day. She knocked on my door Sunday night, scaring me like Eric but not quite as bad. I was so glad to see her, I hugged her after opening the door. I'm sure she thought that was weird, but she didn't say anything. As I stared into those amazing verdant eyes I felt like everything in the world was going to be okay again.

"I'm so glad to see you," I said, trying to sound unperturbed.

"You too," she said. "The drive back was a little rough. It really freakin' snowed up here!"

"I know," I said, thinking about my dorm window. "It never let up. So how was your time back?" I thought if I began with an innocuous question I could lead up to the crazy stuff.

"Pretty good. I got some great gifts for Christmas, and saw some family from the East Coast I'd never met. All in all it was a nice break from Sleepy Hollow. How'd you manage being all alone?"

"It was . . ." I realized I didn't know where to begin. "Hey, could we maybe go to your room to talk about it?"

She gave me a nervous glance, but to my surprise said, "Yes. Let's go."

"I don't know where Sidarthi is," Sarah said as we approached. "Haven't seen her since I got back. I hope she's all right." She closed the door behind us, giving me just enough time to take in the room. I recalled the pink padded futon from before, but there also was a tiny green easy chair tucked away in the corner. Sarah's desk was overflowing with tiny glass trinkets, "Hello Kitty" paraphernalia, and several spiral notebooks. A small glass vase filled with feathers sat on the corner. A wooden loft similar to the one I'd built with my father (but painted bright pink) arched over half the room. Sarah sat down on the futon and patted next to her. This was the moment I'd waited months for, and yet was too terrified to make any kind of romantic gesture. Right now I needed somebody I could trust.

"So, how was your, uh, vacation?" she said.

"Well, it was awful," I burst out. "Truly awful. I saw a side to this place I thought only existed behind curtains, in the books we found, and lurking in every old-ass building on campus. But in fact it lives right out in the open, and it's huge. Speaking of that book . . ." I said, reminding myself as I spoke.

"Yes, I was wondering how long it would take you to ask," she said. "I did get some headway on it. But I want to hear about your time here first."

My shoulders relaxed, and I flattened my body into the stout pad on her futon. I wished I'd had this thing to sleep on instead of Nick's ratty couch. I began to tell my tale. I left out more than what I told Eric, in the hopes that it wouldn't sound too insane. Sarah's eyes widened just like Eric's had as I spoke. But about halfway through my story, a different thing happened: she put her hand on my leg in a gesture of sympathy. A simple move, but in that moment it meant everything in the world to me. I continued with the hooded figure, seeing Justin, and my sequestration on the fifth floor. When I finished, Sarah appeared terrified. We both sat in silence. I tensed up again as I awaited her reaction.

"Mike, I'm . . . that's . . . I'm so sorry," she said. Then she leaned in for a hug. I was so shattered from telling the story a second time I gave in, and we embraced. There was nothing sexual about it but was rather like the hug two friends might share after a long battle. "I can't believe that happened."

"You do believe me, though, right?" I said, my voice shaking.

"Yes, I do. And I believe you about this place, too. I just want to make sure you're okay."

"I am . . . I think," I said, leaning back. The single lamp positioned over the futon reflected an ethereal glow off Sarah's beautiful green eyes. The sight stunned me and made me forget all my problems. The next thing I knew she was leaning into me, her full and pouty lips headed my direction. I was so relieved from letting the story go I gave in to her charms, not even kissing back at first but then allowing the emotional rush to carry me into her arms. We kissed for another few minutes before she pulled away.

"I'm . . . I'm sorry," she said, her face flushed. "I just felt so bad for you. I can't imagine what that was like. I didn't mean to . . ."

"Don't apologize," I said. "I liked it. I like you. That's probably obvious by now. You're the only one who believes me, who believes there's something going on here. We have to stick together."

"All right," she said, still embarrassed. "Now then. Where is that book?" She grabbed her brown backpack from the dorm closet and rummaged until she pulled out the aged, leather-bound tome.

"So, what did you find out?" I asked.

Sarah dove back into her bag and plucked out a single thick wax candle. The edges were rimmed with wax spikes and one side towered high above the other. The center caved down into the middle where a thin strip of string protruded. Sarah took a book of matches from the desk drawer and lit the candle. The aroma soon filled the room, a mix of sandalwood and pine trees. Our shadows danced on the dormitory walls as we moved, silent silhouettes mocking us.

"This is something my dad showed me a long time ago," Sarah said as she opened the book. A rift of dust flew up into her face and she coughed a few times. "Watch this."

She tore out one of the pages of the book. I was about to speak when I saw what she was doing. She held the old document a few inches above the flame. I waited in agony while she sat there, the page a scant bit away from lighting up and bursting into flames. Then I noticed something. Lettering of the kind we'd seen written there in the first place began to come into view. Dark lines from an ancient writing tool came into focus.

"That's amazing," I said, my eyes fixed on our playing shadows. "How'd he know about that?"

"I dunno," Sarah said, shifting her gaze to the carpeted floor. "He . . . just said it was something he picked up long ago."

Sarah sat the page on the floor. The lettering, which had taken on a somber bold font, began to disappear once more.

"Ah, crap, it's going again," I said.

"Yeah, it does that. I'm trying to figure out why. But we can at least read it now."

"I guess. Did you read any of it when you were back home?"

"I read some. And there were some interesting passages that dealt with those people you supposedly met on Homecoming."

"Wait . . . what?" I stammered. "You mean the war veteran who should be dead and the doctor?"

"Yeah," Sarah said. "What was the doc's name? Wind-something?"

"Winograd," I said.

"Yeah, him," she said. "He was a famous alumni here, doctor on the East Coast. He was part of the new society, whatever was built on the ashes of the old one."

"What?" I sputtered. "Where are you coming up with that?"

"It's in the book," she said. She was shuffling through the brown pack again, the peace button shaking with every poke and prod. She pulled out several sheets of paper.

"This covers your doctor friend. Sounds like he led quite a life . . . until the malpractice suits and charges of unnecessary surgery. Then we start getting into horror-movie territory. Except, you know, this guy actually existed."

I stared at the blank pages, wondering what they might hold. "Whoa," was all I could manage. "Can I take these?"

"You can take the whole damn book," Sarah said, shutting it and pushing it into my hands. "I don't want it near me any longer."

"Why?" I ventured.

"Let's just say I don't think it was supposed to leave these grounds," Sarah said, her voice shaking for the first time.

"All right," I said, putting the volume by my side. "I will. And at least we've found how to read it. Thanks for your help."

She flashed me a daring smile, one I had not seen in months. "You know me, always up for a strange investigation into our horrendous school." I couldn't tell if she was joking or not. "I tried calling you about this, but the lines were down."

"Yeah, I noticed," I said. "Yet another impediment to escaping this madhouse over the winter break."

"No kidding," she said. "I still can't believe you went through that. But at least nobody got hurt, right?"

My mind raced to the room a few doors down from Sarah's. "Right," was all I mumbled. "Say, have you seen Amanda since you got back?"

"Uh, no," Sarah said. "That makes two girls on this side who haven't turned up yet. Should I be worried?"

"Well, we are also lacking some guys on my side after the break. Eric told me some kind of 'purge' happens at this time of the year, and a lot of the student body leaves. Don't know why they'd want to leave such a charming campus . . ." I said, chuckling but not feeling funny.

"Wow," Sarah said. "I'd heard rumors about that too, but didn't think it actually happened."

"Yeah, my roommate's gone," I said. "Justin told me he's sending for his stuff."

"Wait, you talked to Justin after that night?"

I hadn't wanted to broach this topic, but here we were. "Yeah."

"And? What did he say?"

"He . . . said Nick wasn't coming back. And that he kicked out Seth and Adam somehow."

"What? How?"

"I don't know. He said he spoke to their parents about their admittedly loathsome behaviour. But who knows how he really did it."

"Hmm," was all she said.

"There's something else," I said. "I looked through the Malworth history book in between my flights of fancy with Justin."

"Oh, did you?"

"Yes. And after what you told me just now, I think we can safely say that this place is haunted as hell."

"What do you mean?"

"Alfred James. I saw him in that history book. In a photograph taken over a century ago."

Her gorgeous eyes widened. "Holy shit," she said. "That makes two of 'em."

"I know," I said. "One from the 'old' society, and one for the 'new.'"

"What do you mean, 'old society?'"

I told her what I'd read near the photograph, about the Malworth Institution of Healing.

"Oh, my God," she said when I'd finished. "That means this school was placed on top of something else . . . something maybe really evil."

"Yeah. Anyways, I was too freaked out to read anything more after that. But I'm sure there is more. Even if it's the 'authorized' version of history according to Dean Moriarty."

"Well, you need to keep reading. Both books. And I'll keep digging, too. We have to get to the bottom of this, Mike. You have no idea how deep this goes."

Before I could ask what she meant by that, Sarah changed course. "Did you see Amanda here over the break?"

I wasn't sure how to answer that. I hoped Sarah wouldn't be upset that I visited another girl on her floor, even if she was now missing. "I stopped at her room one night. I never saw her after that."

"Hold on a second." She got up from the futon, opened her door, and padded down in her slippers to the far end. I poked my head out to see what was going on in the hallway. Every single door was closed tight. I watched Sarah knock on Amanda's door a few times and stand there. After a minute she came back. "Well, that settles it. She's not here. That's really weird. Where do you suppose she went?"

I tried to forget seeing her door ajar with no one inside. "I don't know."

"Huh," Sarah said. "I hope she turns up."

"Me too, but don't hold your breath. Say, do you wanna go get something to eat? It might be a nice distraction from all of this shit. It wasn't very much fun going to the dining hall by myself."

"Sure, just give me a half-hour to finish unpacking. Hopefully I can get it done before Sidarthi gets back. And again, I'm sorry for what happened to you. We're in this together now, Mike."

"I know," I said. "And Sarah . . . thanks for believing me."

We embraced, and she planted a brief kiss on my lips. Electricity flowed from our lips down my spine, and for a minute I forgot all about my nightmarish week in Schuster Hall. I walked back down to my room, feeling hopeful and horrified at the same time.

Second Semester

Chapter

SETH AND ADAM NEVER returned to campus. On Monday I watched as a group of musclebound guys with bandannas rummaged through their room and removed its contents during the first week of the second semester. On Tuesday the same guys approached my door and said they were taking Nick's stuff. I slumped on my ass in the hallway while they disassembled the entertainment center, maneuvered the disgusting plaid couch at an angle through the door and packed up every bit of electronics Nick had, including the immense computer tower, the square television and the mini-fridge. I was left with the small plastic red chair, my clothing, and the shaky loft. With Seth and Adam gone, the rowdiness burned out of our hallway. All that remained was a stony silence.

"Jesus, Sinclair, you weren't kidding about Nick's shit being taken," Eric said as he saw me sitting in the single red chair surrounded by nothing. "No forms of entertainment for you, I guess."

"Yeah," I said, still burning at him from our previous conversation. "Guess I'll just read every night for the next few months. Or study."

"Naw, you don't have to always use your brain," Eric said, turning to walk back to his room. He stopped. "Look, I'm sorry for the way things went when I got back. I'm still not sold on your insane story. But if you ever need a place to hang out that's not completely bare, you know where to find me."

"Gee, thanks" I growled.

"All right," Eric said. "But you're missing out. I've got major *Indiana Jones* on tap for tonight . . . might even watch the extras. Pop on over if you want."

"I might," I mumbled. I sat in the plastic chair and stared at the wall for twenty minutes before I broke down and headed over to Eric's room.

ERIC AND I ARRIVED AT SHULL HALL a few minutes early Wednesday morning and were entertained by some impromptu speech by Professor Deakin as he waved his thin arms around in a cardinal-and-gray sweater.

"I've had it with this place," he said to the half-empty room. Eric had warned me about the "purge," but I never thought it would get this bad. It was like people knew this campus wasn't for them and got the hell out before something bad happened. I found myself strangely jealous for the lost students, adrift in a sea of academia I was prevented from leaving.

"If an institution expects an instructor to achieve tenure in a good amount of time, it needs to incentivize him a bit," Deakin continued his ramble. "Giving him a desecrated hall filled with the remainders hardly qualifies." He had arrived at the point in his speaking routine where his back was against the large blackboard. He gazed around the room to see who was paying attention, and his wizened eyes locked on me and Eric at the front of the classroom. The soft, buzzing chatter of my fellow classmates indicated we were the only people listening. Deakin's left eye blinked shut in a cryptic gesture that was supposed to be a wink. I stared down at my notebook.

Deakin returned to lecture mode, and after a rousing talk on pre-Enlightenment Europe in which I came close to drifting off several times, he dismissed us five minutes ahead of schedule. Eric and I gathered up our book bags, threw on our coats, and headed for the large wooden door.

"Gentlemen," Deakin addressed as we swooped by the lectern. We turned our heads in his direction. "Could you come here for a moment?"

We exchanged worried glances and walked over to where he stood. Up close I could see the stilted chalk lines formed in the outline of a human body from where he had pressed up against the blackboard every few minutes. "Professor?" I ventured.

"You may skip the formalities, Mr. Sinclair," he said with a wave of his hand. "Call me Marvin."

I had never been on a first name basis with a professor. Even Dalton always asked I use "Mr." in front of his name. His formality melted away as he gazed at us with a pleasant and crooked smile. "All right, Marvin," I ventured.

"Gentlemen, this morning's brief outburst was a test to see who in this classroom would pay attention to something as insignificant as an instructor's plight in this damn filthy school." He removed his glasses and began an intense stare that dove into my pupils as he spoke. I had not felt this uncomfortable since he brought up my family on the first day of his class the previous semester.

"I know you must have had some experience that brought you close to the truth behind this school," he continued. "I know it because I saw the same look you now have many years ago. Back when I had a chance to affect things here. At that time, I gave it all up in favor of continuing to shape young minds in the hope they would make the world a better place. A place where institutions such as Malworth serve no function. Alas, my dreams were misplaced, as ours often are, and I was forced to accept the consequences of my decision. But it's clear to me now that things will never change here unless we force them. Do you know of what I speak?"

Eric's bearded face wore an expression of apprehension and mistrust. "I have no freakin' clue what you're talking about, uh, Marvin," he said.

"And you, Mr. Sinclair?" Deakin's sharp, tiny eyes penetrated my soul. Somehow he knew what I'd seen over the winter break.

"I . . . I think I do," I said. "You're talking about this place, and what it really is."

"In a matter of speaking, yes," he said. "Why don't you come up to my office to discuss things over tea? Unless you have somewhere more important to go."

My next class was was with Ellickson over in the English building. I decided I could sit this one out. "Not really . . ." I said.

"Don't you have class?" Eric asked. He was getting annoyed.

"Yes, but this may prove to be more interesting. There's more at stake here than you realize, man." I don't know why I phrased it in such stark terms, but it was how I felt in that moment.

"Whatever," Eric said, shrugging. His giant gray coat raised and lowered as he performed this action. "Go have your tea. Those of us who want to graduate on time will continue with our classes."

I glanced back at Deakin. "Shall we?"

We walked up tiled stairs to reach the top of Shull Hall, our footfalls echoing in the quiet. Deakin's office was at the end of a long carpeted hall near a tall window with an expansive view of the campus. I gazed outside before we entered, noticing how few students were marching through the piles of snow. His office was a sparse room filled with artifacts from all over the world. I spotted an African mask sharing space on a wide shelf with what appeared to be a picture of him with some kind of European official. He motioned for me to sit in the single chair in front of his miniscule desk. He maneuvered his way behind it and slouched into a wooden rolling chair. He raised his fingertips together in front of his drooping mouth.

"I know you saw something," he said. "Over the winter break. I can see it in your eyes."

I wasn't sure what to say. Thus far one out of two people believed my ridiculous story. What if Deakin was part of the conspiracy, trying to hear my side of things in order to see what I'd say? "Yes, I did see something," I said in a low voice. "I don't know how you can see that in my eyes, but maybe that's because I can't shake it."

"I told you, I've seen it before. The last time they were searching for new blood for the society. But I'm getting ahead of myself."

"Not really," I said. "I think I know what you're talking about."

"You might think you know, but no one ever truly does. Some say the Malworthe society originated with the campanologists back in the 1600s, you know, the old bell-ringing society. Certainly gives credence to why that old clock tower wasn't torn down fifty years ago. Others say it's wider and more controlling, that they meet in a secret room every few years and pick the next governor. Hogwash. I think they put those stories out there just to mess with people. The reality is much more devious. They groom people for the roles they might play in American life, or in their homes. They don't produce many, mind you, but every generation there's always one who makes the cut. Who doesn't get crossed off the list. And I know you're on the list."

My eyes exploded open. "You do?"

"Of course. The old fuddy-duddies up in the dean's office still let me in on a few things."

"So what does that mean, I'm on the list?"

"What do you think it means?"

"I have no idea. None of this makes sense. I never wanted to go to this school in the first place."

"Yes, but who did?"

I thought about it for a moment. "My parents."

Deakin smiled. I could see a small hole on the side where a tooth had been removed. "Indeed. And why was that, I wonder?"

"I'm not sure. This was my father's alma mater. It was all he could talk about before they both dumped me here without looking back."

"As I told you last semester, I remember your father. The last time I saw that look, it was in his eyes. I should have intervened back then, but I was young and naive. I thought I had a bright future ahead of me, and so I gave in to their demands. I had no idea I'd be cooped up teaching the same slop to the same fresh-faced group of idiots for forty years. That was the last chance I had to make a difference, or so I thought. Then I found out you were in my class. But I couldn't speak out of turn until you'd seen enough. Today, I knew it was time."

"Time for what?" I said. My mouth felt raw and numb, like I'd been punched.

"Time for tea," Deakin said, rising out of the chair with an audible creak. "I forgot all about it."

He boiled some water on a small stove in the back corner of his office, plopped a tea bag in a cup, and set it beside me on a rickety table. I watched the steam rise up into the air like a ghost. Neither of us said anything for some time. I took a few sips of tea while I watched Deakin stare out the single window in his office.

"I think that's all for today," he muttered, jolting me back to reality.

"What? Why? I want to know more!" I exclaimed.

"I know, I know, but you must be patient," he said. "Their plans were set into motion decades ago. They've got something of a head start on you."

"Who does? Who are you talking about?"

"I said that's all for today. Perhaps on Friday we can resume."

"Fine," I said, gathering up my backpack and shuddering on my yellow coat. "But you will tell me what's going on here, right?"

"Only what I've been able to deduce in my time here," Deakin said. "But it should be helpful."

"All right, see you Friday," I said, and closed the door. My head was swimming, but I still felt like I knew nothing.

ELLICKSON'S OTHER CLASS was the most basic of English courses, but I needed it as somehow the one I'd taken back in St. James didn't count for credit up here. I lucked out in that my health class took place in the same building and thanked the universe that it involved neither physical exertion or a short angry man.

My Tuesday and Thursday classes for the second semester were more of the same, as this grand university used the same professors for most classes in their field. Professor Dalton got me into his Probability class, and each day we'd take our seats in the same high-ceilinged room with the long tables to examine dice rolls and correlate that experience with real life. I approached Dalton at the end of our second class as the ten other students filtered out, none of them speaking or looking at me. He had begun to erase the equations on the white board in slow arcs.

"Mr. Sinclair," he said as he saw he coming. His beard had accumulated more flecks of gray over the break.

"Professor Dalton," I said. "I think I'm gonna need your help with this class."

His brown eyes narrowed. "I think you need help with something else, too."

I stood there in front of him a moment, clasping my book bag and disgusting yellow coat.

"I can see it in your eyes. You witnessed something over the break, didn't you?"

This freaked me out. "Well, something did—"

He held up a single spiny finger, a small wart protruding on the side of it. "You don't have to tell me. I haven't taught here for that long so I'm not as hip to the situation as Deakin. But I sense you've found trouble. The trouble you were sent here to find."

This confused me further. "I thought my parents sent me here to—"

"Oh, I'm sure they gave you some kind of reason," he continued. "Listen, I've gotten to know you pretty well since you came to me asking for help last semester. It's not my place to get involved in your affairs. I'm here to help you pass my class."

"Uh, yeah, that's what I thought too."

"And that's the role I'll serve. But please know you can talk to me about anything. I might not be very clued into the mysteries of this place, but I do feel a connection to them. Everyone who lives here does."

"You live here, too?" I asked.

"Unfortunately, yes. They wrote it into my contract. Ever wonder about that regal guest house building in the east corner? It's nice, all right. Way nicer than your dorms. But it also meant I had to give up my family to teach here. My wife left me years ago."

"Jesus, I'm sorry," I said. "Why didn't you just . . . I dunno . . . leave?"

Here he gave me a long, hard stare, his pupils dilating and shaking behind the wire-frame glasses. "Do you think it's that easy?"

I reflected on how every form of escape from this blasted campus had been denied to me. "No, I guess not," I said, deflated.

"You must know, then. Everyone they want finds out, in the end. Why do you think so many 'rejects' flee at the break? People like you and me, we aren't so lucky."

"What are you talking about?" I was getting nervous. This man had been a beacon of calm during our study sessions over the past few months. Now he was like a different person.

"Nothing," he said, turning back to the white board. He began erasing again in a slow amble.

"Professor Dalton, if you know something you should tell me."
His arm twitched, then came to a stop. "I wish I could. You probably know more than me at this point." He turned around. "I can help you with my class, if that's some small relief for you. The rest of it, you have to figure out on your own."

I considered the import of his statement as I trudged through the snow to the biology building for my second Thursday course. Life: The Natural World 102 once again had the inimitable Professor Langdon presiding in the same laboratory. This grouping also contained about half the amount of students we had last semester.

"Attention, class. Welcome to Life 102," Langdon said from the far end of the room. She had on a purple blouse and a black skirt that went far down her legs. Her stringy gray hair lay around her head like wilted roots. "Those of you who barely passed the introductory portion of this might want to re-think your entry here. You will be doing rigorous academic investigations into the quality of soils, the fauna we have surrounding us, and the state of the universe itself. And once again you will be performing a set of experiments each week. So don't even consider skipping Thursday classes. And make sure you do the readings, because I won't be there to make you." She looked right at me as she said this.

SCHUSTER HALL WAS SILENT as a mausoleum most days. I never saw Justin or any of the other kids that used to walk down the hallway once in a while. Eric always had his door closed, but still welcomed me when I knocked. I thought the fact that very few people remained was getting to him, too. Most nights I sat in my room, alone with my thoughts and the two large books we'd stolen from the library. I borrowed a candle from Sarah to illuminate the text from the book with the hidden script. I revealed some rules for "healing" Whitacre's cult must have performed here long ago. Why it would be written down for posterity was beyond me, but I couldn't stop reading it. These people thought they were onto some new kind of medical breakthrough, but a lot of people had to die to make that happen. Including people like Alfred James. The Civil War had taken a toll on the country's pysche as men and brothers were coming home very much changed. From what I could read in the book, Whitacre was trying to give these families a modicum of solace from the horrific injuries, but going about it in some secretive way that involved ancient rituals. Things got more dicey when people started dying in large numbers, and the powers that were became more interested in what the hell this guy was doing up in Minnesota. The script got incomprehensible after that point, so I'd have to figure out what happened in another way. But what was more important to me at this point was my family's connection to this hell hole.

I approached Deakin's podium after class on Friday morning to see if he had any time to chat. I would have to miss Ellickson's class again, but it was time well spent.

"I think I can fit in some time," he said. "Let's have some tea."

When we got to his office on the top floor, Deakin sat in the wheeled chair behind his small desk and placed his fingertips together in front of his face. For a minute we just sat there, looking at each other.

"I need to know about the history of this place," I said.

"Ah, I suppose you do," Deakin said, leaning forward. "But that's a broad and dangerous topic. You sure you want to travel down that particular rabbit hole?"

I thought about it a moment. "I'm not sure. I really want to know about my father. I haven't even called him since the winter break. Of course, he hasn't exactly reached out . . ."

"I'm afraid I don't know that much about your father's time here," Deakin said. "He was a vastly intelligent man. Almost too intelligent in some ways. I wish I could have provided better guidance for him."

"Look . . . this is difficult for me," I said. "My father and I don't exactly see eye to eye, but it's not like he hates me. True, he made most of my life decisions for me, including who I could date, and made me come to this school. But it's not like he knew what Justin was going to do. I'm just conflicted by what you've told me."

"As you should be," Deakin said, leaning back in his chair. "Your father was not the same man after he graduated. He was the last person left on their list, for one thing. And he was 'encouraged' to send his progeny to this very institution. You have a chance to break the cycle, Michael."

"I don't know what that means. I don't know what any of this means," I said, frustration creeping into my voice.

"I know it is," he said. "And I'm sorry. Perhaps for now we should move to the topic you first mentioned. We can save the rest for another day."

To that end, I decided in that moment I'd call my father, and give him a chance to explain himself. "All right, but I still have many questions. So, the history of this place. Why would the library only have a single book about this place, written by Dean Moriarty?"

Deakin chuckled. It was a raspy, rich sound. "Why indeed? Do you think they ever invited a sociologist to come here and study them?"

"Well, no, but . . ."

"But nothing. How do you think they kept the society hidden? By not blabbing to every reporter and researcher who holes up here. Do you think you're the first to discover the mystery of this place?"

"I'm not sure," I said. "Others have?"

"Indeed. I remember back in the eighties this group of paranormal researchers. They searched every inch of that Castle saloon on the hill, convinced that some ghosts and goblins must be afoot. They found nothing, of course."

"Of course," I said, my mind pondering Homecoming night. "All right, so who was this Dr. Winograd?"

I caught the smallest twitch in the corner of Deakin's left eye. "Who?"

"I know you heard me. Dr. Winograd."

Deakin exhaled. "Where did you hear that name?"

"When he told me," I said.

"He what . . . ?! Impossible. The man's been dead for—"

"Oh, I realize that now," I said, smiling. "I met him Homecoming night. You know how special that evening is around here, right sir?"

The twitch returned to his eye. "Uh . . . no, I'm afraid I'm not that familiar. Most of the students go down to that dreadful hill of bars to get liquored up and strip the clothes off women. Is that accurate?"

"Yeah, close enough. But that's not what I remember from that night. My friend and I went to the Ice Castle that night. It was more like we were escaping a riot. That was where we met Winograd. He led us into some kind of secret passageway that didn't exist afterward."

"This can't be," Deakin said. "You must be mistaken."

"I wish I was," I said. "He was an alumni here, right? Then went out east to become a doctor. A quite famous doctor, according to him. Seems he had quite a fall from grace."

"Yes, he did," Deakin said with a bleak expression. "Black-balled from the medical community for committing some unapproved surgeries. Once people started dying around him, the authorities were called to investigate. But perhaps you know this as well?"

"Somewhat," I said, thinking about what Sarah read in the ancient book. "But he has more or less been erased from history. I wonder what power it takes to do that?"

"I think you know," Deakin said. "He attended school here. This was before I arrived hoping to mold young minds and winding up with years of disappointment. Winograd was the person selected to begin the new society, whatever that meant. And once he graduated he had the pick of medical schools to attend. I've even heard Whitacre's descendants paid for his medical education. And he was quite well known, for a time. But he died decades ago. There is no way you met this man."

"Look, I know it sounds ridiculous. But it happened to both of us. My friend denies it happened, but I know it did. He offered us some whiskey in that back hallway. There was a guy there serving us, too. But when we left, the door we'd gone through disappeared. He was a . . ."

"Don't say it," Deakin said. "I won't hear of this."

"I don't care what you'll hear," I said, ire rising. "I'm sick of people telling me what I did or did not see. He was a fucking ghost, Marvin."

Deakin didn't say anything for a moment. "I'm afraid you're quite mistaken, Michael."

"I am not," I said, getting up to leave. "And if you don't want to believe me, that's fine. But just remember—I believed what you had to say. Don't you think I at least deserve the same courtesy?"

"I'm not sure," he said, leaning back in his chair.

"Well, you'd better think about it," I said as I stormed out of his office.

THE NEXT DAY I WAS ANGRY at myself for thinking I could confide in Deakin, angry at the school for warping him into this crusty old skeptic, and angry at Winograd for appearing before Eric and me, knowing that no one would believe our tale. The notion of calling home had been pushed out by these thoughts, which were roiling in my head as I stepped down the hallway that night to Sarah's room for our study date. I rapped three times on her door when I arrived. When it opened, Sidarthi scurried out in a pair of soft red pajama pants and a white T-shirt.

"Go, fornicate as you will," she said, blurring past me. "I don't care what you two do as long as I'm not part of it."

"Don't mind her," Sarah said. "You know how she gets."

"At least you know she's around," I said, not meaning to sound so dejected.

"Well, there's that," Sarah said. "What's with your mood?"

"Nothing," I said, dropping my book bag on the carpet and plopping on the pink futon. "Yesterday I had a rather unfortunate conversation with someone I thought I could trust. Turns out I can't trust anyone, except you."

Sarah reached behind the small fridge the girls shared and grabbed a thin bottle of wine. She rounded up two wine glasses from the closet and set them on her tiny coffee table.

"I thought we could use a little relaxation," she said. "You do drink wine, right?"

"There's a first time for everything," I said. "Been a beer man since high school. Here I've transitioned to the hard stuff. Wine might seem tame by comparison."

"Not this stuff," Sarah said, pouring me a full glass. "Smuggled it in from my trip out East. Cheers!"

We clinked glasses, and then drank in silence. It was a heady experience. I gulped down the entire glass before I realized it was a drink to be enjoyed at a snail's pace. Sarah laughed and poured me some more.

"So you have Langdon again this semester?" Sarah asked. "You must be in the afternoon class. Does she get more cranky as the day wears on?"

I laughed. "I'm not sure. But she sure was in a sour mood today. I don't know how someone can get mad describing how bees pollinate the world, but she nailed it. I think she hates being here. It's almost like she is forced to be here or something."

"That can't be though, right?" Sarah said. "They can't force their instructors to stay here, can they?

"I'm not sure," I said, thinking of what Dalton told me this week. "But I wouldn't put a single thing past whoever is in charge. There's way more at play here than either of us think."

She stared at me as she took another sip. A slow wave of burning heat creeped into my cheeks. Another began to flow into my crotch. Sarah's eyes flashed a brilliant green in the muted darkness of her dorm room, a mix of confusion and happiness. "So what do you think is at play?" she asked.

"I don't know, but I intend to find out with your help." I reached over and grabbed the mysterious blank book from my pack. Dust spilled from the leather binding as I set it on the coffee table. "What say we do the actual studying we were planning tonight? Then we can worry about Langdon."

Sarah took the large wax candle from its position on her desk. The high side had gained a few inches since I'd last seen it, and the wick looked longer. The sandalwood smell permeated the room as she lit the string. I ripped a few pages out and collected them at the side of the table.

"Shall we?" I asked. Sarah moved the candle to the middle of the table, and I raised the paper above it. After a few seconds the dark script began to show through. After a full minute it was illuminated from top to bottom. "Okay, just hold it like this," I said, standing up to get a good look. I started reading aloud.

The Malworth Society is not open to any who seek acceptance in our fold. Only the pure of spirit and the righteous of soul may bound themselves in eternity with thy brothers and sisters in everlasting harmony with the earth. Only those who posses true skill and talent in their chosen field will be allowed to move on in the trials. Only those whose lives remain a mystery to everyone but themselves may become one with this ancient order. This institution strives to prepare young men and women for their eventual ascension to the ranks of the just, but only those pupils who apply themselves to every realm may feel the embrace of our own.

"This just goes on like this?" Sarah said.

"I guess," I said, taking the page from her hand and setting it down. "Shall we try another?"

"Fine by me," she said. This page contained half the amount of script.

The trials ahead are not for the impure of heart or the faint of spirit. We overseers of the great society must do everything we can to ensure that the next generation of members possess the capabilities required in all alumni: the ability to hide in plain sight and yet remain full of numbers, the ability to teach from afar and yet immerse thyself in the wonders of academia, and the ability to mold young minds in the shape of our forbearers, who will carry on this society for many eons. For such is the way of our movement: always in darkness until the end.

"That last bit sounds familiar," I said. "I think it was the first thing we ever read. Shall I keep going?"

"Are you getting anything from these?" Sarah asked. The light from the candle flickered and threw our shadows on the pale white walls.

"That one made a bit more sense. Let's try one more," I said.

And it is written that each new group shall have a Caretaker, and he shall be imbued with the wisdom and knowledge of successive members of the great society. The Caretaker will watch over his flock to ensure that only the strongest will make it through the trials and ascend to the order. The Caretaker's duties prevail over anything else in his life, and override any previous knowledge that may exist in his mind. The Caretaker's sole function is to ensure that one pupil from each house reaches the end and all other competitors are removed.

"Doesn't this sound an awful lot like Justin?" I asked, trembling as I stood.

The candlelight reflected terror in Sarah's beautiful green eyes. Her pupils shrunk down to nothing. "It sure does. You know, I still haven't seen Amanda anywhere on the floor."

My stomach dropped a few inches. "That's not a good sign. Look, there's something I haven't told you about my two weeks in hell. Something about her."

"Oh, Jesus, you didn't have sex, did you?" Sarah said, punching my arm in a preemptive strike.

"God, no," I shouted. "Although, like you said, easy on the eyes and all that."

"Shut up," Sarah said. "So what didn't you tell me?"

"Well, the day after I saw Justin down in the first floor lobby, I walked over to see if she was all right. Her room was open, but she wasn't inside."

"Oh, shit," Sarah said. "Where could she have gone?" She took another long pull of wine and refilled the glass.

"I have no idea," I said. "But I thought I should tell you, in case she does turn up."

"How could she just disappear like that?" Sarah asked. "It doesn't seem possible."

"I would've said the same thing when I arrived here," I said. "Now all bets are off. You and I are the only people who understand what's really going on. The kids in my classes, they're like zombies. There's no one left on my floor except me and Eric. Justin made sure to do away with anyone who didn't make the cut. Or the list, or whatever."

"Look, I know it's hard to deal with," Sarah said, clasping my hand in hers. "I can't imagine what you had to go through over the break. But

I'm here for you." She leaned in and kissed me. I don't know if it was the wine, or the danger we found ourselves in, or the fact that I'd wanted this girl since the moment I saw her, but I leaned in and kissed her right back. My dream was finally coming true in the weirdest possible circumstances. I leaned over and blew out the candle before we had a fiery mess on our hands. This plunged us into total darkness, the kind of darkness in which clothing becomes optional. We crawled up together to her bed in the wooden loft, which I found to be much sturdier than mine. I'd been lucky enough to get with a few of those short-term girlfriends back in St. James, but looking back I never felt anything more for them than temporary, teenage lust. I felt a whole different set of emotions for Sarah. She was also better at sex than I was, so I let her take on the main thrust of the operation. When we had finished, I lay in her arms, exhausted by pain and pleasure in equal measures. The pain was knowing I couldn't escape this school, the pleasure knowing I could endure it with this girl.

I FELL ASLEEP IN SARAH'S BED. The door opened a few seconds in the morning and I felt the presence of another person. Sarah seemed to possess the same sleeping ability Nick had, so I gave up on trying to wake her.

"Ugh, gross," Sidarthi said as she watched me lope down the ladder in my boxer shorts. "Didn't need to see that."

"Sorry," I mumbled as I threw on my jeans. I gathered up my book bag and headed for the door. "Will you tell her I had to leave?"

"No," she said, not looking at me. That ended our conversation. My face felt flush as I padded down the hallway to the guys' side, but I felt more relaxed than I had in weeks. Still I knew there was someone I had to see.

After twenty minutes of stomping through snow, I was in front of the guest building on the east side of campus. I wasn't sure which one was Dalton's, so knocked on all the doors. Ellickson answered at one of them, and after encouraging me to do a better job attending his class, helpfully pointed me in the right direction.

"Michael, what a pleasant surprise," Dalton said as he opened the door. He had a rumpled look about him, and his beard was coursed through with gray. He wore simple jeans and a hooded sweatshirt. Sunlight shone through the wide window behind him and outlined him with blinding light. "Please, come in. Are you here to revisit those outcome assignments?"

"Actually, no," I said as I threw off my yellow coat and plopped down in the padded easy chair in his front room. "Last time we spoke you said I could talk to you about anything. I came to tell you what I saw over break."

Dalton's eyes narrowed. "I see," he said, his spiny fingers placing his breakfast dishes in the sink of the tiny kitchen opposite the front room.

"You said you saw something in my eyes," I said, blinking. "What?"

"That's tough to describe," he said, letting out a small wisp of breath. "I just know I've seen it before. Must have been one of my students."

"Deakin said he'd seen the same look in my father's eyes," I said.

"I see," he said again. "Well I'm not going to be much service to you regarding your family history. As I said, that was before my time . . ."

"I may have run up against a similar wall," I said. "It seems this place has a way of not allowing anyone to write about it, study it, or gain any kind of knowledge. Although they have tried."

"So I've heard," Dalton said, sitting on a plush couch across from me. "There's a very powerful interest in keeping what happens on this campus away from prying eyes."

"Yeah, that's one thing. Also, you said it wasn't easy to leave this place. I think I understand. But explain it to me anyway."

Dalton's eyes looked like they were glaring at a speck of dust a thousand miles away. "You've heard of the concept of tenure, right?"

"That's when you can't be fired or something."

"Close enough. Well, this place has a very special notion of that word. That is, once you find out too much, they never let you leave. I wound up on the wrong side of this particular unwritten rule. I only came here in the early nineties after a stint teaching math out East. I got into trouble by asking too many questions and antagonizing the wrong people. Simple questions like 'why are my second semester classes always half-full?' I ended up gaining the disfavor of Dean Moriarty, and he gave me a little sit down in his office one day. There I got the message I wasn't going to be leaving this campus. Then, things just kind of happened. My car kept getting flat tires right as I was preparing to leave. Documents that might incriminate people would go missing from my office. And I told you about my wife, right? Just not the whole story. She found some, uh, accoutrements of another female placed surreptitiously around this apartment. She already didn't want to live here and so that was the last straw. She wouldn't listen to my explanations. They let her leave. Not me."

I couldn't believe what I was hearing. "That sounds familiar," I said. "I seem to be receiving the same treatment. I think they want me, too."

"What makes you say that?"

I launched into the shortest version of the saga of Justin and the winter break I could manage. I wrapped up with my strange conversation with the RA before Eric and Sarah came back. When I finished, Dalton's face had taken on a terrifying paleness. Even his beard seemed to contain it.

"Jesus, I never thought a student would get such treatment. Although, from what I gather you seem to have been quite the problem child for them. Can't be gotten rid of like the others."

"Like Seth and Adam? They antagonized the hell out of him, too. I just avoided him until it was too late. Hearing your tale makes me feel that they roll out the same techniques for anyone they need. I lost my car on Homecoming night. I could barely leave Schuster over the break because of Justin and that stupid storm. Variations of a same basic theme."

"I'm glad you told me," Dalton said. "Not that I'm going to be able to do anything about it."

"I've discussed some of this with Deakin."

"So you've said. But something must have happened there. Otherwise you wouldn't be coming to me."

"I guess you're right. Let's just say he didn't believe a very unbelievable part of my story. In fact, it's so unbelievable I'm not even going to tell you."

"You know I would never not believe you, right?" Dalton said. I could see sincerity in his kind brown eyes.

"Right," I said. "But all things the same, I'd rather keep this part to myself." I glanced at the tiny regal clock on his mantel. I had been here for an hour. "I need to go," I said, getting up. "Time to hit the Sunday afternoon dining hall selection. It's a tempting mix of Chinese food and fried chicken."

"Wow," Dalton said. "Dunno how you can think of that right now, but more power to ya. Please know I'm here for you, and it's not as bad as it seems. It's just humans running the show, when it comes down to it. They can be outwitted."

"Yeah, right," I said as I opened his front door. "Humans."

I GOT BACK TO SCHUSTER right at dinner time. Eric was just leaving his room to head over to the dining hall, so I asked to join him. We didn't say much until we sat down at a small, two-person table with flecks of fake gold embedded in its flat top. Eric had created a large cheeseburger with what looked like every topping known to man. Little pieces of cheese kept getting caught in his scraggle of a beard, and I kept having to point them out.

"Thanks," he said, picking out a small piece of cheddar. "This beard is reaching borderline disgusting territory."

"I'd say you reached that milestone a while back," I joked.

"Yeah, and fuck you too," Eric said. "Speaking of milestones, I thought I wouldn't see you for dinner any time soon. You've been hanging out more with professors these days."

"Sorry about that," I said. "I was just bummed you didn't believe me. But it turns out they don't believe me either."

"No shit?" Eric said. "Did you tell Deakin about Homecoming . . ."

"Yes, I did."

"I see. And he didn't believe you?"

"That we were visited by two ghosts of Malworth past? No, he didn't."

"Jesus, you still think that's what happened? You shouldn't be surprised a person of learned academic station didn't believe you. It's sort of his job to be skeptical."

I jammed a few of his french fries in my mouth. "I'm not surprised. I hoped since they've been around a lot longer than us they might believe. Turns out they're more scared of the folks running things than me."

"Wait, why do you keep saying 'they'? Who else have you been spilling the beans to around here?"

I stopped and looked around. We were the single occupied table for fifty yards in any direction. "I've been speaking with my stats prof, too. He doesn't seem to know much, but at least he's nice and he listens to me."

"Hey, I listen. I just think you're full of shit," Eric said, taking another greasy bite. A minute speck of onion lodged in the bottom half of his beard.

"Yeah, I know you do," I said in a malevolent tone. "But I'm okay with that. No one ever believes the true prophet until the time of destiny strikes."

Eric choked on a bit of bread. "What the fuck does that mean?" he spat.

"I dunno, just something I've been pondering," I said. Perhaps the ancient language of the book was starting to rub off on me.

"All right, whatever," he said, downing the rest of the burger. "Look, I can admit we've seen some fucked up things around here. But I don't believe this place is run by some conspirarcy that has some kind of special list we may or may not be on, and that means we're going to join some type of society. When I say it all aloud like that doesn't it make zero sense?"

"I'm more impressed you have actually been listening to me," I said. "Now what say you and I have an excellent Sunday night getting drunk and watching some *Mystery Science Theater?*"

"Holy shit, you read my mind," Eric said, getting up with his empty tray. His freshman fifteen had evolved into more of a freshman thirty.

"And thanks, man," I said, standing with my half-eaten tray.

"You're welcome. Just cuz I don't believe you doesn't mean we can't stay friends."

I hoped that would be true when the shit really started to hit the fan.

Chapter

ELEVEN

THINGS RETURNED TO A KIND OF NORMAL after those first few weeks in January. Eric and I went to class every Monday, Wednesday, and Friday mornings. Deakin must not have appreciated my last outburst in his office because he seemed not to acknowledge my presence in his lecture. I wondered if he was afraid of what else I might tell him. I was still on pretty good terms with Dalton. He was becoming one of the few people besides Sarah I could trust.

My other classes continued on like usual, as if I had never witnessed the cruel underbelly of this university with my own eyes. I found Ellickson's English class a boring facsimile of his Creative Writing course, and my Health & Wellness lecture remained a giant bore. Langdon's class did hold my interest, despite her dour demeanor. Now that we were reaching some advanced concepts of science and biology she seemed to blossom into the teacher she was many years ago. I decided to say something during our last class in January.

"Very interesting class today, Professor Langdon," I offered as I circled past the wide laboratory table she used for her notes.

Her eyes seized on me from above her thick glass frames and underneath her flaxen hair. They didn't contain the anger I saw last semester. "Why thank you, Mr. Sinclair. Thanks for attending my class every day this semester. You know, instead of like the last one."

"You're welcome," I said, feeling awkward as I shuffled toward the exit.

"You're the hope of us all," she said from behind me as I reached the door frame.

I wheeled around. "What did you . . ."

"Oh, nothing, just hope you continue your studies," she said. I swear she winked at me. "That's all."

I turned back around and kept walking.

"THAT FUCKING BITCH, SHE CALLED me out in front of everyone," Sarah said when I got to her room that night, elucidating a quite different assessment of Langdon. I wore my best dress slacks and a button-up white shirt that wasn't too wrinkled. The occasion was a concert on campus mandated by her music professor, who taught an introductory course in the tiny building on the northeast side of campus. Although it was the fourth-largest university in terms of almost anything, Malworth had a gigantic auditorium for music, plays, opera, and any other hoity-toity type activity that most college students wouldn't even glance at. The only reason I was doing any glancing tonight was because Sarah asked me to come. I hadn't broached the topic of our last night together, but it lurked around the edges of our conversation. I didn't want to be the clingy guy I'd seen evolve and never leave St. James, so I decided to play it cool on our first official "date" since we'd known each other.

"Yeah, I hate when she does that," I responded to her jab at Langdon. "Then she like, draws it out so you feel really embarrassed in front of everyone," I concluded, even though that had never happened to me.

"I might not have everything memorized, but I know the material. I was just having a brain fart. Hey, will you help me with this?" She dangled two strands of a necklace behind her neck.

"Oh, uh, yeah, sure," I said. I had no idea what I was doing but got the thing closed somehow.

"Thanks," she said, turning around and blowing me away with her beauty. I had never seen Sarah wear such a copious amount of make up. Her cheeks had a soft rouge glow and her gorgeous green eyes were outlined by dark eyeshade. Her hair had been sprayed with something to hold it up and it contained several shiny metal pins. I moved in for a quick peck on her lips.

178

"Hey," she said. "Watch the lipstick, buddy. What was that for?"

"Because I . . ." I trailed, shuddering at where that sentence could lead. I didn't want her to feel like we had to start some kind of relationship in the middle of the storm of insanity. ". . . because I wanted to," I mumbled.

"All right, mister, but no funny business at the concert," she said. "My professor is playing in the orchestra."

She put on a dainty wool jacket and some heavy boots, slipping her dress shoes into a small carrier. I threw on my hideous yellow coat and followed her down the hallway. Sarah stopped at Amanda's door on our way toward the exit. It was still locked. We braced the frigid air and stepped the several blocks over to the auditorium. This was by far the most modern building on this campus and also one of the tallest, overshadowed only by the campanile. Inky black windows stretched in the center from top to bottom, and a metal vent ran the length on the other side. I marveled how I'd never paid attention to this edifice during all my walks to the English building. Tonight it was lit up from various lights inserted in the ground. Sarah produced two tickets from her purse and gave them to the attendant. We walked through an expansive antechamber, which was half-filled with students not dressed up like us.

The interior performance area was even more magisterial, a huge room filled with padded seats and balconies running on either side. The stage seemed a mile wide and held a hundred chairs for the orchestra. We found our seats on the far right in the lowest balcony.

"Some seats, huh?" Sarah said.

"Yeah, I'll take it," I said. "So, there isn't like a place to get popcorn or anything, is there?"

Sarah gave me a withering look, then smiled. "Sorry to say, there isn't."

"That's okay," I said, bracing myself for another attempt at flirtation. "I have everything I need right here," I said, placing my hand on her tiny shoulder.

Sarah screwed up her face into a look of embarassment, so I removed my arm and decided to change course.

"So, while we have a second, care to discuss other matters? Say, the book?" The look she shot me broke down a little bit as she blinked. "Not now, Mike. We're supposed to be enjoying ourselves. Plus I have to write down the various movements for class next week. So, just for tonight, can we leave it alone?"

I was a little discouraged but glad she had asked me to come along on this excursion. I was enthralled by her presence. I had been ever since I'd first met her in Seth and Adam's dorm room those many months ago. After another fifteen minutes, the orchestra members filed onto the stage to rapturous applause. The lights went down all the way, plunging everything but the stage into darkness. The conductor raised his baton, and we were off. The first half was an auditory tour-de-force, making stops at Mozart and Beethoven's best-known works and ending with a medley of Chopin that blew me away. I found myself surprised that such a hellish school could produce such an amazing group of musicians. I didn't enjoy the latter half as much because it contained music from people whose names I'd never heard.

"Oh, Mike, I can't believe we got to experience that," Sarah said as we filtered out after giving our second standing ovation. "I know I'm not going to remember the various tempos and styles and movements for class, but what I do know . . ." she held out her arms to grasp my bulky coat, "is that I'm so glad I was here with you."

"Me too," I said, staring into her verdant eyes.

We padded back in the dirty snow back to Schuster hand-in-hand. The dormitory was quiet as death. We walked up the linoleum stairs and entered the girls' side of the hallway through the pneumatic purple door. I could just make out some other people entering the far end of the corridor.

"Sidarthi's staying over in another room tonight," Sarah whispered in my ear as we approached her room. Blood rushed to my face and down my legs as she spoke in her hushed tone. And then happiness ceased to exist in the hallway.

"Mr. Sinclair, what are you doing?" The blood that had been flowing became ice in my veins.

"Oh, shit," Sarah said. Her key dangled in front of the lock like a Christmas ornament.

"What do we have here?" Justin's high voice panned down the concrete tunnel. Another RA, quaking in his shoes, took up the rear at a distance. He was taller than Justin but appeared much nerdier, with a pair of wide-rimmed glasses and acne up the wazoo. "You were thinking of entering a female student's room after curfew. And right in front of your RA. They'll find no truck for this plot here, will they Josh?"

"No, sir," came the weak and garbled reply from behind him.

Justin came to a stop a few inches from our faces. It was unnerving. He wore a dull blue track suit and some black work out pants. The RA behind him wore plain blue jeans and a green shirt with some kind of triangle design on the front.

"Shut the fuck up, Justin," Sarah said. I was floored by her response and started laughing. Then I remembered what I saw over the break. The dark pits where Justin's eyes should have been lit up like blacklights.

"What did you say to me?" he growled.

"You heard me. I don't give a shit if it's against the rules, we're not done hanging out. So fuck off." I couldn't believe she was speaking to him in such a manner, and was turned on by her garullous attitude.

"I'm afraid I can't do that, Ms. Jackson," Justin said, but his eyes stayed on me. "Especially not when it comes to this tool in front of me. And come on, what's the fun of creating your dormitory's handbook if you let your charges break the rules?"

"You wrote the handbook?" Sarah said. "Then I'm definitely not paying attention to that stupid thing. C'mon, Mike. Let's go." She turned her key in the lock and started opening the door. Justin moved like a cheetah, clawing at the door handle until he pulled it shut.

"I don't think so," he menaced. "In fact, for this brazen act of disobe-dience . . ." he reached behind him, and I knew he was goint to pull out the small tattered notebook.

"Whatever, psycho," Sarah said. "Just leave me alone. I guess this is goodnight, Mike. Let me give you a kiss." She reached out and pulled my head over, launching into the most charged exchange of tongues I'd ever experienced. No girls in St. James ever kissed like that. I wished I could see the look on Justin's craggy face as we embraced. When it was over, I swore electricity spiked between us.

"Disgusting," Justin said. "Into your room. And just so you know," he did his usual flamboyant work with the ink pen, "you're off the list thanks to this little—."

"Fuck your list," she said, slamming the door.

"They never take the news well," Justin said, smiling at me. It made me sick to my stomach. "Now then, shall we march you off to your room or can you handle it yourself?"

As much as I wanted to respond to him just like Sarah did, I held back. I knew Sarah was never going to stay on the list. Justin had told me as much during our creepy conversation over the break. I felt like I needed to stay on this stupid list of his for as long as I could. As much as I saw it as my free pass out of this terrible place, I needed to see this through to the end. Despite all of this asshole's admonitions and attempts to scare me, he knew my parents sent me here to stay on his list. As long as I didn't provoke him too much I would remain there, and thus remain on campus until I could figure out who was running the show. I needed to bide my time.

"I think I can handle it," I demurred, avoiding his blackened eyes. Even as I stood next to the guy, something about him channeled a very inhuman vibe. I never would have entertained such a thought until I met those ghosts up on the hill. He radiated body heat but also a kind of intense cold underneath which made for an eerie presence.

"Good," was all he said. "Come, Josh. Let's finish our rounds. Quiet hours are in effect."

As I walked past Josh I saw pure terror in his eyes. Sweat congealed at the top of his T-shirt. I shook my head and kept moving until I got to the end of the hall. I headed to Eric's room and knocked on the door.

"Hey, man, what's up?" he said. He wasn't wearing a shirt and had on a loose pair of pajama pants. I could hear the television roaring behind him.

"Hey, dude, I was . . ." I thought about recounting the sorry events of the night, but decided against it. "Um, can I stay here tonight? Just don't feel comfortable in my empty room."

"Sure, man," Eric said. "I thought you were hanging out with Sarah tonight?" Some bizarre cartoon from Adult Swim played on the TV and a bag of Doritos sat open and spilled all over the futon.

I plopped down in my dress attire from the evening, avoiding the cheese dust as best I could. "I did, but we had some RA problems afterward. And that's kinda all I want to say on the matter."

"Oh, shit, really?" he said. "God, I hate that guy."

"You have no idea," I said.

"Well, fuck it," Eric said. "Can't do nothing about it now."

"No, not now," I said. Justin would get his in the end. Even if I had to deliver it gift-wrapped right to his fucking face. We sat and watched TV until after midnight. Then I leaned over to pass out on the giant futon and Eric scrambled up into the loft bed.

THE NEXT MORNING I DECIDED to take up my belated pledge to call my father. I scrambled to the pay-phone in the lobby area fifteen minutes before I had to head out the door with Eric for Deakin's class. I first dialed our home in St. James, and then his insurance office. I got no answer at either location. Bemused and angry, I hung up and trudged back to my room, where Eric was waiting. Deakin hadn't acknowledged my presence in class for a few weeks, so it was a surprise hearing him call my name after his lecture.

"Mr. Sullivan," he called into the scrum of his twelve remaining pupils as we filed toward the door. "Might I have a word?"

I slowed, but Eric kept moving. "C'mon, man, you really gonna give him the time of day again?" he cried.

I thought about it. Deakin might not have believed my very real camp-fire ghost tales, but he also was the closest connection I had to my father left on this campus. I turned toward the elderly instructor.

"Dude!" Eric yelled as he was shoved out the door by the few other kids escaping the classroom.

"Professor Deakin," I said as I walked over to the lectern.

His beady eyes peered out at me from behind the wiry glasses. "It's Marvin, remember?"

"I remember. I just thought that—"

"Thought that you'd scared me off?" he said with a chuckle. The wrinkles on his face contorted, creating a map with diverse lines flowing every way. "It's going to take a lot more than that, my boy. Now, will you join me for some tea?"

"Sure," I said.

He locked his lecture room. Various letters to students and grade postings occupied the glass case next to the door. I stared as if I knew these people. "Did you ever think that your parents sending you here was maybe your last chance as well?" Deakin said, knocking me from my reverie.

"What are you talking about?"

"I've said too much here," he said, glancing around him. The wide hallway contained several other glass cases of artifacts from around the world. The bruised tile floor echoed with students' boot prints as they scrambled to leave the building. Another professor walked down to the restroom at the far end of the hall. "Let's go upstairs," Deakin said.

We entered his office in silence among the many odd portraits and relics that lined the walls. Deakin put on the small kettle and dove into the wooden chair behind his desk.

"So, do you recall our previous point of diversion?" he scowled.

"You mean the fact that you don't believe in supernatural phenomena?"

"That's quite it. I'm still not fully able to grasp what you brought to me. I've taught school at this institution many years, and have seen many students come and go. But I never saw a single ghost in all my years. Never."

"We've been over this," I said.

"Of course," Deakin said. The water on the stove had begun to boil over. He fixed me some tea. "But that doesn't mean you didn't see anything. I never thought I'd have to concede something so ridiculous, but there you have it."

I blew over the scalding liquid, causing a ripple across its surface. "We saw another one that night, too," I said in a low voice.

"You what?" Deakin said, freezing in place.

"Another ghost. This one was from much earlier in the past. He fought in the Civil War."

Deakin remained motionless. "You don't say," he whispered, placing the water back on the stove.

"I do say," I said, trying some of the tea. It burned my upper lip when I drank.

"Who was this other supposed 'ghost' that you saw?" Deakin inquired.

"Oh, no," I said. "You've been cagey enough with me on details. If you wanna hear about this other being, you're going to answer my questions first. Is that understood?" I felt bad speaking so roughly to this man, the one person on campus who might have real answers for me. Time was passing by too fast for anything else.

Deakin stood at his full height beside his desk, his wizened eyes peering at me with an odd mixture of contempt and interest. "I suppose it is," he said, his shoulders collapsing into a shrug. "I at least owe you that."

"I'd say so," I said. "I'll make it quick. Tell me everything you remember about my father."

Deakin plopped into his chair and rolled back a few inches. He stared out the small square window between the desk and the stove. Blinding, snow-filled light poured in from the window and scattered all over the papers cluttering his desk.

"It's a conspiracy of parentage. That's the rub."

"It's a what of what?" I said, confounded.

He turned and gazed right at me. Within his pupils I could see his terror made manifest, the opposite of Justin's burning rage. "You must not breathe one word of this to anyone. Not your friends in the dormitory, and certainly not to that prig of a RA you've got over there. Not one word."

"Sure," I shrugged.

"Not sure," Deakin said. He leaned forward and removed his glasses in one abrupt gesture. "Do I have your word, Mr. Sullivan?"

"You have it," I said.

"All right. Now, do you think your parents were the only group who sent you here to compete for the society's attention?"

I considered it. "Given that I have no idea why they sent me, why not?"

Deakin chortled as he replaced his glasses. "Well, they weren't. Others were thinking along the same lines. In fact, their progeny occupied the very same dormitory you live in now."

I had to rack my brain to remember what the word "progeny" meant, but the memory crackled like a light bulb exploding in my head. "What are you saying . . ."

"They didn't know it, of course, those other rowdy children that made up your dorm hall. They weren't around to recall the unpleasantness."

"The what?"

Deakin let out a long breath that had the anxiety of history behind it. "You see, this competition goes back a long time. Other parents have done the same thing with their offspring, but this time it was different. The parents of Gordon, Baines, Fulton, and Jackson all used to live in St. James. Each family had at least one partner who attended Malworth, in the 1970s. There was a . . . a falling out among their families shortly after they all returned and started having children. Two families left for the northern area of the state, and two headed for the safety of the metropolitan area. Your father was the remainder, his family the only one which retained enough power to stay there. Of course, it was quite diminished after the falling out, and no one ever respected your father in the same way again."

I was stunned, and couldn't even think of the next question I had. "How do you know this?" I stammered.

"That is indeed privileged information," Deakin said. "But it comes from a very trusted source. One who would not be incorrect in these matters as they were set into place many years ago. Shall I continue?"

"Yes," I sputtered. My throat felt very dry, and I took a drink of tea. The liquid burned the roof of my mouth as it slid down.

"This falling out, it was a deep scar on the consciousness of those families but also of the bond of the society itself. In fact, by this point there hadn't been a real winner since your doctor friend."

"Winograd? I thought he was the first member of the 'new' society?"

"First and last. Once word got out of his less than legal ways of operating on patients, well the threat of investigation became too much. Whitacre's descendants knew the awful history of the first inquisition. They did not want another. This tearing apart of the families had to be concealed."

"The families you named . . . you said Jackson?"

"Yes, the very same. I believe you have some familiarity with their daughter?"

"God, yes. She's my . . ." I didn't know how to continue that sentence. ". . . my friend. They all are. Seth and Adam were gone by the semester break. You said Fulton was the other one? He's here, too."

"As I gathered, yes," Deakin said. "Gordon and Baines were hardly a sure thing. You see, part of the renewal of the competition meant that no parents could tell their offspring why they were being forced to attend Malworth. It would have sullied the game, you see. Those two shared the antagonistic streak of their fathers. More promise was seen in you and Ms. Jackson. Fulton was just a given; his parents aren't active in society matters any longer. But you had everything they wanted. The right pedigree, the right name, even seemed to possess some brains. Why do you think you've had such an easy time of it thus far?"

"Easy?" I spat at him. "You call being trapped alone in a fucking dorm building with that madman an easy time?"

Deakin narrowed his gaze at me. "I do," he mumbled. "You should've seen the Caretaker from Winograd's time. You would not have enjoyed him."

"Right," I said. "Justin is a piece of cake. So why me? Why am I so special?"

"You're the last of the line of Sinclairs involved with this place going back to the nineteenth century. I'm sure your parents never mentioned any of this to you, but it's true. This place keeps no real records so I can't show you any proof. But trust me, your family is tied into this place more than anyone else you were pitted against."

"Against? You mean this is really a competition against Sarah and Eric?"

"I'm afraid so," Deakin said, sporting a weak grin. "Doesn't mean you have to join in, though. You see how they handle dissent against the order. But when it comes to someone like you, someone they need . . ."

"I might have a chance," I finished. "I'm sure as hell not going down without a fight. I hope it doesn't have to come to that. I'm still trying to make sense of what you're telling me."

"If that's the case, why don't we switch off? I have more on this topic to enlighten you, but you still haven't given me the information I want."

"Oh, right. The other ghost," I said. I placed all the information flowing through my skull into a separate mental room, which I locked. Any more thought in that direction and I'd go insane. I proceeded to tell the story of Alfred James on Homecoming. How he'd bought us drinks before escaping into the night, passing through other human beings. Then I told him what I read in Moriarty's history book. Deakin's eyes widened as I ended the tale.

"And you're saying you really saw this," he gaped.

"I really did. I wasn't even drunk by that point, "I said, trying to laugh. I looked up at the small clock on the wall. I had spent another hour in this office. Ellickson's class was a distant memory.

"And then he just disappeared?"

"Never to be seen again. He was the last of the 'old' society, then?"

"Something like that," Deakin said. "But I swear to you, I've never heard of anything like this. I mean, it had been rumored among the staff for years. The members returning on Homecoming. But I never thought it actually took place."

"Well, it did," I said. "Unfortunately the other person who witnessed it with me doesn't belive his own eyes."

"You mean Fulton? As I said, he's of little consequence. It's you they want. Strange this presence sought you out. It smacks of being sent."

"Sent? Who the hell sends a ghost to do their bidding?"

"You have no idea," Deakin said with a smirk, leaning back in the chair.

"I don't really want to think about it at this point. Perhaps we should wrap this up for today," I said, my mind reeling from these revelations.

"All right," Deakin said. "And remember, do not tell a soul this information. Do you promise me?"

"Yeah, I promise," I said. I wasn't sure how much of this I could tell Sarah, but I felt like I had to let her in on some of this sick "game."

"Very well," Deakin said. "Mr. Sinclair, I rather like our chats, even if they cover some remarkable territory. Will you come for tea again?"

"We'll see, Marvin," I said. "You've given me a bit of an overload here, and I'm not sure how to deal with it. And I forgot to ask you more about my father."

I saw the little twitch in his eye return as I spoke. "Oh, um . . . of course. I will tell you everything I can recall, if you'll join me for tea again."

"It's a deal," I said, getting up to leave.

"Glorious," Deakin said, closing his office door after me. It took my all not to lean against it and slide to the floor.

THERE WAS ONE PERSON I could speak to about all of this nonsense: Sarah. I hadn't seen her since our little run in with Justin after the concert. I thought about how to broach any of these subjects as I padded down the carpeted hallway toward the girls' side for our Thursday night study date. She knew something was amiss as soon as I entered her room.

"What's going on?" she asked as I plopped down on the pink futon. "You must have had another gab session with that prof in the History building. You were like this the first time you met with him."

"Yeah, I did see Deakin," I said. "I told him about Alfred, too."

"Oh, my God," Sarah said. "And what did he say?"

"He didn't really believe me," I fibbed. "That wasn't what I wanted to talk to you about. But first, I'm very sorry about how things ended after the concert."

"Me too," Sarah said, sitting down. The single lamp on her desk illuminated her verdant eyes. It was an eery sight. "I had hoped there would be some more entertainment afterward," she said. She moved her hand on the inner part of the plaid pajama pants I had donned for this evening. As incredible as it felt, I had to stop her.

"I was looking forward to it as well," I said, placing a palm on her hand. "But I have to tell you something else."

"Oh, all right," she said, slumping back into the futon. "I can see you're not going to be any fun until you get down to business."

"This is some business you're going to want to hear."

I regaled her with what Deakin had told me, excerpting for my own clarity some of the stuff about my father. I made certain to impress on her the historical implications of the two of us being on this campus. She remained more calm than I thought as I spoke.

"You're telling me my family used to live in St. James?" she asked.

"According to Deakin," I said. "They all did. And then they all sent their progeny . . . his word . . . here to compete for the next generation."

"But what happened to make them all leave?"

"I wish I knew," I said. "Deakin was pretty cagey about it, or he didn't know. Either way, I think it may be another solid clue toward this mystery."

"Aw, we could've been next-door neighbors," she said, touching my hand. "We could have gone to school together, had a relationship . . ."

"I think that was what they wanted to avoid," I said. "I haven't spoken to my parents since the winter break. I tried calling a week ago, but no one answered. But I'd wager they wouldn't want to know I've been sniffing around the reasons they sent me here. I'll bet your parents are the same."

"I'm . . . not so sure," she said, averting her gaze. "They were pretty normal when I went home for the break."

"So were mine for eighteen years," I insisted. "Things aren't always as they seem."

"True," she said. "I guess I don't know why I care so much any more. I'm off the list."

"At least you got to stay," I said.

"Oh, yeah, big victory," she smiled. "But I met you."

"That you did," I said. We proceeded to kiss, the strange and mystical properties of our families forgotten in a moment of pure bliss.

EACH DAY AS I STOMPED and stumbled through the half-cleared snow piled up around the cracked cobblestone sidewalks I noticed fewer kids joining me. Were people leaving left and right? Were they being purged? The questions swirled in my brain as I meandered underneath the snow-covered pine and oak trees and avoided large icy spots. By the middle of February the average temperature each day hovered around ten degrees. My room remained devoid of any type of furnishing, so I avoided it most nights. After trudging through the snow and up five flights of stairs all I could do was grab a quick meal at the dining hall and slump over to Eric's room where we'd watch vintage science fiction films. I never laughed as hard as I did those nights, and they were a welcome distraction from everything swirling around me. But they also contained a bittersweet note. I sat next to my friend and knew he was unaware of the great conspiracy tangling up not just our families but Sarah's as well. I wished that Seth and Adam would somehow reappear on the floor like nothing had ever happened so I could fill them in on the news. My Tuesday and Thursday classes relented a bit on the extra work. Dalton's class continued to be a nightmare, but he did his best to mitigate the damage in our study sessions. He hadn't brought up my lurid stories from the winter break, and I never brought them up either. I decided not to let him in on Deakin's recent revelations. It was as if we had a staid understanding of our relationship to this hellish school.

Thoughts of my predicament would fade away when I hung out with Sarah. Just having another person next to me who knew what was going on around this campus was a benefit. We took Deakin's revelation in stride, discussing how our various lives might have been different if we'd just stayed in St. James.

"Maybe we could've been friends, just like in *The Breakfast Club*," Sarah said as we meandered down the long sidewalk toward Schuster on a brisk afternoon. A few snow flakes interspersed among the oak trees and came to rest on the dirty powder around us.

"You think so?" I asked. "I thought about that too. Like we were robbed of the chance to get to know each other. And for what? Some stupid blood feud or other such nonsense. I wish I knew what these guys were really up to behind the scenes."

"Well, why don't we find out?" Sarah asked. "Let's look through the blank book again tonight."

"You think we can find something?"

"I know we can," she said. "Now, race me back to the dorm. You do know college life is supposed to be fun once in a while, right?" She took off at once, scattering wet snow all over the sidewalk.

I gave my best attempt at keeping up with her, but she was a much better athlete. I'd played two years of basketball at St. James High and rode the bench for every game. I pulled up short and watched her run, the dark-brown book bag bouncing up and down on her back as she galloped. I walked fast across the asphalt parking lot on the other side of Schuster Hall, where she met me with a kiss.

"Beat you," she said, smiling in the midday sun.

"Yeah, but you still have to get to the door," I stomped up the small stack of cracked concrete stairs that led to the main entrance. She somehow beat me there, too. "I don't believe it," I said.

"Believe it, Sinclair. Believe it," she said with a lark. We entered, two children alone against the dangers of this world.

That night we sat together on the pink futon in darkness. Sidarthi had once again vacated for parts unknown so we had the room to ourselves. I grabbed the dusty book from my backpack and set it on the table. Sarah sparked the candle and we were ready to divine. I opened to one of the first pages, blank as ever. I ripped it out with a slight feeling of glee, and floated it over the burning flame. Our shadows once again lept around on the pale white dormitory room walls. I watched as the script came into focus, the serifs panning out into ancient black ink. Words began to form into sentences, then paragraphs. Once most of it was complete, I started reading.

> There has always been a Malworthe Society, just as there have always been men striving to better themselves and their societies. The difference being that ours is a legacy that shall never be wiped from the earth. Struggling in darkness, we forever appeal to the higher natures of our being in order to know the will of the ancients who lead us into a new dawn.

"Boring," Sarah said as I spoke. "Let's try somewhere else. I'm sick of reading page after page of bullshit."

"Fine," I said. I flipped ahead and tore another page out. It made a sick ripping noise I enjoyed. I set it above the candle and waited. The usual script appeared on the bottom half of the page. Something else began to form on the top half, the barest outlines of a picture. As it filled in, more lines appeared within the picture. It dawned on me that this was a map of some kind, and I said as much to Sarah. Watching the lines grow and link together jogged something in my mind. I reached over to my back pack and started rummaging through it. I plucked out the map of the campus I had received back in August, and set it next to the page. The similarities were stunning.

"They seem to match up in some way," I said, scanning both maps.

"The buildings line up with these squares on the old map," Sarah said, her eyes dodging back and forth between the two sources. "But look at this . . ." The book's map had its own set of interlocking lines within the grid that my campus map did not. They tangled and wove through the various buildings like a system of roads. Sarah traced a slender finger along the lines, her face a mixture of confusion and intrigue in the glowing candlelight. "These don't match the roads that run through campus. Or the sidewalks."

The old connections converged at a spot in the northeast part of campus. The campus map matched that spot with the small building I had noticed months ago: the one with no label.

"I think these all connect right here," I said, pointing to the building.

"I think you're right," Sarah said. "Jesus, could this be the set of underground tunnels I heard about?"

"They certainly look like they could be," I said. "I thought you said they removed them years ago?"

"Maybe they did," Sarah said. "Only one way to find out."

"You're right," I said. "I've been meaning to check that place out. No time like the present."

"Well, let's wait 'til tomorrow," Sarah said, leaning into me. "I think you have plans tonight." She began kissing my neck, but I still wanted to look at the map. Something else was bugging me. The lines converged in the northeast, but they also came to a point right in the center, where the campanile stood. I considered pointing this out to Sarah but my motivation went away as her mouth moved down my neck. We kissed with passion as the candle flame lapped beside us. I still couldn't get what we'd stumbled across out of my mind. What if those tunnels still existed, and what if they were still used? The answers to these questions terrified me, but I put it to rest for one more night.

I LAY IN SARAH'S BED UNTIL SHE WOKE the next morning. There was no disturbance by Sidarthi this time; Sarah guessed she must have stayed with somebody. I decided our mission was more important than making Deakin's class, though I regretted not meeting with him afterward. We headed from Schuster in our boots and jackets, our course set for the northeast quadrant of campus. This portion held some of the buildings I'd yet to visit, including a Chemistry lab and the small music building where Sarah had class. I had traced the lines from the ancient map onto a sheet of paper. I pulled it out of my jeans with one gloved hand as we walked. I again was struck by how the lines came to a stop in the dead center of campus. The campanile was part of the original institution that resided here, and according to Moriarty's pseudo-history book it made up the steeple of a church that once stood there. We came to a tiny shack that rose about eight feet in the air and had a pair of rickety old doors pulled together. A worn chain was linked between the slats on the doors. A rusty lock held tight at the center.

"Looks like this isn't going anywhere," I said in a morose tone.

"Still, let's look around," Sarah said.

We circled the small hut twice. A single boarded up window sat on the other side. We stomped through the snow and arrived back at the front.

"There isn't going to be any easy way in here," I said, defeated at last.

"Probably not," Sarah said. "Well, at least we checked it out. My music class is coming up, so I'm going to hang around here 'til it starts. Do you want to stick around?"

"No, I've got Ellickson and then Health this afternoon," I said. I hoped that would be cover enough for my true destination.

"All right," Sarah said. "Don't get too bored. Remember, we have a real mystery to solve."

"I know," I said, leaning over to kiss her goodbye. Her warm lips punctured the frigid air and brought life back to my body. "I'll see you later."

She turned and walked up the snow-packed sidewalk to the little music building. I watched her until she disappeared behind the large metallic eighth note that adorned the entrance. I turned and headed for the center of campus, pulling out the traced map as I walked.

I saw the soaring spiral of the campanile before I was even close to its base. The clock tower loomed above me, daring me to interdict its secrets. Tendrils of snow extended from the belfry like giant icicles hanging from the sides of the sheer brick edifice. I reached the base of the campanile and took one last look into the sky. The thing was tall and imposing, and shook me a bit as I appraised its true height. Its base was made of solid concrete and contained a curved space where a decrepit door sat. I walked under the archway and pulled at the door's handle, which didn't give. I stepped back into the wide space before the campanile, a massive expanse of white powder in every direction, crossed by a few dull paved sidewalks. A group of students in thick coats walked down one of these sidewalks toward the dormitories. After another ten minutes of wandering I gave up and headed west to the English building. I decided I should attend at least some class today.

I HEADED BACK TO SCHUSTER feeling defeated and ready to let the school just win already. Figuring out its myriad secrets was a much bigger challenge than I had imagined, and part of me wanted to give up on the whole endeavor. If I didn't have Sarah in my corner I might have forgotten about the whole thing and given in to Justin. I marched up the linoleum stairs and pushed through the pneumatic door. The hallway was quiet as usual. I entered my desolate room and plopped onto the red plastic chair. Since it was Friday, I decided to get drunk. I rummaged through my closet and found another bottle of Jack Daniels I'd secured through Sarah. I twisted the top and poured a considerable amount into a small plastic cup I'd swiped from the dining hall. I leaned back against the hard plastic and considered my options. After a few drinks I had decided to hang tough against this place no matter how much it tried putting me down. I also decided I would find out what this society was once and for all, even if I had to make Deakin break some kind of secret blood oath to tell me. A slight knock on the door disrupted my thoughts and made me jump out of my skin.

"Yo, Sinclair! You in there?" It was Eric. "You aren't jerkin' it, are you?"

I pulled open the door. "If I was, I wouldn't stop for you," I joshed.

"Fucking gross," he said. "You're drunk, aren't you?"

"Maybe," I said, hearing my voice slur. "M-maybe not."

"Bullshit," he said. "C'mon, why don't you bring the party over here? Unless you'd rather sit in a plastic chair by yourself all night."

"I might," I said. "But that sounds better."

I locked my room and followed Eric across the hall to his room, where I flopped onto the padded futon. His television had on some old show from the '70s with no volume. Eric took residence at the desk, staring at his computer screen. A real-time-strategy game flowed on the screen, pitting little space marines against some alien creatures.

"So, this how you're gonna spend your Friday nights now?" Eric said above the din of the computer game.

"I guess so," I said, staring around his room. Jake's stoner posters had all been removed. Eric hadn't replaced them but I noticed a huge new *Star Wars* poster in the corner above his bed. "Do you miss the ol' pothead roomie?" I asked.

"Who, Jake?" Eric said. "Fuck, no. The kid spilled fucking bong water all over my sheets one night. Didn't even apologize for it. I'm pretty sure he nailed his girlfriend in my bed, too, the ass clown. Why would I miss him?"

I watched the television screen flicker against the wall before I spoke. "Just wanted to ask, seeing as how he's gone now like the rest of them. Kicked off Justin's super secret list . . ." I knew I should stop talking, but the alcohol had found purchase in my veins.

"I think it was more that he smoked weed," Eric said in a dry voice. "But hey, you're the one seeing conspiracies and ghosts all around this place."

"You saw them too," I said, too drunk to realize what I was saying.

"I didn't see shit," Eric said, turning his gaze away from the monitor and directing it at me. Anger was rising behind his square glasses. "And neither did you. I thought we cleared this up already."

"Oh, we're clear," I said, leaning into the futon. It felt like two sides of a padded room in a mental institution. "But just so you know, there is way more to this place. Did you know that Winograd character became such an evil bastard that the school had to basically disown him? Turned out he started fucking up operations and . . ."

"Sinclair, I don't give a fuck," Eric said, louder this time. His eyes were back on the screen.

"Well, you should," I said, almost talking to myself. "You're part of the family legacy."

"What did you say?" he said.

I poured over the options in my slushed-out brain. I could bring up Eric's family connection to me and St. James and get my ass kicked out of his room, or I could shut up and try to enjoy the company of the last remaining person on this side of the hall. I sure as hell wasn't going to see what Justin was up to tonight. "Nothing," I said. I poured the JD that remained in the plastic cup down the hatch. "You just have more of a connection to me and this place than you realize."

"The fuck I do," he said. "Now shut up about it before I really regret asking you to come over here."

I sat and watched the mute television while he played his game in silence. "You'll find out," I said. "Just make sure you stay on the list."

"Sinclair, goddam it, get the fuck out of my room," Eric yelled. "I don't want to hear about your crazy-ass drunken conspiracy theories. There's no fucking 'list,' and Justin is not going to come kill you in your sleep. You saw some shit over the break, I'm not denying it. But you're taking this way too far. Now go to bed, sober up or something, but quit bringing it up to me."

"Fine," I said, struggling to get up off the overstuffed bench. "Have it your way." I ambled to his door. "See you around, former neighbor."

"What's that supposed to mean? We're neighbors right now," he said, glaring at me.

"I know. I meant before this," I said. I opened the door just enough to slip out and returned to my side of the hallway.

"You meant . . . what?" I could hear Eric say as I unlocked my door. "Sinclair, what the fuck are you talking ab—" I shut my door on the rest of his statement and sat back down on the plastic chair. It was much less comfortable than Eric's futon. I chugged down another drink as I sat and stared at the concrete wall before clamoring up to my loft bed and passing out in a stupor.

ERIC DIDN'T KNOCK ON MY DOOR Monday morning, and his was locked when I left for class, so I imagined he wasn't in any mood to join me for a jaunt in the below-zero temperatures that clutched the entire area like a freezing pair of hands. Deakin made eye contact with me the minute I entered the lecture hall.

"Mr. Sinclair," he said, not seeming to care about the handful of other students. "Might you be joining me for some tea after class today?"

"I'd be happy to," I said, looking around the room. No one seemed to notice I was having a private conversation with our professor in front of the class. Eric was nowhere to be found, so I grabbed a seat toward the back and buckled in for the lecture. We had just reached the nineteenth century, and I found Deakin's lecture skills much improved the closer we got to the present. I counted how many times he did his little back and forth walk throughout the lecture: twenty-six. When it was over I stayed sitting until everyone filtered out the door.

Deakin wheezed out a puff of air as he erased the chalkboard. "Come, let's go upstairs."

We reached his office and assumed our usual positions: Deakin leaning back in his desk chair, a cup of boiling tea resting on the corner of his desk, me sitting opposite him and staring out the window.

"You are wondering about your father," he said after a minute of silence.

"Yes," I said. "I have not spoken to him since the break. Since I learned he sent me here to compete against a bunch of kids I didn't even know had anything to do with this. I tried calling him a few weeks ago, but he didn't answer. I honestly don't know what I would've said to him if he had picked up."

"You don't have to worry about that," Deakin said. "What I have to say may color your ultimate conversation with your father. I must tell you it pains me to be the one to give you these revelations."

"I need to know the truth," I said. "This man selected almost every aspect of my life for me. This was his last gasp at control. I need to know why he did it."

"I understand," Deakin said. He didn't speak for another moment, but stared out the window. The frosted pane looked like the surface of an ice rink. He pointed a single thin finger out and drew some kind of symbol on the window. It seemed familiar, but I couldn't quite place it.

"When I first saw your father, he was as fresh-faced and naive about the world as you are now," Deakin continued. "The society saw great promise in him. They'd sent Winograd into the world, of course, but they were beginning to have concerns about him. Moriarty himself instructed your grandfather to send Timothy Sinclair to this university against his wishes. Sound familiar?"

"Definitely," I said. "But that's news to me. The way he made it sound when we came here was that he loved every minute of it."

"Oh he did. But that was after . . . the programming."

My eyes widened. "What did you say?"

"How do you suppose Justin became the soulless automaton you see today?" Deakin asked, a grim smile spreading on his face.

"I have no idea," I said. "I know RA's are dorks, but he takes it to a whole other scary level."

"I believe it," Deakin said. "Caretakers were the society's brute force. They accomplished the dirty work so people like Moriarty could meet with the governor and regents once in a while and tell them everything is all right. Justin was charged with getting rid of the other soul that remained in Schuster with you over the break. Do you think anyone is going to ask about her?"

"Wait, you mean Amanda? You know about her? She said her parents died a long time ago."

"In a matter of speaking, they did," Deakin said. "They disappeared during their time here."

I felt the color drain from my face. "Jesus," I said. "How?"

"If I knew, I'd tell you," Deakin said. "That's how good they are. Justin's predecessor, a negative being called Jared, was the Caretaker of Schuster during your father's time. He took care of them somehow. Their bodies were never found, and nothing ever got into any of the papers."

"Amazing," I said. "And terrifying. I wonder what happened to Amanda?"

"Chances are, you'll never find out," Deakin said, closing his eyes. "But we didn't sit down to discuss her, unfortunate as that may be. You wanted to know about your father."

"Right," I said. "And the programming."

"Well, it's what they do to the Caretakers, RAs, whatever you want to call them. Each successor is imbued with the characteristics of each that has gone before. Justin is the culmination of all previous Caretakers, but was programmed to be a normal advisor here at the school. Didn't he approach any kind of normality while you were here?"

"He gave us the usual spiel when I first moved into Schuster Hall," I said. "But it was really weird, like he was a machine spouting off the same crap to everyone. I just notched it up to the fact that he was a dork. Y'know what's funny, I think he has a 'glitch' or something. He kept repeating the same thing about his RA responsibilities. It's like a programming error."

"That could be," Deakin said. "They don't always take their medicine well. It's not easy for them to find souls willing to undergo the process. But this was the only way they could get your father to do their bidding."

A frightening chill tore down my spine. "Wait, what are you saying?"

"I'm saying he was the first of this 'new' society to be forcibly programmed. Until then it was considered an extreme measure to be used only on Caretakers. He had such promise, such beneficial qualities, that they saw no other way. He was like you in the beginning. Trying to find out what was going on even as he was in the middle of it. They were a lot better at it back then. He never had a chance."

I couldn't believe what I was hearing. "So he . . . actually fought them?"

"That he did. I consulted with him about doing so, just as I am with you now. I must tell you, Michael, I regret dearly that I couldn't do anything in his case. Your father was a good man when he came here, just as I know you are. He was ready to take on the world, gain his education at Malworth and then go to get his law degree at Harvard. His path was all set, even if he didn't want to attend this institution. Malworth changed him."

"But he's an insurance agent," I stammered. "Not a lawyer."

"I know," Deakin said. "That was his plan. It never came to fruition, because they got to him first. Your father was their first experiment to put one of their horrid creations into the world. They wanted to see if he would survive and thrive. The unpleasantness I talked to you about in St. James would be the result of that foolish decision. The society lost such trust in him that they wouldn't let you attend school here without the other families' children, too. They insisted on a competition."

"But knowing it would really be down to me in the end," I said. "Justin acted like it was a foregone conclusion that Seth and Adam wouldn't make it. He dismissed Sarah's chances too, and doesn't seem to care about Eric."

"Yes," Deakin said, taking a brief sip of tea. "They knew it wouldn't be much of a competition. But they still had to see what these people had created from their loins. They wanted to gouge the knife in, give the final insult of having their children removed from the institution of their parents."

"It's a game," I said in a meek voice. "That's all this is to them. Well, I'll show them a game they'll never win."

"I trust you will. But you need to know the rules of this game before you can win. And that's where I'm here to help. And I want to atone for your father. You see, he came to me one last time before the programming. I advised him to go through with his plan. I sent him to his fate. Do you have any idea what kind of weight this was on my soul?"

I sat there in silence. The beginnings of tears were forming around his old gray eyes. "I don't," was all I could say.

"You couldn't. No one could. Because no one knows. Just like no one will ever know what happened to that girl's parents. No one will ever know about the truth behind this place unless you get out to tell it. This is my quest for you. You must escape this university."

"What?" I said. "You're kidding. There is no way I'm leaving. Not after hearing all of this. I've got to stop this, got to stop all of it."

"That's the same thing your father said, right before he changed into someone else. I'm not going to let that happen to you."

"You expect me to let all this happen just so I can escape this shitty campus?" I screamed, not realizing it.

Deakin's eyes enlarged at the sound of my voice. He dribbled a little bit of tea onto his slacks and mopped it up with a handkerchief.

"I'm sorry," I said. "I didn't mean to yell. I just can't leave. Not with everything you've told me."

"Ah, but that's the plan," he said, throwing the handkerchief on his desk. "This knowledge must reach the entire state. People who send their children to this school must understand. Many of the students who attend here have nothing to do with the society and are only here to get a sub-par education. Not those who take my class, of course," he winked. "They have no idea what surrounds them. Always in darkness until the end. You must reach them so that they may know what this place is," he continued, leaning forward on his desk. "You must tell them the truth."

"And that is . . . ?" I said, my voice wavering.

"That this place is evil," Deakin said, "and the society must be stopped."

I looked deep into his aged eyes. What I saw there frightened me.

"I understand if this is a lot to take in all at once," he said. "This is your family legacy, Mr. Sinclair. I know you wish it wasn't, but we can't choose our destiny. You can either accept it or not. If there is one thing I know for certain it's this: you must escape this campus. Even if you're the last man to do so."

Chapter
TWELVE

INTER EBBED AWAY and snow fell less each day. The temperature reached a balmy thirty degrees one March afternoon, and the icicles hanging off the brick edges of Schuster started dripping their tails to the ground. There seemed to be even fewer kids on campus these days. On my morning walks to Deakin's class I saw a handful of other students walking in their light coats and stocking hats. I understood the "purge" now as a very real thing, as real as everything else I had seen at this place. I thought Deakin's advice was nonsense, but it stayed with me. The old professor hadn't invited me to tea since our last discussion, and I wasn't sure I wanted to hear any more. The sense of betrayal I felt at my father had evaporated and been replaced by fear and worry. Each day my mind would ponder an event in my childhood, scanning it for traces of weird behavior from my father. So far all I could come up with was some erratic moves on my eighth birthday, but even that I wasn't sure about since it was so long ago. His insistence on my attending this school made more sense now, but everything else seemed shrouded in a dense fog.

The secret map remained embedded in my mind. I kept seeing the confluence of lines at the base of the campanile. I couldn't refute the notion that all of these disparate threads met at that massive edifice in the center of campus. Considering it was one of the few remaining building left from when this institution was a lot more horrendous, it made sense. Each time I walked by the towering structure on my way to the English building I thought about what might lie there. When it rang those giant bells to signify the hour, I considered it a countdown for my soul.

I was heading to Dalton's class one Thursday when I noticed two men standing and arguing at the base of the campanile. I remained inconspicuous as I took the sidewalk that ran on the other side of the long field in front of the clock tower. Two men were gesticulating toward each other. I tried to make out who they were. One wore a long robe that covered even his feet, the other brown work pants and a Carhart jacket. The older guy wore some kind of pointy hat that reminded me of something but I couldn't put my finger on it as I gawked. They continued arguing. I slowed my gait. The side-walk curved toward the campanile and I kept my head down. There was not a single other student within a hundred yards.

The old man came into focus and I saw his white beard. Dean Moriarty. The tri-corner hat was what he'd worn when he gave his speech in the gymnasium back in August—the speech my father enjoyed so much. I watched as he pushed the other guy back with a strength old men don't have. The man almost fell to the ground, then unlocked the dilapidated door I had tried opening. I could hear the creak as it swung open, and both men entered. The workman poked his head out and looked right at me before slamming the door shut behind them. I stared at the sidewalk and increased my speed, making it to the English building in two minutes flat.

I sat through another of Dalton's Probability classes and understood nothing. We went up to his office and through his detailed instructions I learned about half of what I needed. Then our conversation turned toward other matters.

"You look like you've stumbled on some new information since we last spoke," Dalton said from behind his large desk. A stack of ungraded papers teetered on the edge.

"You might say that," I said. "Professor Dalton, I've told you a lot about what I've learned about this campus and you've shared a fair bit of your own history. But what I'm about to tell you must not leave this office. Do you understand?"

Dalton leaned forward. His kind brown eyes gained a seriousness I'd never seen. "Michael, I'll never tell a soul about what you've told me. Do you know what a relief it's been to finally have a student get this place? It's never happened. Half my students either sleep through my class or pretend to pay attention. You actually want to learn what I have to teach! Not once have I ever had a student come to me saying what you have. It's like they turn into zombies once they set foot here. Most of them I never see again. You, I'd love to see again, but I don't see that happening."

I didn't say anything for a moment. "How do you know that?"

"Know what?"

"About . . . my leaving."

"Well, I figured that was your plan. They've never let one of their own go before. You'd be the first."

"That's what Deakin insisted I do."

"Isn't it sound advice?"

"I don't think so. Do you think I'm just gonna pack up and leave, like half the campus has done already? I'm just gonna forget about everything I've seen, and go back to my parents in St. James like everything's okay? They're the ones who sent me here to be . . ." I stopped, not wanting to reveal everything Deakin told me. ". . . who sent me here. No, I've come too far. I'm getting to the bottom of the mysteries behind this place."

"Mike, you need to know what you're getting yourself into."

"I know what I'm getting into, Professor. Better than you."

"What do you know?" Here it was. The remaining unknown. Dalton was a nice, sincere human being, but he wasn't aware like Deakin. I'd continued to keep things from him because, despite his niceties, I didn't want him to get too involved.

"I might as well tell you," I sighed. "But, like I said, it doesn't leave this office."

"Of course."

"All right. So, Professor Deakin knew my father when he attended Malworth in the seventies."

"Your father—"

"It turns out my father was programmed. Just like Justin. Just like everyone else on their list."

"What list? What programming?"

"Just let me finish. My father sent me here not of his own free will, but because he was programmed to do it. My mother either doesn't notice or doesn't care. Either way, they are not on my side. I don't think they ever were."

"What are you saying, Mike?"

"I don't know. To be honest, I haven't spoken with my dad since winter break when he told me he was going on a world cruise. I tried calling him once, but nobody picked up. Now I don't want to call home until I figure out with whom I'd be speaking."

"Good God," Dalton said. "You aren't making this up, are you?"

"Why would I? I know it doesn't make any sense. None of this does. But I need your help now. I need somebody to believe me. I haven't even told you everything. Maybe I'll be able to in time. But for now, I need a confidant. Okay?"

"Okay," he said. "So what can I do for you?"

"Just listen. My father was part of a group of people who all attended Malworth. They all lived in St. James, and they were all friends. They were going to raise their families there. But something happened. What, I'm not sure. But when it happened, everyone moved away. Except my family. I'm hoping Deakin will know so I don't have to ask my father. Whatever happened, the powers behind this place didn't like it. My father, or whoever was controlling him, thought I'd be a shoe-in for Malworth. But because of what happened, there had to be a competition. So each of these families, which had moved all over the state, sent their kids here. And, surprise, we all ended up on the same dormitory floor. The same one my father lived on, I'd wager. Maybe they all did. It was a competition."

"What kind of competition?"

"I don't think we ever had time to actually do it. Two of them got kicked out at the semester break, one got removed from the list, and the other . . ." I wasn't sure what Eric's status was. ". . . he's still here, but doesn't believe any of it. There's something else. There's supposed to be some sort of 'trial' we're meant to go through. I think Justin's administering it. But there was never any question that I would be the one to make it through. It's like they're going through the motions because this is always how somebody's selected."

"Almost as if they know the jig is up, since you understand what's going on," Dalton offered.

"I'm not sure what it is," I said. "But it feels different. I do know one thing. They are not going to let me leave. Not until I play along."

"That's why you need to leave!" Dalton said. "For your own safety."

"I'm not leaving, Professor," I said in a calm voice. "It's too late for that. How would I even get out of here? The cops took my car. I'm pretty sure the police are in on this conspiracy, and I'm sure as hell not going to test that theory by trying to get my car back."

"Damn," Dalton said. "I forgot about that. I don't have a car either. My wife took it when she left."

"So this is where I stand. I need to know I have you standing behind me when things really start to go south. The semester's almost over."

"Of course I will," Dalton said. "I may not be much help, but I'm here for you. I'm always here to listen. And to maybe even teach you a thing or two." He smiled and I could tell he was trying to lighten the mood. It wasn't working with me.

"Yeah, whatever," I said. "I do appreciate your willingness to hear me out. I'm sorry I can't tell you everything, but I hope I'll be able to someday. You've been a good friend."

"Friend?" Dalton said, bemused. "You really think I'm your . . ."

"I do," I said.

"Then can I give you one piece of advice?"

"Sure."

"Why don't you call your parents?"

"What? Are you fucking nuts? Pardon my French, but no way. Not until I find out what's really going on with them and why they sent me here."

"Perhaps you might find out from speaking to them. They don't know all that you've found out here, do they?"

I thought about it. "I'm not sure," I said.

"Well there you go. He may have been brainwashed, but do you think they really are in on what's happening down here? You said they had to do it to him, as if it was against his will."

"That's how Deakin made it sound."

"So, perhaps a part of him is resisting, a part that knows it was wrong to send you here. Maybe you can reach that part."

"I dunno," I said. "It sound risky. What if they are monitoring the phone lines or something?"

"Use my phone," he said. "Or there's another you can use, in town. I don't think they know about it."

"Hm," I said, perplexed. "Maybe you're right. I have to think about it."

"Just not for long," Dalton said. "This might be one clue you've over-looked."

"I used to be so angry at them," I said, looking into his gentle brown eyes.

"Call them," Dalton said. "You might be surprised at what you learn."

"I said I'll think about it." I glanced at the square clock on the wall. "I should go. Don't want to miss tonight's scrumptious dinner. That dining hall is the only thing I will miss about this god-forsaken place."

Dalton barked laughter. "At least you'll always have that. Thanks for stopping by, Mike. And remember: my door's always open."

"Thanks, Professor," I said as I walked out of his office.

I THOUGHT ABOUT WHAT DALTON said on the walk to the dining hall. Him telling me to call my parents, advice any normal college kid would receive, hit me in a weird way. If what Deakin told me about them was true, I never could have known my father as most boys do. It meant my life had been pre-destined by this society, and they thought I didn't have any kind of say in it. As much as I wanted to prove them wrong, I felt helpless to do anything about it. Both my professorial advisers wanted me to leave this place as soon as possible. But they neglected to think about where I would go.

I gorged in a delicious meal of hot dogs and waffle fries in the deserted dining hall. Schuster was silent as usual when I returned through the skywalk. The girls' hallway was devoid of any sound or movement. I recalled how busy this building was when I moved here with my parents. Kids were moving into rooms on all floors, and it looked like a regular college scene. Now it felt like a death sentence. Eric's door was closed tight on our side of the hallway. I couldn't get Dalton's edict out of my head so I sat in the shitty plastic chair in my room and did some reading for Deakin's Western Civ class. It didn't help, so then I tried getting drunk. That didn't help either, but did serve to make me feel worse. The one thing it did was give me a perverse sense of confidence to do what needed to be done. I set the Styrofoam cup on the floor, opened my door, and started toward the fifth floor lobby. I didn't care if someone was listening in on the line; whoever would do such a thing would know more than I did about any of this. The two locks on Justin's door remained shut, and the distinct smell of burned marshmallows lingered a bit as I trundled past his room.

The lobby area was deserted. The crappy old upholstered furniture, which I'd never seen used by any student, remained in the corner by the pay phone. I grabbed the receiver with a shaky hand and placed some change in the slot. I took a large swallow before dialing the number, and made a sharp exhale when I finished. The phone rang for an endless amount of time, and it scared me when I heard my father's voice.

"Hello?" he boomed. A sharp pitch of static ran through the word as it transferred over the line. My drunken mind hadn't been prepared for this. "Hello?" he said again.

"Hello, Dad," I mumbled as the receiver shook in my hands.

"Michael?" he said. He sounded confused and a little drunk. Kind of like the other times I had called him. I remembered I still hadn't told him about the DUI at Homecoming. It seemed like a quaint concern now.

"It's me, Dad," I said. "Your son."

"I know who you are. Long time no calling, son."

"I know. I was kind of mad after you said you didn't want to see me at Christmas."

"That's not quite what happened, if I recall. It's not that we didn't want to see you, we just had this great opportunity to—"

"Yeah, yeah, see the world. When you only get to see your son once a year." I heard the anger creep into my voice but couldn't do anything to stop it. Getting drunk before making this call was a mistake.

"Mike, I'm sorry if you felt like we were abandoning you—"

"Abandoning me?" The way he put it enraged me. "You wanna talk about abandoning people? How about what you did to me? Left me here with a bunch of psychos you knew wouldn't take care of me. Left me to be molded in this place's image while you gallivanted around the globe with Mom. If that's even what you did."

"I don't know what you're talking about," he said. His voice sounded small over the line, like it was a million miles away.

"Yeah, I know you don't," I said. "They did the same thing to you."

"The same thing . . . what are you . . . talking about . . ." Static clicked through each few words and I thought I had lost the connection. "And you'll learn to love it too, Mr. Sinclair." It was my father's voice, but as if he'd dropped three octaves and smoked a pack of cigarettes a day his entire life. I pulled the receiver away in shock as I heard him speak. My father had never once called me "Mr. Sinclair," a title he reserved for himself.

"What are you saying?" was all I could muster.

"You know exactly what I'm saying," came the voice. I heard a glass clink over the line, just like old times. The gurgles of him swallowing some liquor came over loud and clear. "You will learn to love it, just as your father did. Just as his father did. And just as Montgomery Sinclair did when he helped old Ed Whitacre found this place. Back when sons respected their fathers, and authority. Your generation makes me sick. Makes me glad we're almost through with this whole nutty order, in fact."

As he spoke his voice morphed even lower, then regained his pitch. It scared the hell out of me. Then it was back to his normal voice, albeit permeated with static every few seconds.

"All I wanted was for them to shape you into the man I knew you'd be-come." He sounded desperate, as if he was speaking for himself now. "I had no idea they'd had this plan in motion for decades. That they'd roped in the other families . . ."

"You knew about that?" I roared over the line.

"Yes, but only when it was too late to do anything. I'm so sorry. I had no idea they were planning all of this. All I knew is that they'd secured you a nice, normal roommate who had nothing to do with the society. I had no idea Gordon, Baines, Fulton, and Jackson's kin were involved, I swear."

My Jack Daniels-addled mind wasn't quite ready for these revelations, but I knew I had to keep pushing. This might be the last time I ever spoke to my father. "What happened back in St. James that split the families?"

Silence on the other end. I thought I'd lost him, but then he said, "It was an accident. I swear, it was an accident."

"What was?" I strained.

"The Jackson girl . . . she knew she wasn't to go in our garage. She knew I was busy in there working on a project. I told her idiotic parents that they needed to keep her away. But they never listened."

"What happened?"

"I told them to keep her away . . . but they didn't listen, Mr. Sinclair." The low, menacing voice was back on the line.

"Who are you?" I shouted. I gazed around the lobby to make sure no other kids were nearby to see this insane exchange. I don't know why; the entire building was a ghost town.

"I'm your father," the voice said. It was as if somebody a thousand years old had inhabited him. Traces of his gruff voice remained on the edges, and I could hear the ice clink in his glass every once in a while. "Don't you know me? I know you do. What happened to the Jackson girl was no accident. But it had to look like one. Fortunately St. James was imbued with society members from the get-go. It was our second home, you see. People were asking too many questions up in Cold River, so we needed another place to send our wonderful society graduates. But we put too many there. Something had to happen to scatter the herd, so to speak. And Officer Brady was ever so kind enough to obscure the investigation enough with the local cops to make it look like an accident. You remember Brady, right?"

"He . . . he did what . . . ?" I said, my voice meek and afraid. This meant he knew about the DUI in October. More to the point, it meant Brady was connected to all of this, too.

"Son, you have to believe me, it was an accident . . ." my father's voice came through again. It sounded like he was trying to force his way through.

"I don't know what to believe," I said. "Were you ever my father?"

"Yes, of course I was," he said. Every word sounded like a struggle over the frail telephone connection. "I always was."

"Not according to what I've learned," I said. "From what I've gathered, you were never my father to begin with. Not after you left this place."

"Who in blazes gave you that codswallop?" came the debased voice, darker than ever. The static went away every time it spoke. "It was that old fool Deakin, wasn't it?"

I didn't want to implicate Deakin. "No, I found it out . . . at the library." I hoped my reference to the one building my father always asked me about would save my bacon. The voice didn't say anything for a few seconds.

"At the library, eh?" Then, in my father's voice, "We used to pull such pranks there, especially on the fourth floor. Have you been to the library yet, son?"

"Dad, you ask me that every time. Why?"

"Because, it's the center of all knowledge," he said. "The center of all knowledge."

"I don't know what you mean," I implored. "What about the library?"

"Don't mind him," said the voice. "All the memories I had before the programming remain there, in a static state. It's like they never happened, but also like they keep occurring. A delightful little side-effect. You probably saw it in that buffoon of a caretaker they brought in, too."

"You mean Justin?" I said.

"Yeah, whatever the cretin's name is this time around. Poor fool's got so many disparate memories by now that he doesn't know what to do with 'em. Best to put him out of his misery after you get this sorted out. You'll be a good boy and do that for me, won't you, Mr. Sinclair?"

"I'm not Mr. Sinclair. I'm your son!" I wailed. "Dad, you have to be in there somewhere."

"I am," came the voice. "I always am. Don't you see, the programming doesn't just override the consciousness, it melds the spirit. But what am I saying? You'll understand in due course. Moriarty might be a musty old stooge but he knows the ancient ways. The only one who does anymore, I'm afraid."

"So the person I knew as my father . . . is gone?"

"Afraid so, old chap. But don't worry, I'll always be here for you. You're our last hope, don't you see? The world is moving beyond secret societies, skull-and-bones-type nonsense. We have to keep up with the times. And that means a new generation, a new university. You'll be the first to plant the seeds, my young master. This place is old bones; it's for the dogs. It deserves to fall to the ground. This is where I disagree with the old fool Moriarty, you see. He wanted to keep things going the same, always in darkness until the end. That's nonsense. It was a wonder he ever went along with the St. James idea. But that was a mistake. I see that now."

"You said . . . the Jackson girl had an accident, but it wasn't an accident."

"Not that bimbo daughter there with you, if that's who you mean," the voice continued. It sounded more like my father now than ever, as if it was melding with him at last. "Naw, she was put into consideration because of her last name. The second attempt by her family, if you will. The first one didn't end so well, if you get my drift."

"What happened?" I cried. "Did you . . ."

"It makes no difference now, does it? It served the purpose. Got them all to vacate, so I had you alone to work on until we were ready to send you to Malworth. I thought I'd gotten away with it, too. No questions were asked, no formal inquiries. But right after we let you know where you'd be attending college, I got the word you wouldn't be alone after all, that those other fools' progeny would be right there with you. Thank God that care-taker's predecessor was such a brutish fellow. Really lent yours a touch of malice. He still comes out at night. Goes out and smokes in the dead of night, like he's still alive or something. Don't know why he lets him do it."

My stomach droped into my feet. The hooded figure, the one Justin was watching that night in the first floor lobby. His predecessor.

"But this is all redundant. You'll understand soon enough. Just have to make it through the 'trials,' or whatever they're calling it these days. I'm sure you'll do well, Mr. Sinclair. You're my son, after all."

I felt the air seep out of my lungs and couldn't breathe.

"Good luck, Mr. Sinclair. The society's counting on you," said the voice. And then, in my father's normal tone, "I . . . love you, son . . ." I heard the click of the line, punctuated by one final burst of noisy static. I watched as the inky black phone receiver slipped from my hand, swung from the cord, back and forth, back and forth. My mind was exploding, as the alcohol struggled to deal with what I had just learned. I stood there for a full minute, exhausted, aghast.

"Good conversation?" came another voice from behind me. I felt my entire skin crawl. I turned, my legs feeling like they were trapped in mo-lasses. Justin had on the same "Malworth" T-shirt he always wore. The two pits of fire in his eyes seemed to glow in the sparse light of the lobby.

"Fuck you," I spat. It felt appropriate for the moment.

"My, my. Such a tone," he said, smiling. "You'll do better to restrain that if you have any hope of making it through the trials."

"Fuck your trials, you piece of shit," I said. I wanted to run at him but my legs wouldn't obey.

"Fine, have it your way," he said. "I'd hate for Mr. Fulton to come out on top, simply by default. The order wouldn't like it that way."

I glowered at him. When he realized I wasn't going to say anything else, he turned and headed back to his room. "See you soon," he said as he pushed through the door to the study lounge. I stood in the lobby, feeling more alone than I ever had in my life. The phone receiver still hung from its plastic cord, dangling in a two-inch radius. I forced my feet to walk down the hall to Sarah's room. I watched my hand raise up and knock on the wooden door. Her brilliant eyes flashed something awake in me. I knew in my heart now that she was who I was fighting for.

"Mike!" she exclaimed. "What are you doing here?"

"Being a lecherous weirdo, maybe?" came Sidarthi's voice.

"Do you mind?" Sarah said, an edge to her voice. Sidarthi sighed loudly and exited in a huff. "Sorry about her, as always," Sarah said.

"Don't worry about it," I said. "I need to tell you something." I glanced down both sides of the hallway before entering. I made sure she locked her door before sitting on the pink padded futon.

"Is it about the weird building up in the northeast? Because I found out—"

"No, it's not," I cut her off. "It's about my father."

Her dazzling smile faded, replaced by a look of sheer angst. "What about him? You didn't—"

"Call him?" I finished. "Yeah, I did. At first I was wary. But you should've heard his voice. If it even was his. I don't know who I was talking to."

"What do you mean, his voice?" Sarah asked, rubbing my shoulder with a gentle palm.

"I mean . . . it sounded like him, but it didn't. It was the programming. Just like when Justin appears to be a normal human being once in a while. It breaks through. They can't control it all the time."

"What do you . . . what are you saying? What programming?"

"I'm saying my father, however much there ever was of him, no longer exists. He may never have. The person I thought I knew growing up wasn't my father. Moriarty somehow programmed him before I was even born."

"Jesus, Mike. Are you serious?"

"Do I look like I'm serious? I'm sorry . . . I don't mean to snap. It's just . . . it explains a lot, in some ways. Why he never seemed to listen to me, why he and my mother always pressed their interests ahead of mine, why they forced me to come here. But there's more."

"What do you mean, more?"

"It has to do with you, Sarah. Well, your family."

"What has to do with my family?"

"Remember what I said Deakin told me? About St. James?"

"Yeah," she said, gazing down. The tips of her fingers shook as she spoke. "That we all could've grown up friends, all of us. If we hadn't left . . ."

"I found out why your family and the rest of them left. Did your parents ever mention having any kids before you?"

"No," Sarah said, leaning back into the couch. "I mean . . . never mind."

"What is it, Sarah?" I asked, taking her hand in mine. She didn't speak for a moment, but stared straight ahead as if accessing a deep memory.

"It's just . . . I remember seeing pictures in an old scrapbook with my Mom. There was a girl that looked just like me. I asked her who she was. I'd never seen my mother turn that shade of white. She said it was nobody, a distant cousin or something. I never saw that scrapbook again."

"Oh," I said. I had to approach the subject, but hearing this made me reconsider.

"Oh, what?" she implored.

"Look . . . what my father told me—"

"What did he tell you, Mike? You can't back out now!"

"He said there was some sort of accident. It had to do with the child your parents had before you. Something happened in our garage, something my father did."

"What are you saying, Mike?"

"That's all he'd tell me. But whatever happened, it was the incident that drove the other families away. And you know what the sickest part is? My father said he meant for it to happen."

"What? This can't be. I never had a sister, Mike. My parents would have told me."

"Yeah? Well my parents didn't tell me they were sending me to the same fucking institution where my father was brainwashed. There could be some things they didn't tell you."

Sarah began to cry. It started as sobs, but then turned into a full-blown wail. I knew I shouldn't have said it, but I was angry. Angry at my father. Angry at the society. Angry at myself for continuing to be a pawn in this horrid game. "Please, don't cry," I mumbled. This served to make things worse. I felt responsible, so I leaned over and let her tears soak through my shirt. When she finished she blew her nose and wiped her eyes. I saw pain hidden in those green eyes I'd never seen before.

"I think I knew," she said, blowing her nose again. "I'm sorry. I think I covered it up in my heart. There were other signals, stuff I never picked up on at the time. My parents . . . they were always somber on this one day in August. They never told me why. I remember when I was really little . . . stumbling upon them in the kitchen. They had a small piece of cake between them with a single candle. My mother blew it out and hid the piece before I could start asking questions. They must have told me some other fib then, too. Good God, Mike. What's going on?"

As much as I wanted to deny what my father told me over the phone, this seemed to seal it. That voice was telling me the truth, or as much as he thought I could handle. Whatever happened between Sarah's family and mine a generation ago, it led to us both attending this school at this time.

"What else did he tell you?" Sarah said, her voice meek.

"He also mentioned some kind of 'trial' that Justin is going to put us through."

"Oh, who cares, Mike?" Sarah said. "The list, the society, our parents. All of it! It's meaningless, a way to control people! We have to get to the bottom of this before it's too late."

"There's one other thing," I said. "My father . . . he said the society needed to move beyond this place. He made it sound like they were prepping me to be programmed and moved to another school. I think they're planning a takeover."

"My God," Sarah said. "No wonder there are never any students here. They can't sustain it any more. They need fresh blood, and more kids."

"Some place like the University of Minnesota," I said. "That's where I wanted to go originally. I guess I had to be 'in the know,' first, huh?"

"Don't even joke about it," Sarah said. Her eyes were dry but the residue of tears glistened at the edges. "We have to stop them."

"I know," I said. "I'm working on it. But we have to find the right time to strike. I need to figure out what these 'trials' are going to be, what they'll entail. Maybe there's a way to use them to our advantage."

"Maybe," Sarah said, sniffling. She blew her nose a final time and leaned into me.

"The way it sounds, the competition among the families was set up to be a farce from the beginning. They always wanted me. It's my family that lies at the root of this awful tree."

"I'm so sorry, Mike . . ." she said in a faint voice. "So sorry about everything . . ."

We sat on the futon together as I stroked her hair and listened to her breathe. Sarah held me tight until she fell asleep in my arms.

AFTER THAT NIGHT I YEARNED for the monotony of first semester, when my biggest worry was making it to class on time and passing the finals. The necessity of attending class paled before the task ahead of me, the little of it I understood. I made it to Deakin's class every Monday, Wednesday, and Friday, but Eric and I didn't sit together and the old prof didn't ask me up for tea in his office any longer. Each day after class he'd whisper something in my direction about needing to leave campus. I was batting .500 when it came to attending Ellickson's English class and the boring Wellness lecture in the same building. These things didn't seem a priority to me any longer. Professor Langdon retained her cheer when I made it to her biology room once in a while. The urge to ask her what she knew about this creepy campus was harder to put down each time I saw her dour yet smiling face at the end of class. This hit a breaking point at the end of March, when she said something I knew was meant for me.

"Good work today, class, make sure you file your lab reports nice and neat up front," she clamored as we all filtered toward the door. "Good luck in the trials, Mr. Sinclair," she said as I caught her eye.

"Good luck with what?" I said, eying her with suspicion.

"I didn't say anything," she said, looking much younger with her hair upright and stuck behind her head. "But good luck."

"You know about this stuff?" I questioned, getting shoved around by the few remaining students as they dropped off their reports.

"You'd best be going, Mr. Sinclair," she said. You don't have much time." The odd kindness in her eyes masked a deep fear trembling below the surface of the corneas. "Not much time . . ."

Dalton was still a receptive audience, though I didn't feel comfortable unloading everything on him. As we headed up to his office that same week to discuss eight-sided die and their relation to the stock market, I considered what to tell him about my father. We spent twenty minutes discussing the subject before he broke his silence.

"So, you call your father yet?" he asked.

I studied the gray streaks that now encompassed most of his beard before I spoke. "I did."

"And?"

"And, it turns out it's much worse than we thought." I filled him in on the gist of the conversation. Dalton sat there stunned when I finished.

"Damn," he said, stroking the silver beard. It gave him an avuncular appearance he didn't have when I met him in the fall. "So your father is one of them."

"It appears so," I said. "You should've heard his voice. It was him, but it wasn't."

"I think I know what you mean," he said. "I heard Moriarty's voice do the same thing when he sat me down in the office that time. It was like I was talking to him, but also to somebody else. It was terrifying."

"Perhaps some one is controlling him, too?"

"Possibly," Dalton said. "I thought you said he was the real 'bad guy' in all of this."

"That's the assumption," I said. "But I have no idea. I can't trust anyone, to be honest. Not even Professor Deakin."

"I get that," Dalton said. "I still have your back though, right?"

"Of course," I said. "You don't know enough to be dangerous. No offense."

He gave me a warm smile. "None taken. So, what are you going to do with this information?"

"Besides try not to let it scare the hell out of me? Not sure. It's just another piece to the puzzle. Another key for the wall of doors."

"Another what?"

"Never mind," I said. "It fills in a lot of the gaps about why they sent me here, and what happened among the families in St. James. There's one more thing. You ever hear about something called the 'trials?'"

Dalton leaned back in his chair. "Trials? I take it you're not referring to finals week."

"Not quite," I said. "Some kind of competition Justin is putting us through. I have no idea what it could be. The last time I spoke to that asshat he said he'd see me in April. That's a few days away."

"Indeed," he said, scratching his beard in a contemplative way. "Probably a challenge to prove you have what it takes to carry out their orders."

"Grand prize is having your mind erased," I said. "I could've accomplished that up on the hill."

Dalton laughed, a hearty sound in the miniscule office. "You sure could. I'm glad you're keeping a bit of perspective here. Not that it's easy, I'd wager."

"Not really," I said. "I wanted to see if you knew anything."

"I'm afraid I'm not the source when it comes to that kind of thing."

"I know. But Deakin's not talking anymore. He keeps telling me to leave."

"For the record, I agree with that assertion," Dalton said. "But I know that's not an option for either of us. So I'll do what I can to help you."

"Thank you," I said, looking up at the clock. "Well, it's dining hall time again. Is there some way I can train my brain just to remember the excellent food this place features?"

"I don't think so," Dalton said. "Good luck with whatever comes next."

"Uh, thanks," I said, unsure of what to say now that two instructors had given me the same encouragement. "I'll do my best. Let's meet up again next week, if I'm still around."

"I think you will be," Dalton said. "You've made it this far."

"Yeah, thanks," I said as I walked out the door. I would find out how far I had to go in a week's time.

I RETURNED TO SCHUSTER HALL on the first Friday in April after failing a pop quiz in the Wellness class. I opened the door to my room and threw down my back pack. The weather had warmed so I didn't even need a coat walking around campus. The regenerated sunlight I'd missed so much in winter came through the window with a vengeance, spotlighting a letter that sat on the edge of the desk. My full name was written on the front of the worn envelope. I was struck by the frailty of the paper, as if it was about to crumble in my hands. I tore it open it with a single finger, shook out the missive inside, and began to read.

> Dear Mr. Sinclair,
> Your presence is requested in the lobby on the fifth floor of Schuster Hall this Friday, April 5th, at 7:00 p.m. Attendance at this event is mandatory for all invitees. Please do not be late. The society thanks you.
> Sincerely,
> Dean Moriarty

The old man's signature lay below the ancient type. The "H" in Henry was scrawled so large as to resemble a suspension bridge, and the "M" contained menacing grand spikes. I glanced at the small clock on the other desk that jutted out of the wall. It was five o'clock.

An hour later I heard Eric open the door across from mine, then close it. I heard him yell some profanity from within and open the door. Seconds later there came a knock at mine.

"Sinclair, you in there?"

"What do you care?" I said, sitting alone in the red plastic chair.

"Because . . . there was this weird letter on my desk in here. And I know I locked my door when I left this morning."

"You think locks will stop them . . . ?" I said, trailing off.

"What'd you say? I can't hear you. Let me the fuck in here," came his anguished reply.

I stood up and unlocked my door. Eric pushed the door open to reveal his entire frazzled, bearded face. He'd gained another few pounds since I last talked to him, and his beard was encroaching on "out of control" territory. He held a similar letter to mine in his right hand.

"This is what I'm talking about," he said, waving it around his head. The corner of the envelope was reflected in the lens of his glasses.

"Yeah. I got one too," I said in a flat tone. "The trial begins at seven."

"The what?"

"You heard me," I said, my eyes not meeting his quite yet.

"I did, but couldn't believe it. Does this have to do with your nutty conspiracy theories about this place again?"

I laughed. "You still think it's a conspiracy. You never could deal with being wrong, could you?"

"What are you saying, Sinclair? Make sense, Goddammit. Who put this in my room? Was it you?"

"Yeah, I found the key and put in a creepy letter from the dean."

He didn't say anything for a moment. "Okay, it couldn't have been you. Justin, maybe?"

"I thought you weren't afraid of him?"

"I'm not, just . . . he creeps me the fuck out. But who would have access to our rooms?"

"I'm not sure," I said. "But he doesn't need access. Not when he's got Moriarty on his side."

"What does that mean?" Eric said. He was starting to get agitated.

"I tried to tell you," I said. "I tried to warn you about what was going on here."

"The hell you did," he said. "What's going on here? You've been weird as shit since the winter break."

"I told you. You wouldn't believe me. After tonight you will."

"Whatever, man. I'm going back to my room. If Justin or whoever wants to talk to me, they know where to find me. Good night." He turned and fumed back to his room, slamming the door behind him. I left mine sitting open. A half-hour later Sarah stood in the door frame, looking at me. She had another letter in her hand.

"What is this?" she asked, her eyes darting to the letter on my desk.

"I got one too," I said. "So did Eric. They're our invitations to the trial."

"Wait, what?" she said. "That's a real thing?"

"I guess so," I said. "You should consider yourself lucky. Justin took you off the list but still invited you."

"Justin? Mine was signed by Dean freakin' Moriarity."

"Mine too," I said. "Same person, probably."

"They are not the same person, Michael."

"How do we know? How do we know this whole place isn't some kind of grand illusion placed in our brains when we arrived here? How do I even know you're real?"

"Mike, stop it. You're scaring me."

"Join the club."

"I'm serious!"

"Me too."

"Look, I came down here to see what you made of all of this. What happens when Justin shows up at seven?"

"Oh, I'll make sure I meet that asshole right in the lobby," I said.

"Then let's go down there and face this together."

"Fine by me," I said, standing up and grasping her hand.

I didn't hear Eric's door open as we walked. Justin's room was closed, too. The burnt smell wasn't as strong when we passed, but I could still detect a trace in the air. We pushed through the purple door, past the study lounge, still empty of furniture, and into the main lobby. The pay phone I'd used sat in the corner, a reminder of all I had learned in my final days at this college. The lobby was silent as the rest of the building, and the lights were dimmed. We sat on the hideous art deco chairs and waited. Five minutes later a figure appeared at the far end of the lobby. He wore a long hooded robe like monks wore in monasteries. He held a single lit candle in his hands and it swayed back and forth as he walked. He had about the same height and build as Justin, but I couldn't be sure it was him until he spoke as the dark hood obscured his face.

"Welcome to the first trial," the figure said. It was Justin all right, but didn't seem like him. For one thing, he moved very deliberately. Also the timbre of his voice sounded off, like my father's did over the telephone line.

"Justin?" Sarah said. "What is going on here?"

"Ah, Ms. Jackson. So glad you could join us tonight, despite your unfortunate removal from my list. I'll have you know if you put in a good performance tonight you may see your chances at making the society improve."

Sarah looked at me. I had nothing to say.

"And you, Mr. Sinclair," the Justin-voice said. "As lead contender, I trust you know the stakes here. Now where is Mr. Fulton?"

"Didn't you know?" I said. "He doesn't believe in any of this. He thinks it's all some kind of grand conspiracy I made up. It's not real to him."

"I'm quite aware, Mr. Sinclair," the Justin-voice said. "I am gathering him as we speak."

A loud noise occurred down the hallway. It was muffled by the distance and the doors, but Sarah and I both heard it. It reminded me of the noise I heard the day after Seth and Adam put the furniture in front of Justin's door. A minute later the door to the study lounge blasted open, and Eric walked through. He wasn't walking of his own volition. The way his legs thrust forward and back it looked like something was controlling his body. The shock and fear I saw in the eyes behind his glasses confirmed it: he was not doing this on his own. He shifted forward in an awkward dance until he was forced to sit down on the repulsive small couch next to us. He moved his mouth to utter a few choice curse words, but nothing came out.

"Now that we're all here, I can explain the rules," the figure said. "This is a strict competition among the three of you, representatives of each of your families. There's to be no assistance given to anyone, and no interference.

Each has the same objective. Whoever completes the task will be a contender for the next trial. Whoever does not . . ." he waved one robed hand around, ". . . well, we won't worry about that until it's finished."

"What are we supposed to be doing?" Sarah cried. Terror danced around her green eyes as she spoke.

"Ah, I'm so glad you asked, Ms. Jackson," the voice said. "Your first trial is quite simple." He held up a series of photographs for us to view. "You'll recall this little whore as an attendant on the female side of this dormitory." The picture was of Amanda, tied up with rope to one of the plastic dormitory chairs. A gauze was strapped to her mouth and tears streaked down her face. Her eyes screamed more than her voice ever could, and I could only imagine how long he'd had her like this.

"Amanda!" Sarah yelled.

"Yes, whatever her name was," Justin said, sounding like his old self for a moment. "I had her pegged from the moment she arrived here. A slut, just like her mother. Bad manners like her father. We know how to deal with these types around here, don't we Mr. Sinclair?"

Sarah glanced at me, her eyes questioning. It wasn't the right time to mention what Deakin had told me about the girl's parents. I remained silent.

"I know you do," Justin continued. "I placed the whore in one of the dormitories within this grand edifice. It's up to one of you to locate her within the allotted time." He held out three musty and tarnished keys that looked like those we had for our own rooms. "Here are three copies of the exact key that opens the room in which she resides." He threw each key at us. Sarah and I caught ours; Eric's just bounced off his chest.

"Now now, Mr. Fulton," Justin said. His voice had morphed back into the lower one. "You must do things of your own volition. Otherwise this won't be any fun." He flicked his fingers together and Eric leaned forward, writhing in pain. He reached out and grabbed the ancient key from the floor.

"Suck my cock," he managed to whisper between his lips before they were forced shut.

"Now then, the time limit." Justin sat the candle down on the coffee table in front of our legs. "You'll have one half-hour to locate the whore.

If you don't locate her within the time frame, the room she's in won't be conducive for human life much longer. Unfortunately, this doesn't leave you enough time to try every single door. Society members must possess the ability to weigh human life in such a discrete manner. The life of one doesn't always balance out that of another. But I'm sure you'll all figure it out." I watched as a bead of wax dripped off the candle and formed a small circular pebble on the wood paneling.

"You may begin," the Justin-voice said. He turned and headed back toward the door to the study lounge and was gone before any of us could speak.

Panic seized my lungs and I couldn't breath. I'd never seen Eric's face contorted with such fear.

"It's all right, Eric," I said, as if I knew how to comfort him in this bizarre situation. "We just have to make it through this, and then we can figure out a way to go home. I tried telling you—"

"Tried telling me what?" Eric spat. It seemed he had his voice back. "That Justin is a fucking homicidal maniac? That he fucking kidnaps people? No, you didn't tell me that!" he yelled. He stood up and started pacing, once again in control of his own movements. "You're right, though. You did try telling me. And Homecoming night. . . I saw what you saw, I just didn't want to believe it. I couldn't. But this . . . this is something new. Something dangerous. And I don't know why, but I feel like it's your fault."

"What?" I said in anger. "How is this my fault?" Even as I said this I felt a pang of guilt, knowing what I did about St. James. I promised myself if we got out of this alive I would tell him everything.

"As much fun as the masculine posing is, might I remind you there's a girl trapped in here we're supposed to find?" Sarah said in exasperation.

"How do we even know he's telling the truth?" Eric said. "That picture could've been when they were doing some crazy S&M shit, or something."

"I think he's telling the truth, Eric," I said.

"This is fucking insane!" Eric cried. "That's it. I'm going back to my room and calling my parents. Then the police. Enough is enough!" He stomped through the door. I waited another minute to see if he would be brought back by Justin's power, but he wasn't.

"Well, looks like it's just you and me," I said to Sarah. The fear I'd seen around her eyes was replaced by sheer determination.

"We've got our work cut out for us," she said. "If that douche won't come with us, we need to hustle." She glanced at the candle. "Not much time. How are we gonna do this?"

"Uh . . . I'm not sure. How about we each take two floors, then meet up and go through this one, just to be safe?"

"Sounds good," Sarah said. "I'll take one and two. You do three and four."

"All right," I said. "Meet back here in a half-hour, unless we've found her."

"Let's do it," Sarah said.

We headed to the stairwell, which was more silent than ever. I considered my time spent walking through the various hallways of this building, trying to find anyone else who lived there. We split up at the third floor. I broke through the pneumatic door and stared down the bleak hallway. It appeared as if it had been unused in years, worse than when I walked through here in the winter. There were no pieces of paper stuck to any doors, no cork boards listing schedules, no posters, no anything. I struggled to pull the grimy key Justin had given me out of my pocket, and started testing doors. I had no luck until I got halfway down. The room that would have corresponded to Seth and Adam's on our floor seemed to give a little, but not enough to open. I continued on down the hallway. None of the other doors opened, so I headed through the study lounge (this one had furniture, but it was about twice as old) and on to the girls' side of the floor. I ran into similar bad luck on that side, which was just as empty of any personal touches as the men's. I headed through the other pneumatic door and took the stairs. No luck on the fourth floor, either. I got to the end and ran through the lobby to the other side before something struck me. Why would Justin put her in another room? Perhaps he said it could be any room to make us have to check them all. Why wouldn't he just use her room? I stood, indecisive, in the fourth floor lobby. A single light burned in the far corner. A second later I bolted to the stairs and headed up to our floor. My sneakers shrieked on the linoleum stairs as I pounded upwards, sweat pouring from either side of my brow.

I broke through the doorway to the same lobby we'd been in ten minutes ago, now plunged into darkness. Justin wasn't going to make this easy. I remembered I had a mini flashlight in my dorm room, so I sprinted back to my side of the hallway. Eric's room lay open and abandoned when I arrived. I fumbled around my room until I found the damn thing. I dashed back to the lobby, where I almost bowled over Sarah.

"Nothing on floors one and two," she puffed. "You don't suppose he would . . ."

"Put her in her own room? That's what I'm going for," I said between gasps for air. I held up the little cylinder of light. "This ought to help us see what we're doing."

We headed to the girls' side and approached Amanda's room. I pulled out the key and stuck it in the lock. It turned without hesitation, and I shoved open the door. Amanda sat in the same position as the photograph, tied up and immobile.

"Amanda?" Sarah said, shaking her. She didn't respond.

I began to work at the ropes that bound her to the red plastic chair. I wished in vain for a pocket knife. I got one of the strands to loosen a bit, and began pulling. Sarah removed the gauze from her mouth and held her head upward. Her eyes opened wide, scaring both of us, and she let forth with an otherworldly scream.

"No . . . don't . . . it's a trap . . ." was all she got out before the room door slammed shut behind us. I could hear Justin's maniacal laughter behind it. I tried turning the handle but it wouldn't budge.

"Open up, douchebag!" I shouted. "We passed your stupid little test."

"Did you?" came the voice through the laughter. "Think again."

I turned back toward Amanda and watched her tear-stained eyes as they moved to the bottom corner of the room where the heat vent resided. Some type of murky green gas emanated from it.

"What is that?" I asked.

"I told you, it's a . . . trap," Amanda said, struggling to free herself enough to stand. The gas was now pouring over the plush pink futon. "How the hell are we supposed to get out of here?" Sarah cried. She ran over to the window and started pulling. It wouldn't budge. I looked around the room. A large paper weight in the shape of the state of Minnesota resided on the corner of the wooden desk.

"Look out!" I said as I grasped it on one hand. I threw it against the window with all my might. The state of Minnesota flew right through the window, shattering it into a thousand pieces and scattering glass everywhere. The gas began to flow up and out the window. I hung onto the edge of the desk, beginning to feel faint from the gas and my exhaustion. The next thing I knew the door flew open behind me. I turned around to see Justin standing there. He had removed the hood from his monastic outfit and was staring right at me, the two pits of fire that were his eyes blazing in fury. Before I passed out, I saw another ethereal figure standing behind him in a tattered hooded sweatshirt. I couldn't see the face, but I knew who it was.

"Let us go, fuckwad," I slurred, overwhelmed by the situation. My knees began to buckle. "We passed your . . . stupid . . . trial . . ." I fell to my knees. I couldn't see what Sarah or Amanda were doing, but for some reason I didn't care. Then Justin was upon me in the darkness.

I WOKE UP IN A DAZE on the bed in my room. The world around me came into a hazy focus, bringing with it the shattered memory of the previous night. The morning sun shone from the window onto my face, and I raised one hand to shield my eyes from the glare. I swung my legs over the wooden beam of the loft and jumped down to the carpeted floor. I stood there a moment, sunlight splashing all around me, and tried to figure out what the hell happened. I recalled going up to the lobby, remembered meeting someone there . . .

"Eric," I said aloud in my tiny dorm room. As I spoke I whirled and pulled my door open. Eric's door remained open and was empty. I shut my door and jogged past Justin's door at the end of the hall. It was shut tight, both locks engaged. I ran through the lobby and the girls' hallway until I got to Sarah's room. I knocked twice. I heard her voice from within, so I turned the handle.

"Who's there?" came the timid voice from above me. "Mike? Is that you?"

"Yeah, it's me," I said. "Is Sidarthi here?"

"No. And I haven't seen her. Help me get down."

I let her grab onto my shoulder as she jumped down from the loft and held her in my arms as she found her footing. Her thin legs quaked as they found purchase in the carpet.

"Do you remember what happened?" she asked.

"Not really," I said. "It comes in fits and starts. Was that the trial we were supposed to go through?"

"I think so," she said. "I remember some of it. Eric leaving, Justin's weird-ass robe thing, us being too stupid to realize Amanda was in her own room. Then it gets foggy . . ."

"Yeah, I know what you mean. I remember Justin arriving at the end. He could have killed us."

"Yeah, but he didn't," Sarah said. "That must mean he can't touch us while these trials are going on. At least I hope that's what it means."

"Me too," I said. "Any idea how we got back into each of our rooms?"

"Not a clue," she said.

"All right," I said. "Well, I'm glad you're safe. Let's check Amanda's room."

We padded over to the room we'd rescued her in last night. I turned the handle and it opened. The far window still had a hole in it from the paper weight. A slight spring breeze passed through, gliding over our skin. The pink futon had been removed, but the red plastic chair remained overturned on the floor.

"It's like she never even existed . . ." Sarah said. "But there's the hole in the window. So last night really did happen."

"I'm afraid so," I said. Her loft bed was gone, replaced by a thin metal bed frame. The wooden desk was spotless and had not a single girly item anywhere. We closed the door behind us.

"What's going on here, Mike?" Sarah asked.

"I think that's the million dollar question," I said.

"I'm scared," she said. "Scared of what they'll do to us once the school year is over. Scared of what they'll do to us in the next trial. I've never been so terrified, Mike." She leaned into me and began to sob. It was muffled by my T-shirt, but I could feel wetness hit my skin. I'd never seen Sarah so afraid. This entire year she had been the rock I could come to for comfort in trying to understand all this nonsense. Holding her in my arms as she shook from crying, I knew I had to become stronger. Not just for her, but to protect her. She was the only person I had in my corner this entire year.

"There's no way I'm letting anything happen to you," I said, stroking her hair. "I love you." It shocked me as soon as it came out of my mouth, but I meant it. The crying stopped. Sarah rubbed her nose. Her brunette hair fell on either side of her pale face as those emerald eyes stared up into mine.

"You . . . do?" she said.

"Yes, I do," I said, more sure of this than anything I'd faced this year. "You are the only person that matters now. I hope we find Eric and Amanda, but I'm not holding my breath. You and I, we have to stick together. I'm not leaving this place without you."

"I love you, too," Sarah said. "I'm not leaving without you, either."

"I was just thinking now about the one thing we have going for us. That book. None of these bastards knows we have it yet, so let's comb through it to see if we can find anything related to the trials. All right?"

Sarah sniffled one final time and blew her nose on the ragged sweatshirt she wore. "All right," she said. "And, Mike?"

"Yeah?" I said, already starting down the hall to grab the book from my room. She looked very small.

"Thanks," she said, a tiny smile forming on her lips.

WE SPENT THE BETTER PART of the day locked in Sarah's room pouring over the hidden contents of the ancient book. We burned through half the candle trying to read the old script, but found nothing. I snuck out in the afternoon to grab some take-out from the dining hall, but by dinner time I was ready to call it a day.

"Well, this has been a bust," I said, leaning back into the futon. "Lots of information about what they call themselves and why they are so beneficial to this great state. Most of it seems to come from decades ago. You know, something always bothered me about how we found this book. Do you remember? It was propped up, almost like it was meant for us to find it. Do you remember that?"

"Yeah, I do," Sarah said. Her hand shook as she held the candle, wax dripping. "But how could anyone know we'd be the ones who found it?"

"I don't know," I said. "Each time I called my father he mentioned going up to the fourth floor of the library. He said they used to play some kind of prank up there."

Sarah furrowed her brow. "That does seem odd. But I don't know how it's connected."

"Me either," I said, glancing at the clock on her wall. "We need a break from this madness anyways. I'm going to see if Eric's turned up yet. Want to meet up again in an hour?"

"Sure," Sarah said. I left her room and she locked the door. Eric's room was still a single burst of light at the end of the hallway. I turned my head askew a bit to try and see my door, which looked open. My heart began to race, and my muscles tensed. I slow-walked down the rest of the way until I was a few feet from my door. I could hear someone's boots shuffling around behind it. I moved a few cautious steps forward before kicking the door open, only to see Dean Henry Moriarty gaping at me.

"Mr. Sinclair!" he barked. His bearded visage was scrunched together in a weird parody of a wan, wrinkled smile. He wore an assortment of black robes not unlike what he wore the day I saw him by the campanile. "I was wondering when you'd show up. I've been waiting some time to congratulate you."

"Congratulate me?" I said, bemused and terrified.

"For passing the first trial, of course," he said. He winked at me, but used his entire face to create the gesture. Seeing the old man up close I was struck by how frail his body was and the lack of color in his face. He appeared older than time itself. "You did rescue the fair maiden trapped in this dungeon, did you not?"

"Dungeon? What are you talking about?"

"You know what I mean," he said, making the weird wink again. "Or perhaps you don't remember. I'll have to speak with young Jar-, er, I mean Justin about the levels of sedative we're employing in the aftermath. A mere safety precaution, I assure you."

"I remember it. I remember everything this sick university has thrown at me," I said, finding some courage. "I should have known from the beginning. You were telling me about what was to come, weren't you?"

"You catch on quick, my boy," Morarity said. He paced over to the metal window, his slow gait causing his feet to slide along the carpet. "Just like your father."

"What do you know about my father?" My hands tigtened into fists.

"Only that he was a great man. One of the greatest ever to attend this marvelous institution," he said as he stared out the window. "He was our future, you see. Until things ran aground." He turned back to face me, and I was again struck at his pallid countenance.

"So I've heard," I said. "I've found out a lot about this place too, you know." The weird, burned marshmallow smell I'd encountered outside Justin's room now seemed to permeate my entire room.

"From speaking to that old fool Deakin over in Shull Hall? Pshaw," Moriarty chortled. "He knows not of what he speaks. You ought to think better about who you're spending your time with, my boy."

"I don't think that's your concern. Besides, we're getting the hell out of here. And we're letting the world in on this disgusting place you call a university."

Moriarty laughed, a deep barrel-chested sound that had no place within his fragile body. "Are you now? Well, I wish you the best of luck. The society has operated for decades. You think you will do anything to change that? Go ahead." He coughed up a little more of the deep laugh before sweeping beside me. He carried the burned smell with him as he walked, and I felt some kind of transparent pressure pushing me back as he strode out the door. I watched as he shuffled to the left and headed for the purple door. A few seconds later I pushed open the door and gazed down the stairwell. There was no one there. No meandering foot falls, no echoes, nothing.

Chapter

THIRTEEN

ARAH AND I SPENT most of Sunday in her bed, digging through the ancient book for anything useful. We found nothing related to the trials. I couldn't bring myself to tell her about my encounter with Moriarty. I decided to spend Sunday night in my own bed. Eric's room remained open and empty. I feared for his life, but had no idea where to search for him. The back of my mind kept suggesting he was the next object of rescue, but I had to push the thought away.

I felt an obligation to see Deakin one last time. I awoke Monday and headed out for what I thought would be my final trip to Shull Hall. A cool April breeze followed me as I tromped across campus. Monday mornings used to be the busiest; now it seemed as if finals had been moved up and everyone had gone home. I puzzled over this as I approached the giant brick building.

Deakin's classroom was empty. I headed upstairs to his office. At top hallway, I stopped in my tracks. Deakin's office door gaped wide. One of the small filing cabinets he stored under his window jutted halfway out the door jam, its open drawers spilling papers everywhere.

"Professor Deakin?" I called down the hall. "Marvin?" Silence. I expected the room to be a disaster area, but I had no idea how bad it would be. The wide desk Deakin sat behind was turned on its side, its drawers removed. The tiny kettle and stove he'd brewed tea on so many times was destroyed, lying in several pieces on the floor of the office. Inside papers and books lay scattered, the tattered remains of classes taught in the past. I gazed around the office in amazement and horror. I felt a deep shame, thinking my conversations with this man led to his removal. I was about to turn and leave when I noticed something sticking out from the back of an open slot in the desk. It appeared to be an envelope. I reached to the back of the overturned desk and grasped the paper. It was addressed to me. I stuck it in the back pocket of my jeans and got the hell out of the office. I made sure I was clear of the building before ducking into an al-cove near the student union to read the letter.

> *Dear Michael,*
>
> *I don't have much time to write as I fear they are coming for me tonight. I don't know how they found out I was speaking to you, but the revelation will not end well for me. You still have a chance to make good on my plan of escape. Unfortunately there is more to the picture now. I fear in the act of rescuing one of your fellow students you have placed another person in more danger. I believe your colleague Mr. Fulton will be the subject of the final trial. They are going to make you kill him to see if the programming is neces-sary. I don't know how this will happen, or where. All I know is that they are keeping with the traditional schedule for the trials. That is, the first and last Friday in April. You must strive to locate your colleague before it's too late, but never deviate from the primary mission of escape. You must escape this campus, Michael.*
>
> *Give my regards to the scion of Jackson. Thank you.*
>
> *Marvin Deakin*

The paper trembled in my hand as I read it. They were going to try and make me kill Eric? How? I hadn't a brutal bone in my body. I was amazed that even in his disembodied state Deakin still wanted me to leave town. I wished I could get him to grasp how impossible that was going to be. I put the letter in the envelope and stuffed it in the back pocket of my jeans.

I stopped at the student union, a fashion-forward type of building that I avoided most days. I grabbed an overpriced submarine sandwich and read the letter again while I sat in the common area. A gaggle of girls sat at the far corner, laughing every few minutes. I saw a few other students on the periphery. I thought I'd try an experiment. I walked up to the near-est person, an under-dressed kid wearing a large hooded sweatshirt and torn jeans reading a biology textbook. I thought I recognized him from my first semester in Langdon's class. He didn't notice me walk up, so I poked him.

"Hey, what the . . . ?" the kid said. He had wavy blond hair that fell into his eyes and he had to brush away every few seconds. "Who are you?"

"I'm nobody," I said. "But I want to ask you a question. What do you think of this campus?"

"What do I . . . ? I dunno, it's all right. What do you want, anyway?" Quick brush of the hair.

"I mean, what do you really think? Doesn't this place strike you as a little creepy, a little off, somehow?"

"I guess. I mean, the buildings are like a thousand years old. But the teachers are pretty sway. My one teacher lets us do whatever we want every day, and we still get an 'A.' Pretty choice, right?"

I had no idea what he was saying, but I pressed onward. "You mean they don't make you do anything in your classes?"

"Some of 'em do," he said after another swipe of hair. "Like the Coach. Man, he's a real hardass. But most of them are softies. One of 'em stopped coming to class this week. Real old guy over in Shull. Can't remember his name, taught this boring history class I failed last semester."

"I see," I said. "Nothing else around here seems out of the ordinary?"

"Nah, bro," he said. "Now if you're finished with the sixth degree I'd like to get back to my reading."

This kid was an idiot, but at least he was honest. I had a feeling I'd get the same response from the rest of the lackadaisical attendants at the union. Nobody can see the forest when the trees are obscured from view. I headed out of the union and off to the English building.

ELLICKSON WAS CHECKED OUT TODAY as he drifted in and out of his lecture on proper ways to take down footnotes. I tried paying attention, but was too bothered by the zoned-out looks of my fellow classmates. My Creative Writing class had been full of achievers, each striving to be better than the others in the class. This room was full of dullards, some asleep, others staring off into space. It was as if the entire campus was designed to clear the wheat from the chaff. Ellickson let us out with ten minutes left, so I stopped by his desk on my way out of the dim basement chamber.

"Hey, Professor Ellickson," I said.

He looked startled, as if I had broken him out of a trance. "Oh, hello, Michael. Enjoy my lecture today?"

"Yeah, it was great," I said. "Hey, I was wondering if you've noticed something."

"What's that?"

"Does it seem like our class is kinda zoned out today? Like, compared to your Creative Writing class last semester?"

Ellickson peered through his small glasses frames and ran a thin hand over his smooth bald head. "I know what you mean. It becomes so passé to me that I don't even recognize it any more. Have you heard about something called 'the purge?'"

"As a matter of fact, I have. Several people have mentioned it to me. Something about how at semester break people start leeching out of here."

"It's always gone on here, according to my peers. Something happens around that time to cause people to re-think their reason for being here. And everyone who remains, well let's just say you put it diplomatically. They are 'zoned out' for most of their time here. A less kind way of describing them would be 'dopes.'"

"So do you do anything about them?"

"Not really. Most of them do enough to pass with a C, so I just let 'em slide. The rest . . . well maybe college isn't for them."

"I see. Do you think there could be something else at play here?"

"Like what?"

"I'm not sure. Something more devious. Like it's a plan."

"I can't believe that," Ellickson said. "But if it is a plan, it's carried out with ruthless efficiency. These kids get worse every year, and nothing is ever done about it."

"Have you ever brought this to the English department?"

"Naw. I'm too young, and don't have enough years for tenure. That means I don't have any sway. The other faculty never seem to notice anything. Of course, some of them are older than dirt. Uh, please . . . don't mention I said that."

"Don't worry about it," I said. "Well, I just wanted to see what you thought."

"And you don't worry about your grades in my class, if that's what this is about. You're sailing right over the heads of the rest of the dopes."

"Good to know," I said, forcing myself to smile. "Take care, Professor."

I WAS STARTING TO FEEL BAD about keeping my encounter with Moriarty from Sarah. We spent the night together on Wednesday and I bid her adieu in the morning when I headed off to Langdon's class. The professor was back to her usual dreary demeanor so I didn't speak to her after our lab, but went back to the English building. I sat through another hour of impossible-to-solve probability equations and remained at my seat until the other six students filtered out of the room with the high ceilings.

"You look rough," Dalton said when we were alone. His beard was unkempt and he didn't have the greatest smell about him.

"I could say the same for you," I jabbed.

"Yeah, I know. End of the year this always happens. I kinda just forget about my purpose for being here. I suppose you know all about that."

"I suppose I do," I said. "Can we go up to your office?"

"Of course."

We headed up the marble stairwell, our footfalls echoing above us. We reached his office and Dalton threw down his tattered briefcase. Then he flopped down into the chair behind his desk with a loud wheeze.

"Are you sure you're all right?" I asked.

He pitched forward to the desk at attention. "Yes, I assure you I am. Just reflecting over the year. Speaking of which—"

"We'll get to that," I cut him off. "First I want to ask you something."

"Sure," he said, leaning back in his chair, his arms over his small belly.

"How come no other teachers seem to notice anything different?"

"Great question. One I've been seeking for years," Dalton said. "I wish I had a better answer for you. Most of them seem as out of it as the students by the end of the year. I think they put something in the water."

"Really?"

"No, I don't know what it is. It's not like they aren't aware. They just don't seem to particularly care. Hell, even I don't particularly care most years. We still get paid. I don't know how they get the parents of these marks to waste their money on half of an education."

"Me either," I said, gazing out the window. Sunlight poured in over the sheer ledge. "It's not like it isn't noticeable. I ran into maybe five other kids on my way over here today. Five! And your class was the emptiest it's ever been. You're telling me nobody has brought this up before?"

"Well, you see what happens when people ask too many questions," Dalton said. "They nearly ruined my life, made it so I could never leave. I doubt I'm the first person they've ever threatened with that."

"I guess," I said. "It just seems like a lot of willful blindness to me."

"I hear you," Dalton said, scratching his beard. "If you ever find out the answer, be sure to let me know. Now, about the trial—?"

"You're inquisitive today," I said. "You know I nearly fucking died in my own dorm hall?" I felt like we'd reached a point in which I could curse in front of Dalton and he wouldn't care.

His eyes stretched wide and he uttered a choked clutch of air. "You . . . did?"

"Well, it was a close one. Justin had me right where he wanted but did nothing. I think because we completed it."

"What was 'it?' And who else was with you?" Dalton asked.

I gave him the short version of the story, just as I had with various other insanity that occurred within the confines of my dormitory hall. Dalton was silent a long time.

"This really happened?" he muttered.

"Yes!" I said, animated. "Don't you believe me?"

"I do. That's what scares me," he said. "What you endured over the break was one thing. At least you weren't threatened with violence. This is new. I've never heard of one of the trials occurring in such a way—"

"Wait," I said, picking up on what he'd just said. "Last time we spoke you said you had no idea what I was talking about."

Dalton's face burned a nice red shade, and he leaned back in his chair. "All right, you've got me. I have heard of the trials. I just never thought . . . never could have imagined this is what they'd be like. Honestly, I didn't."

This bit of betrayal, small at it was, irked me. I thought Dalton was being honest with me. "What did you think they were?" I cast my line.

"I didn't know," he said. "I just thought it was like a set of challenges. You know, physical, mental, endurance—"

"How about murdering your best friend?" I said, interrupting him.

"What? You can't be serious."

"I am. According to . . ." I was going to let him in on the letter from Deakin, but now I wasn't so sure. ". . . my sources. Apparently I'm supposed to kill Eric. Can you believe that?"

"Not really," Dalton said. "I trust you know what you're talking about."

"I think I do. You should know that by now."

"I do," he said, his eyes not meeting mine.

"Good. It's the final test to see if I need to be programmed. If I go through with it, I guess they assume I'm evil enough to do anything they tell me. And if not . . ."

"I don't want to think about it," he said. "What are you going to do?"

"I don't know," I said. "But for one, I'm not killing anyone. And two, just like Deakin asked, I'm getting the hell off this campus. Even if I am the last one."

"Glad you've got your priorities straight," he said. His eyes resumed their regular shape. "How are you going to escape?"

"That's for me to know," I said. Dalton's little slip about the trials and Deakin's disappearance meant I couldn't trust him.

"I see," Dalton said. "Well, I wish you luck."

"Thanks," I said. "I'm going to need it." I got up to leave. The sunlight had enveloped the edge of the window frame and was now panning across the floor. I split the beam with my leg as I moved away from his desk.

"Is there anything I can do?" Dalton called as I headed out the door.

"Not anymore," I said as I exited.

I GAVE UP GOING TO CLASS. It was a rational decision based on everything that had taken place this year. I figured a passing grade was the least of my worries. Schuster was dead to the world those final days. Eric's room remained open, a horrifying reminder of our night of terror. I didn't see Justin once. The quaint notion of "quiet hours" prevailed, as there was no one to make any noise. I stayed in Sarah's room most days, even if she wasn't there. Sidarthi had disappeared too. Sarah postulated she must have gone home like everyone else.

The week before the last trial, I broke the news to Sarah about my encounter with Moriarty.

"He came to your room? Creepy," she said, her lush eyes gleaming with terror. "What'd you do?"

"Nothing, really," I said. "What could I do?" The ancient book sat on the coffee table. I patted it, and a token puff a dust rose. Just like old times.

As she watched the dust float through the air, Sarah glanced at the floor. "Thanks for telling me. You know, I haven't been entirely honest with you either . . ."

"What do you mean?"

"About the book. Didn't you think it was pretty weird how you found it in the library, open like that?"

"Well, yeah, but I figured someone else must have . . ."

I was interrupted by a loud knock at the door. I jumped a few centimeters off the futon.

"Sidarthi? Is that you?" Sarah asked, a wary pitch to her voice.

"It's me," came the voice. We both knew who it was.

"Fuck off, Justin," I said, newfound courage entering my veins. After what we'd gone through, I just wasn't scared of the asshole anymore.

243

Somehow, I knew he couldn't touch us while we were going through these stupid trials.

"Not the correct response, Mr. Sinclair," came the strange, muffled voice. Sarah's door burst open. The noise sounded like a building falling it was so deafening. Dust rose from either side of the door as it rested on its mangled hinges. "You were saying?" Justin stood in the hazy outline of the doorframe. He was back to wearing his normal college attire: worn out T-shirt and track pants. His fire-pit eyes burned with a seething rage.

"Nothing," Sarah said. She didn't make a move to cover up the book.

Justin's scorched pupils looked downward. "Trying to get answers from old scholars? I'm afraid you won't find much there. Nice try, though."

"What do you want, dickhead?" I yelled, standing up. I could feel a slight pressure coming off his body, forcing me back like a magnet.

"It's more what you should want," came the eery voice. "Your academics are in a sorry state. Shouldn't have taken such a long respite from your classes, Mr. Sinclair. Didn't your father warn you about this?"

"You leave my father out of it," I said. "Besides, I didn't see the point. Now that you've put us aboard the crazy train with these stupid exercises."

"A miscalculation," came the voice. "For your scholastic achievements in this space constitute the second trial. And I'm afraid both of your performances this semester were dismal."

"Who gives a shit?" Sarah said from behind me. A disturbing sensation of wind somehow was blowing her hair backward.

"You should, as my last remaining competitors," Justin said. "You're quite lucky Mr. Fulton bowed out when he did. His grades were much more exemplary than yours."

"I don't give a shit," I said, trying to walk forward but finding I could not. "I don't care about any of this."

"You should. That's one trial passed . . . one failed. You could have saved yourself such agony had you attended your classes. What do you think we're doing here at the esteemed Malworth University but turning out tomorrow's leaders? You felt you had all the intelligence necessary to continue on this journey? Why do you think your father even sent you here in the first place?"

"To fucking brainwash us!" I screamed in anguish, leaping forward. I was able to break through the force field, and my hand found Justin's throat. I grabbed hold with all my might, trying to wrestle my hand all the way around his neck. Justin shrieked, his screams piercing my ear drums. He fell back through the broken frame. His neck felt like a wretched slab of sand paper, and I was forced to let go. The force field came back with a vengeance. I was thrown into Sarah. We both collapsed to the carpet beneath her loft. Justin's wail filled the entire space around us, and I held my hands over my ears. It began to die down and was replaced by the weird voice. "H-haaave it . . . your way, mortals . . . but be warned, the final trial is one of unimaginable pain and endurance. One of you . . . shall not survive. The other . . . shall join usss . . . in the Malworthe society forever . . ."

There was a strong flash of light from out in the hallway accompanied by a roar of strange power. Then all was quiet, just as the entire building had been for most of the semester. I looked over at Sarah, her head resting on the floor.

"I think we scared him," I said. I leaned my head against the concrete wall and lost consciousness.

SARAH STAYED IN MY ROOM the rest of the week since hers no longer had a door. She decided she wasn't going to let Justin's psychotic antics deter her from going to class, so she left me alone most days. I couldn't believe her courage. In the morning I'd tumble out of my loft around ten o'clock. By noon I'd creep over to the dining hall to bring something back to eat. The place had matched the creep factor of the rest of the campus by this point, staffed by a skeleton crew of ne'r do wells who were lifers at this institution. The jovial women who used to staff each area were gone, and the entire building seemed to be running on about half power. It was an eery sight, but I had to get food ingested somehow.

I awoke the morning of the trial with Sarah's arm around my chest. The first brilliant rays of sunlight poked through the metal window and stabbed my eye sockets with their radiance. I lay like that for another hour before Sarah began to stir. I pretended to wake up at the same time.

"Morning," I said, staring into those gorgeous green eyes. They were like two pools of liquid emerald bubbling to life. "Ready to face our destiny?"

"Morning yourself," she said, rubbing her eyes. "And no."

We brushed our teeth in the hall bathroom and came back to get changed.

"I have to go take care of something for tonight," Sarah said, putting on a slim pair of jeans from the collection she'd brought to my room.

"You what?" I asked.

"It's nothing major. Something I think will help us."

"What is it?"

"You'll find out, trust me."

"Trust is in short supply around here, Sarah."

"I know," she said, reaching out and caressing my arm. "But it exists between us. There is no one on this campus I trust more than you, Mike."

"That's how I feel toward you. I need to ask you something else. You were about to tell me you weren't being honest with me right before Justin was nice enough to implode your door. What was it?"

A brief twitch shot through the right side of her face, causing her smile to fleck downward into a frown for a half-second. She ran a single hand through my bushy hair. "You'll find out," she said again. "But right now you need to trust me."

And with that she walked out the door and down the linoleum steps. I listened to the soft footfalls of her tennis shoes until I couldn't hear them anymore. I sat in the red plastic chair for twenty minutes, going over my life and what I had accomplished so far. It didn't seem fair that it would be over after such a brief time on this planet. The feeling of hopelessness I had managed to keep at bay for weeks was now peeking through the outer defenses of my soul, ready to strike. Another thought hit me in this moment, so I got up from the chair and headed down the hallway to the lobby. I picked up the scuffed receiver on the pay phone and inserted my last bit of change. I dialed the number for the dormitories at St. Cloud University. When they picked up, I asked for Ben Mosey. It took some doing, but they ended up locating him and putting him on the line. When I first heard his voice, charred by years of smoking, I felt a relief I'd not known in months.

"Well, what the fuck, Sinclair. Long time no speak, eh?"

I almost didn't know what to say. He was the first person I had contacted outside this horrendous place, and I didn't even know where to begin. "Hey, you fucker," I gasped.

"Whoa, what's wrong over there?"

"Can't even begin to answer that question, Mose," I quipped. "I'm calling to ask a favor."

"What, no 'how's it going over there?' No 'how many chicks you score this year?' What the hell, Sinclair?"

"Not this time," I said. "Look, we'll have plenty of time to discuss that shit. After I get the hell away from this campus."

"Uh oh. That bad, eh? I was wondering why you never called. You missed some wild-ass parties over here man, I'm telling you—"

"Look, can you just shut up for a moment?" It was meaner that I meant for it to sound.

"Yeah, sure. Sorry, man. I bet it's rough there. Have you met any friends?"

"Well, I did, but they're all gone now."

"What do you mean, they're all—"

"For fuck's sake, Mosey, will you just listen to me? I need a favor, and I need it tonight."

Silence on the other end. Then, "All right. What is it?"

"I need you to drive over here and pick me up. Well, me and possibly two other people."

"You what?"

"You heard me. I can't go into the details. I lost my car, and I'm not getting it back. I need a ride out of here, and you're the only person who can do it right now."

"What the hell are you talking about, Sinclair? Are you fucking drunk?"

"Goddamn it, I'm not drunk. Look, things here . . . they didn't turn out the way I thought. In fact, none of it did. You know how I was complaining to you before about this place? It turns out I had way more to be afraid of than I thought. I need to leave. Tonight."

"We have finals next week. I was planning to go to this party tonight . . ."

"I'm sorry you had plans," I said, trying to conceal the fear in my voice but failing. "But I really need you, okay?"

More silence. "Okay," he said. "But why can't your parents—"

"They can't, all right? I promise, I'll explain everything when you get here. I just need you right now, okay?"

"All right, all right, Jesus. Something big must be going on down there. You don't call me all year and then when you do, it's in some kind of panicked state? What the fuck happened to you down there?"

"You don't want to know," I said. "But I promise I'll explain in due time. After we escape."

"You keep saying that, like it's a prison."

"Mosey, you have no idea."

A final, lengthy silence. "All right, fine. Do you want me to leave now, or what?"

"No. Tonight. The trial takes place . . . uh, I mean, we won't be ready 'til tonight."

"Okay, fine. Tonight it is. But just remember this, Sinclair. You owe me big for this. I was about to get on this fine looking beauty from the other side of my dorm hall at this party tonight. I'm sure you have no idea about any of that kind of shit, you panicky-ass motherfucker."

I grinned as I listened. "You never know, Mose. I just might."

"Yeah, whatever. All right, I'll be there. Let's call it eight o'clock?"

"Better make it nine," I said. "Be at the gates of the university in Cold River. You'll recognize them as they resemble the entrance to hell."

"Um, okay. I'll keep my eyes open. And you'd better be there."

"If everything goes according to plan, we will be. Look, I gotta go. You promise me you'll be there?"

"Yes, I fucking promise."

"Good. See you tonight, my friend."

"Yeah. Just remember you owe me big for this. Big!"

"You have no idea," I said again. "Just get here. Goodbye."

SARAH CAME BACK IN THE AFTERNOON. I asked her once more where she'd gone. "Don't you worry about that just yet," she said. "I had to do something I think will help us in the end."

"All right," I said. "I trust you. I called my friend up at St. Cloud State. I couldn't exactly explain this whole scenario, but bottom line is he's coming to get us. Tonight."

"Whoah, really?" she said, impressed by my initiative.

"Yes. I told him there may be a few others coming with us."

"Yeah, like Eric. We have to rescue him, Mike."

"I know, I know. Just as long as we don't murder him. Although how that's supposed to help me go out and tackle the world is beyond me."

"I think that's the point, though," Sarah said, caressing my hair. It had gotten pretty long since the winter break as I'd had no time to get it cut. "I don't think they're sending people out to make the world any better, despite all the propaganda in the book. I think they're sending people out to make it worse. I mean, look at that weird fellow you met at the bar."

"You mean Winograd? Yeah, he turned out to be a real winner. So much that he has to keep haunting the same damn place that created him."

"Exactly," Sarah said. "So it's like the final test—to see if you are capable of murdering your best friend. It's like, 'how evil can we force you to be?'"

"Well, I don't think either of us is capable," I said, looking into her eyes. "Right?"

Before she could answer I heard the soft pad of paper on carpet. I turned and looked at the floor. A letter poked out from underneath the room door.

Sarah followed my eyes. "This is it, Mike."

I got up to grab the letter. It had both of our names on the front. This envelope was much crisper than the last one. I tore it open. We read together.

> Mr. Sinclair and Ms. Jackson,
>   Your presence is requested on the fourth floor of the library tonight at 7:00
> p.m. Attendance at this final great event is mandatory. Please do not be late.
> The society thanks you for your excellent work in the trials.
>   Sincerely,
>   Dean Moriarty

The old man's signature once again menaced the bottom of the letter, the suspension bridge and spikes more prominent this time.

"The final trial," I said. "What do you suppose it will be?"

"Who knows?" Sarah replied. "Have you expected anything that's happened this year?"

"God, no," I said.

"Then we have no idea what we could be walking into. Good news is that I have a plan."

"Oh, yeah?"

"Yeah, you heard me. Where's that map?"

"You mean the map of the tunnels?"

"Yeah, dummy. The one you drew from the book that night."

I rummaged through my closet. The map was wedged between two text books, where I'd stuffed it in anger after we'd investigated the shack in the northeast corner of campus.

"Give it to me," she said.

"Why?" I asked.

"Will you just shut up and trust me?" she said.

I gave her a broad smile. "I suppose."

"And you have to promise me something," she said, gazing into my eyes.

"What's that?"

"You have to promise you'll follow me no matter how weird or dangerous it might get."

"What the hell do you have planned for—"

"Just promise, Mike. Please?"

"All right, I promise. Having a plan is better than not having one, I suppose."

"You're damn right. And I've thought about this one for a while. Haven't told you about it because I don't think it's ready. But we're gonna find out either way."

"I guess we are," I said, pulling her toward me. "We have a few hours before we have to embrace our fate. What say we make the most of our afternoon?"

"Nothing like a little pre-dance-of-death nookie, eh?" Sarah leaned in to kiss me, and it was magic. We transferred our naked selves up to the loft bed for one final moment of bliss before we encountered this night.

Chapter
FOURTEEN

WE AWOKE IN EACH OTHERS ARMS a few hours later. I glanced at my alarm clock for the last time. I had so many memories of that thing blasting me awake for Deakin's class. Now it was a reminder I was about to meet my doom. I wasn't sure what Sarah's plan was, but I had a feeling it didn't involved a straight shot out of here. More like a deep dive into the dark heart of this campus to find some answers, and trying to end it forever. Thoughts of my father danced through my head as I lay waiting for Sarah to awaken. I'd wanted a BB gun for my eighth birthday so bad I could taste it. My father said it was too dangerous. Still my young heart held out hope he might change his mind before the appointed hour. When I arrived in our kitchen I had no idea I was entering the programmed world. A stack of papers and pens stood at the far end of our large dining room table. A calculator sat next to the pile, and some rubber bands.

"See, now you can have your own office," my father chirped in his suit and tie. "You can be just like your old man."

Just like you? Most parents, having endured the constant whining about such a present as a BB gun, would have given in eventually. My father held fast and gave me the most boring gift imaginable: his future.

"You have to promise me I'll never become my father," I said as I watched Sarah's eyes open.

"I promise you," Sarah said, kissing me. "I promise you'll get to live your own life, that you'll get to experience everything your father never did. Perhaps one day you'll even be able to save him."

"Thanks, Sarah. I love you."

"I love you too. Now let's go destroy this damn place."

WE BEGAN OUR FINAL WALK to the library at a quarter to seven. The campus was as dead as I'd ever seen it on a Friday night. An eery stillness covered the area as we walked under the maple trees that shaded the craggy sidewalks. A strong wind picked up as we approached the monolithic edifice. I remembered our first trip here, how struck we were by the building's designs. The campanile may have been the last remnants of a church, but this place seemed like where the real dark magic was done. I stared up in awe at the tall spires as we reached the large oak door with the brass handle. It was very quiet inside. I didn't hear a single cough, mutter, or whisper. The smell we'd encountered on our first journey here was present, but distant. The front area was deserted. The genial old man who'd helped guide us was hunched over at the information desk. We decided to pay him one more visit. I hoped he wouldn't question us about any stolen books.

"Hello again, my young masters," he said as he saw us coming toward him. "Here for the trial, I take it?"

"How'd you know?" I asked.

"Oh, it's all the buzz around the society," he clamored. His silver hair dazzled in the dim light of the library. "You two are quite the oddsmakers up at the dean's mansion. Whoops, wasn't supposed to let you in on that little secret."

"What did you say?" Sarah said, moving toward him.

"Sarah, not now," I implored.

"So where's the trial taking place, if you know so much?"

"Up on the fourth floor, of course," the librarian hissed, flashing some ugly teeth.

Sarah walked past me and headed for the ancient stone stairwell. The torch lodged in the wall held a full, roaring flame. The construction tape had been reaffixed. I pulled it all down. The stench of death returned full bore as we crossed the stone archway, and I had to squeeze my nose shut to deal with it.

"Ugh," came Sarah's voice from beside me. "It's worse now, isn't it?"

"I think so," I said. I pulled the small flashlight I'd used during the first trial out of my back pocket. I shone it down the first lengthy collection of stacks, which remained empty of books. All the construction equipment we'd seen at the far end was gone. A high-pitched scream broke the silence and caused me to jump two inches upward.

"Jesus, what was that?" Sarah asked, alarmed.

"I'm not sure, but I think I recognize it," I said. We picked up our pace as I shone the light down each set of stacks. The farther we got the more decrepit the floor became: the wooden shelves were stacked with piles of dust, spider webs accumulated on every level of shelving, and some entire stacks were broken in half. We sped up until we'd reached the other end of the floor. A large, mold-covered stain glass window resided at this end.

"Now what?" Sarah asked.

"We keep searching," I said. The scream was unleashed again, this time to our right.

"Do you think that's Eric?" Sarah said, her breath tight.

"Yeah, I do," I said. "I recognize that hellish screech from the first day I met him."

We made it to the far corner. I shone my light everywhere, but found nothing, until my light hit the exact corner of the room. Sarah shrieked as it illuminated a skeleton slumped there, its decaying skull at a horrific angle.

"Hey! I'm over . . ." I heard Eric say from the other side of the floor. I turned the light, and we started back the way we'd came. Sarah was holding my hand. We got to the other side in a minute, but found nothing.

"What the hell?" Sarah said, exasperation mixing with tiredness in her speech. "Where are you, Eric?"

We stood and listened a moment, but the room was silent as a tomb.

"I'm behind the wall."

"You're what?" Sarah yelled.

"He said he's behind the wall," I offered.

"What? Where?"

"Where behind the wall?" I shouted as loud as I could. My voice echoed from the ceiling.

"Over here!" it sounded like it was coming from our left. I turned my light onto a wooden shelf at the side of the stacks. It held some dusty glass beakers and jars. A hand-held mirror sat at the very end of the shelf. I scanned the wooden slat above it. Various antique tools were hung there: a saw, a wrench, some woodworking implements, and a vice that appeared glued shut. I traced my finger around them and noticed a screwdriver stuck into the wood at an odd angle. I tried pulling it down when the whole rack itself shuddered. I stepped back as it swung out and moved in a semi-circle backward. Another space opened up on the other side.

"Holy shit. This is like a bone fide secret passage," I said, forgetting the situation we found ourselves in for a moment.

"Yeah, great. Can't wait to tell the Sherlock Society," Sarah cawed. "Go."

I bore my light down the passageway. The beam died in the darkness ten feet inside. I gazed around for any free torch stands, finding one near the entrance. With a little pressure I was able to get it free. I took it to the blazing torch in the stairwell and set it alight. Coming back, I noticed that the brick wall that ended the stairwell served to mask wherever this hidden passage went.

"This ought to light our way," I said, putting the flashlight back in my pocket. Bits of ash fell from the torch and burned into my skin, causing me to yelp in fury. The sound echoed down the dark corridor.

"Be careful!" Sarah admonished from behind me.

We headed down the passage. The stone floor began to angle downward and became stairs. As the torch lit the walls I saw some writing appear. Scrawled notes, some written in a dark color that reminded me of dried blood, marked various dates in history. A bloody hand print stuck to the wall and appeared to have been dragged downward. We passed a few gigantic wooden doors, all of them locked. After walking for what seemed like an eternity we reached a final door. Its large brass handle and warped wood was a mirror image of the entrance door to the library. I grabbed the handle with my free hand. A disgusting layer of grime lay on top of it and it was difficult to move. Sarah laid her hands on it, and after registering her disgust, we both pulled with all our might. The door creaked forward an inch. We kept pulling until we had shoved it open a few feet, just enough to squeeze through.

I was first to go in. The torch illuminated a world of horror. We had entered what appeared to be a medieval torture chamber. A huge rack sat in the dusty corner of the room. A chair with metal spikes sat in the other corner. Various whips and chains were trussed up at the third corner. And in the middle of the room sat Eric, tied to a massive timber chair. His eyeglasses reflected the sheen of the torchlight, but he didn't seem to notice us. His head leaned down at a funny angle, and he didn't move. My mind began to wonder how we were able to hear him yell if he was stuck down here when the gigantic door slammed shut behind us. Once trapped, the full measure of the death smell permeated my lungs and I struggled to breath. Sarah almost dropped the torch. She held it up, and we noticed a figure standing behind Eric. It was Justin, wearing the same robes he did at Schuster Hall during the first trial. For a few seconds we stood in place across from each other.

"Welcome, my worthy competitors," came Justin's voice, which was once again tuned down several octaves. "I'm glad you found your way to the final challenge. As you saw, not everyone makes it this far. But you two have some . . . advantages the others didn't. Now then, I shall instruct you in the final trial."

"Instruct away, sicko," Sarah said from behind me. "And when you're done I'll be happy to lodge this torch as far up your ass as you'd prefer."

The Justin figure laughed. It was a sound not from this earth, a growl mixed with a howl. "You'd like that, wouldn't you? You don't fathom how lucky you two are. I begged and begged the master to put both of you out of your misery in your sleep. I considered poisoning your food from the dining hall. I had a legion of plans for how to deal with the spawn of Sinclair and Jackson, all for naught. You two spoiled brats don't know how good you've got it. Used to be we'd toy with competitors for hours down here, just to see who was the stronger warrior. Each of these tools were so enjoyable to use. But no, they told us proper society has moved on from such things. Not my society. If it was up to me you both would burn for your various sins. But that's not the deal, is it? Not if I want to finally escape this hellhole. I have to babysit the idiot twins." His voice fluctuated back up to his regular pitch as he spoke these last lines, then modulated down. "I have done my duty. The master will surely recognize this."

"Are you ever going to shut the fuck up?" Sarah shouted.

"Silence, wench!" came the voice. "Now for the rules of this trial. Once again you will be pitted against each other. Mr. Fulton's reticence to partake of the last challenge will be his undoing, as one of you must destroy him. Whoever manages to accomplish this task shall be richly rewarded with a permanent place within the Malworthe Society. The other . . . I'm afraid won't live. Such a pity. This hallowed place has seen such great competition over the years. I hate to see it imperfected by the likes of you two imbeciles. But this is the price we must pay if we are to ever expand. You two should be so lucky. The last competitors this place shall ever see. Make us proud!"

The not-Justin lifted a robed arm. A very inhuman hand poked out of the end. It looked like a scaly lizard claw, and the fingernails were garish spikes. The freakish thing clamped onto Eric's shoulder, and he jolted upward. His eyes opened behind the glasses, and even in the brief light of the torch I could see they were not his eyes. These were programmed eyes.

"Good luck," came the voice as it retracted its claw. The not-Justin faded backward into the shadows of the room. "You may use anything in this room to destroy one another . . ." the voice said from everywhere.

"Eric?" I called out. "Are you all right?"

The torchlight continued to reflect off his glasses. "I'm more than all right," he said as he rose from the giant chair. "I'm ready to kill you."

The next sound I heard was Sarah screaming and dropping the torch behind me. I was thrown backward as Eric barreled into me at full speed. My head flew backward and hit the stone floor with a hard smack. He felt like an iron safe on my chest. The weird specter of his face rose above me, the torch on the floor casting it in a bizarre light.

"Eric, listen to me!" I shouted as he raised his fists. "You don't have to do this!"

"Shut up, Mr. Sinclair," came the voice, modulated several octaves down. The usual high-pitched utterances I used to hear as we watched bad sci-fi movies in his room had evaporated. He brought his fists down on either side of my face, and I thought my jaw had shattered. "Just accept it, Mr. Sinclair," came the disembodied voice from above me. I noticed the torch light was no longer reflecting this sadistic creature, and flinched as I felt his weight shift. He lifted his fists up once more. The next thing I remember was a figure brandishing the torch and pushing him. Sarah had shoved Eric off me and slammed the torch into his chest as she made her move. I lifted myself onto my elbows and squinted ahead of me. Sarah had the torch steady in her hands and was standing over Eric in the darkness. I glanced around me for any sort of weapon. In the corner sat a large wooden bat with a few metal spikes stuck into it. Sarah's torch illuminated it each time she swung it in my direction.

"Stay put," she cried, dodging out of the way as Eric tried grabbing her from the ground. I saw her kick him in the forearm, and he stopped. "Mike, where are you?"

I lurched to the corner and grabbed the wooden mace, then turned back toward Sarah. "I'm over here," I shouted. Her eerie shadow stood in the middle of the room, but I couldn't see Eric. "Sarah, watch out . . ."

I watched like a helpless animal as she was bowled to the ground from behind, the torch flying out of her hand once again. It settled into a crack in the middle of the stone floor and illuminated her flailing body. She didn't scream this time, but lay there. I could see the outline of Eric's wide body stomping toward her. I cinched my grip on the object and ran forward. He had his own weapon now, a rusty sword that belonged on a pirate ship. He lifted it above his head as I advanced. I had just enough time to react as he brought the searing blade down into the thick middle of the mace. He tried pulling it back but it wouldn't budge, so he ripped the entire mess out of my hand and threw it behind him.

"It's futile to resist, Mr. Sinclair," Eric said, a hellish grin spreading on his face. "You know this as well as your father did."

"You shut up about my father," I shrieked. "He never had a choice."

"Of course he did," Eric said as he danced around in a circle. I pivoted to watch him move. "There is always a choice. Sometimes the society has to make it for you." He lunged forward to grab me. I pounced backward. The back of my foot brushed against the torch. I leaned down to grab it, but it was stuck. I pulled with all my might, and just as I got the thing loose and swung it, Eric was upon me. I put the torch forward with a clumsy shove, and it surged a flame all around his face. For a moment I saw the real Eric Fulton appear there, terrified and alone. I shoved the torch forward and he backed off.

"Sarah?" I called to the darkness. No response.

"It's over, Mr. Sinclair," the figure said. "You have to kill me, remember? The rules of the game and all that. Such a pity, if this kid hadn't turned into such a worthless slob he might have been the winner of all this. Now he'll have to die."

I stood there for a moment watching him speak. His face contorted, and for a moment the real Eric seemed to take control.

"Mike," he said. "Is that you? What the fuck's going on down here?"

"Eric, listen to me," I said. "You've been captured by the society. They're using you against us. They're trying to make us kill you. You must not give in. Do you hear me?"

His face contorted again. "I hear you fine, Mr. Sinclair," the voice said as he was rushed toward me. I had no choice but to shove the flame forward into him. Eric let loose a horrendous scream and ran off at a tangent away from the flame. I could hear his sneakers stomping around the outside of the chamber. I searched for Sarah near the huge wooden door we'd entered.

"Mike . . ." came a tiny voice. I ran over to her and knelt down. "You've got to . . . finish him . . ."

"No," I said. "I can't. Not him. I don't care if it gets us out of this. I'm not killing the only other friend I made here."

"Not . . . your friend . . ." she said into the stone floor. I didn't care what she said. This guy may not have believed much of what we'd witnessed over the year, but it was going to be a cold day in hell before I murdered the guy. I lifted the torch and saw him coming this time. I side-stepped, leaned out my foot and tripped him. He went sprawling into the dusty floor. I walked over behind him, raised the torch and clocked him in the back of the head with the stout handle. He slumped and didn't move.

"Motherfucker," I said to no one in particular. Then, "Sorry, Eric." I nudged the limp body with my toe. He didn't move. I helped Sarah to her feet and we walked over to Eric.

"Jesus," she said when she saw the sight. "He got burned pretty bad."

"Yeah, unfortunately," I said. "It wasn't his fault. He didn't want to be involved in any of this, but they didn't care. Just like my father."

"What are we going to do with him?" Sarah asked. I turned the torch-light her way and saw an inch-long gash above her eyes.

"Sarah, are you all right?" I asked. She followed my eyes in the torch light and reached up to touch her forehead.

"I'm fine," she said, staring at the blood on her fingers. "You should be worried about him."

I gazed at the form before us. "We'll have to carry his ass out of here."

"You mean you'll have to," Sarah said. "If it was up to me, I'd leave him."

This was a vindictive, uncaring side I'd never seen in Sarah. "We're not leaving him," I said. "I'm carrying him out of here. Here, hold the torch." I reached down and pulled Eric up over my shoulder. His chest had a major burn on it, which was warm to my hand. I felt even worse about what I had to do to subdue him. I tried setting up his feet on the floor but they kept sliding. "Let's go," I said.

The massive door that had shut behind us was closed tight. We moved around the creepy chamber, feeling for a way out among the horrid spikes and whips. I found a much smaller door at the far end. I was able to pull it open, and hoisted Eric's body through the frame. Sarah followed with the torch and closed the door. We were in another long corridor like the one behind the secret passage, but this one had a much lower ceiling and tons of disgusting bugs. I inched forward, Eric slumped over my shoulder, for what seemed like years. We ended up in some weird antechamber which led to the balcony that overlooked the first floor of the library. Sarah threw the torch, now almost burned out, on the floor of the chamber. I took a few cautious steps forward and peered over the splintered wooden railing. I could see the reference desk, where the creepy old man sat. A puff of cigarette smoke hovered in the air behind him, wafting from the first floor stacks. My heart dropped as I saw its source: the hooded figure I'd seen outside Schuster (and again at the end of the first trial). He wore the same ratty hooded sweatshirt and paced down the corridor between the stacks. I backed away from the railing, but it was too late. The figure raised up his smoke to the hood for another drag, but stopped. My foot had trampled upon a loose board on the balcony and caused a horrendous snap.

"We have to go, now!" I said to Sarah. I started dragging Eric. She struggled to pick up the slack. We shuffled to the stairwell that led to the first floor. I peered over the edge of the railing once more. The old man sat behind the reference desk, and the hooded figure was nowhere to be seen. We hustled down the steps, the torch holders on the walls casting a strange glow on our passage. We reached the archway on the first floor, just as eerily silent as upon our arrival here. I didn't see anyone. I glanced at Sarah, then froze when I saw beyond her. The figure stood at the second floor stairwell. A single cigarette dangled between its gloved fingers.

"What is it, Mike?" Sarah said, terrified.

"Just run," I said, and pulled Eric forward.

We reached the hallway that led to the massive oak front door, which was now sealed shut. The hooded figure stood at the other end of the hall. I turned back to the door and had Sarah hold Eric's shoulders so I could gave the front door a massive heave. It hardly budged. The figure was moving toward us, a trail of black smoke billowing from his hood.

"Shit," I said, putting my back into it. The door moved a few inches, but not enough to slip through.

"Mike, hurry!" Sarah exclaimed. The cut on her forehead had sprouted a trickled finger of blood that curved toward her ear. I'd never seen such a determined, intense expression in her verdant eyes.

"I'm trying!" I said, my breath terse. "No wonder this thing is always open when we get here."

The figure was a few feet away. It reached a gloved hand toward Sarah.

"Go away!" she screamed. I shoved with all my might and pushed the door out a few more inches, then turned to face the figure.

"Fuck you!" I shouted, swinging a balled fist with all my might. I clocked it right in its "head," which felt like no other human head I'd ever known. It felt hard as a rock, but the figure took a step backward. "Push him through!" I yelled at Sarah, motioning to Eric.

She pushed his limp body through the opening in the door. His feet were stuck together so she had to disconnect them. I turned away from this sight in time to watch the gloved hand reach for my neck. The leather smelled ancient, like from another time. My breath began to close off. I grabbed its forearm, sinew that felt like stark concrete. The grip tightened, and my vision began to sway. A thick cloud of smoke billowed out of the black hood and enveloped my coughing mouth.

"Such a pity, this one," a voice like gravel emanated from the hole. "Such promise. You were going to be our new society, born from the ashes of the old. So unfortunate."

The grip tightened, and I began to black out. I remember a flash of light that tore right in front of my eyes. Then the glove slipped loose. I doubled over, my hands at my throat. I looked up in time to see one of the giant rusted metal chandeliers come pouring down from the ceiling and land right on the hooded freak. A torrent of dust flew in every direction. A hand grabbed my shoulder and pulled backward out the huge oak door. I kept moving until I tripped over a lump on the ground which I realized was Eric.

"Careful!" Sarah said from beside me. "He's still breathing, I think. Can you help me pick him up?"

"I think so," I said, hoisting myself upward. I reached down and grabbed Eric's shoulders. Sarah helped me slump him over my back. More puffs of dust flowed out of the door of the ancient library. I heard a pained shout from the old librarian inside.

"Wh-what happened?" I asked, in daze.

"I saved you," Sarah said, a hint of pride in her voice. "I grabbed another torch from the entrance and lobbed it at the thing. It was pure luck the chandelier chain gave loose."

"Holy shit," I said. "You did save me. God, I love you."

"I know," she said, leaning over to kiss me. It was awkward as we were both holding Eric, but worth every second.

"Now let's get out of here," Sarah said. I pulled Eric along on my back as we shambled away toward the student union. Most of the tall lamps that lit the concrete paths had burned out so it was difficult to see where we were going. I slumped Eric's body against one of them. He was covered in soot and dirt and I wiped off his face with my shirt.

"Now, let's get the hell out of here."

"Not yet," Sarah said in a firm but gentle voice.

"What?" I said. "I know I was dead set against leaving. I wanted to get to the bottom of all this. But we almost died just now, Sarah. I'm ready to leave."

"Didn't you hear what the freak show in the library said?" Sarah asked. "You were kinda like their last hope. They're placing all their hopes on you to start the society anew in another location."

"Wait, what are you saying? How do you know this?" I questioned.

"Don't worry about it right now," she said. "We have to finish this once and for all," she said. "Just like you wanted."

"Oh, God," I said. "Is this part of your plan?"

"You better believe it," Sarah said. "Now help me get him up. He's not coming with us for this last bit. We need to find a safe place to dump him. Hopefully he'll make it through tonight."

I reached down and pulled Eric's body up on my shoulders. His mouth was still moving, and I could feel his chest move.

"This way," Sarah said, heading up the northeast corridor behind the student union toward the music building.

We reached the small white shed in a few more minutes. It appeared the same as the last time: rusted red chain pulling the two front doors closed, paint peeling even worse after the winter, the roof tiles torn asunder and falling off the top.

"Set him behind this," Sarah instructed. I followed, heaving Eric behind the shed under the single, boarded-up window.

"We're comin' back to get him, right?" I asked.

"Of course, we are," Sarah said. "Assuming we survive."

"Ah, right," I said, not amused. "I can't believe you're trying to walk us right into the belly of the beast. How the hell are we even going to get into this . . ."

I trailed off as Sarah went to the other side of the shack and returned with a small pair of bolt-cutters. She placed them on the rusty chain and began to apply leverage.

"Where'd you get that?" I asked instead of trying to help her.

"Tool shed on the other side of the greenhouse," she said, flexing. "Don't tell me you've never seen it?"

"No,"I said. "Then again after each class with Langdon my main goal was getting the hell out of there. Wait, was this what you went to go do earlier today?"

"Nothing gets past you," she said, struggling to close the pincers. "Say, a little help?"

"Oh right," I said. I placed my hands above hers and we gave a mighty squeeze. The first links of the chain broke free. We proceeded to notch through each of two more layers until the entire rusty mess fell to the ground. Sarah pulled on the wooden door, and it almost fell off its hinges. Inside was a typical garden maintenance shed—some pruning sheers, some rakes, some watering cans, and a gasoline-powered lawn mower.

"There doesn't appear to be any passageway," I said, somewhat relieved. "Well, at least we checked it out. C'mon, let's go."

"I don't think so," Sarah said. "Remember the work bench in the library?"

"Yeah," I said in a sheepish manner. "I do."

"It's probably like that. You had the magic touch last time, so why don't you try again?"

I looked around inside. There was another wooden bench on the side with various newer tools all over it. I pulled on some vice grips, a pair of pliers, a screwdriver, and a few others. Nothing happened.

"Keep trying," she said, prodding the other side of the shed.

I searched around for something else that might be a lever. I walked over to the lawn mower, shifted it into neutral and pulled it backward.

"Holy shit," Sarah said, looking amazed.

"What?" I said. "It's only a lawn mower. My father had one of—"

"No," Sarah interrupted, pointing down. "There."

Underneath where the lawn mower sat was a small wooden door with a metal ring. It appeared to be some kind of trap door.

"Bingo," Sarah said, walking over to it. She pulled on the ring and it opened. A disgusting smell not unlike the library's emerged, making us both step away and cough.

"Jesus," I said. "This hasn't been opened for a while, I'd gather. Like the last century."

"You're gonna have to get over it," Sarah said between coughs. "We're going down there."

"What about Eric?" I said.

"We'll put him in here. Go grab him."

I went back outside, picked up Eric once more, and brought him into the shed. Sarah closed the wooden doors behind me. I slumped him against the work bench. Sarah was already climbing down into the hole.

"Be careful," I said as I watched her disappear. I pulled the flashlight from my pocket and shone it down the passage. She was descending a rusty metal ladder. I couldn't see the bottom of the corridor.

"I will," she said, beginning to disappear from sight. "You coming?"

"Yeah, yeah," I said. I turned to Eric. "If we make it out alive you and I are having a serious talk about this place. All right?" His head lolled to the side. "I'll take that as a yes. And if I don't make it out . . . farewell, my friend."

I placed one foot down, then another. Soon my head had gone below and I was plunging into the netherworld beneath this horrific campus. I climbed down thin metal steps until my feet touched rock solid ground. I plopped down and shone the light around me. For a brief, panicky instant I thought Sarah had disappeared. Then I saw her at the far end of the tunnel.

"Sarah!" I called to her. My voice traveled down the ancient brick tube. Moss gathered around the corridor and the dank stench of death permeated everything. The single light was from my flashlight.

"Over here," Sarah said. "Get out your map."

"Oh, right," I said, pulling out the tattered piece of paper. I poked the spot on the map where the white shed was, then traced my finger down the diagonal tunnel to the center. The campanile. I caught up with Sarah and showed her the map. We stumbled down the tunnel, lowering our heads and trying not to step on the bodies of dead rats. A small trickle of water flowed down the center of the stone floor.

"Remember when I first told you about these?" Sarah said as we marched.

"I think so," I said. "But if I remember, you said these didn't exist anymore."

"I know, but I had a feeling they did. I just never thought I'd have to find out."

"Sarah, what's the plan here?" I asked, shining my light on her back.

"We get to the campanile, first. The person we need to see to finish this will be there. He always is on the night of the final trial. He'll be waiting for Justin to deliver us to him."

"Wait, what are you talking about?" I said, bemused. "How do you know all of this?"

Sarah let loose a deep exhale. "Look, like I tried telling you before, I haven't been completely honest with you. I can't get into it right now, but just know I'm trying to help you end this. My family wants it finished as much as you do."

"Your family?" I said, starting to feel numb. "So you knew about the St. James stuff?"

"Not all of it," she said. "But more than I let on. I didn't want to confuse you any more than you already were."

"Well, I'm pretty fucking confused now!" I shouted. My panicky voice stretched down the corridor.

"Let's get to the campanile and finish this," Sarah said. "I'm on your side, remember? And if we make it out of this, I swear I'll tell you everything I know. All right?"

"All right," I mumbled. "You better promise."

"I do," Sarah said, turning to face me as we approached the first tunnel crossing. "I love you, Mike. That's one thing nobody expected out of this. The two families connecting like this after so many years. We can start anew, without all the baggage of the society or Moriarty or any of it. And I promise once this is finished, I will tell you everything. Now, which way to the tower?"

I looked down at the ragged map I'd traced. "This way," I said, pointing. "And Sarah . . . ?"

She turned back toward me.

"I love you too," I said.

Somehow in this dark pit of insanity her eyes retained their amazing glow in the gaze of my flashlight. "Let's go."

We marched down another tunnel. The walls continued to constrict and I had to keep bending my head down. We came through to an open area where other tunnels emptied onto a broad stone platform. Another rusty ladder stood in the center. I pulled out the map again.

"This must be dead center," I said, pointing at the intersection. "The clock tower is right above us."

I followed the ladder. It led upward through a hole in the ceiling of the room.

"That must be it," Sarah said. "Come on."

She started up the ladder. I waited until she was through the hole before I started climbing. The metal rungs were very rough. I gazed up into the black hole and saw nothing. I kept going until I heard a door open above me. Sarah had pushed open another trap door very much like the one in the maintenance shed. Her body was enveloped by a small square of light as she climbed out. I followed, climbing up to find myself standing in the bottom room of the campanile. I looked upward to see a twisted wooden staircase leading around to the top, where a wide sheen of concrete indicated the belfry. I could hear the low knocking sound of the huge pendulum above. The curved door that I'd been unable to open sat to my left and Sarah stood to my right, eying the staircase to see if it was safe.

"Let me guess, we're climbing this now?" I asked.

"It looks secure to me," she said. "You're not giving up on me now, are you?"

"Of course not," I said. "It's just . . . we've been through a lot, and . . ."

"We haven't even seen the worst yet. Are you sure you're ready for this?"

"Well, I wasn't ready to find out my father sent me here to be brainwashed. And I certainly wasn't ready to find out my RA was a lizard man who likes to run sadistic trials on people. And finding out you knew about St. James wasn't easy to take down. But I made it through all that, didn't I? Who's to say I can't make it through more?"

Sarah laughed, a weird sound in this situation. "Not me," she said. "Glad you have the right perspective. Now let's finish this." She gripped the splintery railing and headed up the stairs. After another peek upward, I followed.

The stairwell was attached with rusted metal plates that pulled loose from the wall a bit as we climbed. I felt like I was Batman in Tim Burton's 1989 film, ascending the cathedral in the final act. With each new set of tremulous stairs we could hear the slow tick-tock of the pendulum grow louder. Every minute the hands on the outside clock thrust forward with a loud thunk that shook the walls. We stopped on a small wooden platform just underneath the concrete belfry.

"Are you ready?" Sarah asked again, staring at the final trap door.

"As I'll ever be," I said. The noises of the pendulum swaying were even louder up here.

Sarah climbed up the final rust-stained ladder and pushed through the trap door. I pulled myself up the ladder, careful not to cut myself, and came upon an odd scene. Sarah stood next to the opening looking at a figure sitting in the middle of the concrete room. The large bells that marked the hour hung like two giants on either side of the figure. I recognized the hair from behind: it was Deakin. He was facing away from us, tied to a small wooden chair. I was moving before I even realized it.

"Professor!" I shouted above the noise of the whirring machinery.

"Mike, wait . . ." Sarah said from behind me.

I whirled around, anger in my eyes. "What?"

"Doesn't this seem the slightest bit like a trap?" she said.

"I don't care," I said. "I have to save him." I started forward and called him by his first name.

"Mr. Sinclair? Is that you?" came the weak voice.

"Yes, Marvin. It's me," I said. "We're here. I got your letter."

"Then you obviously didn't follow its dictates," Deakin said as I came around to face him. "I told you to leave this place, Michael. Not come back to the center of its evil."

"The center of what . . . ?" I said, struggling to untie him.

"He said it was the center of its evil," came a powerful voice that reverberated off the huge iron bells before it drilled into my brain. "Thank you for the demonstration, Marvin." I watched, my mouth agape, as the taut ropes slackened and fell to Deakin's feet.

"Michael, I'm sorry. Please forgive me," Deakin said, his eyes wet with tears.

I was blown back by a force I'd felt before, in my dorm room. It was the strange, mystical magnetic field of Moriarty. The man of impossible age sauntered out from behind the iron bell. The old beard stretched longer than I remembered, and he seemed taller. He wore a variation of the dark robes I was used to seeing him wear, but another blood red velvet sash hung over his chest. He wore the same tri-corner hat he'd worn during his speech in the gymnasium. His beard turned from ash gray to pure white, and back again, as he walked forward.

"Mr. Sinclair," he said in that sinister, low voice. "What a problem child you have been this year. We had such high hopes for you." I stood there stunned as he ambled over to Deakin and put a single wrinkled hand on his shoulder. "Marvin played his role well. I knew you couldn't resist rescuing your source of information."

"Marvin?" I said, my voice wavering. I had lost track of Sarah. She wasn't standing by the trap door any longer. "What is he talking about?"

"I tried to tell you, Michael," he said. His voiced sounded small and far away. "I told you to leave this place."

Moriarty laughed, a deep-throated guffaw that bounced off the concrete walls of the belfry. The minute hand on the clock face near us struck again, scaring me. "Leave? You ought to get it by now that it's impossible, you old fool. No one leaves the society. Especially no scion of the Sinclair family. We have big plans for you, my boy. Of course I wished you would be doing this voluntarily. Marvin never had a problem with it."

I stared at Deakin, but he wouldn't meet my eyes. "What is he saying, Professor?"

"Oh, back to formality, I see," Moriarty roared. "Yes, what am I saying, Professor?"

Deakin moved his eyes up to mine, then darted them back to the dirty floor. "It's true. I too was programmed. Back when I started here. But it didn't take, just like your father. Or at least not as well. Which is why they needed somebody younger. I got further and further out of their reach over the years. The old magic isn't as strong anymore. But they still exercised some control."

"That's right," Moriarty said, raising his right hand. I watched in horror as Deakin's right hand raised too. "Don't you see, boy? Once you're in our society, you're in for life. Just like your father."

"You shut the fuck up about my father!" I yelled. I had never felt such rage course through me. The one person I thought I could trust besides Dalton had been working both sides the whole time. I knew it wasn't that simple, that Deakin was trying to help me, but the rage blinded me to any nuance. I was pissed at everyone who had any connection to this god-damn place.

"Such anger, such hostility," Moriarty growled. "Your father passed on some good traits. You'll do well when the new expansion begins in the fall."

"You mean moving from Ancient Greece here to some other univer-sity?" I said. "I think not. You'll just have to kill me."

Moriarty barked laughter. "Don't tempt me, Mr. Sinclair. I have con-sidered it. But you're our last hope. Don't you see? Sending your father out into the real world was a mistake. We understand that now. But you are our great salvation. The last of the old society births the new. It has al-ways operated as such, remaining in darkness until the end. You are our great new hope. Get up, Marvin."

Deakin made an abrupt stand from the chair and walked over to Mo-riarty's side. He didn't appear to have control of his own movements.

"Sit down, Mr. Sinclair," Moriarty said, pointing.

"No," I said. "Fuck you."

"I said, sit down."

I felt myself moving forward, my legs bending, my ass moving downward. Then I was on the chair, Moriarty standing in front of me. I still had not seen Sarah anywhere. I hoped she had escaped this horrifying situation.

"You see, you are hardly the first to go through such a procedure," Mo-riarty uttered, swaying in front of me. Mr. James? You may come out now."

I shuddred as I heard the name, and my blood ran cold. Then my entire body was freezing, but this wasn't from terror, but because a figure was materializing right through me. Alfred James came into transparent being in front of me. He wore a disgusting leather coat that had been through a war. A dusty, torn cowboy hat adorned his head, his ratty hair poking out from various places. His mustache bristled as he saw me.

"Alfred was our last experiment in the old days," Moriarty said. "Why don't you tell him yourself?"

"You think I don't know all about him?" I spat, thinking of the history book.

"You might think you do," Moriarty said. "Why don't you fill us in, Alfred?"

"Gee, didn't know you were the one when I first met ya on the ol' night of Homecomin' there," the ghost said as he ambled before me. "Just thought you were one of the dumb ones. We get plenty of them. I jus' thought you two was thirsty."

"We weren't asking your opinion," Moriarty roared. "Why did you come back on that night?"

"Well, sir, I was a veteran of the war of southern aggression, y'see," Alfred said. "Caught some bad cases of the gout after my time on the battlefield. Thought I'd have to lose my leg. I heard about this here institution up on the plains, heard it might be able to help. Well, they helped all right, helped me right into an early grave. But that's all right. Up until I died I felt much better."

"We tried everything to save him," Moriarty said. "But our prayers to the demons below and our applications of the advanced wizardry of his day didn't work. Alfred didn't recognize it, but he was the beginning of the end of the Malworthe Institution of Healing. Seemed ol' Alfred had some powerful relatives on the East Coast. Once they got interested in his death it was all over. We didn't exist again until the university was founded in the next century.

"I know all of this," I said, struggling to move any part of my body.

"Yes, yes, you're so well-sourced on the matter of our society. Well, it had to undergo some changes after the first tearing down. And now that I've considered your plight after all these years . . . Alfred, you are free of the pull of this land."

Great happiness coursed through Alfred's translucent eyes. His entire body faded out of existance just as it had just faded into being a few minutes ago. I felt warmer just by his absence.

"As I was saying, we had to change," Moriarty continued. "From the ashes of the ancient priests came the new regime of instructors. A new sheen of respectability had to be created out of the previous generation. And all the records from that time had to be burned. But we knew the society could continue if given the right motivation. That imbecile Winograd was our first attempt at sending a recruit out into the real world. Unfortunately, that didn't turn out well."

I felt a chill in the air again, much cooler this time, and my stomach felt like it dropped into my feet. Winograd materialized next to one of the huge bells.

"You called, oh, great and pious one?" the doctor mocked. He was wearing a pinstriped suit with a bowler hat. His monocle remained in his right eye, and he carried some kind of walking stick.

"Churlish goon!" Moriarty raged. "You can stay yoked to this land for all of eternity. It was very unwise of you to visit him in such manner." Moriarty then turend to address me, as if Winograd had never appeared. "He is not someone to be looked up to, even if he did do good work for the majority of his career."

"Couldn't stop the whole human experimentation angle, eh? Couldn't quite repress it?" I prodded.

Moriarty's eyes bubbled with rage. "That wasn't the problem, my boy." He glanced back at Winograd, who was now polishing his monocle. "The problem was weakness of spirit. Dr. Winograd took the wonderful innovations of our society, the fact that we were on the cusp of reanimating human beings even as they perished, and reveresed course. He made a mockery of our vision."

"That's one way to see it, ol' chap," Winograd said, placing his monocle back in his eye. "I was releasing these fools from the torment I'd had to go through to get to this point. You thought you were so beneficial to the world, that your craven 'mission' would never cease. Not once did you even consider the damage it could have on my reputation, on my life's work!"

"Be gone!" Moriarty bellowed, a deafening sound in the concrete room. He stretched out his hands and some kind of power emanated from them, blasting Winograd into nothingness. "Don't worry, he's not going anywhere. His punishment is to reside here for all eternity. The same weakness of spirit he had would prove to be most problematic with your father. Weak-willed should have been tattooed on his cowardly back."

"You shut the fuck up about my father!" I screamed.

"And why should I? Your father was our next attempt to see if anyone could make it outside of the society. St. James seemed a suitable destination. Not very populated, and full of idiots who kept to themselves. We programmed others to keep watch over him as he was our prize student. But of course, you know what happened next."

"No," I said. "I don't. Something happened between my family and the Jacksons. I never found out what."

"Really?" Moriarty said, rubbing his hands together and glaring at Deakin. "How delicious. I'd hoped there might be some part to this tale you hadn't puzzled through. It was our first discernible error in programming, you see. This was before we understood the extent of our problems. This will all be corrected for your programming, of course. But your father's was embedded too deeply. He thought the Jackson girl was on some kind of reconnaissance mission rather than simply coming over to borrow a tool for her parents. She had the misfortune of coming upon your father when he was working on his chainsaw in the garage. She startled him, see, and . . ."

"Enough!" I yelled. "I don't want to hear it. This can't be true!"

"Oh, but it is," Moriarty said with menace. "He regretted it, of course. Never could quite come to terms with what he did. Used the self-programming techniques we bequeathed him to bury it while we used our own Officer Brady to bury the deed. St. James is a small town, and nobody had to know what really happened. Our people knew, of course. That's why they had to move away. It could have been much worse, but we decided to take our losses. We had one final chance to make it up with you. And so we have."

"Stop it," I said, struggling to move from the chair. "Stop it!"

"Not a chance, Mr. Sinclair," Moriarty said. "This is our last, glorious opportunity to make it right with you. Once you undergo the programming, once it becomes part of your essence, you will transfer to the university down on the river bank. There you shall start the society anew, begin your infiltration, and by the time you are ready to graduate that place will fall like a bloody domino. It's almost too easy."

"Fuck you!" I yelled. "I won't do it!"

"You won't have a choice," Moriarty said, edging closer to me. "Now then, Marvin. Would you do the honors?"

Deakin had stood behind Moriarty for his entire rambling speech, his complexion turning more bleak the more he had to listen. His old, wrinkled hands shook at his sides.

"Marvin?" Moriarty said. "Will you please?"

"No," Deakin said in a solemn voice. "I won't do it. You've done enough to this boy's family. It ends here, Henry."

Moriarty's nostrils flared, and his eyes opened wide into pools of liquid fire. "You won't? You old fool." He turned and reached out his hands once more. Deakin was shoved backward by an invisible force toward the open brick window of the tower. He hit the stone wall and his torso flew through the open space. His old legs flew up behind him, losing one polished shoe as they went over the edge. I let out an agonized scream as I watched, struggling with every fiber of my being against the force holding me to the chair. I was able to get up and started running toward Moriarty, who had his robed back turned toward me as he watched Deakin fall. I got within a foot of him before I was shoved back into the chair. It almost fell to the floor with the force of my frame. Moriarty turned with one swift motion, his eyes seething with rage.

"He had it coming," he said in the low, crawling voice. "And so do you. You're lucky I don't toss your delinquent ass right off this tower. If I didn't need you, I would, you ungrateful little . . ."

He gave a menacing stomp forward, and I braced for the end. Before I closed my eyes I saw him raise both hands, like he was about to cast a spell. The air around me grew still, then began to blow my long hair back, and then it stopped. I opened my eyes and saw Moriarty standing right in front of me, but looking off to his left, where Sarah stood between the two monstrous iron bells. Her gorgeous eyes, that I'd spent so much time daydreaming about over the last months, glowed like emeralds. She opened her mouth and muttered a phrase I didn't recognize. She spoke it again, louder this time. The fury in Moriarty's face had been replaced by pure fear. It was not an emotion I was expecting to see there.

"You fool!" he cried, raising his hand toward her. I could feel the unseen power start to materialize as he aimed right at her head.

"Don't you dare!" I yelled. I realized the force holding me down had again lifted. I did the first thing that came to mind, which was kicking my leg out as hard as I could. It caught Moriarty right in the gut, and he fell back. I could hear his old bones strike the solid concrete with a sickening snap.

"Sarah!" I cried. "Are you all right?"

She came running toward me. "Yes," she said. "We have to go. Now."

The floor began to shake underneath my feet. I had never felt a real earthquake before, but I imagined it was very similar to this. A dull throbbing noise began to fill in the entire space around my ears. Moriarty was struggling to pick himself up. I thought about moving in to kick him once more, but was pulled back by Sarah. The entire tower shook and a large piece of stone dislodged from the ceiling, landing right on top of him. It made a disgusting popping noise as it hit, and horrific black blood spurted out from either side of the slab. I turned away before I vomited from the sight.

"I told you, we have to go!" Sarah shouted. She pulled me between the bells, which were threatening to come loose from their yokes and crush everything in their paths. Sarah pulled open the trap door and shoved me into it. I grabbed onto the ladder and started down toward the wooden platform. Sarah jumped down from above, using agility I didn't think she had. She shoved me forward once she landed. We climbed down the wooden staircases until we reached the bottom, where the shaking was much worse. I could feel the entire campanile move as I stood, and I knew the thing was about to come down. The curved door had been sheered open by the force of the quake, so we bolted through the gap. We ran about fifty yards into the open field before we both turned around to watch the campanile stagger and collapse to the ground in a giant blast of sound and rubble. A giant rush of dust flew from the debris toward us. I knelt down and covered my face with my hands. When it had passed I looked at Sarah.

"What the hell did you say?" I asked, struggling to comprehend what was happening.

"Don't worry about it," she said. "I'll tell you if we survive this."

"Did you do this?" I asked.

The emerald glow I'd noticed in her eyes was still there, but faded. "Yes," she said. "Now let's go. We have to get Eric and meet your friend."

It took me a few seconds to figure out what she was saying. "Oh, right. Yeah, let's go."

We ran across the campus toward the white shed on the northeast side of campus. I squinted as I saw a figure standing in front of it. Eric was waving his hands and shouting at us.

"Oh, shit," Sarah yelled. "Remember, he might still be programmed!"

I could just make out what he was saying, and it was full of the bluest of words. As we got closer I could hear sentences. "What the fuck . . . is happening . . . ?!"

"No time to explain," Sarah said. "Do you remember anything?"

"No," Eric said. Pure terror outlined his eyes. "Being in my room at Schuster was the last thing I remember, then . . ."

"We'll fill you in later," Sarah said, agitated. "We have to get out of here. You sure you're all right?"

"Yeah, I'll be fine," Eric said, but didn't look it. The front of his shirt was blackened beyond recognition, and the beginnings of a horrific burn poked out from where the shirt had been obliterated. Sarah turned and started running south.

"What's going on, fucknuts?" Eric yelled as we watched her move away.

"It's a long story," I said in between puffs of air. "But we almost had to kill you. Sorry about the burns, by the way."

"I was wondering who beat the shit out of me, "Eric said, his chest heaving.

We scooted around the student union and made it to the small paved road that ran through campus and headed to Schuster Hall. We ran toward the huge metal gate that signaled the entrance. I could see the small gravel path that led to Cold River, and beyond that I could just make out a pair of car headlights.

"It's Mosey!" I shouted. "He came!"

"It's who?" Eric shouted, confused as ever.

"My friend from St. Cloud State," I said. "I asked him to come pick us up once I knew the shit was going to hit the fan. I can't fucking believe he came!"

"You can believe it later," Sarah said. "Come on!" She motioned for us to go through the giant gates as she swung them open. I made my way sideways through the gap, and Eric followed. I sprinted over to Mosey's car, a wood-paneled station wagon he'd inherited from his father. His thin visage sat grasping the wheel, his eyes wide as he watched us race toward him. I helped Eric get in back, then I opened up the passenger side door and threw myself inside.

"What the fuck is going on, Sinclair?" Mosey shouted in my face.

"Mosey, you're a life saver," I said, leaning over to hug him.

He shrugged me off. "Oh, no. Not until you fill me in on this shit show."

"Dude, I will in time. Right now we need to get the hell as far away from here as we can. Here comes Sarah."

I watched as Sarah stumbled through the space in the metal gates and ran over to the car. She opened the door opposite of Eric and jumped in the back seat. "Drive, dude!" she shouted.

"Fine by me," Mosey said. He threw the station wagon in reverse and started back up the driveway. When he reached the end he whipped the wagon around with a brief flick of his wrist.

"Where to?" he said, as if he was a cabbie.

"Away from this town," Sarah said.

"I guess that's a given," Mosey said. "Then you'll tell me why Sinclair made me ditch the biggest fucking party of the year to come pick up you stragglers?"

"Yes, yes," Sarah said. "Just get moving."

Mosey threw the car into drive and the wheels spun out on the gravel. He headed down the main street where I'd been pulled over in the fall. We weren't met by a single other car as we reached the dark pewter sign at the town's edge. The night's events were like a nasty dream I would never forget. I leaned back into my ripped cloth seat as the patched highway rushed toward the car in waves of pavement. I exhaled a breath I didn't realize I had been holding. It released it in a whoosh of air as I gazed out at the bland countryside of Minnesota in the wan light.

"So my question again," Mosey said, letting off on the accelerator. "What in God's name did you get into here, Sinclair? My freshman year consisted of bong hits, booze, and a few ladies whose names I've forgotten. Oh, yeah, and getting educated. You seem to have majored in destroying some kind of clock tower and almost killing your dorm-mates." I could see his eyebrow arch over his glasses as he stared at Eric in the rearview.

"It's a very long story," I said, my eyes fluttering as I struggled against the urge to sleep. "I'd love to tell you in depth, but first we need to figure out where we're going."

"Right," Sarah said. "Any chance we could hide out with you for a while?"

"Uh, it's doubtful, but we can sure try," Mosey said. The twang in his voice hadn't been removed by college, just subdued. His small eyes glanced in the rear view mirror again to scan the passengers I'd brought along. "Can't you all just go home, or something?"

"Unfortunately it's not that easy," I said, exchanging glances with Sarah.

"Okay," Mosey said. "How about you, baldy?"

"You got me," Eric said, the first he'd spoken since we'd left Cold River. He appeared small and terrified in the back seat. "Sorry, I'm still in shock from almost getting killed tonight." He stared out the window and didn't look back for a long time.

"All right," Mosey said. "I guess we're going to my school. As long as you promise not to destroy any more buildings."

"Very funny," I said. But the comment got me thinking. I turned my head back to Sarah. "So what the hell did you say up there in the campanile?"

She stared at the darkened fields rushing past her window. "It was a phrase in Latin. That's what triggered the quake."

"The what?!" I said. "You . . . you did that?"

Sarah flashed her gorgeous green eyes, back to their usual sheen, right at me. "Yes, I did. It was a phrase my father gave me. I had it memorized for that moment."

"You've had it memorized?"

"That's what I said. I suppose this opens up a whole bunch of questions in your mind?"

"Well, kind of," I said, bemused. I felt like I was speaking to somebody I had just met.

"I'm sorry, Mike. I couldn't risk you finding out what I had planned. I wasn't sure it was even going to work."

"I'm glad it did," I said. "But you could have told me, all the same. So what else have you been keeping from me? You said you hadn't been entirely honest with me. We never got to finish that conversation."

"I'm so sorry, Mike. My father told me a lot of stuff before I came to Malworth. Stories about you and your family. There were so many times I wanted to break down and tell you. But it became impossible. We got too close, and I couldn't endanger your life anymore."

"So . . . you knew about our families in St. James?"

She gazed at the ratty carpet of the car. "Yes. Well, most of it. The other families kept this from their kids, or like your father were programmed. Seth and Adam's parents weren't programmed, and never told them a thing. Didn't care about the society, what it might do to their kids. Eric, your parents were programmed, but according to my folks it sort of wore off and they just forgot about it."

Eric twitched at the sounds of his voice and made some kind of gutteral noise, but didn't take his eyes off the darkened farmland as it roared past his window. Mosey stared straight ahead at the pavement, doing his best to appear invisible.

"My parents told me the truth about this place, about what the society had done to your family, and charged me with taking care of it. I wish I could have told you, I really do."

"I see," I said, watching the blackened earth of a cornfield slip by my window. "So what else didn't you tell me?"

"Mike, do we have to do this now? I always had your best interests at heart, I swear."

"Well it doesn't quite feel like it, Sarah," I said. I was beginning to feel angry.

"What do you mean? I was with you every step of this journey."

"Apparently you weren't. Not when I was having to scrap together evidence of this fucking conspiracy through Deakin. Who's dead now for his trouble, might I remind you?"

"I was there, Mike. I remember."

"Next thing you're going to tell me is that you set that book up for me to discover on the fourth floor of the—" I broke off when I saw her stricken face. "You . . . that was you?"

"I had no choice. Somebody was rummaging around up there when I was first examining it. I didn't have time to think about closing it. All I could think about was getting the hell out of there. And then when you had the same idea, I figured I'd just go along."

"I can't fucking believe this," I said, crestfallen. "Was there ever a time when you were truthful with me?"

"Yes, yes!" she cried. "When I said I loved you, for starters. I told you, that complicated things."

"Boy, did it ever," I said. I knew Mosey was glancing at me as he drove, but I didn't care.

Eric had fallen asleep. I gazed past Sarah's head and into the rear window. As my vision focused, I noticed two distinct dots of color behind floating on the horizon. They looked like cat's eyes in the faded light.

"I don't think you even understand everything, Mike," Sarah said. An ominous tone had become attached to her voice. "I heard what Moriarty said up there. About your father, and the sister I never had."

"I heard it too," I said, my voice creaking. "Don't think it doesn't disgust me."

"I don't, but it wasn't somebody from your family that had to die. He stole her from me, Mike. I could have grown up with her, gone to school with her, gone to camp. I could have gone to Malworth with her, taken on this whole place together."

"Yeah, I bet you would've loved that," I shouted, wishing instead I said something to comfort her. "Then you wouldn't have had to connive me to get what you wanted."

"Don't say that," Sarah cried. "I'm so glad we got to do this together."

I took a deep breath. "I am too. And . . . I'm really sorry for what happened. For all of it."

"I know you are. But your father isn't," Sarah said. Dark storm clouds gathered within her voice. "He will be when I'm done with him."

"What are you saying, Sarah?" I stammered. For the first time since I met this girl, I was afraid of her.

"We need some time to lay low up in St. Cloud. Once I'm certain nobody from the society is tracking us, we're going back to St. James. And I'm going to kill your father."

Blood rushed out of my face, and I felt nauseous. I felt like I had shared my life with a complete stranger. I was about to bluster a response when I saw the two dots of color I'd noticed earlier had more form this time. Now they were two bulging red and blue lights. I trained my eyes below and saw they sat on top of a vehicle of which I had a sickening recognition. It was the police cruiser that had pulled me over Homecoming night in Cold River.

"Oh, fuck," I said, my stomach sinking.

"What?" Mosey asked. "What is it?"

"We're being followed," I said in a quiet, toneless voice. "Just drive, Mose."

He glanced in the rearview. "We're being followed by that cop?"

"He's no ordinary cop," I said. "We don't want to be stopped by him."

"Damn, and I've got an expired license," Mosey said, chuckling. "Sorry I neglected to mention that."

"Just fucking drive," I said. My whole body seethed with anger and contempt at Sarah. Beneath this feeling was pure, unadalturated fear. I turned back to face Sarah. "We're not done."

"Of course not," she uttered, her face blank. She didn't seem one bit concerned about our situation, which made me even more irate. "And we'll never be done with the society. Not by a long shot. Taking out their leader was a big deal, a game changer. Things will never be the same after this night."

I gazed behind her. The shiny cruiser lights began flashing, creating rolling waves of red and blue that brightened the pavement behind Mosey's car.

"You sure I shouldn't stop . . . ?" Mosey asked in a tentative whisper.

"I'm sure," I said. "Just keep driving."

Mosey hit the gas and the wagon shuddered forth on the lone highway, pointing south toward St. Cloud in the darkness.